BROTHERHOOD of the FALLEN

WHITE HAVEN HUNTERS BOOK SEVEN

TJ GREEN

Brotherhood of the Fallen

Mountolive Publishing

©2024 TJ Green

All rights reserved

eBook ISBN: 978-1-99-004781-7

Paperback ISBN: 978-1-99-004782-4

Hardback: 978-1-99-004783-1

Cover Design by Fiona Jayde Media

Editing by Missed Period Editing

Contents

One   1

Two   11

Three   22

Four   34

Five   50

Six   63

Seven   78

Eight   89

Nine   98

Ten   108

Eleven   120

Twelve   131

Thirteen   142

Fourteen   156

Fifteen   166

Sixteen   179

Seventeen   187

Eighteen   199

Nineteen   212

Twenty   222

Twenty-One   234

Twenty-Two   247

Twenty-Three   258

Twenty-Four   280

Twenty-Five   293

Twenty-Six   306

Twenty-Seven   316

Twenty-Eight   332

Twenty-Nine   345

Thirty   356

Thirty-One   373

Author's Note   385

About the Author   387

Other Books by TJ Green   390

One

Gabe settled himself against the curve of the church's domed roof, the starlit sky spread above him, and focussed on the shadow-filled courtyard below.

He was in Florence, Italy, with Niel, Ash, Nahum, and Shadow, waiting for the man they suspected was an agent for Belial, the Fallen Angel. It was the end of February; two months since they had defeated Black Cronos, and since then, this search was all they had spent their time on. Two months of achingly slow progress, with this the only lead. It was an opportunity that most of the team hadn't wanted to miss out on. However, despite their eagerness to participate, they all knew the importance of caution. Consequently, Eli and Zee were still in White Haven, Barak and Estelle were in Yorkshire, investigating Jacobsen's church again, and Lucien was in London, working with Jackson and Harlan as they continued to track down leads. They were all trying to keep Olivia out of it because she was pregnant, but she was not happy about it.

The patter of footfalls on cobblestone made him hold his breath, but the giggles of a group of girls made him realise the noise came from outside the church, bouncing off the thick stone of the surrounding buildings. The church was in one of the oldest neighbourhoods of

Florence, at the centre of a spiderweb of streets, with small squares sandwiched in between the ancient buildings. The place was old, creaking with knowledge and secrets, this thirteenth-century church more than most.

It was after midnight, and they had been in Florence for two weeks, becoming familiar with the area and their quarry's movements. Only Shadow had been inside the church, the rest of them wary of being discovered and alerting their suspect, an elderly deacon called Salvatore Amato. So far, they were sure they hadn't been. Shadow, because of her natural fey magic and stealth, had followed his movements on foot at night as far as the entrance to the crypt, but was reluctant to explore further as she detected unearthly angelic power. Caution had won over curiosity, but it was enough to convince them to question the old man.

Niel's voice cut across his thoughts, through the earpieces they wore to keep in contact. "I see him now, approaching from the south. He's heading to the door that leads to the courtyard, just like normal. I estimate another few minutes before he arrives. Stick to the plan. Copy?"

The murmured responses from his brothers and Shadow confirmed his message, although Gabe knew Niel would have more trouble following that instruction than anyone. *Follow Amato, seize any jewels with Belial's power, and question him. Do not kill him.* Gabe carried a wooden box in his pack, spelled with protection, and designed to hold any Fallen Angel jewellery they found. Its weight reassured him.

Gabe glanced to his left. Ash was a short distance away, also perched on the roof, where he sheltered in the shadows of the ornate stonework. Shadow waited below, cloaked in darkness in a corner of the courtyard. Niel circled overhead, keeping watch, while Nahum looked out over the front of the church. They would both now adjust their positions to join them. *Just questions*, Gabe reminded himself. *Don't kill him, no matter how much he irritates the crap out of you. And be wary of Belial's trinkets.*

Gabe took a deep breath and exhaled slowly. *They were so close.* It was Jackson who had found Salvatore after tracking Jacobsen's movements—the vicar who had peddled around the reliquary that contained Belial's jewellery. He had investigated his various addresses over many decades and found that he spent a lot of time at this church in his youth. It seemed odd that a vicar of the Church of England should frequent a Catholic church, but something must have piqued his interest. That led them to do more extensive research, and they had found something very interesting. While many staff moved around, a few older members had worked here for decades, but Jacobsen had kept in touch with only one of them. *Salvatore Amato*. But what had confused them was that there were no sporadic outbreaks of violence in Florence. Another mystery, if Amato was an agent.

The click of the lock in the door alerted them to his arrival, and Gabe braced himself for flight.

The figure was slight, innocuous in many ways, but his movements were sure and swift as he locked the door and crossed the courtyard to the side door of the ancient church. *Just like clockwork*. Every Sunday, Tuesday, and Thursday night he would come here for at least two hours before leaving again. They waited for him to enter the church before swooping down, and then all four Nephilim landed in silence, although, Gabe noted again with a grimace, Ash's newly golden wings reflected the tiniest bit of light. An unexpected gift from Belial, and no doubt unintended. Shadow was already at the door, and they soundlessly followed her inside.

The scents of incense, cold stone, and a whiff of mustiness struck Gabe as they closed the door behind them. Amato had already disappeared, but Shadow led them down the passageway and into the nave. It was huge, a domed roof high above them, with rich reliefs on every single wall. At the far end was a spectacular altar, a gilded cross towering over it. There were angels everywhere. Huge, winged creatures that looked on from paintings and sculptures.

Gabe's skin prickled with unease, but he hadn't time to think about it. Shadow led them behind the altar to the choir area, then halted at the steps that led to the crypt. Gabe felt Belial's presence like a punch to the gut. He gently eased her aside, shot a warning look to his brothers, and led them down the steps.

The staircase descended further than he expected, the smell of dampness mingling with Belial's distinctive power. The ancient wooden door of the crypt was open, candlelight leaking through. A low-roofed space stretched ahead, filled with tombs, iron railings, niches, and statues. They faltered for a moment, still unable to see Amato, but light from a side corridor drew Gabe onwards.

With every step, Belial's power swelled around them, until Gabe was sure that he was actually about to face him. A palpable air of worry had settled over all of them, and Gabe gripped his sword for reassurance. Finally, they arrived at the threshold of an ancient round room with a domed roof, carved with hundreds of angels. A place of worship to a master who didn't deserve it. An altar dominated one side, an enormous marble statue of an angel with outspread wings looming over it. It was draped in jewels. A long, golden necklace with a heavy pendant rested on his broad chest, a silk-lined fur cloak flowed from his shoulders, and bracelets and torcs were fixed around muscular arms. In his outstretched hand was a real sword made of tempered steel with a rich, engraved hilt. *So much jewellery. So much power.* Amato was nowhere in sight, but he must be here somewhere.

Wary of traps, Gabe glanced down the corridor that continued past the small chapel, but it lay in darkness with an air of disuse. He tentatively stepped inside the room and had progressed a few steps only when he was suddenly struck by Belial's power. It was as if a giant weight was forced upon his shoulders, and unable to resist the unspoken command, he fell to his knees. By now everyone was inside the room, and his brothers followed suit. Shadow suddenly vanished. Panic swirled through Gabe as he struggled to master his movements, but he was utterly powerless. Unable even to speak.

Salvatore Amato emerged from behind the statue, black clothes billowing around him. His eyes glowed with a maniacal gleam. "It is fitting," he crowed, his thin, reedy voice swelling with the power of Belial, "that you kneel before him. You are nothing compared to his power and majesty."

Gabe's panic multiplied as he struggled to respond, his jaw tight, every muscle seized. *Idiot. Why did he step inside?* All four Nephilim were in a loose semicircle, darting eyes their only movement.

"You will swear your fealty to Belial or die," Amato continued, stepping closer. "I know who you are. You murdered poor Jacobsen and have used Belial's jewellery for your own ends." He shook his head as he paraded in front of them, then suddenly pulled a wicked, curved blade from his gown, glinting with angelic script. "And you," he paused before Ash, whose golden wings glowed within the candlelight, "even used his power to save yourself. You are already his. Perhaps I should ask you to kill your brothers. Stand."

Unexpectedly, and clearly against his will, Ash stood, sword gripped in clenched fist, muscles flexing. He towered over Amato, but the man stood before him, resilient, unyielding. *If he commanded Ash to kill now, would he?* Niel and Nahum were within easy reach, both furious and frustrated.

Trying not to let fear and anger overwhelm him, Gabe focussed on slowing his breathing and regaining control of his mind and body. He forced himself to look at the statue of Belial. He had no natural human form, but from his many incarnations, he recognised his narrow-eyed stare. The look of superiority. The vindictive smile. It might only be marble, but white fire seemed to flame behind his eyes, the skin taking on a luminous glow. His presence felt so strong, Gabe was almost convinced that he was actually contained within the statue, but that was impossible. And it was impossible that they should be restrained by him. He scanned the room, taking in the scored marks on the stone floor and its mirror image above them. He had been so distracted by the hundreds of angels that he hadn't seen it. A trap, but not for demons. For Nephilim.

Amato was toying with them, and despite all their stealth and care, the bastard had known where they were all along. But did he know about Shadow? And where the hell was she?

As soon as Shadow entered the shrine, she detected another level of magic, and it didn't come from Belial. It came from the sigils etched on the floor and roof, and she instantly knew what they were. Fortunately, they did not affect her actions, and she stepped into the dark, where the candlelight couldn't reach, and pulled her fey magic around her.

She felt an instant relief as Belial's insidious whispers muted, and the stone and earth around her offered her soothing comfort. *I am fey. As old as the Earth and her mysteries. I am not cowed by you, Belial.*

She was only just in time. As the four Nephilim fell to their knees, Amato stepped around the statue, and she moved silently behind him, back to the wall, assessing all other dangers. But there was no one else in the room. As well as the jewels on the statue, rings were heaped upon the altar amongst half a dozen candles. She also scented blood. Old, dried blood. *Sacrifices.*

Amato began to speak, his voice assuming power that was not his own. Shadow was torn with indecision. If she killed him now, they would learn nothing from him. No, she would wait and hope he would reveal more of his plans. He would not harm the Nephilim. *Not yet, surely.*

"Should I have you kill your brothers?" Amato asked Ash. "It would be so easy. You lift your sword, and you stab the one to your right." He raised his hand as he spoke, and Ash lifted his sword and struck at Niel, the blade missing his throat by a whisker. "If I willed it," Amato said, a thin-lipped smile creasing his face, "he would be dead by now."

Shadow flinched at the demonstration of power. She couldn't deny it was impressive. *But that was too close.*

Amato stepped back, and Ash sank to his knees, sweat beading on his brow. Amato whirled around, placing his dagger on the altar, then studied the Nephilim again. "I need answers. How did you find me?

What else do you know? Who works with you? You!" he commanded Nahum. "Speak."

"Screw you, old man," Nahum ground out between clenched teeth. "You might control my body, but not my mind."

"Ah! The father of the Nephilim child. Belial is aware of it. She and her mother have the protection of the Goddess, which is rather annoying."

She?

Nahum stuttered, his blue eyes flickering with uncertainty and a flare of pride. "I'm having a daughter? I swear, if you touch her, I will kill you."

"You are in no position to threaten me, and certainly not Belial."

"Don't be so sure about that."

"You have no power here, so your threats are pointless."

Salvatore Amato looked utterly unconcerned. For an old man, he radiated health and vitality. In fact, he might actually be much older than they suspected. A gift From Belial. It would explain how he could assume the Fallen Angel's power and carry it so effortlessly. And this place certainly reeked of age. It was as old as the church above, maybe even older. Perhaps the church had been built over it.

He continued, his voice dropping and filling with Belial's power again. "How many others?"

"There are only us."

"Lies. Perhaps if I kill one of your brothers, you will speak the truth. With every lie, I kill one more." He studied the four prisoners. "Kill the golden-winged one."

Nahum unwillingly stood and lifted his sword, slowly advancing on Ash.

Shadow couldn't afford to wait any longer. She had hoped that Amato would give away some of his secrets willingly, but it was clear he would not. They would have to coerce him, and somehow break his power over the Nephilim.

She materialised out of the darkness, wrapped one arm around Amato's thin shoulders, and placed her dagger at his throat. "End it now, or I end *you*."

The old man roared in shock, and before Shadow knew what was happening, he seemed to swell in size as he emitted a blinding white light. It threw her off her feet and into the wall, her dagger falling to the floor.

Fortunately, it had thrown the Nephilim back, too. All four lay crumpled against the walls. But that was as much as she saw, because Amato snatched up his cruel-edged knife and flew at her with lightning speed.

She rolled to a crouch, her other blade already in her hand, facing him. "You are more than you appear, Amato. You must carry a trinket to have that much power."

"Who are you?" he spat. "How dare you enter my sanctuary!"

"I dare to enter anywhere I choose."

He flew at her, dagger slashing where she had stood, but she had already moved, keeping easily out of reach. "Release the Nephilim."

"I will kill them first."

Rather than lunging at her, he sprang at the closest Nephilim, all four still lying helplessly and unable to move. He reached Gabe first. His knife slashed his arm in a vicious jab. Shadow tackled Amato, rolling over and over across the stone floor, feeling his sharp blade slice her side. It was as cold as ice, yet it burned with the power of the sigils.

She landed on top of him, knee pinning his hand that carried the blade to the ground. She punched him repeatedly, his head striking the stone flags. But he was strong with angelic power. He rose up, trying to throw her off him, desperate to free his knife. With an unexpected surge of strength, he rolled, slamming her into the ground, blade slashing down. Shadow wanted to slit his throat and be done with him, but they still needed him for answers. Instead, she stabbed his arm, slicing through tendons, and with a horrified yell and a splatter of blood, he fell backwards, then scrambled away on hands and knees.

"Glad to know that you still feel pain, you bastard," she yelled. She struck again, cutting the back of his legs and slicing his Achilles tendons with another splatter of blood.

He screamed, eyes wild, foaming at the mouth as if with some religious ecstasy.

She edged back, knowing he couldn't move, and checked her team. They were still where they had fallen, limbs tangled. Gabe's arm was bleeding profusely. He stared at her, his emotions a mix of fury and gratitude. And confusion. Deep confusion.

Not surprising. This place was all kinds of unexpected, and so was Amato. The wound at her side ached, and she pressed her hand to it, trying to stem the blood flow. Amato was muttering something, eyes closed, his power building. Much like the unexpected surge of power when she had attacked him.

What now?

Two

B arak eased the door open and slipped inside the rectory that had once been Jacobsen's home, Estelle right behind him.

It was the first time they had been able to enter it after his death. There had been, understandably, a lot of press interest in the death of a vicar slain in his own church, and as yet there wasn't a new one assigned to the area. The weekly service was instead delivered by a visiting vicar. When the police investigation ended, they seized their chance.

"Do you feel any sign of Belial?" Estelle whispered.

"Not a thing." The loud ticking of a wall clock marked the time as Estelle threw a few witch-lights above them. They illuminated a short hall, and doorways to either side. "He'll have a study somewhere, a place where he would have written his sermons and seen visitors. Let's hope it's where he kept his secrets."

Together they opened doors and progressed through the house, investigating the living areas and kitchen before finding a large, square study at the back of the house overlooking the garden. The house was cold and dusty, and it was obvious that no one had been in since the week Nahum had killed him. A Christmas tree wilted in the front room, dead pine needles spread across the floor.

"Do you think he'll have a folder of co-conspirators?" Estelle asked, half laughing.

"Let's hope so. It will make our life easier." Barak shut the curtains and the door and flicked on the light switch. Fortunately, the house still had electricity, and light flooded the room revealing bookcases, a small fireplace, a desk and chair, and an armchair by the fire. "So far, so ordinary."

"It's hardly like he'll advertise his allegiance to Belial. Apart from the gigantic painting of an angel, of course." An angel in typical Biblical style was portrayed with spread wings, looking down at the Earth. "It's unnerving. I think his eyes are following me."

Barak laughed. "*Great.* A possessed portrait. That's all we need." He turned his back on it and started going through the drawers in the large, battered desk. Papers were spread over it, along with the remains of the powder the police used when dusting for fingerprints. "Old sermons, notebooks, pens, pencils. Just the usual crap."

"Is there an address book?"

"Not so far."

Estelle hunted through the bookcases, and for a while there was silence between them. Barak placed a couple of notebooks in his pack, but the desk otherwise held nothing of interest.

"Here are some more old notes," Estelle said, handing them to him. "We can check them later, and there's also an address book. Pretty scant pickings, really. All of the books are religious, apart from a few thrillers."

"What about those?" Barak asked, turning his attention to a few photographs on the wall. "He's young in them. Looks like he's fresh from religious college, or whatever they call it."

"A seminary, I believe."

"Let's take them, too. They might direct us to important connections."

Estelle was transfixed again by the oil painting. "We should look behind that. I have a feeling about it."

"I've learned never to ignore a witch's intuition." He lifted the painting down and turned it against the wall. There was nothing on the back of it, but set into the wall was a safe. "Time for your magic again." Within a few moments, the door swung open, revealing a bundle of pages inside, and nothing else. He flicked through them. "It's a manifesto."

"You're kidding me!"

"No. Some claptrap of bringing Belial's power to Earth. Bollocks." He looked at Estelle, seeing her confusion mirror his own. "This is bigger than we thought. Much bigger."

"Shadow!" Nahum drew her attention, relieved that he could still speak after Amato had lifted part of the spell. "Can you drag us out of the room? That's the only way we'll regain control. It's some kind of trap."

"What if I can break it?"

"I don't think you have time. We need to get out of here. Amato is summoning *something*."

Power was building again. The whole room resonated with it. It was so strong that Nahum felt sick, and he realised that the trap was making them more susceptible to it.

Shadow staggered to her feet, and grabbed Niel beneath the shoulders, the closest Nephilim to the door. But he was too heavy, and while her fey abilities gave her superior speed, they did not make her strong.

Shadow grunted. "I can't. You're all too big. Herne's fucking horns!" she yelled in exasperation. She slumped against the wall, blood pouring down her side again.

Amato cackled despite his pain. "You can't break the trap. It's burnt in by Belial, scored deep into the rock. He's coming now. He looks forward to seeing you."

"Impossible," Nahum said, sounding more certain than he felt. "He cannot walk this Earth again."

"He can through me." Amato pushed himself upright and dragged himself back against the wall, smearing blood along the ground. "This is one of his most sacred places. He's coming. I have called him. Even my death will not stop him. And when he sees you?" He laughed again. "You will all be recruited to his cause. You cannot resist."

Shadow limped to his side, unsheathing her Dragonium sword. "I'm willing to test that by removing your head. How many other sacred places are there?"

"You think I will tell you? Fool. Too many for you to find. There are more involved than just me and Jacobsen. So many more..." His voice was a rasp now as his strength finally started to ebb. Power continued to build, though, a pale glow seeming to light his skin.

Then Nahum spotted a chain around his neck. *Another trinket containing Belial's power.* "Get rid of his necklace. Don't touch it with your hands!"

She used her sword to slice through it, flicking the broken chain across the room, the ruby pendant clattering against the stone. A huge ring also adorned his finger, and she cut off his whole hand, kicking it across the floor, too. He didn't even scream.

"Shadow!" Nahum summoned her attention again. "Get the box from Gabe's pack, and put as many jewels in as possible! It should stop whatever is happening."

She hauled Gabe's pack from under him, rolling him awkwardly "Sorry, my love."

While Shadow raced around the room, sweeping as much of the jewellery as she could manage into the box, Nahum studied the trap. He'd be damned if he was going to die down here or become Belial's accomplice. *He was going to be a father. He was going to have a daughter. He would not leave Olivia to care for her alone.* Renewed hope surged through him. *There had to be a way to break the trap.*

"I can't get the rest of the jewels." Shadow gestured to the jewellery on the statue's arms. "Not unless I touch them. The box is near full, anyway."

"*No!* Do not touch them." Nahum's voice was sharp. "You are resisting all of this so far. We can't risk you succumbing to his power, too. What do we know about traps?"

"That if you break them in some way, then you interrupt their power. Strike out a sigil, or break the circle." She spun on her heel. "But Amato is right. These are scored deep. I'd need an axe, and even then, if they're made with angelic magic..."

"Niel has an axe."

She rolled her eyes. "It's huge! I doubt I can even lift it! It's almost as big as him, the big lump!"

Niel's only response was to glare. *If looks could kill...*

"Wait!" she said, almost jumping with glee. "JD's weapons! Why the hell didn't I think of that sooner?"

Nahum groaned with relief. "Of course! Belial is clouding our thoughts. There's one in my pocket."

"Don't worry." Shadow patted her fatigues and withdrew a sleek metal object from her pocket. "I have mine."

Nahum scanned the room again, deciphering the many sigils scored into the rough stone. As usual, the trap was circular, stretching to every wall. However, in the centre, was Belial's seal. Monstrous in size, it echoed the same design in the ground, and connected to all the other sigils. He pointed at it. "That one! Take it out, above and below."

"That sounds suitably alchemical."

Amato hissed. "*No*! You risk burying us alive!"

"Shut up!" Shadow commanded. "I'd rather that than be a puppet. However," she raised a sleek eyebrow at Nahum, "floor first! Close your eyes."

As Shadow retreated to the doorway, Nahum was relieved that at least he could close his eyes. His leg was buckled under him, and one arm was twisted behind his back. He lay half on top of Ash, and Gabe and Niel looked similarly squashed from the little he could see of them through his peripheral vision. *Please work.*

He clenched his lids shut just as Shadow blasted the seal with short, controlled bursts of the weapon. Rock and dust blasted into the air, pelting his face and body, and he knew he'd be covered in a myriad of cuts. The blasts continued for several seconds before it finally fell quiet.

"I'm done."

Nahum cautiously opened his gritty eyes and saw Shadow standing over the mess.

"It hasn't completely gone, but I've taken a chunk out. Round two." She took a breath, looking at all of them. "I'll make it as quick as I can." Her gaze lingered for a moment on Gabe, and then she headed back to the door again.

The next blast felt so much worse. Chunks of stone rained down, and rocks bounced over him, one striking his temple. Dust went up his nose and despite his best intentions, he swallowed some, too. He wished he'd thought to tell Shadow to cover their faces. *But what with?* Their clothes were in packs squashed beneath them. But then he realised that the air felt cleaner, and the sticky, cloying power of Belial had lifted. He carefully moved his arm and relief flooded through him.

Ash groaned. "That's my face. Ow!"

"I think I've dislocated my butt," Gabe said. "Is that even possible?"

"Sorry, Ash! Shadow, you bloody superstar! You've done it." Nahum brushed debris from his eyes and opened them slightly, but he could barely see anything. Dust filled the air, and he started coughing. "Are you okay? Why are you so quiet?"

"I think you should move. *Quickly.*"

"What the fuck have you done?" Niel bellowed.

"The roof is cracking, and so is the floor."

As if to emphasise her point, an ominous shudder shook the entire room.

Niel grabbed the stone door frame as the floor buckled beneath him. He was only just in time.

With an enormous *crack*, a chunk of rock dropped out of the ceiling and shattered the slabbed floor as it crashed through it. A section of the floor tilted precariously.

Niel flung out his other hand and grabbed Ash on his right. "I've got the door! Hold tight!"

In seconds his brothers had all gripped each other, forming a chain, but Gabe was the furthest from the door and was sliding towards the gaping hole as Nahum clung to him. A chunk of slab had upended, and Gabe braced himself against it as Niel gripped the frame with increasing desperation.

"I'm okay!" Gabe yelled. "For now. Shadow! Where are you?"

"Over here, trying to help Niel." She was flat on her belly, half in the corridor, arms wrapped around Niel in an awkward embrace as she tried to help, her legs braced against the frame. "The passage seems unaffected—so far, at least."

"Well, that's something, I guess," Niel complained, as her head wedged under his armpit to get a better grip.

"Can anyone extend their wings?" Ash asked, his voice strained. "I have no room."

"Me neither," Nahum said. "Where's Amato?"

Niel grunted as he twisted to see across the room through the settling dust. "I think he's under a pile of rubble. Yep, I can see his leg. At least the floor's stopped moving." He was trying to reassure himself more than anything. Although he was strong, he was carrying most of the weight of his brothers, with only Shadow and the slab Gabe was wedged against helping him. If he lost his grip now, Shadow would not be able to stop him from sliding.

"I might be able to open my wings," Gabe said, tentatively bracing himself more carefully. "I can't see into the hole, though. I don't know how deep it is. It might only be a couple of feet down."

"Or it could open into a cavern system, and we're screwed," Ash suggested. "But I guess we might be able to fly then."

"Bear with me." Gabe twisted again, testing his weight against the slab, and digging the fingers of his free hand into the cracks around him.

Niel took stock of the room as the dust cleared. It was a wreck. The altar and Belial's statue were covered in debris, and both were tilting precariously. The hole in the roof where the seal had been revealed a solid mass of earth and rock that could come tumbling down at any moment. *They had to get out of here.* He tentatively tested his strength, pulling against the door frame, but he barely moved an inch.

Gabe adjusted himself once more. "I'm going to open my wings really slowly."

It seemed that everyone held their breath as Gabe's wings carefully unfurled, catching chunks of stone as they did so. He slid for the briefest movement and then stabilised again, and finally they were fully extended. Niel felt the weight he was supporting ease. But they all knew the next step would be the hardest. The room was barely large enough to encompass his wingspan, and for him to fly he needed to move his wings.

Niel braced himself again, renewing his grip on the door frame and feeling Shadow tighten her grip around his chest.

Then everything shifted. Suddenly, Gabe was airborne, his wings filling the room, and the turbulence sent whirls of dust around again. Niel hauled himself upwards as the weight of his brothers reduced. Shadow squirmed backwards, helping to drag him to the passage.

It was impossible for Gabe to lift either of his brothers, and as Ash and Nahum started to inch backwards too, Nahum asked, "Can you see what's below us, Gabe?"

"There's a narrow seam in the bedrock, and it goes down a good way, from what I can see. It looks like the part you're on is solid. The weight of the falling seal must have broken through a weakened section. I think you're right, Ash. It's some kind of cave. Or it might even lead into old sewers or something."

Niel resisted looking at him, focussing instead on dragging them backwards, and with relief he cleared the door frame with his shoulders. In a few more minutes, they had wriggled clear and were wedged into the passage, covered in sweat and debris.

"That was too close," Nahum said, breathing heavily. "Gabe, is it worth trying to get down there? Could there be anything related to Belial?"

Gabe shook his head. "Unlikely. I don't trust the roof not to collapse further, either. But I want Amato, if he's still alive." He carefully landed on the more stable part of the floor and removed debris from the man's prone form. "Bollocks. He's dead."

"Is there anything we can salvage?" Shadow asked. "Anything on his body? Or can you get the remaining jewellery?"

He didn't answer as he patted the corpse down. "Just his knife. If the box is full, it's pointless for me to take the rest of the jewels."

"We can't just leave them here!" Nahum protested. "Others must come down here. Maybe more of Belial's disciples."

But the second the words came out of his mouth, the statue started to topple.

"Gabe! Move!" Shadow cried out.

Gabe had mere seconds to leap out of the way and take to the air when the statue crashed to the ground, taking another chunk of the floor away. With an ominous *crack*, the rock beneath them split again and the huge, winged angel plummeted into the gaping hole, Amato's body tumbling in after it.

"Time to go!" Gabe yelled, angling towards the door as everyone made room for him to land.

Without a backward glance, they all fled from the destroyed shrine, and Niel could swear he felt the ghost of Belial's presence pursue them.

Three

"Two months," Jackson said, "and scarcely any leads."

"Did you honestly expect anything else?" Harlan asked, incredulous. "Belial has been here for centuries. Millenia, even. His agents are resourceful, and no doubt well hidden."

"You keep saying 'agents.' It's depressing."

"You know I'm right. It won't be just one person—or a paranormal *whatever*—supporting him. Belial will have backup. And besides, what we have is better than nothing. Stop being so negative."

Jackson ran his hands through his shaggy hair, making it even more messy than usual, and stared at the large world map pinned on the wall of his office in The Retreat, the base of operations for the Paranormal Division that sat beneath Hyde Park and Kensington Palace in London. "But it's so tenuous! This is like searching for Black Cronos all over again."

"Well, we found them, and we'll find these agents. At least Gabe and his team had some success last night. And Barak and Estelle found a damn manifesto! That's huge!"

"True. I'm just impatient." He sighed and headed to the shelf where he kept his tiny kitchen area to make a pot of tea. Knowing Harlan hated tea he asked, "Coffee?"

"Please. Strong."

It was Friday afternoon, and the working week was drawing to a close. Not that it meant anything to him or Harlan. Their hours were erratic, and although he'd take some time off over the weekend, he would continue researching. Both teams had phoned that morning with news of their overnight success. Amato's death was unfortunate, but at least Jackson could continue to hunt down his connections. Shadow and Gabe had gone straight from the church to Amato's city flat and searched it, knowing that the police would be notified of his disappearance very soon. Unfortunately, as at Jacobsen's house, there was little to find.

"I presume," Harlan said, "they'll investigate Amato's country house?"

"Heading there now." He handed Harlan his mug of coffee. "It will take them a couple of hours to get there, but they should arrive soon."

"And Belial's jewels?"

"Safely tucked up in the spelled box. I have a feeling we'll need one the size of a treasure chest next time." He dropped into the chair behind his desk, weariness washing over him. "The amount of jewellery there was worrying."

"Maybe it's a good thing. Perhaps most of it was there, and now some of it is down a very deep pit, forever." Harlan grinned. His relentless good humour was exhausting. "I mean, how much bling can an angel have, right? He sounds like a rap star."

Jackson laughed. "Well, that's one way to look at it, but I suspect that he has a lot! By the sound of it, the Fallen liked to preen. But we can't forget the manifesto." The mere thought of it banished his smile. "It's big. Organised."

23

"Not necessarily. Lone bombers have manifestos, too. If it was really so big, there'd be a lot more crap happening. I'm still convinced it's a small group who just love to spread unrest." Harlan sat in the chair opposite him. "We didn't even know about this until Olivia stumbled upon the reliquary. It's not great, but it's not huge, either."

Jackson sipped his tea. "You're right, I guess. I need a good sleep to get this in perspective. This place is getting to me again." He meant the unending corridors of The Retreat. Sometimes it was oppressive. It seemed especially so only a couple of months after Russell's death, the Deputy Director of the PD. He was killed by Layla Gould of all people, after Russell murdered two PD staff and was about to shoot Maggie Milne, the DI of the Paranormal Policing Team. "It's still unsettled here."

"Of course it is. You have new staff, increased security, and people are still grieving. Yourself included. You need to cut yourself some slack. *You* are still getting over the news about your grandfather too, never mind the scientist and that nice kid, Petra."

Harlan's statement depressed Jackson further. Petra *was* a nice kid. *Too young to have been murdered by Russell fucking Blake.* "I can't deny that their deaths haunt me. Petra's more than anyone's. I've convinced myself my grandfather wouldn't have known anything once Black Cronos changed him. But Petra? That's shit. I've seen the camera footage. She was screaming and terrified, and he shot her like she was nothing. Maggie and Layla are heroes for stopping him."

"So are you." Harlan considered him, a thoughtful expression on his face. "You need to get out of here. Maybe out of London. Strictly speaking, you don't need to be involved in the Belial stuff. Maybe you should pick up a case and work on something completely different."

"Waylen wants me to stick around. He's invested in finding Belial now, too. Plus," he gave Harlan a wry smile, "despite everything, I like it here. It's in my blood. And I owe Waylen. He needs me here. They all do."

Working for the government's Paranormal Division went back years in his family, and he had always worked for them in some capacity. Harlan didn't know half of it, although he suspected it.

Harlan nodded. "If you're sure. What's happening with the Deputy Director's job?"

"Waylen offered it to Lyn, the scientist and alchemist, but she refused. Said it would take her from the lab too often. Too much management crap that would get in the way of her research. He's disappointed, but understands her reasoning."

"Because Russell was a scientist, right?"

"Yes. So then, he offered it to Layla, and she said yes, but only until he has someone long-term. She says she's too old to deal with managing egos. It leaves Waylen with a dilemma. He doesn't feel the other scientists are up to the job, but he really wants a scientist who understands the lab and the research. He's very resistant to bringing in a completely new person for such a role. I mean, we have new staff, obviously, but not in such a senior position. So, he's considering asking someone else…" Jackson massaged his temple just thinking about it. "JD."

Harlan spluttered coffee. "You're kidding! JD? That grumpy bastard, managing people? No!"

"My sentiments exactly. I've objected—strongly. I suggested he keep him as some kind of special consultant instead. He could oversee the work, but not manage the staff. He likes that idea, and that has led to another scenario." It was another reason he didn't want to abandon Waylen and The Retreat right now. "He asked me to do it."

"That's amazing!" Harlan said, shooting upright in his chair. "Congratulations! You said yes?"

Jackson shrugged. "I'm thinking on it."

"What's there to think about? You'd be great! You're friendly, personable, balanced, and you know the PD well! Everyone likes you. This is a fantastic compliment."

Jackson ran his hand through his hair, feeling awkward. "But is it me? I mean, I'm a bit chaotic. Laid back. Scruffy." He meant it, too. Management to him meant suits and meetings, performance reports, and other such crap. "I hate evaluations and stuff. Just the thought of it is depressing! But it's very flattering, too, right?"

"Of course it is. He wouldn't ask you if he didn't think you could do it." Harlan smiled, his expression sympathetic. "I get it, though. You'd be responsible for others. But you know, you kind of do it anyway."

"I do? How?"

"You liaise with everyone. The analysts, Barak, Estelle, and Lucien. You brought the Nephilim in. You have contacts that Waylen doesn't. And you're relentless, my friend. You survived being kidnapped by the count! The more I think about it, the more I think you're perfect for the job."

Jackson was momentarily speechless at the unexpected response. "Really? I did not expect you to say that."

"You thought I'd talk you out if it? No way. Oh, man! Maggie will be so pleased to have the ear of the Deputy Director!" Harlan laughed, and once he started, he couldn't stop. He wiped tears from his eyes.

It set Jackson off, too. "Why am I laughing? It's not funny. She'll drive me insane."

"It's so brilliant. You'd even be JD's boss—kind of!"

Despite his initial reluctance, talking to Harlan helped clarify a few things. He did do all those things. "Perhaps I should say yes."

"Yes, you should! Do it now! Then we can celebrate. It's approaching beer o-clock!"

"Slow down. I'll give it more thought over the weekend. I can't drink too much, anyway. I'm meeting Barak and Estelle later. They're travelling back today and should arrive at Chadwick House soon. Lucien is already there, of course." Chadwick House used to belong to William Chadwick, until he was killed. He'd left it to The Orphic Guild in his will. Harlan's boss, Mason, was happy for it to be used by their contractors, and Lucien was living there for now. He was searching Chadwick's study for anything that might be relevant. As an occult collector before his death, he had many arcane volumes there, and they thought it prudent to check them all. "Want to join us?"

"I've got a date with a pregnant woman."

"Olivia? What are you two up to?"

"She's seeing Morgana for a check-up. I thought I'd offer some moral support."

Jackson noted his friend's earnest expression. "You're taking your uncle role very seriously."

"I can't help it. I'm worried, and with Nahum away, I don't want her to be alone. I know the Moonfell witches are great and everything, but, you know..."

"I know. She's okay, though?"

"She's great. Excited!"

"Even more reason to find Belial. Give her my best."

Harlan nodded, rising to his feet. "I will. If you find anything of interest in that manifesto, let me know. But accept the job! You'll be brilliant at it."

"Thanks, Harlan. I appreciate it." Jackson watched him leave, thoughts immediately drifting to Amato. He had a few hours to investigate his background. He'd see what else he could dig up.

"Are you sure she's all right?" Olivia asked Morgana, scrutinising her expression for anything that might suggest otherwise.

"I'm not lying!" Morgana pursed her lips, but then immediately softened as she ran her hand a few inches over Olivia's still-flat abdomen again. Olivia could feel the witch's magic like a gentle warmth. It comforted her. "She's perfect. Stop worrying." She stood back, her examination over.

"And still hardly a bump!" Harlan noted. He squeezed Olivia's shoulder as she sat up. "You look radiant."

Olivia adjusted her clothing, glad she could still wear her skinny jeans and silk blouses for a while longer, and then patted her stomach. "I thought I'd be feeling sick by now, but I'm fine!"

"That's Nephilim blood for you."

The three of them were in Morgana's private consultation area on the south side of Moonfell house, comprised of just three rooms—an examination room/office, a herb preparation room, and a bathroom. It had its own private entrance that was tucked into one of the building's many nooks and crannies. There wasn't even a door into Moonfell's interior. The better for privacy, Morgana told them. That explained why Olivia had never seen the rooms when she had wandered the house before Christmas. However, they were still decorated in Moonfell's flamboyant style. Morgana was a witch, after all, and used magic to help her clients, not science.

Morgana jotted a few notes into a file on her desk and then turned to face them. She looked a little less severe than usual. Her long hair was loose, and she wore a dark blue dress instead of her customary black, but it was still loose fitting and long, with a thick, colourful cardigan to add warmth, the sleeves rolled up to her elbows. "I must admit that I'm not sure what to expect of a Nephilim baby. Potentially, it could grow much quicker than a normal child, or will be bigger. I have chatted privately to Nahum about this though, and he reassures me that previous pregnancies have all progressed like any normal, human-fathered one."

Olivia recoiled in shock. "I didn't know you chatted to him alone!" Nahum certainly hadn't said so. It made her feel like a child. "You can tell me these things!"

"Of course, and I'm telling you now. But, if the pregnancy was moving along quicker than expected, we would all have had to adjust. I wouldn't have wanted you worried, or your energy depleted. Fortunately, though, all is as it should be." She smiled as she leaned back in her leather chair. "It's given quite the bloom to your cheeks."

"I know. Everyone keeps telling me how well I look, and they have no idea I'm pregnant. I haven't told anyone yet. Not even my best friend." Olivia felt horribly guilty about that, but thought it best to stick with regular time frames. "I won't tell either, not until the first scan. I'm hoping Nahum will be around for that."

She felt Harlan stir, knowing he was worried about their relationship. He'd become oddly protective lately, which was sweet, but unnecessary. And Maggie was being Maggie. Belligerent and forthright. Although, she had already brought her a pack of newborn baby clothes, unexpectedly revealing Maggie's tender yet practical side. Jackson was wonderful, like an indulgent brother, and that reminded her of Nahum's brothers. *Blimey.* They were something else, and her reception at New Years when she went to stay with Nahum at his Cornwall farmhouse... Well, she was treated like a queen. Not that they were together, of course. She had her own room, and he was courteous and solicitous, and very much at arm's length, when all she wanted to do was get him naked again...

Morgana's lips twitched with amusement, as if she knew exactly what Olivia was thinking. "I'm glad Nahum is being supportive, but I would expect nothing less. He's extremely charming. How is he? I gather he's off chasing Belial."

"They're in Florence, Italy. The team had a run-in with one of Belial's agents last night. He's dead now. The shrine was destroyed—accidentally, of course," she said, watching Morgana purse her lips.

"I'm not disapproving. I'm frustrated. Did they find anything out before he died?"

"Just that there are more of them."

"And," Harlan added, "that there was a lot of jewellery there. They managed to take some of it and place it safely in the spelled box that the Cornwall witches supplied, but some of it was lost forever. Well, we hope forever." Harlan ran through the events, and they coincided with what Nahum had told Olivia, which was good. At least he hadn't held anything back.

Morgana's eyes widened in surprise. "They were caught in a trap?"

"Yeah." Harlan huffed. "Seems to be the season for them. Shadow had to break it with JD's weapon."

"The priest, Amato, said that Belial had scored the trap into the rock?"

He nodded. "Do you think he was lying?"

"If he wasn't, it's very worrying! He's either found a way to act here, or it has been here for millennia."

"It was a very old shrine, hidden deep beneath a church," Olivia informed her, "so yes, perhaps it was that old. I think the shrine was hacked out of bare rock." She felt dizzy with it all. "If I hadn't found that reliquary, we would have known nothing. Surely that means whatever is happening is on a small scale? No one even knew!"

"No one knew about Black Cronos, either, and there was nothing small about that. But," Harlan said, "actually I agree, and as I said to Jackson, there's no reason for us to get panicky."

Morgana snorted. "Have you forgotten the night we banished him?"

"How could I? It's imprinted on my brain. But a few lone religious nutters spreading his word might not amount to anything."

"Bollocks to Belial!" Olivia was sick of hearing about him. "I'm pregnant. I want positive thoughts around me. Morgana, should I be doing anything? Or can you detect anything? Does the baby have wings?"

"Good grief! I hope not. You don't want to give birth to *that*." Morgana laughed. "It's a baby! Although, I will admit to feeling a strong spirit, and most definitely a whiff of Nephilim magic."

Olivia felt a fool for confessing, but... "I've never considered that they have magic. Not like you."

"Because it's not like a witch's magic, or fey magic, either. It's their own, angelic magic. Diluted, of course, being half-angel, and their human part is dominant, but supernatural strength, healing, speed—and wings—are all magic."

Perhaps this should have reassured Olivia, but instead it set off another wave of worry. "I'll have a magical baby! How can I be a mother to that?"

"Just like you would be a mother to any other baby. You will shower her with love, keep her warm and safe, give her boundaries, and educate her. Quite honestly, Olivia, I think you'll be wonderful. You're strong and feisty, and no one's fool. I doubt Nahum would have slept with you otherwise. I think he must have had a sixth sense that you were the perfect mother. Not that he was planning to impregnate you, of course."

"I'm not a test tube!"

"I meant that some creatures, paranormal ones in particular, know when they've found the right mate. That's all."

"But they are not *mates* like some fated mates bullshit," Harlan said a little too forcefully. "They are fuck buddies!"

Olivia slapped his arm. "One time does not make a fuck buddy! And please don't use that term again. It was a tryst! A late night comfort. That's all."

Morgana's eyes sparkled with intrigue. "Of course, Olivia. Just a tryst. Now, I have a packet of herbal teas that I want you to drink regularly. Just one cup daily will suffice. It will strengthen your immune system, help you sleep, and generally support the pregnancy.

It's a slight change to the last mixture, just a tweak to adjust for the growing baby's needs. Okay?"

"Thank you." Olivia glared at Harlan once more before turning back to Morgana. "You're very kind. I feel much better for having your support."

"And mine?" Harlan asked.

"Sometimes! You can take me to the pub for dinner, and that will make up for slurs!"

With luck, it would also take her mind off Nahum, wondering what he was up to, and whether he was thinking of her at all.

Four

"It's unusual that a man such as Amato should have such a grand country residence, don't you think?" Nahum asked his brothers and Shadow as they finally located the building in the wooded valleys around Palazzuolo sul Senio, a small town to the northeast of Florence.

"I think it's probably his reward for decades of service," Ash said, staring beyond the locked gate and down the drive. It was dark now, close to seven in the evening, and the country lane was quiet. "It's impressive, without being overbearing."

"And very well concealed," Shadow added, craning her neck out of the window. "It's impossible to tell from here whether anyone lives there or not."

Gabe just huffed. "Another late visit, then."

"I need to get out and stretch my legs," Niel complained. "Two hours stuck in a hot car with you guys is driving me insane. No one will spot us."

Gabe obligingly pulled onto a grassy area just past the drive entrance, and they all exited on cramped legs. Nahum rolled his shoulders, taking deep breaths of fresh evening air and strolled down the verge, needing a little space to clear his thoughts. In the end, they had left Florence later than originally planned, after deciding they should stake out the church where Amato had worked and died. They had wanted to see who might be involved and whether anyone would arrive at the church that looked suspiciously upset and panicked. Unfortunately, or maybe fortunately, nothing untoward had presented itself.

They had carefully locked up the crypt after leaving the previous night, and nothing appeared to have been damaged on the upper levels of the church after the destruction below. They had hoped that with luck, no one would find his body for days. Maybe even weeks. His disappearance would be suspicious, but far less so than his death—especially in such a place and such a manner. Eventually, however, after the day proceeded as normal at the church, they decided that delaying any longer would be dangerous, especially since there was nothing else to learn.

No one talked much on the journey. They had all been shaken by what they had found, and they had barely slept when they returned to their hotel after their encounter and collective near-death experience. It was only now that they all seemed to be shaking it off. Belial, as usual, had slid under their skin. Nahum wondered what would have happened if they hadn't spotted the necklace around Amato's neck and the ring on his finger. *If Shadow hadn't removed them, would Belial really have manifested through Amato's body?* The glow of angelic light was real enough. His annoying cackle and superior laughter suggested inside knowledge. He knew who all of them were. *Was someone spying on them?* He glanced uneasily overhead, as if Belial's presence was close. It didn't help that they had a stash of Belial's trinkets in the boot of the car, either. They may be wrapped in protective spells, but they were like magnets, always drawing their thoughts. Well, Nahum's at least.

As always lately when thinking of Belial's trinkets, or whenever in fact his mind drifted at all, Nahum thought of Olivia and their child. *Their daughter.* Having that news delivered by Amato infuriated him. It wasn't as if he didn't want to know, but he did not wish to be told by *him.* Information Amato could only know through Belial. He had taken pleasure in revealing something Nahum should have learned with Olivia. He had phoned her as soon as he could with the news. It seemed only fair. Of course, he had checked with her before revealing the fact, but she had wanted to know, and could barely contain her joy. *A daughter.* Nahum closed his eyes, imagining Olivia's expression. The curve of her smile, the tease in her eyes, her smooth skin.

He had kept his distance at New Years. It was one night of passion. That was all. With lasting consequences that were unexpectedly good. *But once their daughter was born, what was he to do?* Unable to deal with that right now, he returned to his team and their conversation.

"Of course," Ash mused in a low voice, "if Amato had accomplices at that church, they may already know where to look for him."

Shadow nodded. "True, but would they want to make it obvious that they knew exactly where to look? I wouldn't. Someone will stumble on him in a few days, I'm sure. We should keep our eye on the news reports to see if anyone in particular found him. It might be another clue."

"Or, of course, no one will report the death at all," Nahum suggested. "His body did fall into a big hole. Or maybe they'll make sure it seemed to have occurred well away from the church."

"There's that *they* again," Gabe complained.

Ash laughed at Gabe's grimace. "He did say there were more of them. We can't ignore that. That shrine was significant. It could involve the entire church. There were a lot of angel motifs as decoration."

However, even as he was saying it, it didn't ring true to Nahum. They were all sure that Amato had worked alone there.

Niel, ever impatient, stripped his shirt off and extended his wings. "We should take a quick look around while we're here. If the place is empty, then we don't need to return later. If he has a housekeeper or someone else lives there, lights will be on now."

"That's logical," Nahum agreed.

Gabe considered the suggestion and then nodded. "Okay, if it looks deserted, come back and we'll join you. Be careful!"

"I'll come, too," Nahum said, stripping and extending his own wings, anxious to dispel his circling thoughts of Olivia.

"I'll move the car under that stand of trees," Gabe said, gesturing down the road. The forested slopes pressed closely along the lane, and the wind in the trees sounded like whispers.

"We won't be long," Nahum promised, and in seconds he followed Niel's lead and flew over Amato's grounds.

Amato's country house was a stocky building with a square tower and was actually much smaller than Nahum had anticipated. The grounds were heavily wooded, with the trees ending in a circle around the property. It would be menacing here even in midsummer, the air close and thick. And it was dark. No lights glowed in the windows, and there were no cars on the drive. They landed on the flat roof of the tower, and up close it was obvious why the house was deserted.

"This place is a wreck," Nahum said, noting the cracked masonry and general air of dilapidation. "I don't think anyone has lived here for years."

Niel peered over the parapet onto the roof of the main house. "I agree. Everything needs to be repaired. There are holes in the roof, and cracked windows. But why? What happened here?"

"Maybe nothing. Amato could have preferred living in Florence."

Niel scanned the woods, and then finally looked at Nahum. "There are secrets here. Or were once, at least. It feels ominous."

"I don't like it at all. I sense evil."

"We might as well investigate it now, then."

Nahum nodded, distracted. *What was it about this place that was so unsettling?* "Fine. You get the others. I'll wait by the main entrance."

He flew over the woods again in the time he had spare. There wasn't a break in the trees, or any sign of a building under the canopy. The grounds were obviously as neglected as the house. When he finally set down before the double wooden entrance doors, one was already ajar, the frame warped by the weather. He shivered, unable to shake the feeling of unease, and waited for his brothers to join him.

It was then that he spotted Belial's seal over the door, and felt a prickle between his shoulder blades. He spun around, sword raised. The dark woods presented an impenetrable wall behind him, but was something in there, watching him?

He turned his back, convinced that whatever had once been here was long gone, but Belial left dark shadows, and he did not relish stepping into them.

Lucien spread the manifesto out on the study table, the half a dozen pages lined up next to each other, and weighted their curling edges down with the objects closest to hand. A few peculiar glass paper-weights, a brass hand, and a bronze egg in a stand. Objects he had become very familiar with once he had settled in at Chadwick House.

His attention, however, was on the manifesto, as was Estelle's, Barak's and Jackson's.

"It's handwritten," Jackson observed. "I didn't expect that. Old, too."

Lucien nodded. "An old-fashioned ink pen wrote this. It looks to be centuries old. I've seen similar papers that are stored in Chadwick's collection. Personal histories, some of them. Diaries of occultists. Not manifestos," he added hurriedly, in case anyone got the wrong idea.

Lucien felt very confident, compared to how he had been a couple of months before. Defeating Black Cronos had reinvigorated him, and he had mastered his shifts to a super-soldier. It also helped that he was now living at Chadwick House, with his own room and agenda, and no one watching his every move anymore. He hadn't really liked the house to begin with, but he had acclimatised well enough, and it was free to stay there. He had consequently immersed himself in the occult, researching Chadwick's collections, and familiarising himself with the study and the books it housed. He had grown to like it. The house's old walls creaked and moaned, but it was also secure and warm, and for the first time in months he relished his privacy. He felt that he had become the house's custodian. *Stupid, really.* Mason Jacobs, the Director of The Orphic Guild, was actually in charge, but only in name. He didn't live and breathe the house like Lucien did. Lucien had begun to think that this place was part of his destiny. He was a member of the paranormal and occult world now. He may as well embrace it.

Estelle agreed with his suggestion. "Yes, Barak and I thought it was old, too. It makes us think that Jacobsen must have been a valuable part of the organisation for him to own what looks like an original manifesto."

"Unless, of course," Jackson suggested, "this is an old copy of an even older manifesto. I need to study it properly, but the language is old-fashioned, the phrasing weird."

"Angels were always deliberately obtuse," Barak said, grimacing. "The more fanciful they could be, the better. It's tiresome, but at the time, it was just the way things were."

"You think Belial wrote this?" Jackson asked, eyebrows shooting up.

Barak shrugged. "Dictated, perhaps? I don't know. He was always fond of his own voice. I think it's likely he had a hand in it."

"Which means he had a strong connection to whoever wrote this." Jackson straightened up, gazing about the room but not really seeing it. "A mental connection, or was he actually, physically here?"

"I'd have said that was impossible," Barak said uneasily, "not for millennia, at least, but after what my brothers have seen lately, I'm not so sure."

Lucien rubbed his tattoos as he studied the manifesto, a habit he'd developed when he was first turned by Black Cronos. Now it just seemed to be something he did without thought. "I thought I'd got used to occult language, but that's gibberish!" He glanced at Barak, who like all Nephilim could read any language, but it wasn't the language at issue here; it was its obvious attempt to confuse and obfuscate. "Anything strike you?"

"No, other than the obvious. Ash might make more sense of it. Or JD, perhaps."

The manifesto started with a declaration, a promise to return the exalted Belial to his true position, after his selfless plunge to Earth as one of the Fallen. It stated that he had fought side by side with Samael, otherwise known as Lucifer, the devil, when he started Heaven's rebellion and left God's side. Together they sought to cleanse the Earth of the less than worthy, and reward those who were deserving. Those that followed him.

"That's bollocks," Barak said, pointing at the line that Lucien had just read. "He never rewarded anyone. He made them think he was going to, but it was all smoke and mirrors. He was a cruel, thankless master. Not many of the Fallen liked him. Unfortunately, you could never ignore him, either. His own Nephilim of course followed his every word, until they too finally rebelled."

"So, just to clarify," Jackson asked, "every Fallen Angel had his own Nephilim?"

"Yes, they all fathered lots of us. Remember, they could take the form of any man, for a while. Some women wouldn't even have known they weren't sleeping with their husbands, because the angel inhabited their skin."

"Which is horrific!" Estelle said, her hands clenching as if trying to contain her magic. "Treating them like a breeding machine!"

"And the men like a dedicated stallion," Barak pointed out. "Having an angel inhabit your skin was not pleasant, I can assure you. There were no winners in that scenario. We called ourselves Houses. I was from the House of Kathazel. Gabe and Nahum, the House of

Remiel. As you know, my father had healing skills. Raphael was the most powerful healer. An Archangel. Kathazel was not as strong."

It was dizzying to hear ancient names uttered with such familiarity. Dealing with the immortal Comte of Saint-Germain and JD seemed strange, but this... Lucien focussed on the manifesto, and pointed out a few lines that were confusing. "What's this about angels of the First Sphere and the Second Dominion?"

"They were classes of angels. Belial was of the First Sphere. The most powerful of the angelic hosts." Barak grinned. "Even Heaven had a class system."

"The good thing," Estelle said, taking a seat at the table, "is that the manifesto seems unconcerned in general with any of the other Fallen. It only speaks of continuing Belial's work in cleansing the Earth by using his own brand of destruction—sowing the seeds of madness and causing destruction from within."

"A little hands-off for Belial," Barak stated. "He enjoyed getting his hands dirty, but he would like this, too. The insidiousness of it all."

"He does have a physical stake in all of this," Jackson reminded them. "His jewels that contain his power—his essence. How have they survived all this time? Gabe and the team found lots more beneath that church in Florence. That's what's troubling me more than anything. The manifesto is nothing without them. Just a bunch of words and promises that have no teeth without them. It's his trinkets, as you call them, that make the manifesto so threatening. You've read it. Does it give us any clues as to how they are here?"

Barak looked uneasily at Estelle. "There is a passing reference to the House of Belial, and the assistance they offered in distributing the jewels. Couched in flowery language, of course, but the meaning is clear."

"Are you saying that there are other Nephilim walking the Earth right now?" Jackson asked, face draining of colour.

"Not exactly! It suggests that there were at one time. That could have been hundreds of years ago. We are long lived, not immortal."

"But it's possible?" Lucien asked, shocked.

"Well, we're here, and the world is a big place," Barak conceded. He took a seat at the table as if all his energy had left him. "I've been mulling on it all day, trying not to see something where there is nothing, but it's in the manifesto. I don't think we can ignore it. It mentions certain jewels by name, too, and names his sword. They were names known only to his House."

"Why?" Jackson asked.

"Names confer power and knowledge. I mean, obviously I don't know if that *was* his sword's name. Someone could be making it up, but it sounds plausible. Especially because it's written in angelic script. It means *Justice Bearer*."

"Have you told your brothers?" Jackson asked.

"No. I didn't want to unduly worry them until I was sure. I also wanted Ash's opinion. He's good at this kind of thing."

Jackson looked astonished. "I can't believe you haven't warned them after what happened last night."

"Dealing with other Nephilim is a walk in the park compared to Belial. We have all done that thousands of times. And," Barak held up a hand to stop Jackson interrupting, "I'm not worried. We would have seen signs by now."

"But if there are other Nephilim, even one," Lucien pointed out, as astonished as Jackson by Barak's decision, "who wields Belial's jewellery, like you all did, you know how it changes your abilities."

"They would not reveal themselves so soon. There is too much at stake for them."

Jackson snorted. "I hope you're right, Barak, because otherwise your brothers could be marching into a death trap."

Ash was as unnerved as his brothers as they searched Amato's abandoned country residence. Its obvious decay was surprising. *Why let such a place fall apart?*

"Perhaps something illegal happened here," he wondered aloud. "Maybe that's why he let it rot."

"You mean there might be bodies on the grounds?" Niel asked. "That wouldn't surprise me from the look of the place. Or under the floorboards, perhaps. Maybe even bricked up in the walls."

Ash rolled his eyes. "Good grief, you have a vivid imagination."

"Would you put anything past Amato, or any of Belial's acolytes?"

"I guess not after last night."

Ash and Niel were alone on the ground floor of the house, while the others searched upstairs. So far, they had found nothing untoward, but the place was undoubtedly creepy. Old furniture was shrouded in covers, including the paintings that hung on the wall. The air in the house was thick with dust, cobwebs cluttered the corners of the rooms, and there was evidence that animals had been inside, and maybe a tramp or two. Although the gate at the top of the drive was closed tight, the woods would probably provide a way into the grounds. The scent of decay was strong, and when Ash pulled the covers from some paintings, they saw that mould had started to creep across the surfaces.

"Perhaps we're assuming too much, and this was never a base of operations. It might have been an inheritance. Can you remember what Jackson said?" Ash asked.

"No, not really. All I heard was that there was a house we needed to check out."

They progressed slowly through the ground floor, investigating each room carefully, occasionally hearing their brothers and Shadow shouting to each other. There were holes in the ceiling where the joists had rotted, and Ash hoped that no one would come crashing through. The kitchen was still very old-fashioned, and it seemed it hadn't been updated since the early 1950s.

"Fancy cooking in here?" Ash asked Niel with a smile.

"Only if I wanted to poison everyone. It's filthy. I like modern kitchens, not clunky old ranges." He stood at the window and looked out on the dark forest, which seemed very close to the house at this end of the building. "Maybe Amato did inherit this house. He might have inherited his responsibilities to Belial, too. There's nothing to suggest it's not a family affair."

"True. The Fallen always liked to keep their Houses tightly knit. Maybe the same applies to Belial's human followers."

"I think," Niel said, pointing at the forest, "that something is in there. I think that's the start of a path."

"But you saw nothing from overhead."

"No, but look how dense it is. It's like Ravens' Wood. We're looking in the wrong place, I'm sure of it."

They exited through the side door into the wreck of an old kitchen garden, and followed the faint remnants of a path to the wood. When they reached the trees, they could see a faint trail heading away from them, although the start of it was overgrown.

"Well?" Niel cocked an eyebrow at Ash. "Looks likely."

"I agree, but let's wait for the others. I'll phone Gabe."

In a few minutes' time, the rest of the group joined them. "Nothing of interest on the upper levels," Shadow declared, "but I like the look of that path! I'm going first."

"Shadow!" Gabe started to complain.

She shushed him with a look. "I'm not susceptible to Nephilim traps, and the woods are my strength. Follow me, and keep quiet."

Ash knew better than to argue, and before anyone could complain, he squeezed through the undergrowth that she so effortlessly skirted, and followed her down the path, single-file. It looked like an animal track, and perhaps animals had maintained it, of a sort, all these years. Tiny tracks branched off it, and the hoots of owls accompanied them as they walked.

Shadow, as she always did, virtually vanished in the deep shadows beneath the trees, treading silently but quickly, her bow ready should she need it. His brothers, for all their size, were almost as quiet behind him. She led them unerringly onwards, only pausing once when a similarly sized path crossed the track they were on. She searched the ground, scratching away the earth, and then turned to follow the new path. Ash had no idea what had made her change direction, but he followed her up the gently sloping ground.

Suddenly, she halted and pointed, her voice soft like the rub of leaves on the wind. "There. A building."

Ash squinted. He prided himself on having great eyesight, but for a long moment saw nothing. Finally, he spotted a vine-covered column that looked just like a tree. "How the hell did you see that?"

"I am fey. I feel it as much as see it."

His brothers crowded behind them, and she waited until they had seen the column, and then progressed ever slower. In a few moments, more columns became distinct from the trees, and it was evident that they created a temple. A circle of them, now covered in moss and ivy, rose majestically towards the canopy, but there was no roof. The temple was open to the sky, although thick and twisting tree branches grew over the whole place now. The central space was sunken into the ground, a few deep steps leading down to a circular area, almost like a mini amphitheatre. It was hard to see its depth as it was filled with fallen leaves, but in the centre was a huge, winged statue of an angel.

"Herne's hairy bollocks," Niel whispered. "A temple in the forest."

"Ionic pillars," Ash noted. "Greek, not Middle Eastern. It might mean nothing, of course. Temple designs in England often lean to classical antiquity."

Shadow went to walk onto the upper step, when Gabe pulled her back. "Check the perimeter first."

"It's an old, abandoned temple, Gabe."

"Just listen to me for once!"

They fanned out, exploring the edge of the temple, finding stone slabs beneath the leaves that created a path around the columns, but many were cracked and broken, roots pushing their way through.

Saplings even rose up through the central space, throwing the statue into deep shadow.

"Happy?" Shadow asked them all. When no one objected, she said, "I'm going to investigate down there, make sure there are no traps etched in the centre."

"Why is it abandoned?" Nahum asked, glancing around, hand clenched, like all of them, around the hilt of his sword.

"Places become unpopular. Newer temples supplant older ones. It's the way of the world," Ash said. "This place is creepy, though."

"It's on higher ground," Niel noted. "Might have had quite a view, at one point."

Shadow shouted, "It's all clear down here. No Nephilim traps or anything, just cracked stone. Marble, I think. The leaves are half a metre deep, sludge at the bottom, so it's slippery."

Ash waded through the leaf detritus and stood in front of the statue, checking every detail. "It's the same as the one in the temple last night."

Gabe was next to him, eyes lifted to stare at Belial's head. "I think you're right. It's uncanny. It looks just like him. It captures his haughty, heartless expression."

"His eyes are fixed behind us." Ash turned, looking in the direction that Belial faced, but the way was blocked with trees. "It's facing northeast. The same as yesterday's statue."

"Why is that important?" Shadow asked.

"I don't know that it is, but the fact that they are both facing the same way suggests it has significance. If it was just east, I wouldn't question it. Facing east was a common part of Christianity, and other religions, actually. It was Godly, the direction of the rising sun. But northeast?"

Niel stood next to him, also staring through the trees. "A direction for a reason, perhaps? To mark the way to somewhere of significance?"

"Perhaps."

Nahum was scrabbling about the base of the statue, moving leaves. "There's a big, square plinth down here, with an inscription. A large one." He pulled his torch from his pack and shone it on the surface, as one hand cleared moss from the words. "It's some kind of call to action. Lots of text."

Ash frowned. "A manifesto, perhaps? Like Barak found?"

Nahum looked up, surprised. "Maybe. Help me clear it."

Over the next ten minutes, they all cleared away the debris, scraping back moss to reveal the text that ran across the base, and Ash started taking photos. "I think it is. Whether it's the same…"

He trailed off, trying to comprehend what it meant.

"Niel," Gabe said, summoning his attention, "shine your torch straight upwards. I'll see if I can climb through the canopy and then fly. I want to orientate myself up there, see where he's looking."

"I'm going to explore further afield," Shadow said. "Check if there are other buildings or temples. Don't worry! I won't be long."

"Half an hour," Gabe instructed, "and then we're out of here. If necessary, we return in the light, tomorrow. There's nothing to worry about now that we know it's deserted."

Ash nodded, and once satisfied with his photos, focussed on the marble floor. He wanted to inspect every inch of this place, just in case something happened, and the wrath of Belial brought the place down over night.

Five

G abe peered over Ash's shoulder as he expanded a map of Europe on his laptop screen.

"So, we're where?" Gabe asked him.

"Here," he said, entering the name Palazzuolo sul Senio into the search bar. A small, red triangle popped up. "That's where we are right now. So northeast is roughly *that* direction."

It was Saturday morning, and Gabe, Shadow, and his brothers had just eaten breakfast and cleared the table in the small villa that Jackson had arranged for them to stay in for a few days. Nahum was phoning Jackson and Olivia with an update, and Niel and Shadow had returned to Amato's house to search in daylight.

Gabe nodded as he orientated himself. "Where is the church in Florence?"

"There," Ash said zooming out and scrolling across the page.

"Bollocks!" Gabe traced a northeast route from the church to their current location. "It's on the same line."

Ash swore in Greek. "I'd like a physical map to mark it out properly, but it's damn close."

"It must be significant, right?"

"I don't know. Perhaps?"

Gabe sat back, rubbing his stubble, and wishing he'd had more sleep. Unfortunately, his dreams had been plagued with memories and visions of Belial, and he'd slept poorly. "Two statues don't really make a case, do they?"

Ash turned to face him properly. "No, and as there was nothing significant to see—within easy view at least, last night—we're at a dead end for now."

Gabe had flown across the entire grounds of Amato's country house and then beyond it the previous evening, specifically searching the northeastern route, but nothing presented itself. No unusual buildings, or churches, or anything of note. "Potentially, there could be something that's miles away. Florence, after all, is an hour or two from here."

"There could be, yes. However, we should focus on the text for now." Ash pulled up the photos he'd taken the previous night and transferred to his computer. Then he accessed the photos of the manifesto that Barak sent. "The manifesto is convoluted and verbose, but there is that unnerving reference to the House of Belial."

"From what I can gather, Jackson was pretty cross that Barak didn't tell us about it yesterday, but I think Barak is right. Surely, we'd be aware of Belial's Nephilim by now." Gabe phoned Barak earlier and had a long discussion about what that reference could mean.

"Or maybe we're being naïve. Why should we know? We keep a low profile, why wouldn't they?"

"Perhaps." Gabe considered the implications of their use of the Fallen Angel's jewellery. "However, using his jewels has alerted someone to our presence. It certainly alerted Belial. He attacked Olivia, and had to be expelled. And Amato knew about us!" That had chilled

Gabe more than anything. He felt under scrutiny again, as if Belial were watching him from afar.

"True, but no one has come for us. If anything, you would think his acolytes would go into hiding, but Amato didn't. He knew we were following him and set us up."

"But he underestimated us, and he—*they*—didn't know about Shadow."

Ash laughed. "Our secret weapon."

"Herne's horns! She loves that. It's no laughing matter, though, Ash. Without her, we'd have been stuck in that trap, and it did seem as if Belial was trying to manifest through Amato. How long do you think that temple under the church has been there?" They had barely talked about it afterwards, focussing only on searching Amato's apartment in Florence, and then his country house. Gabe had pushed it to the back of his mind, but he couldn't ignore it any longer.

"Hundreds of years, maybe over a thousand. It was old, hacked out of rock, deep beneath the church. Maybe something stood above it once, before the church was built. Or there was an earlier version of it."

Gabe voiced something else that had struck him. "It couldn't have been carved by Belial, though. It was hewn by hand. Belial would have made something like The Temple of the Trinity if he could." Memories of Raziel's temple still haunted him.

"Agreed. So it was carved by humans, or Nephilim."

"But that was after the Flood, so if they're responsible, some Nephilim must have survived."

"That's a reasonable assumption. It doesn't mean they're alive now, though," Ash reasoned.

"I think we have to consider the fact that they might be, however unlikely. Best to be prepared."

"Perhaps we should always carry one of Belial's jewels, just in case they are here."

"Perhaps." That was a last resort as far as Gabe was concerned. It had taken him only a few hours to shake off Belial's influence after destroying the count's castle, but it was long enough. Barak and Estelle had argued about it, and even Shadow wasn't impressed with the effect it had on Gabe.

"Come on," Ash said, turning back to the laptop. "Let's consider the manifesto and what's written on the base. They are similar, but the manifesto is much longer. They both essentially say the same thing, though. They exalt Belial and proclaim themselves his acolytes. But there is a different word used on the base of the statue in the woods." He pointed at a portion of text on the photo, difficult to read in the light of a phone torch, especially with dirt still ingrained in it. "It says *fraternitas*."

"Brotherhood. It sounds organised." Gabe sipped his coffee and then grimaced. It had gone cold. "We need to know more about that house and who owned it before. I want a proper history. I also want more information on the church above the temple in Florence. And we need more on Amato's contacts. Is there anything we can do in the meantime?"

"I will scrutinise the manifesto and inscription to make sure we haven't missed hidden meanings, but we should also explore places along that northeasterly line."

"So, we need a map. A big one." Gabe reached for his phone. "I'll get Niel and Shadow to pick one up."

Ash lowered his voice, looking through the partially open doorway to the hall beyond. "How do you think Nahum is holding up?"

"He's okay. Worried about Olivia, of course, and his daughter. It's a lot to take in, isn't it? Even now. And of course, we can't forget that Amato knew the sex of the child, either." Gabe raked his hand through his hair, exasperated. "I must admit that I'm worried, too. Nahum likes her more than he's letting on." *That much was obvious.* Over the New Year, he could barely take his eyes off her.

"I can tell. He's fretting, and that is very unlike Nahum."

"He's really excited by this whole opportunity. His past marriage was not based on love. He endured it, but this thing with Olivia... He says it was something that just happened, but it was more than that—for both of them. Now she's pregnant, well, that's something else."

Ash gripped Gabe's shoulder in an attempt to reassure him. "Olivia is strong and smart, and has plenty of friends who know the paranormal world well. If anyone can handle it, she can. I like her, and she fits in well with us. She already feels like part of our family. You know that I never had children?" Gabe nodded. He and Ash had known each other reasonably well in their old life. "It was never anything I missed, you know? But I am looking forward to being an uncle. These are strange times, Gabe." He smiled. "But good. We must not mess it up. We would all be devastated if anything happened to Olivia or our niece."

"I'm beginning to think one of us should be with her right now, considering what we know."

"Then send Nahum back to London. It should be him."

"He wanted to come with us!"

"Bravado. A need to be of use to us, and play down his feelings for Olivia, but I think we both know where he needs to be now. So does he."

Gabe laughed for the first time in what felt like months. "It could be quite a reunion."

Ash rolled his eyes. "They will dance around each other for days. Go tell him, I have work to do." And with that, he turned to the computer, and Gabe went to speak to their brother.

Harlan was in his kitchen making breakfast when someone pounded on his front door. He went to open it, knowing exactly who it would be.

"Maggie! I'm not deaf!"

She grinned, looking bright-eyed and cheerful. "You might have been lying in."

"And had I been, you would have woken me up!" He swung open the door to let her in. "As it is, I have already been to the gym."

She inhaled deeply. "Bacon! Delicious."

"Yes, there's enough for two." He led the way back to the kitchen. "To what do I owe this pleasure?"

"I can't just visit my friend?"

"Of course you can, but you don't." He started the coffee machine. "I presume you want one of these, too?"

"Yes, please. And you're very mean. We go out for drinks and coffee sometimes. It's not always about work."

He wagged a finger at her. "But it is today, I can tell." She had an air of purpose about her. And something else. "Did you go to Storm Moon last night?" A flush of guilt swept across her cheeks, and he smirked. "Yes, you did. Chat with Grey, by any chance?"

"I chatted with lots of people."

"And yet you look like a naughty schoolgirl caught up in a crush."

Her eyes narrowed. "What are you insinuating?"

"Maggie, it's okay. You like Grey. I can't blame you. He's a big, good-looking unit. Handy with weapons. Dry sense of humour. Doesn't mind prolific swearing, either. Just your type."

"I don't have a type, and no, I don't *like* him. I mean I do, but not in that way!"

"So why are you blushing?" He passed her a coffee, enjoying her discomfort. Teasing Maggie was always fun. Better, even, than teasing Olivia, and that was lots of fun at the moment.

"I'm not blushing!" She snatched her coffee, narrowly missing scalding herself. "I like Grey, of course, as I do all of Storm Moon's staff. It's a fun place to hang out."

"Has he asked you out yet?"

"No! He doesn't need to."

"You're a modern woman, why wait? Ask him yourself."

"Harlan! Pack it in!"

"But I'm enjoying myself."

"Fuck off!"

He roared with laughter, and then reached into the fridge to get more eggs. "I knew it!"

"We are changing the subject." Her sunny disposition had vanished, replaced by a scowl.

He wasn't giving up that easily, but he shrugged. "Shall we talk about what you want from me, then?"

"Peace and bloody quiet!"

"And?"

She stood at the kitchen window, sipping her coffee as she watched him over the rim. "I wanted to ask you about your Rome office. The Orphic Guild's, that is."

"Does this relate to a certain church and country house in Florence?"

"It might."

"I thought Jackson was looking into that."

"Jackson is looking into the church, and something about northeastern directions. I'm helping in my spare time. I have resources, but they're limited. I need more background on Amato's country house, and it's not the type of thing I can really ask the local police about. I have no connections there, nor with the local councils or whatever they call them in Italy."

"Herne's horns! I go to the gym for an hour, and so much is going on! You better bring me up to speed." He started to crack the eggs. "Scrambled okay? Your eggs, I mean, not your hormones."

Her eyes narrowed. "Harlan!"

"I thought that was funny!"

"It wasn't, and yes, scrambled!" She leaned against the counter and updated him on the statue and manifestos, and The Brotherhood. "So, we need to know more about that house! Who are Amato's family? Did he inherit the place or buy it? If so, who from? It has a bloody great temple on the grounds!" Her voice rose indignantly.

"Isn't this out of your area of jurisdiction?"

"Yes, but I want to help. It's important."

"I know. I have a couple of people I speak to in the Rome office, so I'll call once we've eaten. Then I'll chase up JD. I'm wondering if he's found anything that could help in his extensive library." He didn't mention the Emerald Tablet that JD was still experimenting with. Although he could trust Maggie, they were keeping the information about its existence to a very small group. Instead, he said, "He was obsessed with angels, and hearing about Belial has set him off again."

"Any little clue would be useful." Maggie had never met JD, and for that Harlan was grateful. They would be at odds, he was sure.

He plated up the eggs, bacon, hashbrowns, and mushrooms, his brunch treat after the gym. "All right. Let's eat, and then I'll make a few calls."

Shadow grimaced, hands on her hips, as she stared up at the statue of Belial. He looked imperious and patriarchal, and she already loathed him.

"I hate bullies," she said to Niel, who stood close by. "He must be one of the biggest. I thought Herne was, but I think Belial is worse."

"He was a nightmare." Niel had been clearing away some of the undergrowth with his axe, but he paused to catch his breath. "His Nephilim were the same. To be honest, we were all entitled, but they were nightmarish. Worse than Samael's followers."

Shadow nodded. He'd suggested as much before, and she'd had long conversations with Gabe about it. "We should smash his statue. I don't like to think it's still standing here, waiting for adoration."

"I like that idea, but perhaps we should take lots of pictures before we destroy it. Something about it might hold clues."

That brightened her mood. "You promise?"

"It's funny how the little things please you, sister," Niel said, laughing.

"You're the same," she shot back. "You and that axe are never apart."

"I'm not disagreeing. We have the same appetite for destruction and swift justice. I just temper it now."

"So do I, but it's hard when it's what you've done your whole life." She studied the statue's details. It was twice Niel's height, as was the wingspan's width on each side, and the feathers were painstakingly carved. "Someone took a great deal of care on this. Do you think it's the same one as was in the temple at the church?" The events had unfolded so quickly that she wasn't sure.

Niel paced around it. "The design is the same, I think, but this one is bigger. His features have been worn by the weather, too."

Belial was rendered with sculpted muscles, his chest bare, and a skirt low on his waist. He wore calf-length boots, and carried a raised sword as if ready to dispense justice. But he clutched something in his other hand. She pointed to it. "Niel, what's that? Is it a horn?"

"I think so."

"Did he usually carry one?"

Niel frowned. "I'm not sure. Perhaps. They were common, for some angels. A way to start a battle or summon a withdrawal of troops. Or just plain instil fear and awe. Their sound was unearthly."

Something else struck Shadow, and she clambered onto the plinth, and rubbed some moss away. "The jewels that were on the statue under the church are actually carved on this one. Look! The long necklace around his neck, the torcs on his arms, the rings on his fingers." She scrubbed at more of the moss, peeling it away to reveal the design beneath, and then dropped back to the ground. "And the sword looks to be the same as the one he was holding."

"You're right. That is interesting! Well spotted." He looked at her, eyebrow cocked. "Significant?"

"Perhaps. The only object I don't recall seeing that night was the horn. Admittedly, it was a bit chaotic in there, but I'm sure I'd have seen it on the table. I crept around the back while Amato was talking to you." She wasn't seeing the open temple dappled in half-light under the trees anymore. She was in the subterranean temple again, prowling around the perimeter unseen. The jewellery glittered on the stone altar, and she could scent the rich incense that hung about the cloak on his shoulders, cleverly arranged under the wings. There were a dizzying number of runes and sigils marked on the floor and roof, but no horn. "No, I'm sure of it."

She withdrew her phone from her pocket and started to take photos, working her way methodically around the angel. "Have you found anything inscribed in the marble flooring?"

"A couple of compass points on the outer perimeter. South and west so far. I'm heading to the northeastern part to see if anything is there."

She looked at the area he'd cleared. The marble was stained green and brown from decades of mud and leaf detritus, but south and west were clearly scored into the marble that formed the base of the mini amphitheatre. "Interesting. No altar, though, is there?"

"What do you think happened here?"

"It doesn't strike me as a meeting place. Belial's statue is huge. It hides big sections of the seating, especially on the upper levels, but it is imposing. The whole place, I mean. When clean, everything must have dazzled in sunlight and moonlight. Everything is made of white marble. Imagine walking up the path and catching a glimpse of Belial. Plus, you're right—it is on a rise."

"It's a place of initiation." Niel spoke with conviction, and he nodded to himself. "Yes, I'm sure of it."

"Really?" She looked around, considering his words, imagining the new believers being brought here and sworn to The Brotherhood. The steps that doubled as seats could have been for other members to watch. "It's possible, I guess."

Niel attacked the northeast quadrant with renewed vigour, and putting her phone away, Shadow joined him. They quickly cleared a large section to reveal the final two compass points, but there was nothing significant to mark the northeasterly direction.

As if reading her thoughts, Niel said, "You wouldn't spell it out, though, would you?"

"No." Something tickled at the edge of Shadow's mind. "A temple of worship, and this, a place of initiation. Could it be a sort of path of enlightenment, or some such bollocks? And maybe it's not northeasterly, but southwestern? You move from one point to another, through various tests designed for you." She shrugged, frustrated. "Do you know what I mean?"

"I think that sounds very interesting. Have you been spending time with Ash?"

"I am quite capable of working things out, too!"

He grinned, face smeared with dirt and leaves stuck in his hair. "You are so easy to wind up."

"Piss off."

"No, I think it has to be northeasterly because of the way he's facing, but I guess he could be looking back towards the beginning?" He huffed. "Lots to consider. Or, of course, we're seeing something where there is nothing."

"No, there's something. Can we smash it now?"

"I presume that's my job?"

"We'll do it together. Just a little push!"

"All right. Stand well back." Niel extended his wings and flew a few feet above the ground, until he was face to face with Belial. He gripped the head and rocked the statue back, roaring with effort. It wobbled off its plinth and smashed on the ground, cracking the marble underfoot. Chunks of the statue rattled across the rock, and something skittered out of the debris.

Shadow knew what it was, even from a distance. *Another piece of Belial's jewellery.*

Six

N iel carried the newly discovered ring back to their Tuscan villa that was tucked into a fold in the countryside, trying to ignore Belial's whispers and entreaties while they completed the shopping Gabe had requested.

They had smashed the statue into tiny pieces, Niel using his axe, Shadow using her Dragonium sword, eager to ensure they were leaving nothing behind. Fortunately, the ring was the only trinket embedded into the statue. It hadn't reduced their unease, though. They were both quiet on the journey home.

Ash was working on the computer when they entered the kitchen, but Gabe and Nahum were discussing flights.

Niel placed the ring, a huge ruby set within an ornate gold mount, on the kitchen table. "Another one."

Gabe and Nahum's conversation ended abruptly as Nahum asked, "Where did you find it?"

"In the statue that we smashed to pieces. There was nothing else."

Ash looked up, alarmed. "You smashed it? Are you mad?"

"We took photos beforehand," Shadow informed him. "Besides, isn't it good that we did? We found *that*!"

It pulsed with power. Niel could feel it, and felt sure if he could see auras, there would be a dark one around the ring. "It's just like the others. It whispers evil."

"We can hear it," Gabe said, answering for all of them. His jaw was tight, eyes fixed on the ring. "How many more will we find?"

"There could be hundreds more." Ash pushed away from the table. "I'll get the box."

"Why are you discussing flights?" Shadow asked.

"Nahum is returning home to look after Olivia."

Niel grinned. "Look after her? Is that what we're calling it now?"

Nahum glared at him. "Not funny. And not my idea!" His glare shifted to Gabe.

"It's for the best!" Gabe replied. "Look at what we're finding out. I don't think we should leave her alone right now. What if this bloody Brotherhood goes after her? Or do you want me to ask Lucien to be a bodyguard? Or Barak? Or Eli, perhaps?" There was a glint of amusement in Gabe's expression now.

Niel's grin broadened, and he expanded the tease. The ring was egging him on, urging him to unsettle Nahum. "I'm sure Eli would be only too pleased to comfort Olivia while you're away."

"I know what you two are suggesting, but I'm pretty sure that Eli wouldn't seduce Olivia while pregnant with my child!"

"But her hormones will be raging, brother," Niel said, "and she looked radiant at New Year. A good-looking woman! No wonder you couldn't help yourself."

Ash intervened, sweeping the ring into the spelled box as Nahum's hands clenched into fists. "Let's get rid of this, shall we? Before tempers flare."

The box shut with a bang and Belial's whispers instantly vanished.

Chastened, but only slightly, because Niel was enjoying getting his own back after all the teasing he had endured over Mouse, he said, "Gabe is right. All of us would hate for anything to happen to her. Maybe you should both leave London for a while. Find a place no one knows about."

Shadow smirked. "A love nest?"

"Shadow!" Nahum took a deep breath, a resigned expression crossing his face. "I know you think this is funny, and yes, you can tease me. Go ahead! I slept with her—*once*—and now she's pregnant. I didn't foresee this, and if I had known, well, I wouldn't have. I'm ruining her life." He sank into a chair, staring at the table. "The last thing I want to do is crowd her."

All of them stared at each other over his head, and compassion swept over Niel. He sat down next to him. "That's not true. You are not ruining her life. She could have chosen to abort her, but hasn't. She wants this, Nahum, and that means she wants *you*—and all of us, too—in her life. When she visited us, she was happy! She fitted right in. I think you're more worried than she is."

Nahum looked up, eyes locking with Niel. "What if I'm not father material? Or even a good partner, in whatever capacity that is? I've never done this before. My marriage was a sham. This life was supposed to avoid that."

"Then you would have been avoiding *living*. You cannot completely avoid connections, or love, or lust, or else you'd be dead! Or merely existing. And love and relationships are painful." He looked across at Shadow and his brothers, who had also sat at the table now, their mood sombre. "You all know about me and Lilith, but I wouldn't have missed all of that for anything. It's life, in all of its messy, glorious strangeness. It's what we fought to eradicate, and then fought to save. It's why we're hunting down Belial and his damn Brotherhood. It's meant to be, Nahum." He felt a bit emotional, as he always became when dwelling on such things. It's why he channelled his feelings into aggression half the time. It kept his ridiculous romantic side in check. "I want to be an uncle, and you will be an amazing father."

Nahum's eyes filled with tears. "Brother."

"Oh, you two," Shadow sniffed. "You're even getting to me."

"I'm serious, though," Nahum continued. "Should I suggest that I stay in a hotel room?"

"What good will that do?" Gabe asked, rolling his eyes. "You have to move in. I'm not saying forever, just for now! I could phone her, if that's what you're worried about? I'll tell her it's my idea, and she can't say no."

"No!" Nahum took a deep breath, pulling himself together. "No, I will. It's all taking some time to get used to. You know, how all of this will work."

Shadow's natural sarcasm returned. "You better get a move on. Seven months to baby time."

"Yes, thank you for that reminder." Nahum didn't move, though. "I can't just sit in London and do nothing. I must help in some way."

"I'm sure Jackson has a list of things to follow up. Or even JD," Ash said. "If I think of anything, I'll let you know. Maybe look at the map and pursue the northeasterly idea. Did you buy one?"

Shadow extracted the item in question from her pack. "It's the biggest we could find. Niel and I had a few ideas while we were smashing things. Ooh! And we discovered that Belial's statue was carrying a horn. Do you think that's important?"

Ash blinked. "A horn?"

"Yes, and jewels were carved onto the statue, just like the ones under the church. They were identical! It must mean something."

Ash turned to Gabe. "You must remember his special horn? It induced a type of madness any time he blew it—triggered a bloodlust among his Nephilim, as well as everyone else. It's what made his battles so...horrific."

Gabe narrowed his eyes, gaze distant. "I do, actually, but strangely I'd forgotten about it until now. I never heard it, though. I just heard about it through others."

"Have either of you?" Ash asked. Niel and Nahum shook their heads. "Well, I heard it. It was unearthly, and like his jewels it got under your skin and into your brain. If that exists here, we're in big trouble."

"Why?"

"Its sound carries for miles. It would have a far wider ranging effect than the jewels. It could be devastating."

"Surely that means," Niel reasoned, "that they haven't got it, or they would have used it already."

"Unless they have a specific time they are waiting for," Nahum suggested. "Although, I'm sure its effects would be devastating whatever time it was used."

Gabe stopped their conversation. "This is just supposition. We'll keep the horn in mind, but we focus on The Brotherhood." His phone started ringing, and he frowned when he saw the caller. "It's Theo! I'll take it outside."

"Theo?" Niel asked, excitement building. "It must be about the Templar treasure!"

Theo Carmichael was the rich owner of Temple Keep, and as the name suggested, it had once belonged to the last Master of England who served the Knights Templar. Theo had instigated the search for the lost Templar treasure, and they had found some of it deep beneath the church in Temple Moreton. Not without running into descendants of the Templars, however. After a fierce battle, the Nephilim had given them the instructions to find other caches, and Theo had generously agreed to split the money they would earn for the treasure. It had been in the British Museum for months since then, being evaluated.

Ash moved his laptop and spread the map across the table. "Perhaps they have come to a decision about money! That would be good news in the middle of all this. Now, let us search this northeasterly line."

He put a cross on the map where the church was in Florence, and then marked the position of Amato's house. "Okay, so roughly, if I draw a line to the northeast through these two points, and focus on the bigger cities, we cross the edge of Venice, head into Austria, skirting Linz, and on from there into the Czech Republic, and then Poland. If we go southwest, it will take us to Corsica, Algiers, and Morocco. After that it's the Atlantic, and north is Finland. Do those places suggest anything to you?"

Niel shrugged, "Not particularly."

"Perhaps," Nahum said, "they'll mean something to Jackson."

"We could at least research big churches and cathedrals," Shadow suggested.

"There'll be so many," Ash told her. "And there's no guarantee there will be any churches involved. We need more to go on."

Gabe entered the room, more cheerful than Niel had seen him in weeks. "Good news! The British Museum has agreed to an amount of money to award us, and we have Theo and his influence to thank for that. I think it would have taken a lot longer otherwise."

"How much?" Shadow asked, cutting straight to the point.

He named a seven-figure sum. "That'll do, right?"

"Are you for real?" Niel asked, the map forgotten. "That's huge!"

"The find was worth billions, and that's not even factoring in its cultural significance."

Shadow whooped, jumping up and down. "Lots of lovely gold!"

"Money in a bank account, actually, Shadow," Ash said.

"But I can buy gold with it, right?"

Nahum laughed. "You want a nest of it?"

"Could I?" Her eyes gleamed with the prospect.

Gabe shook his head. "Please stop giving her ideas. However, they need a signature from one of us. We need to meet Theo on Monday morning. Harlan too, because he'll get a share, of course. All of us and Shadow are all named as beneficiaries, so any one of us can do it. I suggest that you," he looked at Nahum, "or Barak go. Probably you, seeing as you want something to do, and Barak might have other leads to follow up. Or you can both go."

Nahum nodded enthusiastically. "Of course. Do we get to see the treasure again?"

"I believe so. Some of it, at least."

Shadow's mouth dropped open. "I want to see it!"

"Sorry, you're stuck here with us!" Gabe stuck his hands in his jeans' pockets. "I'm a bit gutted I can't go, actually."

"Why don't we all go?" Ash suggested. "It's a short flight."

Niel considered the jewels they had found, and the statues, and the likelihood that there'd be more. "I don't think we should. One of us should stay here. I'm happy to do that. Hopefully it won't be the only opportunity we get to see the hoard again. Plus, I want to get back in that house, in case there's something we missed."

"Unfortunately," Ash said, leaning back in his chair, "I agree."

Gabe nodded, disappointed but determined. "Yes, we'll stay here."

"Okay, then." Nahum headed to the door. "I'll organise my flights, and someone will need to take me to the airport. With luck I can get one this afternoon. I'll take Olivia with me on Monday. She'd love to see the hoard."

"I'll drive you," Niel told him. "What about the jewels? You may as well take those. We don't really want them with us." The spelled box would also get the jewels through customs without alerting anyone, much the same as the one they used to transport the emerald discs out of Egypt.

Nahum's lips tightened. "I'm not keeping them in Olivia's place. No way!"

"JD's house, then? Or The Retreat?"

"No!" Gabe's strident voice cut across Niel's suggestion. "Only *we* look after them. JD wouldn't be able to help himself."

"A trip to Cornwall too, then," Nahum said, nodding. "Leave it with me."

When Harlan arrived at JD's estate, Mortlake, on Saturday afternoon, he was buzzing with excitement that he knew even JD wouldn't dampen.

He'd be signing the paperwork on Monday morning to receive his Templar treasure finding fee, and would be seeing some of the treasure again. He'd been so overwhelmed when he first saw it under the church that he'd barely been able to take it in. Not helped, of course, by being captured and at great risk of imminent death. However, on Monday he would see it properly, with hopefully most of it catalogued. His imagination was working overtime just thinking about the stories the treasure could tell. It would be good to see Theo again, too. Out of courtesy, he'd tell Mason Jacobs, his boss. He would have to go during work time, after all. He had a feeling that Mason, who knew Theo well, would also want to go. He hoped The British Museum's staff would be accommodating.

Plus, he'd phoned his contacts in Rome, and had successfully talked to an Occult Hunter called Romola Falco. She had agreed to look into Amato's house and the family for him. Romola was a voluble woman in her mid-thirties, passionate about her work and effusive about everything Italian—food, cars, cities, fashion, and of course, its vast history. She was even named for the myth about Romulus and Remus who had founded Rome after being suckled by a she-wolf as babes, and then raised as shepherds. Romola was the female derivative of Romulus.

Harlan had kept the details about a Fallen Angel's jewellery out of it. He'd just said it was religious iconography that he was chasing down. She'd pressed him for details, and once she heard about the Florentine church, she'd told him she'd investigate that, too. He passed the good news on to Jackson, hoping that might encourage his friend to take time off, as well as Barak, Estelle, and Lucien. All of them had been obsessing over Belial for weeks, and this was a chance to rest for a while, and recover from their bruising encounter with Black Cronos, too. Like the rest of the team, he couldn't really believe that the count was really gone, but for now, he was enjoying it.

Since Christmas he had dedicated himself, more or less, to his job. He'd had a few old texts to track down, a rumoured cursed statue, and a few auction jobs to attend for clients. He'd only been sidetracked when a demon had rocked up in Wimbledon, courtesy of a witch who'd tried to fool the Storm Moon Pack. More fool *him*. Now that was over with too, and his thoughts circled back to the Emerald Tablet of Hermes Trismegistus.

Anna, JD's assistant, answered the door as usual, her gaze sweeping disapprovingly over him. He had no idea why she seemed to dislike him, but took heart in the fact that she looked at everyone except JD with that same tight-lipped air of intolerance. "He's in the marquee," she said, heading up the stairs and leaving him to find his own way to the garden.

"Thanks!" he called sarcastically after her.

He walked quickly through JD's Elizabethan manor, exiting onto the long back patio with the expansive lawns beyond. Right in the centre was a huge, white marquee that looked as if JD was preparing for a wedding. He wasn't, though. It housed the tablet.

Harlan shouted as he neared the entrance, not wanting to surprise him. "JD! It's Harlan. Okay if I come in?"

"Just watch your step! And shut the door after you!"

Warily, Harlan unzipped the entrance flap, pushed his way inside, and then stopped in shock. "Herne's horns! What the hell is going on?"

Electric cables snaked across the ground, and strings of lights were suspended overhead. Benches were set up in a circle around a central area, littered with scientific equipment that looked utterly baffling, like some kind of Frankenstein's circus, with JD as the ringmaster. Plus it was stiflingly warm from the array of heaters around the place.

"What do you think I'm doing, imbecile? I am testing the tablet."

Harlan ignored the insult. He was used to it. Besides, JD said it more out of habit than real meaning. That was what he told himself, anyway. "Now?"

"*Yes*! For about the hundredth time." JD was wearing one of his Elizabethan smocks that made him look like a mad Renaissance artist, and he turned, hand on hips. "In fact, to be precise, this is my one hundred and thirty-eighth test. It's all in there." He gesticulated to a large book on one of the tables.

"So many?" Harlan weaved through the tables, focussing on the Emerald Tablet displayed on a large, stone block. A wheel of correspondence was a few metres away, set up by some kind of control centre. "Is this the one from your lab?"

"Yes. I brought it all out here. Took a week. To make another one would take far too long." JD's beard was unkempt, and his hair was brushed rakishly in the wrong direction. "I've been testing since just after Christmas, once I knew we got rid of that old devil." He meant the count.

Harlan turned the pages of the book that JD had referred to, seeing reams of confusing notes and diagrams. "Why so many?"

"There are a million permutations of the wheel, but my investigations have narrowed down the possible combinations to several thousand instead. However, I am getting close. At least I know which disc fits now."

"You do?"

"It's already in place."

"It is?"

"Yes. It took a few attempts, but then I realised it had to be done at a certain time—planetary alignments, stars, etcetera. Well, one of several special times."

"How did you discover that?" Harlan was aware that he was asking an endless number of questions, but the last time he had discussed this with JD was weeks ago, and he hadn't achieved any of this.

"Mathematical calculations based on potential dates of its construction, the alignments of the cosmos, plus the properties of emerald, and the text itself, of course. It didn't make sense that it could just be resurrected at any old time. There needed to be a key, and not one that was accessible once in a thousand years, either. When I cracked it, it slid in like warm butter in a pan. You can't even see the edge where they join anymore."

"It's heavy! How did you manage it?"

"Anna helped me. So now I'm focussing various resonances at it using gemstones—much like I used in my weapons."

"Like a laser beam."

"If you have to use that term." Harlan studied the circle of tables again and saw that an array of objects was pointed at the tablet. JD followed his gaze. "Yes, I use all of them. I manipulate them using the wheel, and they direct energy at the tablet."

No doubt about it. JD was a genius. Harlan could feel the hum of *something* around him. "It could still take years."

"No. Days, I estimate. Maybe even today."

Harlan's mouth dropped open. "You mean that thing could grow *today*? Reveal its secrets?"

"Perhaps. There could be many stages, or just one. And whether I understand what I see... Well, that remains to be seen. Or, it might not grow at all!"

Harlan stared at the cloudy interior of the Emerald Tablet, considering the fact that it always reminded him of the solar system. Up close, it made him dizzy; at a distance, it just seemed threatening. "And what if the power it contains is like a nuclear bomb? Or even just a small bomb. You'll be dead, and you'll blow up the house."

"Or half the county. Or the whole country?" JD shook his head. "No. When I unlock it, it will be because I've done it correctly. It won't explode. I will have earned its secrets."

Harlan turned his back on it with a great effort. He'd forgotten how mesmerising it could be. "What about Belial?"

"Ah! Our Fallen Angel. Yes, I have found something. A reference in an old book written in the nineteenth century by another alchemist, actually. I believe it refers to The Brotherhood, although he doesn't call it by that name. He calls it The Consortium."

"That's great! Does it mention any names or places?"

"A *palazzo* in Venice—a grand residence. He had gone there on the invitation of a rich family who sought help with the object in question. A jewel that had strange properties." JD's eyes had taken on his usual, feral gleam. "I came across that book about a hundred years ago, back when I was still obsessing about angels. I followed that lead and came up against a dead end. I hadn't associated it with Belial. Now, however, things make sense. I'd forgotten all about it until this whole thing with Belial's jewels cropped up."

Harlan could barely contain his impatience. "Why a dead end? The house was destroyed? Family dead?"

"Oh, no. They were alive. But no one would answer my calls. In fact, I was hounded out of Venice."

"But what about the original alchemist that they invited?"

"Oh, he spoke very coyly of the object of power after the visit. He was Italian, too. I've left the book out in the library for you, with a translation. I don't suppose Gabe would let me see the jewels they have found?"

"Not a chance." Harlan already knew Gabe's view on that topic.

JD tapped his lip with an ink-stained finger. "I suspected as much. Well, if they need assistance, you know where I am. I will say, however, that they are probably far more dangerous than that." He pointed at the tablet. "But we shall see... Would you like to see my next test?"

"You know, I don't think I would." Harlan backed away. "Happy if I head to your library, though?"

"Of course. But stay the night, Harlan. I do want to show you a few other things, too."

Harlan wasn't sure how he felt about that, but he nodded anyway. He'd planned to meet up with Jackson, Maggie, and Olivia for drinks and a meal, but JD had a story to tell, and he needed all the details he could get on the mysterious *palazzo* in Venice.

Seven

Olivia had been fretting for hours, ever since she'd received Nahum's phone call telling her that he was coming back to effectively guard her.

He hadn't used those words, exactly. In fact, she couldn't remember quite how he'd put it. Something about how Gabe and his brothers had decided that with things being so uncertain, and with the latest developments, he had been sent to look after her. *Sent.* He hadn't volunteered. It was like she was a mission. *And that was fine*, she told herself. One night of passion and a child on the way inferred no obligation beyond what they had talked about already.

Nevertheless, it irked her, and she tried very hard to shove that feeling aside. She had suggested that Barak and Estelle could look after her if they were that worried, or Lucien, the super-soldier. *Surely, he was skilled enough to defend her?* But Nahum had hurriedly shot that down. So now, here she was, having cleaned her flat, plumped various cushions, and prepared the guest bedroom, as if royalty were coming to stay. She'd even stocked beer and nibbles such as soft cheeses and pâtés, the things she couldn't eat now that she was pregnant. *By the Gods, she needed a glass of wine. No, a bottle.*

She was just touching up her makeup, the barely-there look that smacked of time and effort, when the intercom buzzed from the main door downstairs. *Nahum.* She really needed to give him the code. She took a deep breath and exhaled, and then let him in. In minutes he was in her hallway, looking devastatingly handsome, and far more self-assured than she felt.

"I feel terrible that I've arrived so late," he admitted, following her into the kitchen. "Have I kept you up?"

"It's ten o'clock at night, not three in the morning! Besides, I'm a night owl. You know that." She smiled, trying to look relaxed. "I feel guilty that you've been travelling so late."

He shrugged. "Night owl, too."

"Beer?"

"I'd kill for one. Travelling is thirsty work. Sure you don't mind, though, seeing as you're not drinking?"

"The whole world can't stop for me. I'll sniff it and pretend."

"Thank you. You look well." He almost drank her in, and that set her to blushing.

She patted her stomach. "Yes, this little one is being gentle. I feel fine. But look, get settled first. I've put you in here." She opened the door to the guest room that suddenly seemed far too small for Nahum. It wasn't really, but his presence was so overwhelming. *Breathe...*

"This is great!" He put his bag on the double bed, taking it in quickly. He'd never been in her flat. Since her New Years visit to Cornwall, they had stuck to phone calls. "It's a nice place. Roomy."

"Well, I earn enough money, and I hate pokey flats. Come on, though. My room is opposite, with the ensuite, and there's a main bathroom, too—that's yours. And this is the living room and kitchen-dining area. All in one." She was gabbling and she knew it. She also had another room she could use as a nursery, but there was no way she was discussing that now. *Calm the fuck down!* For a while she bustled about, glad to keep herself busy. "I've bought lots of food. I know you eat like a horse."

"Okay. Rule number one. I pull my weight around here. I know it's your place, but I can cook, pour my own beer, make my own snacks." He gently took the can and glass from her hands, and the touch of his skin was like electricity. "I'm imposing, but well, things are weird..."

"You're *not* imposing! Please don't think that." She took a breath and smiled at him. This was Nahum. They were friends before their night of awesome sex. He was moving in for a while, and she couldn't deal with this awkwardness. "Yes, things are weird. But, like I said before, I wouldn't change a thing. This," she gestured between them, "will be something we'll work out. We're friends, right? We were before that night, and still are!"

"Of course. Friends." A trace of some emotion Olivia couldn't quite work out flashed across his face. *Relief, or regret?* "So, you have cases, I presume? I can help you with them. I really should be with you all the time, so..."

She made herself a cup of herbal tea to keep busy. "Yes, a few cases. The early stages of some, wrapping up others, but nothing urgent. I will have to go into the office at some point. I'm not entirely sure what I should say to Mason, though. No one at work knows I'm pregnant, and even if they did, I can't explain a bodyguard easily."

"But Mason knows all about us, and the paranormal. Does he know about when you were possessed?"

"Yes, actually. I had to have time off. He was very sweet about it."
Mason could be prickly, but she'd always got on well with him.

"Just tell him we're worried he'll come for you again. That should
suffice."

"True. I think I already have baby brain."

He laughed. "I'm sure you haven't. I've got a few things I have to
do, actually, and wondered if you'd like to come with me. I need to
go to Cornwall tomorrow to deliver the collection of jewels we found.
My brothers will caretake them."

Her eyes widened. "You found more?"

"Yes, lots. I'll give you all the thrilling details if you want. It involved
a near-death experience, so that was fun."

Her heart almost skipped a beat. "Near-death! Why am I surprised,
though? Yes, of course I want to know!" *More jewels, and they were
here.* "It might sound odd, considering what happened, but I'd like to
see them. No touching, obviously."

Nahum shook his head. "No. Sorry. I don't want to give him any
quarter at all. You and our daughter are too precious."

"I like being precious! It's gives me a fuzzy, warm glow." She
couldn't resist a tease. It was in her nature.

"Well, it's true. My brothers will kill me if I let anything happen to
you. And I'd never forgive myself." He held her gaze for a moment,
and her brain emptied of everything except a desperate urge to kiss
him. "So, do you fancy a trip tomorrow? It's a long drive, though.
And we can't stay overnight," he rushed onwards, "because I have to
go to the British Museum on Monday." He briefly outlined what had
happened.

"I can go with you?" Vision of golden, jewelled treasures filled her head. "Holy shit! Yes, please! Templar treasure! An enormous finder's fee!" All embarrassment vanished. "Sit and tell me everything about what's going on."

"So, you see our problem," Zee said to Alex Bonneville as they were cleaning the bar of The Wayward Son in White Haven after a busy Saturday night. The other staff were well out of hearing range. "A box won't cut it anymore. We have too many jewels."

"Oh, no! What a terrible dilemma!" Alex shot Zee a wry grin. "So much gold!"

"Funny, if they weren't so dangerous!

Alex poured them both half a pint of Skullduggery Ale. "I'm kidding, obviously. You need another spelled box. Or a treasure chest, at this point."

"More like a bunker. Me and Eli have already prepared a place in the cellar. We've dug a pit. It was a rough brick and dirt floor anyway. We've lined it with slabs and made a trap door to go over it. Can you spell that?"

"Bloody hell, mate. How much stuff are you expecting?"

"Prepare for the worst, and all that." He'd already told Alex about what had happened to his brothers and Shadow in Florence. "There could be more. Weapons, too."

Alex's grin vanished. "I'd rather it be in your cellar than anywhere else. I'll come round tomorrow with the whole coven. We'll set up a protection spell."

Zee knew that Alex would help, but it was good to have it confirmed. "Thank you. I don't like us having them. Feels like we're sitting on dynamite, but like you said, better with us than anywhere else."

"You're sure you don't want to be with them? Your brothers, I mean."

"No! It's important that me and Eli are here to keep everything safe, and besides, I like my new job."

"Good, because you're great at it." Alex raised his glass. "And way easier to deal with than Simon!"

It had been two months since Simon, Alex's previous Bar Manager, had left and Zee had taken over the role, and he loved it. He also loved the fact that he had use of the flat upstairs. A partial sharing arrangement with Abigail Kendall, the DS on Newton's team. He was currently spending half his time there, and had debated whether to fully move in, but with more of Belial's jewels arriving now, he couldn't really.

"Cheers, Alex. That's good to know. Any idea what we can do with all of his stuff long-term, though? We can't keep it forever."

"There are a few options, I guess," he mused while he sipped his beer, "but the more you accumulate, the more overall power you'll have to contain. Digging a hole is a great idea. Maybe the best yet. However, with all your newfound wealth, you should have a proper safe installed. A big one."

Zee blinked in shock. "I hadn't considered that. The kind we can walk into, like in a bank?"

"Pretty much. You can then add spells to it, and you'd have double levels of protection. Make sense, right?"

"We could convert half the cellar!"

"Absolutely, if that's the best space. Reinforce the walls, etcetera. I bet Caspian can recommend someone. He'd know companies who could do that."

"That's a brilliant idea. Nahum is arriving tomorrow. I can talk to him and Eli, and call Gabe. He'll agree, I'm sure." The more Zee thought about it, the more he liked it. There would be no need for it ever to leave their house, and seeing as Gabe had bought the farmhouse and the land for all of them to use, it made sense.

"I bet," Alex added, as he put his beer down and loaded glasses in the dishwasher, "that your alchemist friend, JD, could recommend metals you could use for extra insulation, too."

"Alex, you really are a bloody genius! That's a brilliant idea."

Alex winked. "I know. I might not be able to search for Belial, but I'll do what I can."

It had been a great source of frustration that Alex couldn't use his magic skills to find Belial in other worlds. He couldn't touch the jewels, and even if he could, they couldn't risk him encountering such a powerful presence. It would kill Alex. Plus, there was nothing else they could use to find his agents. *Until now.*

"What about the manifesto?" Zee asked. "It will have been handled by people other than Jacobsen. Could you use that?"

"Of course, but isn't that in London with Barak? Why don't you ask Estelle to do that? It's one of her specialities."

"That's actually a great suggestion. I don't know why they haven't considered it. Unless they have, and it failed. I'll call Barak soon. He'll still be up."

"Hold on!" Alex held his hand up. "There'll be other spells you can use, not just finding spells. Objects contain impressions, and the stronger the emotion, the stronger the impression is. A manifesto will have lots! A skilled witch should be able to draw out the emotions of who was writing it, maybe even where. I have a few spells in my grimoire. They all vary slightly, but hopefully one will work." He grimaced. "I tried one on my own grimoire, but there are too many years, too many individuals to separate. It gave me a headache. The manifesto, however, could be perfect to try."

"Really? That's possible?"

"Perhaps. It's worth a shot if you're at a dead end."

"We are for now, but we're working on options." Zee forgot all about cleaning the bar, excited by the prospect of unlocking the manifesto's secrets. "Wow. If we could pin down who wrote it, even if it's years old, it would tell us something. Surely though, a psychic witch like you would have better results?"

"Maybe." Alex pulled his long, dark hair out of his top knot and rubbed his head as if it ached. "Confusing, isn't it? I don't know what hidden talents Estelle has, but she might have success. Or, what about the Moonfell Witches? Olivia was telling us about them when we saw her at New Years."

They'd had a big New Years Eve party at the farmhouse, and all of their White Haven friends had attended. The witches, Newton's team, the PCs from the town, Stan, and Ghost OPS. It had been epic. A way to celebrate after vanquishing Black Cronos, and to toast Olivia's pregnancy, of course.

"They saved Olivia," Alex continued, "and I gather Odette saw Nahum's wings. She sees the truth of things. It sounds like she works a little like I do."

Zee nodded. He'd never met them. In fact, the only Nephilim who had was Nahum. "I guess we could ask them if Estelle needs help—*if* she'll admit it!"

"She's not a fool. She'll ask if it will get all of you further along."

"I like working with you, though."

Alex laughed. "Thank you! We are glad to help, but they're closer, and I think you can trust them, too. You need all hands on deck for this."

Zee sat heavily on a bar stool. Everything seemed so big, with so many moving parts. He thought life might get less messy after Black Cronos, but it seemed even more complicated than ever. He felt like he was back on the battlefield, and could almost taste the dust and feel the sweat running down his face, and scent blood and death in the air. He took a deep breath to dispel it all. The images vanished, but it left him knowing something he'd rather not.

"We're going to become Belial's keepers, aren't we?"

Alex nodded and sat down, too. "If you mean you'll have to guard his shit forever? Yes."

"Forever is a long time."

"If you break up The Brotherhood, no one will know. You keep them in your big vault and forget about them. You think only of your future, which is for you to design as it pleases you. Like being here, for now."

"I've got a lot going on in White Haven. That stupid pact with the dryads with Eli. My flat share, my job, my friendships. A shit-ton of money coming our way, too!"

"Always nice!"

New resolve filled Zee. "Yes, we build a huge, fuck-off vault spelled with everything, and sit on it like big Nephilim dragons. And we make sure we celebrate everything else. Like pregnancies and weddings."

"Wedding! *Just one*!" Alex rolled his eyes. "That's enough."

"One for now!" Zee laughed, glad to change the subject. "Having fun with Reuben as his best man?"

"Fun is one word for it." He swept his hands down to his old rock band t-shirt, jeans, and boots. "Do I look like a suit man?"

"You have to wear a suit? Wow. Which means Reuben is wearing a suit for the wedding? *Wow,*" he repeated, unable to imagine Reuben dressed in anything so formal.

"Of a sort."

"But he wears board shorts all year round. Are you kidding?"

"No. So that means we have to start suit shopping."

Zee, on the whole, had stayed out of the handfasting discussions, mostly because Reuben wanted to surprise their guests. He normally exhibited an air of insouciance, but lately that had been replaced with distraction, and endless list ticking on his phone notes. Of course, his surfing habit remained ever present.

"So," Zee asked, now very curious, "this is going to be quite big, by the sound of it. I didn't expect that."

"Neither did El, nor Reuben, to be honest." Alex smiled. "He's determined to make this the best handfasting *ever*."

"So, where are you shopping for a suit?"

"I have no idea! But who does wear a suit very well?"

"Newton? And Caspian!"

"Exactly. I mean, I wore one for Gil's funeral, and so did Reu, but that's a funeral! This is very different—and Reu has *ideas*!" Alex made air quotes. "So, because I'm the best man and I can't duck out of these things, we four musketeers are going suit shopping. This fucking wedding is sprouting horns!"

"Oh! That's priceless!" Zee started to laugh. "But Reu is happy, and so are the girls."

"So happy." He drained his half pint. "Avery is only a bridesmaid, and yet we are knee-deep in bridal magazines! Even Kendall is involved!"

"I confess that I have heard some flower chat." Living with Kendall, it was inevitable. "But Kendall is being cagey."

"Avery is not cagey enough for me!"

"You, mate, need a night at the farmhouse, killing stuff on video games. It will do wonders for your soul."

"I might take you up on that."

"How long to go? A month?"

"More or less. The longest month of my bloody life."

"You love Reuben! You don't mean that."

Alex groaned. "No, I suppose I don't. I'll make him pay with my best man speech. I have many stories to share!"

Zee stood up. "Well, we better make sure most of this is under control before then, because I don't intend that I or any of my brothers or Shadow will miss that wedding. I'll phone Barak right now."

Eight

"I just wish I'd bloody thought of that," Estelle Faversham said, feeling cranky as she prepared a cup of coffee on Sunday morning. "Trust Alex to think of unveiling spells to use on the manifesto!"

"My love," Barak said, standing behind her and nuzzling her neck, "he's helping, and you should be grateful."

"I am! And that's even more annoying. I can't believe I'm actually friends with them."

"The dreaded 'F' word. Oh, no! You do know that you're coming to the wedding, right? With me."

"Yes." She giggled as his lips moved along her neck. "It's impossible to stay mad when you do that."

"I know. I can do it more often."

"Not in the kitchen!"

"No, not in the kitchen!" Lucien remonstrated from behind them.

Estelle turned around, laughing as she pushed Barak away. "Sorry. Barak is incorrigible."

"You don't normally complain."

"We don't normally have an audience."

"I'm not watching like a peeping Tom," Lucien said, horrified, as he headed to the cupboard to get a mug.

"I know! It's just an expression." Sometimes things got lost in translation.

Barak started to get food out of the fridge. "I was cheering her up, because one of our very good friends," he shot her sideways look, "has come up with a brilliant suggestion for that manifesto."

"Really?" Lucien was as frustrated with it as they were. "Like what?"

"Like a spell to unlock its secrets." Estelle checked her phone—again. "He's sending through some spells I can use on it. The only thing is, I might not have everything to hand here. Or it might be beyond my skill set. We may have to ask the Moonfell Witches for help—specifically, Odette."

"But you cast a finding spell," Lucien said. "Is that different?"

"Yes. The results were confusing." She had cast it the previous night, and watched the smoke trail across Yorkshire, and then over Europe and into Italy. But then it diffused, pinpointing nowhere in particular, and leaving her very frustrated. She had tried several different variations with the same result. Perhaps the Fallen Angel's presence had confused things, or maybe it indicated that several hands had designed it. Alex's suggestion certainly sounded intriguing. "This could tell us so much more, but I've never cast such a spell before. If I damage the document, then I might not be able to use it again. Magic can be tricky."

As she was talking, her phone buzzed with incoming messages, and she quickly scanned them. Alex was concise. He'd sent photos of the original spells and written transcripts.

"Have you got a printer here, Lucien?"

"In the study, upstairs. It's new, like the PC. The Orphic Guild installed it." He shrugged. "It's a sort of backup office here."

"Good. I need these printed off so I can study them better. Barak, will we be seeing Nahum today?"

"No. He's taking Belial's tokens to Cornwall with Olivia. Why?"

"In case I need the Moonfell witches. That's okay. He can phone them and tell them who I am. I hate to cold call." Estelle might be abrupt on occasions, but there were ways to do things, and rocking up on someone's doorstep asking for magical help as a stranger was not the way to go.

Estelle didn't often eat breakfast, so she left Barak and Lucien to it, and took her coffee upstairs to the book-lined study, filled with occult and arcane ephemera. She'd never met William Chadwick, but she had a sense of who he once was. Old-fashioned, obsessive, fastidious in his research, but chaotic in every other aspect of his life. He probably had his own, organised system that was confusing to everyone else. His occult collections in the series of rooms downstairs were meticulously displayed and organised, but here, in his inner sanctum, the place was a mess. Apparently, Mason Jacobs had started to organise the study, but hadn't got very far. From the piles of books on the floor and notes in Lucien's handwriting, it seemed that Lucien was keeping himself occupied by trying to organise the place.

After a few moments of fiddling with settings and Wi-Fi, she synced her phone to the printer and printed off the spells Alex had sent her. They were all long and complicated, and while she had the ingredients for one, she didn't have them for the others, and the herbs required were unusual. There were plenty of witchcraft shops she could buy supplies from, but that would take time.

Alex had also suggested spells that would reveal hidden writing. A message within a message. One used fire, but the other was far more unusual. Hating herself for doing it, she called him. After exchanging pleasantries and her thanks, she said, "You suggested a spell using Nephilim blood? Where did you find that?"

"I didn't. It was Avery's idea." Estelle rolled her eyes. *Of course it bloody was*. Alex continued, "She's good at making new spells, and she thought seeing as Nephilim are the sons of angels, their blood might unlock some secrets. It might not do anything, of course, but well…"

She finished the sentence. "It's worth trying."

"I found hidden messages in one of my spells once, unveiled by fire, which is my element. It worked. It was a bit risky, but seeing as you're dealing with Belial, they might have used the power in his jewellery to hide something. It's just a thought."

"It's a good one, too," she said. "It might even be why my finding spells aren't successful."

"But you should take all precautions. Set up a circle." He hesitated. "I don't like the idea of you doing that alone, Estelle. You're powerful, but Belial is a Fallen Angel. Who knows what weird crap might be wrapped in that manifesto. Can Caspian help?"

She shook her head, though he couldn't see her. "He's tied up with the business."

"We can't help, either. We're placing protection spells around a big hole in the farmhouse cellar today. A bunker for jewellery. Zee and Eli want to be prepared for anything."

She laughed, and the thought of the farmhouse, and Alex's Cornish accent, made her suddenly homesick. She had an urge to see the Cornish moors, and feel the cool air, and scent the sea. London was exciting, and travelling was fun, but it wasn't home. She shrugged it off. She had a job to do. "A bunker? I guess it's wise, all things considered."

"It is, and you should be careful, too. Ask the Moonfell witches. Don't do it alone."

"It had already crossed my mind."

They chatted for a few more minutes about ways to cast the spells, and potential issues, before ending the call. She walked over to the table where the manifesto was still laid out, and picked a page up, stroking the paper, and trying to discern what, if any, magic could be in it. The more she thought about it, the more foolish it seemed to presume that this was just a manifesto, despite the fact that it felt innocuous enough. The message aside, of course. The call of mad men to invoke more madness should not be taken lightly.

Their day was open so far. She would phone Nahum and get him to call Moonfell, and while he liaised with them, she could try a few spells, study Alex's spells, and generally prepare herself.

"You," she said, tapping the manifesto, "will tell us what we want to know, whether you like it or not!"

"Venice? How sure is he?" Gabe asked Harlan on the phone while he paced around the old attic in Amato's house.

"Very sure. I've read his diaries about it. You know JD. He records everything. It's worth pursuing."

"I have no doubt about that. I'd chase anything right now." Gabe gazed out of the dusty windows, not seeing the forest and overgrown grounds, but a *palazzo* in Venice that might contain secrets of The Consortium. *The Brotherhood*. "You have an address? A name?"

"The family is called Lamberti. I contacted Romola Flaco yesterday, a friend who works in our Rome office. I had asked her to investigate Amato's house, so this morning I asked her to look into this place, too. But there's a problem. The Lamberti family is rich and powerful—she knew the name straight away—and there's no way that you can approach them directly. Romola will double check the Venetian house to make sure it still belongs to them, and that we are talking about the same family, but she strongly suspects it will be them. Apparently, they have used The Orphic Guild in the past. They like arcane objects."

"That's brilliant!" Ash looked over at Gabe's excited tone. "But will that be an issue? I mean, might Romola warn them of what we want?"

"I damn well hope not! They're a client, and they pay for our help for individual jobs, and then we move on. Unless Romola is on some kind of retainer. But she shouldn't be, that's not how we work."

"Good. So how long will that take her?"

"A few hours, maybe? She said she'd call you directly. Is that okay? I gave her your number."

"Sure. She doesn't know what we are though, right? Either us or Shadow?" Gabe liked to keep the fact that they were paranormal beings as quiet as possible, despite that Romola worked for The Orphic Guild.

"No. Not from me, at least. I doubt Mason will have told them, either."

"Thanks. I'll start looking for accommodation there. I think we've wrapped up here." Ash gave him a thumbs up sign. Niel and Shadow had continued to search the grounds.

"There's nothing else in the house?"

"Nothing useful. It's abandoned, and has been for decades. It's dusty, mouldy, and rotten. I can't help but wonder what happened to make them abandon it."

"Romola might be able to help there. Of course, even if the Lamberti family had an item of Belial's jewellery, it doesn't mean they still have it now. And one more thing. JD thinks he's close to unlocking the Emerald Tablet."

"How close?"

"Days, maybe hours."

Gabe sat on a dusty windowsill, the rotten wood creaking beneath him. "Seriously?" He turned the speaker on and beckoned Ash over.

"Is this a bad idea? I mean, could he unleash some kind of Biblical apocalypse?"

Ash answered him. "If I believed that, I wouldn't have given him the tablet."

"But did you actually think he'd unlock its secrets?"

Ash looked uneasily at Gabe, his gold eyes darkening. "Probably not, but we helped him get the disc, and we know he's resourceful. It was always a possibility. This soon, however..." He trailed off, and Gabe knew exactly what he meant.

They had given the Emerald Tablet to JD thinking it was the safest place for it, and believing it would be decades, maybe even centuries, before he could truly understand it, but now, a deep unease settled over him. However, other hopeful possibilities presented themselves, too. "Harlan, it's worrying, but it may offer a way to completely negate Belial's jewels. And anyway, is it likely that you could stop JD?"

"No, but one of you could."

Gabe shook his head. "No, like we said months ago, too much knowledge has been locked away. I won't gatekeep it again."

"But if it's as dangerous as Raziel's book?"

"Raziel was an angel who had recorded the world's first spells that underpin life. Hermes Trismegistus was not an angel."

"But," Ash said, "he was thrice Hermes, which meant he was Thoth, too, and Thoth is an Egyptian God."

"And the tablet," Harlan pointed out, "is supposed to contain the secrets of life and immortality."

Gabe sighed, seeing resignation in Ash's eyes, too. "I think we have to let this play out. For a start, he already knows the secret of immortality. If he opens it, it's because he's worthy of the knowledge."

"That's what he said." Gabe could almost hear Harlan's eyeroll. "Anyway, back to Venice. I can get you a place to stay there. Orphic Guild connections. Do you want me to organise it?"

"Yes, brilliant. Thank you."

"Will do. Okay, I've got to go. I'll keep you updated."

Ash sighed as Gabe ended the call. "I am sort of excited by the possibility, you know? The tablet, I mean."

"Say he does make it bigger. It doesn't mean he can understand it! That could just be one step of many."

"True." Ash walked over to his pack where the map was stored. "Let's focus on Venice. You know where it is, right?"

"Vaguely."

"I have a feeling," Ash said, unfolding the map and laying it across the duty floor, "that it's northeast. There!" He jabbed the map. "I was right. It's roughly northeast from here. About a three-hour drive."

"It must be related to all this!" Gabe didn't see the point in wasting time. "We've exhausted this place, right? Let's pack up and get moving. I'll call Shadow."

Nine

H arlan ended his phone call with Gabe and looked through the window of his first-floor bedroom at the enormous marquee that loomed out of the thick mist that had descended on the chill February day.

It looked innocuous enough, but it housed something so powerful that Harlan could barely comprehend that JD might actually unlock its secrets. He should get back to London and prepare for the week, but the marquee beckoned.

The previous evening, JD had delivered as promised. He had told Harlan of his conversations with angels—the celestial kind, not the fallen ones—and had looked so earnest, Harlan wanted to believe him. But he couldn't. Having read all about his dubious friend who had enabled his conversations, the man who history had decried as a fraud, the spiritualist Edward Kelly, he questioned everything JD said. He knew that Gabe had endured long conversations with him in the past, and that he doubted JD's experience, too, even though he had designed—revealed, perhaps—Enochian language. According to the Nephilim, though, that was not the language of angels that they were familiar with. It didn't mean that the angels hadn't taught him another one, though. One accessible to humans.

JD had also described his various quests for knowledge and outlined his visit to the Lamberti's. They lived in a centuries-old Venetian palace that sat on the Grand Canal. It was magnificent, apparently, with frescoed walls, ornate plasterwork, cavernous rooms, and decadent furnishings. Well, the part he had seen of it, which wasn't much. A reception area only before he was escorted off the premises. They had denied knowing anything about such a jewel, and accused JD of being a madman. *Nothing new there.* He had faced that accusation many times.

It must be hard, Harlan thought, *to be an immortal genius.* To have to live amongst people so less gifted than himself. No wonder JD was prickly and odd. He'd had to survive lifetimes of such experiences. Being around normal people, though, who understood him, was important. It grounded him. *Sort of...* Perhaps being a scientific advisor to the lab at The Retreat was a good thing. He was so isolated here. By choice, of course, but nevertheless... Harlan found he had enjoyed their conversation. JD talked to him properly for once, as if they were of equal intellect. It wouldn't last, of course, but his stories were fascinating. A window into the past, from someone who had actually been there.

Harlan decided to see his progress once more, and leaving his packed bag on his bed, headed downstairs. He was halfway across the lawn when the ground rocked, and a wave of *something* passed through him. It was so powerful that Harlan was blasted off his feet and onto his back, leaving him looking into the mist, and wondering if he'd lost his vision.

The wet grass soaked into his jeans and jacket, and the back of his head, and he could see the moisture hang in the air with crystal clarity.

Time stood still. The power of the earth rose up and the crush of air pinned him to the ground, and yet he didn't panic. He could see so clearly. The millions of moisture particles hanging above him, both beautiful and surreal. He could feel them on his skin, and see them settle on his own eyelashes. And then the weight of air and the feel of earth vanished, and he floated, weightless, able to see and feel the minute breaths of wind as they passed over and under him. And the colours! He twisted like a kite on a breeze, seeing the garden spread below him, and the thick press of trees and shrubs, all with a strange, vibrant glow.

Wait... What?

His body was lying motionless on the lawn, and Harlan realised he wasn't breathing. *Holy shit. I've had a stroke. Or maybe a heart attack. I'm dead, and my soul is leaving my body.* Regrets raced through him. That he wouldn't be around to support Olivia. That he wouldn't see the Templar gold again. That there were so many places in the world that he still wanted to see. That he hadn't spoken to his mother recently.

His soul was leaving his body and going somewhere.

Then he saw the marquee that was glowing with a brilliant green light, and he knew instantly what had happened. JD had unlocked the knowledge within the Emerald Tablet and killed him. *That mad bastard!*

The knowledge triggered a visceral physical response, and he thudded back to the ground and into his body with a thump. He took a sharp intake of breath, sat bolt upright, and yelled. "I'm alive!" Struggling to his feet, his body feeling strangely familiar and unfamiliar all at the same time, he ran across the lawn, yelling, "JD!"

But as soon as he reached the door to the marquee, he skidded to a halt. From the outside the marquee looked as normal, but a strange, ethereal light was visible through a chink in the flap that served as a door.

"JD! Are you okay?" It was deathly quiet, with no sounds coming from the house or the huge tent. "JD!" Unzipping it as if it might explode, and half expecting to see JD dead, he peered inside. "*Holy shit.*"

The Emerald Tablet had vanished, as had JD, and in the centre of the tent was a cavernous entrance to what looked like an emerald cave. The rest of the tent was unchanged—the tables, the scientific equipment, and even the wheel of correspondences were all still there. Tentatively, Harlan stepped inside and zipped the door shut. *Had Anna felt the ripple of energy? Would she come and investigate?*

Not knowing whether he should be terrified or excited, he crossed to the cave's entrance, feeling a wave of power emanating from it. A passage ran ahead, far too long to be encompassed in the marquee. It was a gateway. He called JD again, half wondering if his body had been turned to dust, looked back at the world he knew and might never see again, and stepped inside.

"I see what you meant about a bunker," Nahum said to Zee and Eli. "We could bury a body in there."

"Just being prepared." Zee winked at Olivia. "We put the bodies elsewhere."

"I don't believe that for a second," Olivia shot back.

Eli leaned against the wall, looking as usual, incredibly seductive. It was like sex just oozed from him. He gave Olivia a rakish grin and Nahum subdued a scowl. *No. He was not letting Eli look after Olivia.* "You should. The field out there was strewn with bodies just before Christmas. We had to put them somewhere."

"Oh, stop it!" Briar said, horrified. "The police took them all. Olivia, ignore them!"

"I try, but they're very naughty," she said, teasing. "Something I am already used to."

The farmhouse's cellar was crowded with the five White Haven witches, the three Nephilim, and Olivia. There was, despite the gravity of the situation, almost a party atmosphere. Nahum and Olivia had arrived about five minutes earlier and found their way to the cellar, where the witches had just completed their protection spell. It was good to be home again, and Nahum was looking forward to catching up with his friends and brothers.

Nahum placed the heavy, spelled box that contained the jewels on to the ground. "I should probably get this box back to Gabe somehow. If they find anymore of Belial's stuff, they'll need somewhere to store it."

"I thought they had a smaller box?" El said, confused.

"They do, but we're finding more of his crap than we expected." He studied the runes and sigils that had been burned onto the slabbed interior and sturdy wooden lid by witch-fire, reassured that it would suffice. "I'd like to leave everything in this one, though, as double protection."

Reuben, the water witch, pointed to the corner of the room where another spelled box was lying ready. "Already done."

A huge weight lifted off Nahum's shoulders. Carrying the box had started to bother him, even though it was spelled with strong magic. It was as if Belial's power could still leak from it, and even though he knew it wasn't, it was like his insidious whispers were in his head anyway.

"Fantastic. Let's do it. You lot, though," he gestured to the witches and Olivia, "need to go upstairs."

"Actually," Alex said, "I'd like to feel the effects once you open it. I won't touch anything, obviously, but it might help me get a feel for all this."

Zee was emphatic in his response to that request. "*No!*"

"You asked for my help, and what I can give is limited. We felt the effects of the other jewels and were fine. This will be stronger. It could help."

Avery shuffled uneasily. "Alex, we've talked about this. What if it kicks off one of your weird, psychic premonitions?"

"Which it could totally do," Eli agreed.

"It's my risk, and I'm used to managing psychic energy. You'll have to trust me on this. I won't do anything to risk hurting myself."

"You'd better not!" Reuben said, indignant. "We have wedding stuff to do."

Nahum exchanged worried glances with his brothers, and resigned, they both nodded. Alex wasn't a child. "Fine. But everyone else, especially you, Liv, out!" He had slipped into using the shortened version of her name, and found he quite liked it. She seemed to, as well. She was dressed informally today, in her jeans and t-shirt, and still looked good. *Focus.*

"I'm going." She headed up the stairs. "I'll make drinks."

"We should go to the pub," Reuben said, trailing after her. "The Wayward Son does a great Sunday lunch."

In less than a minute, only the three Nephilim and Alex were left in the cellar, and after casting a worried look at Alex, Nahum flipped the lid open. Immediately, Belial's insidious whispers seeped into the room, as if there were hundreds of him crammed inside, and his power radiated outwards, too.

"Herne's horns!" Alex exclaimed, staggering back as if he'd been punched. "That's insane."

"Are you okay?" Zee asked.

"I'm fine. Just taking a moment to shut my psychic awareness down."

Nahum and Eli lifted out the jewels, one by one. It was tempting to upend the box and throw them inside without touching them, but Nahum had made an inventory, and he wanted to check that they were all there.

Eli frowned as he lifted a necklace. "This looks and feels important."

"It was placed on the altar, and nowhere near as big as the one draped around his neck," Nahum explained. "Do you think he actually wore this?"

"Perhaps, on one of his visits. It makes my skin crawl." The huge sapphire mounted in silver filigree seemed to blink like an eye, and Eli lowered it into the new, larger box the witches had made.

Nahum quickly transferred the rings, loose gemstones, and bracelets, ticking them off his list. "The necklace on the statue ended up in the hole that opened up when the temple collapsed."

"Was it as bad as it sounded?"

"Worse. I've never been so powerless in my life. I couldn't move. Couldn't speak, even, except when Amato willed it."

"And this one?" Zee held up the broken necklace.

"Taken from Amato's neck. Shadow cut it with her Dragonium blade."

"Impressive, I didn't know it could cut through metal."

Nahum hadn't really stopped to consider it. "That's true. Neither did I, but I didn't take the time to consider it in all the drama."

"Her sword was undamaged?" Zee asked.

"Must have been, or we'd have never heard the end of it."

Alex crouched close by, careful to keep his distance. "It's a pure fey blade, right?"

Eli nodded. "Forged in the Otherworld. Dragonium is made from dragons. It's a pretty gruesome process. Makes the best weapons though, apparently. Even the dryads talk of it."

"You chat to dryads about weapons?"

Eli smiled. "About all things related to the Otherworld."

Alex just nodded, thoughtfully. "So, the fey blade can cut through angelic jewellery and not be damaged. Interesting. And Shadow went undetected by Amato."

"And Belial, I presume." Nahum sat back, glad to see Alex was coping with Belial. "When we first met Jacobsen, the jewels whispered that I was there. He turned and saw me. That didn't happen with Shadow. She was using her fey magic, of course. She kept to the darkness, and I couldn't see her, either. You know what she's like in her stealth mode."

Alex sat cross-legged on the floor. "She talked about Raziel's magic back when you found the temple. Of how the old God tried to stop others from using magic, and laughed. She said it was impossible. That magic is everywhere, especially in the Otherworld."

"I remember. She said writing it all in some big book and then locking it away was madness. She wittered about the elements."

"Yes, the fundamentals of life. The elements that we access." Alex smiled. "It's a weakness."

Nahum had been ticking off jewels and throwing them into the new box while they talked, but now he froze. "What do you mean?"

"I'm not sure, but I know it is."

Nahum went to speak but Zee shushed him. "Wait!"

Alex was quiet for a few moments. "They don't have control of it. Magic, I mean. Especially Otherworldly magic. It's wild, and not of our world. The world of fey is like magic on speed, right? That's how it almost seems to me. It's like having it on tap. Raw and unfiltered, unlike our world where it's hidden. Muffled." He laughed, eyes widening almost maniacally. "Oh, wow. They can't read it. Or could once but can't now. Or Belial can't, anyway. He's tuned to his own angelic magic, but that's different."

Nahum stared at his brothers, glad to find they looked as baffled as him. Well, Zee did. Eli laughed, too. "The dryads have no truck with Gods or angels. They are just other concentrated forms of energy to them. Dryads are a bit smug, actually. They consider their own magic the purest because it's of the earth."

"And the old God, the Christian God," Alex continued, "had no sway in the Otherworld."

Nahum nodded, seeing what Alex meant. "Shadow used to think that we're some kind of sylph, but now she knows we're not. They are air spirits. We're similar, but from a different mould. A different magic."

"The same root, but a different branch. He has no sway over Shadow at all." Alex grinned. "She's your secret weapon."

"But if she touched his jewels?" Eli asked. "We've been very careful to keep them apart."

"Probably wise, but I don't think they would have an effect on her."

Nahum had another idea. "Could her blade destroy these?"

"No. Break them, yes. But there'd always be pieces of them."

"So," Zee said, "we're back to being dragons again."

Confused, Nahum said, "Dragons?"

"I'll explain over lunch. Alex, are you getting anything from the jewels?"

"Let me sit quietly with them for a few minutes and I'll let you know. Then it's time for a pub lunch."

Ten

So, this was Moonfell, Barak thought, as the huge front door opened to a colourful hallway of rugs and burnished wood.

An older woman with a thick mane of white hair greeted them, elegant in a dark red dress, displaying a beaming smile and shrewd eyes that took them all in. "Welcome to Moonfell. Come in quickly, out of that nasty February cold." She shut the door behind them and shook their hands. "I'm Birdie. Estelle, I presume?"

"Yes. Thank you, Birdie. We really appreciate your help."

"A fellow witch is always welcome." She kissed Estelle's cheek. "Well, most of the time. We had an issue with one only recently. Anyway, you must be Barak and Lucien."

Lucien had been at a loose end and was as anxious as them to see the outcome of this visit, and the witches had welcomed all of them when Estelle had called for assistance.

"We're in the kitchen at the moment," Birdie said, leading the way down the hall, "the heart of the house, but we'll head to the tower room for the spell. Time for tea, first."

Barak followed her, soaking in the magic of the house. Now he knew what Nahum meant when he said the Moonfell witches were very different to the White Haven witches and Estelle's family. Although the Cornish witches had strong family histories of witchcraft, they lived fully in the present, especially Estelle and Caspian, who were doing their best to forget their father's influence completely. Already he sensed that the inhabitants of Moonfell kept a foot in the past, as well.

Birdie chatted to Estelle as she led them down the hall, and Barak observed the bohemian décor. He had no doubt that the characters who lived here were as colourful as the house. It reminded him of his old palace in Ethiopia. The wall hangings, the rich furnishings, and the sense of opulence. It was nothing like his ancient home, and yet it was, too, even down to the scent of incense that hung on the air. A wave of homesickness hit him like a blow to the stomach, and he stopped for a moment, images unspooling before his eyes like an old film.

Birdie turned and smiled. "It has that effect sometimes. It will pass."

She knew. "I'm okay. The past catches up with me sometimes."

"As does the heartache." She smiled at Estelle. "But that will pass, too. He has new things to love now. And you, Lucien, well, you have been through a lot. Morgana can help with that."

"You read auras," Estelle said, eyes narrowing. "I've never been able to do that."

"I can turn it off, but sometimes it's so strong that I can't help it. All of yours are strong. That's good, and to be expected from such powerful individuals. Now, here we are."

Suddenly they were in a large, spacious kitchen, with grey February light illuminating the shining surfaces of a very modern, yet still very Gothic kitchen. Two women were in there, one with long, dark hair who was making a pot of tea, the other younger, with thick, auburn, wavy hair, who was seated at the table reading a magazine.

"My granddaughters," Birdie announced. "Morgana and Odette."

Odette, the young woman seated at the table, rose to her feet, mouth falling open in astonishment. Her unblinking gaze seemed to see right through him. "Another Nephilim! By the Goddess, look at you! Your wings are like the wings of night. I can almost see stars in them."

Barak laughed. "My brother, Nahum, warned me about you. You have the Sight."

"Of a sort. And a sister witch." She moved around the table to hug Estelle. "You're not a hugger, I can tell, but you need one right now. And you!" She took Lucien in. "Metals course your veins and pattern your skin." It was like a storm swept over her clear features. "Such a violation. But you have mastered it. You are strong and will get stronger still. All will be well."

"Good grief, Odette," Morgana said, ushering them into seats at the table. "Let them get settled first before you blast them with your insights."

"I can't help it!" She smiled an apology. "Sorry. It's out before I know it sometimes."

"You can see the metals?" Lucien asked, face creased with confusion. "How?"

"*See* is the wrong word. It's a sense I have, really."

Barak could tell Lucien was itching to ask more questions, but they sat at the table as Morgana carried over a pot of tea and a plate of biscuits, and then set out the cups.

"So," Birdie said when they all had drinks, "you have a manifesto that you wish to prise secrets from."

Estelle nodded as she extracted it from her bag and put it on the table. "Yes, this is it. I have tried a few finding spells on it to work out where it could have originated from, or the person who wrote it, but I think I'm blocked somehow. Potentially by Belial himself, or perhaps by the power his agents wield. I know you saved Olivia, so you're familiar with him." She pointed to one of the cut edges. "That was my doing, where I took a portion for spells. I'm scared of doing that too much in case I damage it."

"Far too familiar, unfortunately," Birdie agreed, thumbing through the pages. "But I doubt you could damage these significantly." She closed her eyes briefly as her fingers ran over the paper. "Yes, I can feel angelic magic. Odette will feel more. But not yet, Odette," she said turning to her. "You will feel it more strongly, so I suggest we wait until we're in the protective circle."

"You're an empath," Barak said to Odette, certain he was right.

She nodded. "That, too. It's a strange mix of powers that I have."

"Do you think the spells that Alex has suggested will work?" Lucien asked as he sipped his tea.

Morgana answered as she too flicked through the manifesto now that Birdie had finished. "Perhaps, but using a protective circle is wise. If we lift the magic on the manifesto, there might be consequences." She smiled at Estelle. "It was wise to seek assistance. The circle is already prepared. We have added a few little extras to it," she eyed Odette and Birdie, amused, "after what happened last time."

"This will be nowhere near as dramatic," Birdie said.

Morgana laughed. "I'll reserve my judgement."

For a few minutes, while they drank tea, the witches questioned the group on their search. Barak felt relaxed around them, sure of their support and friendship. They were open and honest, and he understood why Olivia liked them. They had looked after her well, and Harlan trusted them, too. It was good, considering what they were up against. When Birdie was satisfied that they had all the background they needed, she led the way along passages and up flights of stairs, until they came to a curious tower room. The floor and ceiling were marked with a pentacle and edged with sigils and runes, as were the window frames and doorways. When Birdie closed the door, Barak noted the sigil on that, too. The only furniture in there were a couple of chairs, a small round table, a long table used as an altar, and a bookcase filled with old texts pushed against the wall.

"Wow!" Estelle said, clearly impressed. "A full protective circle. Permanent!"

"Our ancestors deemed it wise," Birdie said, gaze sweeping around it. "A seventeenth-century addition. All the glass was broken during our expulsion of Belial." She gestured to the huge, Gothic windows. "Cost a fortune to replace them."

"You couldn't use magic?" Lucien asked.

"We were exhausted," Morgana explained. "Plus, it would have taken too long. As it was, they were boarded up for a month. Besides, they were very old. It gave us a chance to eliminate the draughts properly. As you can imagine, it's an old place that requires a lot of upkeep, even with our magic."

"It's beautiful," Estelle said, relaxing for the first time since they had entered the house. She had been nervous about visiting, despite Birdie's assurances on the phone. Barak knew how self-reliant she was, and how she had hated to have to ask for help. "It has such a lovely feel to it. The entire house, I mean."

"It depends on the visitor." Birdie's smile was mischievous. "It likes all of you. Those whom it doesn't it has no time for, and they feel unsettled. Again, that was reinforced only too well recently. Anyway, let us prepare. Estelle, join us, please. Gentlemen, amuse yourselves."

With a word of command, the candles flared to life, casting the grey February light into a warm, yellow glow. The circular tower meant that there were no shadowed corners, and Barak paced the room's perimeter, half watching the witches' preparations as he looked out of the three windows.

The garden sprawled below in all directions. Unusual topiaries populated the grounds, along with shrubs and trees, winding paths, and flower beds, mostly bare at this time of year. He caught a glimpse of unusual moon gates, too.

"This place is amazing." Lucien spoke quietly at Barak's side, taking in everything. "I hope they let us watch."

"We wouldn't be here if we couldn't."

Lucien pulled the cuffs of his jacket back to look at his tattooed arms. "Can Odette really see the metals? They would be tiny specs. Powders!"

"But they have been alchemically enhanced, and they've changed you. That is what she must see. The traces of magic." He frowned at Lucien's discomfort. "No one else can see it. Don't worry."

"I feel exposed. Naked!"

"It wasn't intentional, although I feel exposed as well," he said quietly, unwilling to offend Odette. "She sees what others cannot. It must be unnerving for her, too."

The table and one chair were now in the centre of the circle, and Odette took her seat, the manifesto on the table. The spells that Alex had sent were in Estelle's hands.

Birdie carried another grimoire that she placed on the altar. "We also have spells that might work. One is very similar to what your friend sent through. That's an ancient text," she noted, head cocking as she looked at the papers in Estelle's hands.

"We all possess very old grimoires."

"Impressive. Ours are downstairs in our library. The texts in this bookcase are regular spells we use in here. Those of banishment, as well as protection. None to unveil. Perhaps we should remedy that." She looked across to Morgana who was placing out a range of ingredients for the spells on the altar. Gemstones, herbs, jars of what looked like oils, and more candles. "Ready?"

"Just the incense." Morgana lit a bundle of sticks with a word of power, and then proceeded to place them about the room. "For clarity," she explained to Barak and Lucien as she passed them. "I suggest you wait by the bookcase. Do not interfere, no matter what happens."

Barak nodded, but called Estelle aside, suddenly terrified for her safety, despite her power. "Are you okay? Really?"

She cupped his cheeks with her hands, her smile warm and reassuring. 'I'm fine. I've checked the circle. It's well constructed and will protect us, and I know we can trust these witches. I feel it." She reached up and kissed him. "Stay back, but watch carefully, both of you. We will be focussed on the magic, and you may see something we don't."

Reluctantly, Barak did as he was bid, joining Lucien by the bookcase. He stood, arms folded across his chest, leaning against the wall, as the witches made their final preparations. Three of them stood around the circle, the Moonfell witches carrying huge wooden staffs, but Odette remained seated at the table.

"Is Odette staying in the circle?" Barak asked, alarmed.

"Just for now," Birdie said. Odette's eyes were already closed, hands in her lap, the manifesto spread on the table. "She's going to get a feel for it with her senses and then touch. She has personal protection in place, but her response may be strong. It's hard to know. We won't perform any spells until she's with us. Don't worry." She considered her next words. "He may detect you—if he's hidden in the document. You are Nephilim, after all. Do nothing. Say nothing. Understood?"

"Morgana has already warned me. I understand."

Birdie looked into his eyes as if reading his soul, and then, satisfied, stood between Estelle and Morgana.

Barak took a deep breath after the intense scrutiny, and looked at Lucien. "You heard her. We do nothing."

"I'm okay with that, but are you?" Lucien asked, eyebrows raised.

Ignoring him, Barak focussed on the witches. Birdie raised the circle of protection, the sigils and runes that ran around the double ring flaring into light.

Odette's eyes were closed, but she could obviously tell the circle was complete. She leaned forward, not touching the manifesto, but running her hands a few inches over it. For a couple of minutes she did nothing but that, and her breaths deepened. "There are levels of magic here," she said, her voice low, but sure. "I feel it in the paper and the ink. There is a seal, too. Another level of magic. Angelic, of course. But it's subtle. It doesn't surprise me that you couldn't feel it easily, Estelle." She inhaled and sighed. "Myrrh. Sandalwood. Something else that evades me right now. I will touch it now." Barak braced himself following Odette's announcement. She opened her eyes and started with the first page of the manifesto, her fingers lightly brushing across the surface. "I sense many have had a hand in this—the making of the parchment, and the preparation of the ink. One scribe only. I see a dark, shadowed place, lit only by lamplight. A quill made from an angel's feather. Given willingly to impart magic."

Barak frowned. Surely not Belial's—or any angel's, for that matter. It could not have survived. *Could it?* He was desperate to question her, but it must wait.

"It is older than it seems," she said, continuing to the second page. "Ancient parchment and old ink stored in a sacred place for such an occasion, but written more recently. They are at least a thousand years old. The quill..." she took a deep, shuddering breath again. "Ancient beyond reckoning. The scribe is...different. Strong enough to handle an angel's feather. It is pure white, almost silver. A celestial light." She closed her eyes and drew back. "So bright!" Odette steadied herself, and opening her eyes moved to the final page where the seal was embossed in the parchment. Her fingers hovered over it. "The seal is where the power is strongest. Power is infused into the wax."

For long moments she did nothing, and Barak realised he was holding his breath. What she had seen seemed impossible, but she spoke with such conviction. *Was it a hoax?* Something to confuse them and send them astray. He could hear Belial's whispers again, so low, so insistent, he had missed their arrival. He shook them off. Belial was instilling doubt where there should be none. The room seemed dark now, despite the candlelight.

Odette placed the tip of her finger on the seal, screamed as if she was being tortured, and fell forward, motionless.

Harlan progressed slowly down the emerald passageway, fingertips touching the walls to reassure himself that they existed. The surface was rough, unpolished, and although he was no gemstone expert, he was sure it was raw emerald, glowing within from some unseen power.

He paused and looked back, relieved to see that the marquee was still there, looking reassuringly normal. But it was so far away. He took a deep, steadying breath. He was an explorer. He hunted occult objects. He was used to this. And then his inner voice rebelled. *No, you aren't, you moron. Not like this. You are inside the Emerald Tablet!*

The knowledge hit him like a blow, and he staggered backwards. *He was in the tablet.*

"JD!"

No answer.

He quickened his pace. Either JD was now dust as a result of the wave of power that had knocked Harlan off his feet, or he was up ahead. Within a few more paces, the passage turned and opened into an enormous cave, and he paused on the threshold, taking it all in.

"Herne's fucking horns! This is insane."

The entire cave was made of pure, polished emerald that reflected the lights of a thousand candles, torches, and lanterns. Hundreds of pillars filled the space, rooted to the ground and reaching to the roof high above. Some were square, some were round, while others twisted like spirals. The one thing common to all was the writing that covered every surface—script he couldn't understand, but that looked ancient. In addition, it was as if he'd stepped into a Middle Eastern bazaar.

The lanterns were made of silver, bronze, copper, or gold, designed with intricate patterns, with coloured and clear glass, and suspended on long chains from the ceiling or the pillars. Rich, Oriental rugs were scattered through the space, and occasional low seating was dotted throughout. It was so enormous that he couldn't see the far side.

One thing was clear, though. This was a gargantuan repository of knowledge.

He started to walk through it, noting the feeling of timelessness, but also of antiquity. The words on the pillars were inscribed in thick, bold, and curving strokes. Faultless and immaculate. And all of it waiting for the one who had the skill to open it.

"JD! Where are you?" Harlan's voice echoed back to him, and finally he received an answer.

"Harlan, I'm over here! In the centre."

The scent of incense and a bright, orange glow drew Harlan onwards, and he found JD staring at a column of flame that blazed from the centre of a six-pointed star inscribed into the floor in what looked to be pure gold.

"As above, so below," JD said, turning to Harlan with a beaming smile. "Can you believe it?"

"No! What the actual fuck, JD? What did you do?"

"I unlocked it!"

"I know that! But..." Harlan's gaze swept around once more. "This is insane. We're in a cave! An emerald cave!" His voice rose with indignation and shock.

"No. We are in the *Emerald Tablet*." JD spun on his heel, his arms stretched out. "Look at all this knowledge. A lifetime's worth. I don't even know where to begin."

"So, one of your calculations worked. JD, you really are quite brilliant."

JD's eyes had taken on a fervent gleam. "There will be a pattern to the knowledge. A system. I just need to work it out."

"Can you read all this?"

"Ancient Aramaic and Sanskrit are the two languages I've seen so far. Yes, I understand some of it." JD fixed Harlan with his piercing gaze. "I will look for angel-related information first, but if one of the Nephilim could help, perhaps?"

"Nahum and Barak are staying in London. Well, Nahum will be back from Cornwall tonight. They'll only be too happy to help, I'm sure." He reached for his phone automatically, and then saw there was no signal at all. *Of course there wouldn't be.* "I'll head outside. Do you think it's stable?"

"For now."

"That wasn't the answer I wanted!"

"It's all I can give you right now. The field is stable. Nothing should disrupt it. It has waited for millennia. Tell no one else, though! Just our small team!"

"Of course! I'm not a moron."

JD just nodded, his attention now on other things. "I need papers, pens, notes, filing supplies, all of it..."

Harlan left him muttering to himself, hoping the outside world was still there.

Eleven

Lucien was relieved to see Odette's eyes flicker open. "She's okay! Give her air!"

He had reacted even quicker than Barak when Odette had fallen forward in a faint. Birdie had dropped the protective circle, and Lucien had rushed in and picked her up, gently depositing her on the floor outside it. Her pulse fluttered faintly at her throat, and her eyes moved restlessly beneath her lids.

"Here, let me," Morgana said, kneeling at her side as everyone else stepped back. She laid a hand on her brow. "Odette, can you hear me?"

Odette's gaze was distant, as if her vision was blurred, and then she blinked and focussed on Morgana, and then Lucien on the other side. "I'm fine, thank you. Help me sit up."

"Water and chocolate!" Morgana commanded.

"All ready," Birdie said calmly.

Lucien smiled at Odette as he supported her weight. She was feather-light, almost insubstantial. "Take your time."

"Thank you, Lucien." She accepted the water and snack from Birdie, and after a few sips and a bite of chocolate, her colour returned. "Sorry, everyone. It was a strong image I saw from the seal. That's all. It was like a cobra strike." She gave a shaky laugh. "I feel a bit embarrassed now."

"Let's get her in a chair, Lucien," Morgana said.

After she was settled and had taken a few deep breaths, Odette smiled. "I'm fine. We can carry on soon."

Barak crouched opposite her. Everything about him was clenched tight—his jaw, his fists, and his corded muscles. "What did you see? Belial?"

"Yes, and someone else. The scribe. Belial was fleeting. A flash of his eyes and then he was gone. But the scribe was intense. I couldn't determine his age, but he was one of you. A Nephilim."

Barak's black skin turned grey. "Surely it can't be possible."

"I know what I saw. Not pure angel. Belial was his father, I'm certain."

"Of the House of Belial. That's bad news." Barak sat back on the floor heavily, looking at Estelle and then Lucien, absolute confusion on his face. "It shouldn't even be possible. You said the parchment and ink were old, but the manifesto was newer. So that means the scribe is of more recent centuries, too?"

"Yes. Well, I think so." Odette's gaze flickered to her coven and Estelle. "I don't see things with crystal clarity, but I can usually trust my intuition."

Birdie nodded. "Yes, she can. We have all learned to trust what she sees."

"So, what we—me and my brothers—have feared, is true. We had hoped it was just human agents that he possessed, but I suppose it was the only logical conclusion, really."

"Is it so bad?" Morgana asked, puzzled. "You are Nephilim, and you are here!"

"Well, human agents are easier to fight, that's for sure. Of course, we have battled other Nephilim many times over the years. That is not the issue, either. It's how he is here, now! We died in the Great Flood, and found our way back through an open portal. But him..."

Birdie nodded. "I see. He either survived for millennia after making it through the Flood, or was brought back another way."

"And if he did survive," Estelle said, meeting Barak's worried look with her own, "how many others also did?"

"Exactly." Barak regained his feet. "No matter. That is not for you to worry about. We will deal with that. It's even more important now to get more information from the manifesto. You've already told us so much, though, Odette. Thank you."

"It's my pleasure." She too stood up. "I'm afraid that fainting is one of my standard responses when I'm psychically overwhelmed. It's a defence mechanism that shuts down my psychic awareness. However, I am okay, and we can continue."

They settled back into their positions, this time with Odette outside the rune circle. While they set up, Lucien studied Barak. He looked preoccupied, his jaw tight, and he attempted to reassure him. "It will be okay. We will find them and stop them, no matter how many there are."

"Belial's sons fought dirty."

Lucien laughed. "So do we. And we have JD's weapons now, too."

"You want to help?"

"I'm here, aren't I? What else will I do with my time? I have all this strength and speed that I'm finally getting used to using, thanks to you."

His thoughts drifted as the witches cast the protection spell around the pentacle on the floor and started the first spell. Birdie led them, the High Priestess of the Moonfell Coven, and Estelle seemed happy with the decision. Lucien was used to her twisted lips that denoted disapproval. She had always been kind to him, but there was no doubt she was abrupt when things did not go her way.

The truth was that Lucien still wasn't sure how he'd live his new life, long-term. He wasn't looking ahead for more than weeks at a time. For now, he was enjoying his freedom, and enjoying living in Chadwick House. He could maybe ask The Orphic Guild for a job, or get a contract with the PD. Jackson had actually suggested it once, but he said he needed time. Now, as life settled down, it seemed like a good idea. He could get paid and find his own place. He couldn't live in Chadwick House forever. Or perhaps he could move back to France. Perhaps the Paris branch of The Orphic Guild could offer him a job there. Although, for now, London pulled him. He had friends who knew about his situation. That was worth more than anything.

Estelle took her place around the circle again, happy to let Birdie lead. It was her house, of course, and her coven that she was working with.

For the next hour, the witches worked their way through the spells, first starting with Moonfell's own that Birdie and her granddaughters were more familiar with, and then moving to Alex's. She was used to working with other witches, and lending her magic to a spell, and this was no different—in theory, at least. Birdie's magic was rich, like a fine, aged wine. So far, they had extracted no further secrets from the manifesto. The pages lifted and turned sometimes, and once a spell caught them in a kind of whirlwind before settling the pages back on the table. Estelle became more and more frustrated, but Birdie calmly continued, moving steadily through the spells in the order she had chosen.

There was logic to her actions, starting with the familiar ones, and then the simplest, leaving the more complex to the end. Estelle was sure which one would work, though. She had been ever since Alex had sent it through. The one to which he had suggested they add Barak's blood. Finally, after another failed attempt, Birdie gave Estelle a long, measured look. "Blood it is, then."

She summoned Barak and pierced his finger with a sharp-bladed knife, adding a few drops to a potent herbal mixture that also contained herb oils and a thimble of potion, then smeared it on the edges of the manifesto before setting the circle up again.

They took their positions once more, at the four points of the compass, Birdie remaining at the altar in the east. As Birdie commanded the manifesto to unveil its secrets in Middle-English, the space within the circle darkened, as if she had conjured a storm. A haze descended on the pages, and they lifted into the air and hung there. The text lifted from the parchment and swirled like some sort of alphabet soup. Estelle's breath caught in her chest as she struggled to contain her power. The spell was drawing it in, like a giant sink hole.

Then Birdie shouted words of command again, and images began to form in the circle's centre, like a flickering film or a hologram, and finally the manifesto began to give up its secrets. A large sandstone cave, and then a temple, blazing with candles, an angel with outstretched wings and sightless eyes. A casket overflowing with jewels. A heap of weapons. A desk stacked with parchment. A library of scrolls. All passed by so quickly it was hard to keep track. A cityscape unfolded. Old buildings, undulating roofs, towers, and houses. Then the letters that had swirled aimlessly started to rearrange themselves into words.

Names.

Out of the corner of her eyes she saw Barak and Lucien scramble for paper. Birdie dragged her attention back, her voice rising as wind whipped up in the circle.

And then something exploded out of the images, shredding the manifesto and sending the letters tumbling. A wave of power rolled outwards, hit the protective shield, and rebounded like a wave. Out of the midst of it came the sound of a haunting, mournful call of a trumpet, accompanied by the flash of tawny wings edged with gold. Blinding white light exploded outwards. Estelle closed her eyes but stood firm. The circle would not break. Not while she still drew breath.

The trumpet sounded again, the white light pressing on her closed eyelids. She felt Birdie's steadying presence, and then Morgana and Odette's. The circle held firm, until the light vanished, and silence fell.

She opened her eyes, terrified she had plunged into a void, but the witches were still there, blinking in the candlelight, as half blind as she was. As her sight returned, she saw the table and chair in the centre of the circle were now splintered wood, and the manifesto was a confetti of tiny pieces spread across the floor.

She whipped around to stare at Barak and Lucien, who looked similarly dazed. "Did you see who it was, Barak?"

His features were mired in confusion. "It was Belial's commander. And he carried Belial's horn."

Olivia felt as if she didn't have a care in the world as she enjoyed a pub lunch at The Wayward Son.

A weak February sun illuminated the small backroom of Alex's pub, a fire crackled in the grate, and her food was delicious. It was the company, though, that sealed it. The witches were fun and welcoming, and the three Nephilim joked and teased Reuben about the wedding. Not his fiancée, though—El, the stunning, blonde-haired witch. But maybe that was because Reuben seemed particularly obsessed with it.

El smiled at Reuben affectionately. "Enough wedding talk before you drive us all insane! I can barely think straight!"

"That's all right, my love," he said, kissing her fingers. "I have it all in hand."

Alex rolled his eyes. "Yeah, right. As much as I'm pleased for you, no more midnight phone calls!"

"I had an idea!"

"Save it until morning!"

El sniggered. "And that applies to me, too."

Reuben gave Olivia a sly smile. "Yes, but if it's a killer idea, I can't wait, right?"

He was sweet for including her in this, and she smiled. "Maybe you should, though, just to keep your friends happy? After all, a few more hours won't hurt."

Reuben clutched his hand over his heart dramatically. "And I thought I had an ally!"

"You've missed your calling, mate," Nahum said, laughing. "Maybe you should swap surfing and your garden business for wedding planning."

Briar threw a piece of her bread roll at him. "No! Stop encouraging him."

"If anyone would be into this, I would have thought it was you, Briar," Eli said, teasing her.

A glint was in her eye. "Because I'm a woman?"

"Because you're excited. I see it every day! You can't fool me."

Of course, Olivia had forgotten that Eli worked with the earth witch.

"And the stack of wedding magazines on the table," Eli continued, "makes your enthusiasm very clear."

Alex snorted. "Not there, too! We have a forest of them at our place."

Avery batted his arm. "Shut up! *Men!*"

Looking lofty, Reuben ignored them all. "Just wait until it's your turn." He frowned at Olivia, and for one heart-stopping moment, she thought he was about to ask what was happening with her and Nahum. But no, all he said was, "Did we invite you to the wedding?"

"Er," she looked awkwardly around the table, "no, but that's okay. I mean, I barely know you!"

He waved her reassurances away. "Consider yourself invited. You're family now! I mean, you're carrying a little Nahum package, and they're all going to be uncles! I consider myself one, too—for the record!"

Nahum spat his pint out, showering his thankfully empty plate with beer.

Zee threw his head back and roared with laughter. "A Nahum package! Oh, that's priceless." He caught Olivia's eye, tried to stop laughing, and failed. "Sorry, but it is."

The whole table was laughing now, but Avery squeezed Olivia's arm. "So sorry. Reuben's mouth runs away with him sometimes."

Despite her blushes, Olivia laughed. "It's fine. It *is* a Nahum package. Mine too, though."

Reuben, clearly enjoying himself now, and with a big twinkle in his eye, suggested, "You should have a joint name. Like celebrities do. For example, me and El could be Reuspeth, or Elben. I think Reuspeth is better. Avery and Alex would either have to be Avex, which sounds like a car rental company, or Alery, and that's not much better. You two, though, could be Navia. Or Olivum." He grimaced. "Olivum sounds gross. Navia, however, is great! You could name your daughter Navia!"

Nahum was still struggling to get his breath after almost choking, his face flushed. He glared at Reuben, who ignored him completely.

Olivia tried to remain composed. "I don't think we've decided anything yet, but obviously we will consider it carefully!" What she didn't say was that mashed names denoted a couple, and that was one thing she and Nahum were not. She focussed only on the baby's name. "But thank you for the interesting suggestion! And the invitation, of course. I must admit, I do love a good wedding, as long as I'm not intruding." And by that she meant on Nahum's friendships. He might not want her there. She would discuss it with him later, and if he looked like he hated the idea, she would back out.

"Anytime. I'll send you an official invitation. Or I could just add a plus one to Nahum's invite." He cocked an eyebrow, amused, and now she knew he was shit-stirring, and so did Nahum, who looked ready to throw something at him.

"Perhaps," Nahum said, finally finding his voice, and shooting an apologetic glance at Olivia, "we should talk about our issues with Belial."

"Excellent idea," Alex agreed.

Reuben smirked. "If you insist."

"I do."

The conversation turned to Alex's theory about Shadow being impervious to Belial's power, and how to use that to their advantage. Olivia breathed easier. With no idea how their relationship was going to progress, the subject always felt awkward with others. Never when they were alone, though. Well, not once they had got past their initial awkwardness, at least.

Avery, however, the pretty red-haired witch who sat next to her, had other things to talk about, and she lowered her voice. "Sorry, Olivia, Reuben is a dreadful tease, and I hope he didn't embarrass you. I could hex him sometimes."

"No, of course not. It's a weird situation, isn't it? I can't deny it." She glanced around the table, relieved that no one was listening to them. "I'm sure everyone is wondering what will happen with us, but the truth is, I don't know. Other than of course being parents, and we'll make it work. Somehow."

"Of course you don't know. It just happened, as some things do. I'm a big believer in fate though, especially after our tangle with Wyrd last year. You two, and your baby, were clearly meant to be. Of course, it's impossible to say what will happen in the long-term, but you know," she hesitated and then rushed on anyway, "he watches you. In a nice way, obviously. And discreetly, of course. I think that says a lot."

"Like what the hell have I done, and how do I get myself out of this mess?"

"No! Like how do I make this thing work without scaring you off? Sorry, I shouldn't have said anything, because I'm interfering, but well..." Avery smiled. "I thought you should know. The men won't say anything. Maybe Zee would, but they wouldn't want to interfere directly. Reuben—obviously—is a massive tease. I, on the other hand..."

Olivia laughed, still feeling awkward, but she knew Avery meant it for the best. "Well, thank you, I'll bear that in mind."

Avery pulled back, leaving her to her thoughts, and Olivia was relieved when her phone rang. *Harlan*. She excused herself from the table.

"Hiya. Is everything okay?"

"No! Yes. I have news, Liv! Big news, and if possible, I need Nahum's help."

 *Twelve*

J ackson studied the group of people gathered in Chadwick
House's study, wondering how best to manage all the information
they had to follow up. Initially they had struggled for leads, and now
it seemed they had too many.

It was Sunday evening, and Nahum and Olivia had returned from
Cornwall, Harlan from Mortlake with what was, quite honestly,
shocking news, and Barak, Estelle, and Lucien, had cracked the manifesto at Moonfell. Sort of. All of them looked tense, not surprisingly.
It was too much. However, they needed a plan, and they needed to stop
arguing. Right now, Nahum and Barak were standing by one of the
bookcases, locked in fierce debate as what to tackle first. Harlan and
Olivia were in chairs by the fire, chatting quietly. Estelle and Lucien
were seated at the table with Jackson, its surface covered with notes.

"Clearly," Jackson interjected, trying to calm Nahum and Barak
down, "we must split things up between us, which includes the others
in Italy, and Maggie, too."

"Which means," Harlan said, breaking off his conversation with
Olivia, "telling her about the tablet. Is that wise?"

"I trust her! Don't you?"

"Sure, but it's the *tablet*! It's huge news!"

"So is Belial," Lucien pointed out, "and we trust her with that. She *is* the lead detective of the Paranormal Policing Unit."

"Plus," Jackson said, "we don't know what effect that tablet may have on things in general. It could carry paranormal repercussions. She needs to know, which is why I have invited her tonight. She'll be here soon."

"I have no problem with that," Nahum said, shrugging. "She's always helped us in the past. Like making sure we don't end up with criminal records, despite the body count."

"Good." Jackson massaged his temple. Keeping secrets was his job, but keeping them from his friends who could provide valuable help was annoying. He was tired of monitoring his conversations as to who knew what. "I suggest you get her up to speed, Harlan, when she arrives."

"Sure, will do. It will be a relief, actually."

"Well," Barak said, taking a seat at the table, "we must go to the British Museum tomorrow. That cannot be avoided. We have to sign the paperwork, and I want to see that treasure! We were holed up in France at the time."

"I want to see it, too," Estelle added. "It's not like we're wasting time. It'll be over by midday."

Jackson gestured to Harlan, Olivia, and Nahum. "You three are going, too?"

Nahum nodded. "After that, I will happily go to JD's place with Liv to see the Emerald Tablet that is now a cave." He stared at Harlan. "You're not winding us up, are you?"

"No! It really is a giant, emerald cave. I would never kid you about that!"

"Which means that we," Estelle said, including Barak and Lucien in that, "can focus on what we saw in the spell at Moonfell."

They had already updated all of those present with the images the spell had lifted from the manifesto. Jackson wished he'd been there to witness it. Everyone now took a seat at the table in the centre of the room, keen to formalise their plans.

Olivia tapped the loose papers covered in scrawled names. "These were in that spell?"

Lucien nodded. "Yes. The letters lifted off the page, rearranged themselves, and made the names. They just hung in the air! But it was too fast to catch all of them. We missed some."

"We missed a lot," Barak virtually growled. "There were dozens of them. Maybe hundreds."

"But potentially," Harlan pointed out, "that could be a list that has accumulated over decades. Centuries, even. They could be dead by now."

"Not if they're directly related to the manifesto we found. It's only a few decades old. Jacobsen's signature was on it."

Estelle drummed her fingers on the table. "That's an interesting suggestion, Harlan. The parchment and the ink are old and imbued with angelic magic. Odette said so, and I don't doubt her. One of the images showed piles of parchment on a desk, and scrolls stacked on shelves. Therefore, any individuals that contributed to their making, storage, or anything else, were probably part of The Brotherhood years ago, and could well be dead now. The spell pulled up everyone's names."

"It's a fair point, Estelle, but we shouldn't assume," Jackson mused. "Any names you recognise?"

"Amato's, but that's all," Barak said.

Harlan grinned. "I recognise one. The Lambertis. That's the family in Venice who own the fancy *palazzo*."

"The family mentioned in the old text JD found?" Olivia asked, becoming excited. "Which means we're on the right track."

Jackson made notes as they talked. "I'll let Gabe know."

"Let me," Harlan offered. "They should be in Venice now. I set them up in an apartment belonging to The Orphic Guild, and I want to make sure everything is okay. Plus, I need to chase up Romola." As he spoke, the doorbell rang, and he rose to his feet. "And that's Maggie, so I'll get her up to speed, too. Drinks, anyone?"

A chorus of requests rang out, and Harlan left them to it.

"I want to identify that city," Barak said. He stood and started to pace. He'd been visibly unsettled ever since Jackson had arrived. The big man was always so calm, but not anymore. "I have a feeling it's where Jiri is."

Belial's commander. "Why? It could mean anything," Jackson said, swivelling to watch him pace.

"Jiri was always in the thick of things. He wouldn't skulk in a country house, or a small village. He would want to be near entertainment, easy travel, everything."

Nahum nodded. "That's true."

"But it was an ancient-looking place," Estelle pointed out. "It could be long destroyed by now."

"There are plenty of old cities left, or old quarters, at least. It looked Middle Eastern, or Greek, perhaps. Maybe even North African."

Jackson sighed. "That still leaves a lot of cities. Tell me more."

"Red sandstone buildings, or red brick, at least. Red tiled roofs, too. A flash of the sea. Maybe even mountains," Barak said, struggling to recall.

"Sounds more Mediterranean to me," Olivia suggested.

Barak nodded. "Perhaps. Estelle and I could look along that north-eastern line the statues indicate. See if anything fits."

Jackson looked across to Lucien. "We could search through the names you've written down. It's a huge task, but we can't ignore them!"

"Of course. But I've been thinking about your offer, and my future."

Jackson smiled, knowing what was coming. "You want a job?"

"It makes sense, yes? I know The Retreat. I can help. Perhaps be a type of field agent. I have too many skills to sit behind a desk forever. Besides, I'd go mad. Hopefully, for now, I can continue to live here."

"Of course. We'll work something out." Jackson felt a renewed sense of excitement at his own job offer. He liked Lucien, and was keen to help him find a new role in his altered state. "I suppose that helps me make my mind up. I've been mulling over it all weekend."

Estelle spun around. "What?"

"I've been offered the Deputy Director role at The Retreat. I have ideas, and in that role, I could really develop them."

Olivia gasped with delight, ran around the table, and hugged him. "That's brilliant! You'll be so good at it!"

"Thanks Liv. I'm not so sure, but..."

She cut him off. "No! You will be great. How fantastic."

A flurry of congratulations followed, and Jackson was anxious to stop them. "Thank you. I guess it means my occult-hunting days will be at an end, for a while."

"Unless I help with that, too," Lucien offered.

"Thank you, but let's finish with Belial first. I'm still looking for the remnants of Black Cronos, too." *Always so much to do.* "Now that Maggie's fully on board, let's see if she can help with that list of names."

"Harlan is always guaranteed to put us in a great apartment," Ash said appreciatively, as he took in the old, frescoed walls of the living area. They had been expertly restored, with decorative mouldings on the plaster work, opulent colours, and rich furnishings in the room. "It's amazing."

"And the view isn't bad either," Shadow said. She was out on the terrace overlooking Venice's Grand Canal, her slender silhouette black against the lights of the opposite buildings. "A city on water. I like it."

Gabe stood next to her, his arm sliding around her waist. "We should explore later. Find the *palazzo*."

"And food!" Niel said. "I'm starving."

They had arrived only a short while earlier, after taking their time on the drive. Navigating Italian traffic was sometimes tricky. Their apartment was on the top floor of an old *palazzo* on the banks of the Grand Canal. The view was of the rooftops, ancient churches, and the winding canal that was filled with boats and gondolas. The sun had already set, and lights blazed across the city.

Ash left the sumptuous living area and joined them on the terrace. He leaned on the balcony, taking it all in. "There are lots of little trattorias on the back streets. We'll eat and then find the Lamberti's place." He checked the address and searched the map on the search engine on his phone. He took a moment to orientate himself, and then pointed to the left. "It should be that way. Not too far, actually."

"But what do we do once we find it?" Niel asked. He was lounging in a chair, already drinking a beer, his feet propped up on another chair. "I presume we'll break in later?"

"Perhaps," Gabe said, joining him at the table. "I'd rather scope it out tonight and wait for Romola to contact us. Getting some background on the family will be important if we're to avoid what happened in Florence."

Ash nodded. "You think we might encounter another Amato-style character. A vessel for Belial?"

"Perhaps. Or another temple in the cellars, and a Nephilim trap." He cocked an eyebrow. "I'd rather not go through that again."

Shadow played with her blade, sending it twirling around her fingers so fast it was a blur. "But I'm your secret weapon. Maybe I should go alone."

"No way!" Gabe scowled at her. "We wait. And we can't presume anything. After Florence, they may have found a way to detect your presence."

Niel huffed. "The mysterious *they* again. Don't we mean Jiri?"

They had all been updated on the latest events from London. The news that JD had unlocked the Emerald Tablet was shocking. Ash had honestly never thought he would do it. No one had. He was desperate to see it and help reveal its vast knowledge. However, knowing that Jiri,

Belial's ruthless commander, was out there, somewhere, was a blow, and this had to take precedence. However, Ash had to admit that he was intrigued, too.

"How has he survived?" he asked. "Jiri, I mean. And I don't just mean the Flood! I mean all the years since. We don't live for thousands of years!"

"Unless," Niel suggested, "Belial's magic has sustained him. The use of his jewels, perhaps."

"He must have found a high mountain," Gabe reasoned, "and shelter. Somewhere to wait out the Flood and the years afterwards. Then he found a way to integrate himself into society, like us."

"Not necessarily," Shadow said, finally putting her blades away. "What if he escaped through a portal, like you? We know that witches can open them. They use them to communicate with Otherworlds, or summon demons. Or send them back! It's unfortunately common. We know that from Harlan because it happened recently, and Alex has done it a couple of times, too. Plus, we know that demon conjuring was very popular hundreds of years ago. You can't presume that you are unique."

"True," Ash said with a sigh. "He, and maybe other Nephilim, could have seized their chance, like we did."

"Or were summoned deliberately." Niel sipped his beer, eyeing them all grimly. "People are obsessed with angels, even more so in Medieval times and the Renaissance. Look at all of the art dedicated to them. If Belial was stronger in the past, he could have encouraged someone to do his bidding. And this place," he cast his gaze beyond the balcony to encompass Venice, "is very religious. Angel iconography is everywhere. In fact, the more I think about it, the more I'm sure that's what happened."

Silence fell, and Ash stared down at the dark waters of the Grand Canal, the cool night air ruffling his hair while he considered Niel's words. *Yes, that was the most likely scenario.* "Wait." He swung around to stare at the others again. "Belial's jewels. Where did they come from?"

"Perhaps Belial had news of the Flood," Niel suggested. "He always was a schemer. He had agents everywhere, even then. Maybe word reached him of the old God's plans, and he decided to plot for the future. He could have buried his jewels in a cave in the mountains. Left Jiri—and maybe some other Nephilim—with instructions of how to find them, should the opportunity arise. If he protected them with his magic, then they could have survived anything. He may even have assumed he could get them himself. I guess none of them foresaw what the Igigi would do."

Gabe nodded. "And remote mountaintops wouldn't be razed to make room for new cities. It's a good idea, Niel."

"You know," Shadow said, kicking out a chair and taking a seat on the wide terrace, "it's always bothered me as to why there were Nephilim weapons in the Temple of the Trinity. It made no sense. Why would Raziel have stored them there? You," she addressed Niel, "thought it was because he was screwing with you. What if he knew of Belial's plans, and he was offering you help?"

"Without any explanation?" Niel snorted derisively. "That would be typical!"

Ash exchanged worried glances with his two brothers. "It's a possibility, I guess. I never really considered why they were there. I was too worried about getting out of the temple at the time. And after, well... I didn't care."

Gabe stared at Niel. "You saw them better than I did. Whose were they?"

"There were a few different Houses. Tiril, Tumael, Baraquel, Meresin, and others I can't remember." He frowned as he sorted through his memories. "None particularly ominous. There were swords, shields, daggers. I considered taking a couple and then decided against it. Like you said, Ash. There was a lot going on."

The terrace was dark now, the last rays of the sun had dwindled while they talked, and only a dim lamp from the room beyond and the city lights illuminated them. Shadow placed her sword on the table, and pale light glinted along the blade. "Were they as strong as this is? Imbued with magic and special metals?"

"Not fey-made, if that's what you mean," Ash said, picking up her sword. He had handled it before. It was incredibly light for its size, and perfectly weighted. The blade was engraved, but the hilt was plain except for a curl of a dragon's tail engraved around it. "But yes, they had Fallen Angel magic. None were as fine as this, though."

"Forged on Earth, that's why," Niel said. "However, they were stronger than the weapons we have now, even though El has woven magic in them. I didn't want one though, if I'm honest. We carry enough of our past with us."

"A gift, nevertheless," Shadow said. "He knew, or suspected. He was arming you for a fight."

"Well, he should have left fucking instructions!" Gabe said viciously. "Damn angel games."

"It's done," Ash said, suddenly tired of the discussion. "Ultimately, it doesn't matter whose weapons they were, or why they were there. We have no access to them, and don't want them. What we have now is more than enough. As to how Jiri is here, well, no doubt we'll find that out when we find him. We should also assume that if he's here, others could be, too. It will make our job a little harder, that's all." He smiled at his brothers. "I take heart from the fact that they haven't achieved world domination, and Belial does not stride amongst us." He stood up. "Come on. Let's eat, find the *palazzo*, and scope the area. Then we should have a quiet night while we can get it. The beds look too good not to sleep in."

Thirteen

"I'm sorry about Reuben's teasing, yesterday," Nahum said to Olivia over breakfast in her flat on Monday morning. "He just gets carried away."

He'd mulled over Reuben's jokes all night, hoping Olivia wasn't about to run for the hills and decide to have nothing to do with him at all. Nahum had a good sense of humour, but he'd just felt awkward yesterday. It was stupid, really, because Olivia seemed to handle it well. Everyone liked her. And she'd been invited to the wedding. *As his plus one!*

"He's a tease," she said, laughing. "*Navia!* Cheeky sod!"

"He's always the same with everyone. He's a joker."

"He means well. He's not malicious. Just naughty. I like naughty." She gave him an impish grin, and his breath quickened. He still hadn't got used to seeing her in her silk pyjamas and bathrobe, bare of make-up, and with her hair tousled. Although, it was brushed now, and he could smell the minty toothpaste from across the table. It felt intimate with breakfast laid out between them. Breakfast he'd insisted on preparing.

"Please don't feel you have to go to the wedding, either," he continued. "I mean, of course you're welcome, but he might have put you on the spot."

"If I'm honest, I'd love to go. A hand-fasting! I've never been to one before. I can't wait. Are you sure you don't mind? I don't want to intrude. Our lives have become very enmeshed lately."

"Well, you are carrying my 'Nahum package.' They'll be even more enmeshed soon." He grinned. "Unless, of course, Reuben and my brothers have scared you off."

"They are all amazing. It's a long way off though yet." She patted her flat stomach, but her smile faded. "I must tell Natalie. She's my *best* friend, and I'm keeping everything from her. I won't mention what you are, but I have to say something. It's killing me not to."

"Of course you have to tell her. If she wants to meet me, I'll play normal."

"Thank you, but she'll pepper you with a million questions, so we'll put that off for a while. I need her to acclimatise first." She glanced around her eclectically decorated flat that was full of occult objects and treasures from her travels. "At least you haven't had to rescue me from anything yet."

"And won't. It's a precaution." He checked his watch. "We have a few hours before we have to sign the paperwork at the British Museum and we become insanely rich. Anything you want to do first?"

"Actually," she said, buttering her toast, "why don't we go to the museum early, and check out the displays? They have a huge amount of ancient Mesopotamian and Assyrian treasures, and also the Sutton Hoo treasure. I love it there. Who knows, we may even see something useful. They even have JD's old scrying glass. Mason has given me the time. I checked with him yesterday." She laughed. "I think he thinks that with me and Harlan there, we might get on the news and drum up more work for The Orphic Guild. He's probably right, too. I'm amazed he's not coming."

"Do you really think it will be on the news?"

"Today? Maybe. They could see this as stage one of their publicity plan. Having authenticated the treasure, they will be planning a huge display, and when they announce the news to the public, it will be enormous. Newspapers, TV. Everywhere! You found Templar treasure!" She stared at him, amused. "This has been debated over for hundreds of years, searched for by countless numbers of people, and you found a large part of it. In fact, I'm probably underestimating the impact this might have. It could well dominate headlines for weeks when it breaks. They've sat on it for months while they catalogue everything, but now? All bets are off. Knowing Theo, he might have organised some publicity, too. The village will be inundated with visitors. Are they opening the church vault where you found everything?"

Nahum looked at her, baffled. "I haven't even considered that!"

"If they've preserved the place, and I'm sure they will have, it will be a huge money maker. They'll probably open it for tours."

"Well, it's certainly possible to organise access from the crypt, but they'd have to make it more accessible, and yes, organised tours only, I'm sure. Wow!" Nahum sipped his coffee, remembering the fight with the Knights of Truth and Justice, the Templars' descendants, the huge, vaulted space beneath the church, the traps, and the riddles. "I've been so busy with Black Cronos, I hadn't considered any of it, but of course they will open it up. I'm sure Theo will have been working on it for months! I'm such an idiot!"

Olivia laughed. "Having missed out on all that fun, I know I must visit it! And I can't wait to see the treasure this morning. *If* they show it to us. They could be cagey about it, even now."

"I didn't consider that." He returned to her suggestion that they might be on the news that morning. "Say the publicity machine does start today, I'm not sure we should be photographed and splashed over the papers. We might be recognised by Jiri."

Olivia froze. "He knows you?"

"It's possible." Nahum shrugged, trying to cast his uneasy feelings aside. "Unlikely though, right? I mean, there were hundreds of us. It's not like we all knew each other. Sorry." He smiled, trying to make light of it. "I'm just paranoid."

"I might be wrong, too. There may be no press there at all. Besides, you will get to choose whether you want to be photographed or not. Theo will choose to be, I'm sure. So will Harlan. It means you're off the hook, as long as they have *someone* for photos!" She bit into her toast, chewing slowly and looking thoughtful. "As for The Brotherhood, it's unlikely they have photos of you. I mean, no one knows we were involved with Jacobsen's death. However, we can't forget that Amato knew about Gabe and the others."

"But Belial *saw* us," Nahum reminded her. He'd never forget the look on Jacobsen's face as he whirled around in the nave, eyes wide with terror. "Not like a photo, but through the connection with his jewels and Jacobsen, and he will have told Jiri and whoever else. He can connect with them, mentally. They would know what we look like. We have all carried his jewels." He tried to suppress the shudder that ran through him at the memories of using them at the farmhouse. He and Eli had channelled Belial's power and had become incandescent with his angelic magic, allowing them to crush many Black Cronos soldiers. *He would have known.* And Ash had survived because of Belial. "He warned Jacobsen that I was behind him, and he would have detected that his jewels were used. Plus, he obviously knows you and our baby. He possessed you!"

"But really," Olivia persisted, "would he have known what we looked like? He doesn't have eyes. He wasn't *in* Jacobsen, or Amato, from what you've said. He felt your presence. Our energy."

"But he's a Fallen Angel. He would see what others couldn't. They set a trap for us, under the church in Florence." Nahum glanced uneasily around the room as if he was watching them now. He rubbed his jaw, feeling the clenched muscle. He really was becoming paranoid and over analysing everything.

Olivia sat back, as thoughtful as Nahum. "He's the Angel of Death and Destruction. The bringer of madness. Maybe you feeling paranoid is exactly what he wants. I don't think he can know what we look like!"

"So how do you explain what happened in Florence with Amato?"

"Like you said. You touched his jewels, and he registered your presence. He alerted The Brotherhood. Perhaps they can attune to your energy if you're in close proximity? He clearly has a level of consciousness, which is why Jacobsen knew you were behind him in the church. And of course!" she said, rolling her eyes. "You said Amato was wearing his jewels that Shadow removed. He would have whispered to him as he did to Jacobsen, knowing you were watching him in Florence." She smiled, pleased with herself. "That must be right! You're the angel expert. What do you think? Logically! Let's not get paranoid."

He huffed, resigned to her suggestion. "Yes, that is the most likely scenario. When we carry his jewels, it's like we're wiring ourselves to him. An even better reason not to carry them. Now I'm even happier that they're in the cellar, under levels of spell protection. Hopefully my brothers are now invisible to Belial again, although I'm sure they are searching for us. I'm sorry that you were dragged into this."

"I was the one who dragged *you* into this! Anyway, it's done now, and we have to deal with it." She leaned forward, squeezing his hand. It was the first time she had touched him in days. Weeks, even. They had kept a wary distance, apart from an awkward hug in greeting. A hug that said, *I'm pleased to see you, but we're just friends.* Her touch was electric, and they both felt it. To her credit, she didn't pull back. "We're in this together, and I don't regret a thing. Not what happened between us, or our impending child. We'll get through it."

"Yes, we will. I promise." He wrapped his fingers around hers, fighting back the urge to lean in and kiss her. To lose himself in her soft skin and warm embrace again. He didn't want to think about how their daughter might not survive, or how he'd feel if the worst happened. How the loss would strike both of them like a blow. For now, their futures were entwined and ripe with possibilities and promise.

Silence stretched between them, their gazes locked, words bound behind their uncertainty, both unwilling to say more and risk everything. Then Nahum's phone rang, shattering the silence, and he wasn't sure whether to curse the interruption or welcome it.

Shadow studied their unexpected visitor, Romola Falco from The Orphic Guild, who Niel had just admitted to their apartment, hoping that they could trust her.

"We were expecting a phone call, not you in the flesh," Niel said, eyeing her warily. "Is everything okay?"

She beamed at him, eyes roving over his impressive physique before resting on his face. "Everything is great, but I decided that what I had to share should be said in person, rather than over the phone. All of this is fascinating! Especially the Lambertis." She tapped the leather briefcase she carried. "I have lots of information in here. Sorry if my arrival has upset your plans." She cast a quizzical look at all of them gathered in the lounge, watching her with narrowed eyes.

Shadow exchanged an uneasy glance with Gabe and his brothers. It was midmorning, and they had risen late after a night spent exploring Venice and finding the *palazzo*. They had just finished breakfast and were actually debating whether to phone Romola when she had arrived, unannounced.

Despite her apology, she didn't look sorry at all. Romola was a striking woman with long, dark hair and flashing, intense eyes that were almost black. She had a light tan, and wore an elegant black trouser suit, tailored to fit her good figure. She was the epitome of an Italian businesswoman. Her smile was broad as she took them all in, no doubt noting all the details about them, too.

Gabe folded his arms across his chest. "It's just unexpected, that's all, and we take our privacy—especially in business matters—very seriously. But I guess that's why you just turned up. If you had asked to visit, I would probably have told you not to."

To her credit, she just laughed. "You've found me out! What's the expression?" she asked in her heavily accented English. "Sorry, but not sorry! And you'll be glad I did. Can I sit? Get a coffee? I'd love to go through what I've found, but I had an early start."

"Let me," Ash said, gesturing for her to sit and giving Gabe a look of resignation. "Nice apartment, by the way. I gather we have you to partially thank for that?"

"Yes, this place is one of our assets. Venice is packed with history and intrigue, so it's not surprising how often we have to come here to sort acquisitions of one type or another. Harlan," she said, placing her paperwork on the coffee table, "is very complimentary about you. We were happy to help a colleague." She sat on the sofa, at ease amongst strangers.

Shadow decided she didn't like Romola. It didn't mean they couldn't trust her, but she had dismissed Shadow with a tight glance, focussing all her attention on the men. A deliberate attempt to undermine another woman as she flashed her beaming smile around. Shadow had come across women like her before. She never liked them. They saw other women as a threat. To what, she wasn't sure. *Their feminine power? Their ability to control the room? Their wish to have all men's attention?* They were especially dismissive of other very attractive woman. Less attractive women could be humoured, but Shadow was good looking with a killer figure, and that would rile Romola more than anything. *That was fine.* Shadow liked being a threat, and was more than happy to play on such insecurities. She would remind her of her presence when it was needed. For now, she would stand back and watch.

"Have you been travelling all night?" Gabe asked as he sat opposite her. "You are based in Rome, I believe."

"Yes, but there's a fast train to Venice. A few hours' travel only, and very convenient. I caught the early train." She tossed her hair, leaning forward and beaming. "Is it your first time in Venice?"

"First time in Italy."

"And yours?" She turned to Niel, who had taken a seat, too.

"I came years ago. It has changed since I was last here."

"Same for me," Ash said, entering the room with a tray of cups and a pot of coffee. "I hardly recognise the place."

Shadow suppressed a smile. *Like several thousand years ago.* He had told her that Rome had just been a tiny village on a hill then.

"Well, I'm happy to take you all on a tour."

"Unfortunately," Gabe said, "we're not here for pleasure. We need to know more about the Lambertis. Then, we need to meet them."

Suddenly, Romola was all business. She lifted half a dozen sheets of paper and passed them to Gabe. "An outline of the Lambertis who have owned the *palazzo* over the years. I can confirm that Harlan was correct. The reference in the book that he found refers to the same family who own it now. I have focussed on *only* those who have lived there. The family is large and spread across the area. They were very powerful at one point. Now, less so." She wiggled her hand. "But still rich. They had connections to the Borgias once. Houses in Rome, the Amalfi coast, and Umbria. The *palazzo* here, though, was always considered the seat of the family." She accepted a cup of coffee from Ash, inhaling appreciatively. "Arabic?"

"Yes. It's how we prefer our coffee."

"Excellent. No complaints from me."

It was the one regular thing the Nephilim liked when they travelled, and they always packed a bag of ground coffee in their luggage. A quirk.

"Anyway," Romola continued, while Gabe and Ash scanned the list, "they have had less success over recent decades, and over the years a series of family deaths. I know because, as I said to Harlan, we have had dealings with them in the past. We all have our own clients, and the Lambertis aren't mine. Their contact within our branch retired years ago, and because we hadn't received work from them for years, they were never assigned to a new collector. Past purchases include religious statues and relics, mainly Christian but not all, old volumes of occult knowledge, nothing overly significant."

"And by that," Niel said, smiling, "you mean vastly expensive."

"Well, if you put it like that, yes. But over the years, it mounted up. Until twenty years ago. That's the last time they contacted us for anything."

"Any idea why?" Gabe asked.

"The son inherited the estate after his father died. The father, Enzo, was ancient. In his nineties. The eldest son, Tommaso, took over, and well, it seems he wasn't the collector his father was. He is now in his late eighties himself."

"You have been thorough," Ash noted.

"It's my job. Besides, we keep extensive records on our clients. The London office does, too. Anyway, I have decided to try to recruit them again. It will be a good excuse to visit them and get you inside." She smiled again, pleased with her ruse.

Gabe leaned back, the list ignored now that Ash had it. "I don't think so. We work alone. I'll pay you for your effort, of course."

Romola just smiled. "I know these types of families. You won't get in without having some kind of connection. I'm it. Although I'm sure they speak English, speaking Italian will also be helpful. Being one of them."

Gabe rattled off something in fluent Italian, and Romola gasped. There was a rapid exchange, during which Niel and Ash joined in, before Gabe switched to English again, for Shadow's benefit, of course. "So, you see," he said smugly, "communication will not be a problem."

"Well, aren't you dark horses." She turned for the first time in a while to look at Shadow. "And you?"

"Oh, I have my own hidden abilities."

Romola assessed her silently and then turned back to Gabe. "Nevertheless, you still won't get in without me. If you try and fail...well, you might not get a second chance."

"Neither might you if we go alone and upset them. I think your altruism is a ruse." Gabe leaned forward, elbows leaning on his knees, eyes locked with hers. To her credit, she didn't withdraw. Gabe wasn't being overtly threatening. He just was without even trying. "You need us, too. We only want information on one jewel. A ring. How will you help us?"

"I will ask about it, upfront. Say that we have been approached by a buyer who has heard of this ring and wants it. I will offer to broker a good price for it. One of you will be my assistant."

"Not the buyer?" Ash asked.

"No! We broker. We never introduce the buyer to the seller. How would we get our cut?"

Niel shrugged. "Sounds like a plan to me, Gabe. I presume we can ask questions, Romola?"

"Of course, although we should discuss what, first. We can ask to see it, too."

"He won't show it to you," Shadow said. "Not a chance. If they value it so much as they have in years past, he won't even admit to having it."

"We shall see, won't we?" Romola replied, gaze fixed on Gabe. Silence fell and she said, "I know what you're thinking. You're wondering if you could break in and find it. These *palazzos* guard many secrets, theirs probably more than most. We should at least try it my way first."

Gabe sidestepped the question. "What have you found out about Amato and his country house?"

"Ah, that! Well, that's where it gets interesting. It took a lot of digging, too." She reached for another set of papers. "It actually belonged to another member of the Lamberti family. One of Tommaso's nieces."

Gabe exchanged a jubilant glance with Shadow and his brothers. *Another connection.*

Ash set the list down and reached for the other set of papers. "Why did Amato end up with it?"

"I can't tell you *why*, of course, but I can say that the house belonged to her father, Tommaso's younger brother, for years. It passed to her the same year she got married. A wedding gift, I presume. That would have been forty or fifty years ago. But twenty years ago, just around when Enzo died, it ended up in Amato's name." Romola spread her hands wide. "I have no idea why!"

"Well, it can't be a coincidence that it was the same time that Enzo died," Niel said. "But why give away a house? A really great house!"

"Not just any house, though," Ash reminded him without elaborating.

A house with a temple to Belial in its grounds.

Gabe pressed her for more information. "For the last twenty years the family fortunes have been diminishing, according to you, Romola. Any idea why?"

"No." Romola eased back into her seat, legs crossed to give a flash of very expensive high-heeled shoes. "There's something you're not telling me. I can help—if you let me in on it."

Shadow was standing out of Romola's eyeline, and she shook her head at her brothers. Not that they needed her advice. Gabe was already answering her. "There's nothing to tell, other than this ring is rumoured to possess strange powers. Nothing you haven't experienced before in your line of work. It interests us. But more than the ring, we want to know how it came to be with the family in the first place. It connects to other avenues of our investigation."

"Your investigation," she repeated, her eyes sparkling. "This is getting more interesting by the minute."

"Nothing other than what you will have experienced before," Gabe reassured her. "And like I said. *Our* business. However, you have found out some great information, and we're very grateful. I take it your retired colleague couldn't elaborate?"

"I tried to contact him, but couldn't." She sighed with resignation. "Frustrating. I checked his files, of course. All paper, nothing on the computer from that time. However, there were no personal notes to cast any light on anything you asked me to find. My offer still stands, though." She looked at each in turn, Shadow included. "These old families are as cagey as you. They won't give up their secrets easily. As complete strangers, you won't have a chance. Me, with my connections, it's possible. I am used to keeping secrets. Just like Harlan."

Ash spoke quickly before Gabe could decline. "She's right, Gabe. We should accept her offer. We just need to decide who goes with her."

"I should," Shadow said, "for obvious reasons."

Gabe shook his head. "I know, but even so, I'm going. If we're not out after an hour, then you three come in and find us."

"Make that two hours," Romola said, shooting forward, eager to help, before Shadow could argue her point. "You can't rush these things. We will no doubt have to wait, then go through formalities. Niceties."

"Two hours!" Niel exclaimed. "That's nuts."

"Rich families like to keep people waiting," Romola shot back.

"An hour and a half," Gabe suggested. "A compromise. When do we go? Do you need to call to make an appointment?"

"No! That is one way to find our visit barred. We just go. I suggest this afternoon at three. A good time for afternoon coffee. It will give me time to shop for a gift. Something to go with a little present I already have." She smiled broadly as she stood up. "An artifact Tommaso won't be able to resist. A lovely religious icon I have been saving for a special moment such as this."

"You think of everything," Gabe said, unable to suppress a smile.

"I try. I'll return at half past two. I'm staying downstairs, in a smaller apartment, so nice and close. In the meantime, enjoy Venice."

Fourteen

"Theo! Good to see you," Harlan said, crossing to the old man's side and shaking his hand. "It's been a while. You look well!"

Theo beamed. "I've had plenty to keep me busy, and well, the anticipation of all this has kept me very happy!" He swept his arms out to encompass the Great Court of the British Museum. "We're on hallowed ground, old boy!"

Theo, despite his advancing years, was irrepressible. As usual, he was dressed in immaculate tweeds, no doubt bought at Saville Row, and his moustache and beard were oiled and groomed, his exuberant facial hair in sharp contrast to his bald head.

Harlan laughed. "I suppose we are. Any idea what we should expect today?"

"Aside from the large cheque, you mean? Hopefully champagne and a little publicity. My solicitor is already up there checking the paperwork. Can't be too careful!"

"You think the press will be here?"

"The British Museum's marketing team! I've been keeping in close contact, you know." He tapped his nose. "They have opening dates set for the summer. June, I think. Not sure which gallery yet. Guaranteed, though, this will draw a lot of attention. I intend that Temple Moreton will get lots of it."

"Won't that make your small, pretty village horribly busy?"

"We need the money. The church is desperate, and the local businesses will benefit from increased tourism. I will, of course, donate some of my money to the church for a new roof. We've already done some work in the crypt for accessibility."

Harlan had fond memories of the pretty village in the Weald of Kent, although not the fight with the Knights of Truth and Justice, or being held captive. Or having to cross the death trap that was the map room with the trick-slabs. "I must admit that it will be good to see the chamber well lit, without fear of my life."

"Oh, it's all safe now. The mechanisms have been disengaged. The access secured. We've even repaired the broken tombs." Theo's eyes shone with excitement. "It's quite something, you know. Obviously, it's not half as impressive without the vast quantity of treasure in it, but it's an impressive structure regardless. The other passage is still blocked, but has been secured with gates, and the roof has been repaired. Don't want anyone scurrying about under my keep!"

"So, you were able to reach an agreement with the church?"

"After a bit of wrangling." He rolled his eyes, and then his face cracked into a huge smile, directed behind Harlan.

Harlan turned to see Nahum and Olivia crossing the floor towards them, Barak, Estelle, and Lucien a few steps behind. Seeing Olivia and Nahum strolling side by side, relaxed and at ease, a certain closeness between them despite the fact that they weren't touching, he realised they were already a couple. They just didn't know it yet. He'd been worried that Nahum would do something stupid and abandon Olivia in a rush of fear or denial, leaving her alone. It had fuelled his own protective instincts. He now, however, realised how utterly stupid that was. Nahum wasn't going anywhere. It both reassured Harlan and left him feeling disappointed. He'd envisaged that he and Olivia might eventually end up together, their lifestyle aligning them, but that door had firmly closed now.

As for Olivia's job with The Orphic Guild, despite her protestations otherwise, that might well change, too. He smiled broadly as he greeted all of them, and he introduced Barak, Lucien, and Estelle to Theo.

"So, another brother," Theo said to Barak. "I take it you three were busy in France at the time?"

"*Oui*! Rescuing me," Lucien said as he shook Theo's hand. "You don't mind that I come to see the treasure?"

"Of course not. At least, I hope we'll see it. I take it that you," Theo addressed Estelle with a twinkle in his eye, "also have special skills?"

"You could say that." She smiled enigmatically, no trace of sarcasm in her tone. *Barak had indeed worked wonders.*

"Playing your cards close to your chest! Wise. Well," Theo said, all business, "now that we're all here, we'd better head to the main desk."

In a few minutes' time, they were escorted by a young woman through a door marked *Private*, along corridors, and upstairs, all well away from the public spaces, finally ending up in a large, spacious meeting room with half a dozen men and women gathered in earnest conversation. Reams of paperwork were stacked on the table, and a couple of men with cameras hovered nearby. Champagne and glasses waited on the side, and even a few select treasures were in the room, along with security staff.

Once the paperwork was signed, it was obvious that the marketing of the Templar treasure was about to begin.

"This is impossible," Maggie declared, throwing the list of names onto the table in Jackson's office, and glaring at Jackson. "I can't do anything about those! Have you lost your fucking mind?"

Jackson scowled. "I was hoping for some creative input!"

"I'm a police officer! I work with facts, not mumbo-bloody-jumbo!"

"They are not mumbo-jumbo! They are names of people who are involved with The Brotherhood!"

"Yes, Belial's bloody henchmen, I know!" She stabbed viciously at the page. "First name! Last name! Incomprehensible name! Do you think I have a list of bad guys in my desk that I can mix and match?"

Jackson rubbed his face wearily. "I know it's hard, but among those names we might strike gold. We already recognise the Lambertis."

"Well, jolly bloody hockey sticks!"

"Maggie! I argued to bring you in on this, the least you can do is stop ranting."

"And that's another thing! Why couldn't I be trusted with knowing about the Emerald Tablet?" That rankled more than anything. She had been so pleased to hear about it the previous night that she had just got on with it, but overnight she had seethed about it. "I should have been told straight away!"

"For fuck's sake, Maggie. Will you shut the fuck up and sit down!"

Maggie stepped back, gobsmacked. Jackson had never raised his voice to her before. He hardly ever swore, either. It was that more than anything that calmed her down. She had really pissed him off. "Sorry. I'm frustrated." She sat heavily in her chair, annoyance vanishing. "And thank you for arguing to include me. I just don't like being the last to find things out."

"You are not the last! Hardly anyone knows about this. It's The Emerald Tablet! Something of inestimable value and power. You don't just bandy it about in any old conversation. Your sergeants will never know about this, or I will never include you in anything again."

"Of course they won't! I'm not an idiot."

Jackson glared at her. "Are you done, then?"

"Yes. But I'm still right. That list is impossible. The best we can hope to do with it is recognise names as they crop up during research. Didn't you say that they could go back generations?"

"Yes." Jackson also sagged back in his chair, looking suddenly exhausted and defeated. "And span countries. They only recorded a fraction of them, too."

"I'm sorry. I really am. I know you've obviously put great store in these. Of course I'll bear them in mind, but Irving and Stan are busy on other cases. You've only got me. Let's focus on things I can do, like look at Jacobsen some more. Or look at the northeastern line, the direction the statues face. You say Barak wants to identify a city?"

"Yes, but that's insanity as well. I have nothing to show you. It's not like they took photos! Only Barak can help there."

"But, say that line is important. We can at least narrow down cities on it. Historical or current."

Jackson nodded as he pulled a folded map from the drawer in his desk. Like all the furniture in this room, it was of art nouveau design, complimenting the style of The Retreat. Maggie found the whole place suffocating, but the warm tones of the wood, and the soft light through the stained glass windows situated in the interior walls alleviated some of that. *Mostly.* When she wasn't ranting about stupid lists.

After clearing space on the coffee table, Jackson unfolded the large European map, and Maggie saw he'd already drawn a line in pencil partway across it. "This," he said, "is where the church is in Florence, and that spot is Amato's country house. I've extended it to Venice, but stopped in Poland when I hit the coast. I find it hard to believe anything will be so far north, but I could be wrong."

"Yorkshire is further north," Maggie pointed out.

"I know. It's not on the line, either." Jackson ran a hand though his shaggy hair. "I realise that Belial's agents could be anywhere, but the statues, I think, are part of something else."

"The root of everything," Maggie said, understanding his thinking.

"Yes. If we trace that line back, we hit Corsica. I thought it was Sardinia at first, but the line was wrong. Then we hit Algeria, Mauritania, and Senegal. I don't think we should focus there."

"Why not?"

"It feels wrong."

Maggie snorted. "*Feels* wrong? We need facts, not feelings."

"What can I say? I have a hunch. I think this is a European thing." He jabbed at Corsica. "I'd like to look there more closely."

"Why?"

"The description of the buildings that Barak saw makes it sound Mediterranean. It's French, but used to be Italian, and we have a lot of Italian links in this story."

Maggie patted his arm. "We work with what we have, and we don't make too many assumptions. We can't make our hunches fit facts that aren't there. That's one way to ruin any good investigation. It's called unconscious bias. You cast your net wide with Black Cronos. That's why you had success. We should do the same here."

Jackson gave her a wry smile. "Since when did you become so wise?"

"I always have been. Cheeky shit. Now, tell me about Corsica."

"Well, it's a French island..."

"Something I don't know."

"If you'd stop interrupting! It's the fourth largest Mediterranean island, and it has a long history of human habitation, the most notable being the Carthaginians and the Greeks. There's lots of prehistoric monuments there. The Etruscans were there for a while, and then the Romans took over."

"Wow. You have done your homework."

"The important thing is that there are old cities there. Maybe that's what Barak saw."

"Maybe. Let's not get ahead of ourselves. What about later years?"

"The Vandals and then the Byzantine Empire ruled. Then it became the Kingdom of the Lombards."

Maggie sighed as she settled into a chair. Jackson had become far too caught up in research and had lost track of his goals. "Let's focus on what we know, Jackson. Belial might be as old as the hills, and his jewels, but his agents are a more recent thing. At least as in the last few hundred years. That means we focus on closer timeframes. The church in Florence may have been a few hundred years old—"

"The temple underneath it, too, don't forget! The Nephilim said it was carved from rock."

"Yes, I know, but it could have been used for other things years ago and they repurposed it. The trap could have been added later, too. Amato's country house is also modern. Have you got a date?"

Jackson's face scrunched up as he considered her question. "No, but Harlan would know. I think three or four hundred years old, max."

"And again, whoever owned it could have been recruited at any point. Maybe even a hundred or so years ago."

Jackson smiled at her. "We focus on the last couple of hundred years, then."

"We consider it. No unconscious bias, remember. We also have to consider the relic that started this off, the one Olivia found. That's been around for hundreds of years too, but again, from the research that she did just to find it, she believes that the jewels were added only in the last hundred or so years. Why they picked that reliquary is still a mystery, but I guess that's something else we should add to the list." Maggie liked talking things through. It helped her thought process-es. The more she talked, the more clarity she gained. She nodded at Jackson. "Yes. Let's focus on the last couple of hundred years. We won't exclude anything, but the facts are pointing in that direction. What might have happened a couple of hundred or so years ago to precipitate this?"

"Someone opened a portal and a Nephilim came through, if our discussion last night was correct."

"Perhaps. Why was there such a big hoard of jewels in the temple under the church?" Jackson just stared at her, puzzled. "I mean, why not spread that around, too? If the jewels are so destructive, why keep them there?"

"Maybe they hadn't found places for them."

"Perhaps. Or maybe they liked the collection of power there."

Jackson huffed. "Stop suggesting more things! This isn't helping!"

"It is. We must look at all angles." Her thoughts returned to their earlier conversation. "You say Romola gave Gabe a list of Lamberti family members?"

"Yes, and a list of a few other properties. Like Amato's place."

"Which we know was only passed to him twenty years ago."

"Yes."

"The names that Romola identified. Any of them on our list from the spell?"

"No."

"But that family is clearly involved. Or was. We know they were a couple of hundred years ago."

Jackson grinned for the first time in hours. "The alchemist. The one JD said went to the house about the jewel 'with strange properties.' That information is why we sent Gabe there now."

Maggie returned his grin. "Exactly! Now that's something tangible! Let's look at the dates in that diary." She stood abruptly, seized with conviction and the need to act.

"What? Now!" Jackson asked, rising to his feet, too.

"Yes. That family is involved! How did *they* get the jewel? And then why give the house away? They were involved, possibly deliberately, hundreds of years ago, and then something happened twenty years ago. Come on. We're going to JD's." Plus, she had an ulterior motive for going there. "Which means that we can see the amazing emerald cave, too!"

Fifteen

B arak smiled broadly for the camera, wishing he could put his fist through it instead.

The last hour had been tedious beyond belief. Guided by Theo's solicitor, who had examined the contracts in great detail for all of them, thankfully, he declared himself satisfied with the terms and amounts agreed upon. They had signed the paperwork, Nahum and Barak acting on behalf of the Nephilim and Shadow. Harlan and Theo each had their own identical agreements, as did the church representative from Temple Moreton who had arrived before all of them. Theo had been right. The amount of money involved—even for a portion of the agreed value, was astonishingly huge. They were all stupidly rich.

After the formalities were completed, the champagne flowed, and photos were taken. The museum staff were thrilled with the find. All of them who had been involved in its discovery were peppered with questions. There was a lot of lying involved. Of course, there was no mention of the knights and the near-death experiences, although the tricky episode in the map room was relayed—with reservations.

Even though Barak hadn't been there, he was part of the team who had, and of course Nahum had experienced the whole thing. Theo took centre stage, and that was fine with all of them. Barak posed for one final photo with Nahum and Theo and then retreated to stand with the others, who watched and chatted to each other, clearly amused by the whole event.

"I just want to get out of here," Barak confessed to all of them.

Estelle laughed. "Enjoy the champagne and the warm, fuzzy feeling of all that money, and just keep smiling."

He rolled his shoulders, trying to ease out kinks of knotted muscle. "I'm not a signing paperwork sort of guy."

"Neither am I," Lucien said, "but for that amount of cash, I'd stand here all day long. I was half expecting them to hand you a giant cheque, like on the lottery."

"Darling," Olivia drawled in an exaggerated tone, "this is the British Museum. It's far classier."

Barak smiled with his new sister-in-law of sorts. "Yes, it was just a big, whopping bank transfer to our account."

"Olivia!" Harlan called over. "Come and get a photo. A little extra publicity for The Orphic Guild."

She rolled her eyes, but clutching her orange juice, she crossed to his side. Nahum watched, face creased in concern. Barak understood his reservations. They were all paranoid about Belial and his agents, but that didn't mean they should put their lives on hold. Even though Olivia was pregnant with a Nephilim child. A first for thousands of years—or so they presumed. Lucien drifted away too, to examine the treasures laid out on a side table, and immediately a museum worker engaged him in conversation.

"You're getting as bad as Nahum," Estelle said softly, her gaze on Olivia, too.

"Are we paranoid?"

"Yes, but you have every right to be. I gather the Moonfell witches have made her an amulet, though. She's in good hands. And Nahum will keep her safe." Her dark eyes that glowed with passion for him alone now flashed with amusement. "He watches her like a hawk."

"I cannot find fault with that, or with the fact that he is falling in love. It's made me a happy man." Estelle's face flushed with pleasure. Barak angled his broad back to the room, hoping to put off anyone who might want to approach them, and leaned in for a sneaky kiss. "I've been mulling over that image of the city I saw in the spell yesterday. I can't place where it could be! Can you do anything to narrow it down?"

"No, unfortunately. The image was dragged from the manifesto, along with every other image that we saw. There's no way I can replicate it." She saw the disappointment in his face and squeezed his arm. "I'm sorry. I'm as frustrated as you. Why don't we focus on Jiri? What do you know about him that could help?"

She had asked this the previous evening, and he'd spent the night thinking over what little he knew. "Well, like I said, we didn't know each other, but he was based all across the Middle East. I was born in Africa, and I spent most of my time there, too. But that means nothing now. Look at us. We're in England!"

"True." Estelle huffed with disappointment. "The horn, then. Maybe we focus on that. There's nothing in the other images we saw that we can track down, interesting and informative though they were. Why did Jiri's image burst out of the manifesto, though?"

The flash of his wings filled Barak's vision again. "I think it was his power that was baked into it."

"You know, there is a group of very well-respected researchers behind you." Estelle nodded to the museum staff. "There are several different departments involved in the Templar treasure display. I doubt they'd have much to do with the time period we want. However, they might point us in the right direction."

Barak frowned. "You mean, someone might know about angelic horns?"

"They might. There are lots of Babylonian and Assyrian statues and art here. You saw them!" He couldn't miss them. It was as if he'd stepped back in time. "What if one of them knows about some special horn that was found on some dig?"

"That's nuts!"

She folded her arms, lips tightening. "Who cares? We should ask anyway. It would be stupid not to, now that we're here."

He too looked around at the gathered experts. "All right. I'm game. It beats kicking our heels while we wait to hear from Gabe."

They approached a middle-aged man dressed in a suit he looked very uncomfortable in. He ran his finger under his collar as he tried to loosen his tie. At the sight of Barak and Estelle approaching, however, he stood upright, beaming as he gripped Barak's hand. "I'm Samuel Dugan. I can't tell you how exciting this is. I have spent my life pouring over Templar documents. For you to have found a portion of the treasure is just breathtaking!"

Barak smiled and nodded, letting the man wax lyrical about the treasure before turning the conversation to more ancient matters.

Samuel frowned. "You're interested in ancient history? The Sumerians and Babylonians contributed much to our society. The true founders of the modern world. Not my specialty, of course."

"There is someone here, I presume, who we could talk to?"

Estelle flashed a huge smile. "Not in the room, we realise, but somewhere in the museum?"

He floundered for a moment at the change of subject. "Er, of course! We have a large department devoted to that era. Jenkins is the head of that particular team. I'm sure he would be happy to spare a few moments to speak to you."

They waited while Samuel called his colleague using a phone in the corner of the room. When he returned, he looked apologetic. "He can't see you right now, unfortunately, although he is thrilled to meet you! He suggests this afternoon. Would three o'clock suit? He can meet you in the main entrance."

Barak glanced at Estelle, and she nodded her agreement. "Excellent. This afternoon it is." Which would give him time to shake off the paper signing, eat lunch, and celebrate their enormous commission.

Gabe stood outside the main entrance of the *Palazzo* Lamberti, noting what he had failed to see the night before. That the old building was crumbling with age.

Romola clearly shared the same thought. "This place looks run-down. Neglected."

"Perhaps Enzo's death years ago precipitated a downturn in their fortunes."

"Perhaps. That could be why they no longer use our services." She wiggled the gift bag in her hand. "Let's hope that this is still well-received anyway."

They stood on a narrow street, one of many that laced through Venice, waiting for someone to answer the door. The bell had tolled deep within the house before falling silent. The Grand Canal was on the other side of the building, and Romola had told Gabe that the large entrances that many *palazzo*s had on the water were seldom used now. These small lanes crossed a multitude of narrow canals, and the scent of brackish water and dampness drifted around them. They stood in deep shade, the bulk of the surrounding buildings blocking out the light. Somewhere around them, well out of sight, were Shadow, Niel, and Ash.

The *palazzo*, however, despite its neglect, was magnificent. A mix of Byzantine and Moorish design, with embellishments over windows and doors. Gabe doubted that the interior would be as well preserved as their apartment, if the exterior was anything to go by.

Just as Romola lifted her hand to call the bell again, the door swung open, and a thin, sharp-eyed woman answered the door. She looked at them suspiciously before launching rapidly into a conversation designed to send them away. Just as effusively, Romola introduced herself and argued her point, before lifting the gift bag. Like any Italian conversation, it was voluble and full of gesticulations.

The woman sniffed, and then grudgingly let them in with an instruction to wait. Romola took a deep breath, sighing out her next words. "Well, that was harder than I thought."

"But we're in."

They stood in an imposing hall with a high ceiling. The plasterwork was detailed, and the paint was rich in colour. Deep reds on one wall contrasted with deep blue on another. But it was faded in places, and the glimpse offered through open doorways to either side showed that the rooms were devoid of furnishings. Still, it had a grand atmosphere that begged to be restored.

Romola explained, "The lower levels can flood, and were used for deliveries. They are hardly ever furnished. Everyone lives on the upper floors. Unless, of course, extensive work has been done. Flooding is an ever-present issue in Venice, as I'm sure you can imagine. St Mark's Square floods constantly. Have you been there yet?"

"We walked through it last night."

"You must visit St Mark's Basilica. It's magnificent."

Gabe wasn't sure he wanted to see such a monument to the old God he despised, despite its magnificent exterior that dominated the square, but he nodded anyway. *Perhaps he should. Beautiful artwork and creation should always be appreciated.* "Of course. We'll go before we leave."

He fell silent, both hoping and dreading that he should feel Belial's presence, but he felt nothing. A sharp voice called them from above, and Gabe realised that the housekeeper, if that's what she was, had summoned them. On reaching the next floor, everything changed. Opulent rugs covered sumptuously tiled floors, and oversized light fittings dangled from magnificently high ceilings. Furniture dressed in brocades, silks, and velvets was everywhere, as were the rich patinas of wood, Venetian mirrors, and huge oil paintings. Unfortunately, age tarnished everything, despite its cleanliness. There was visible wear and tear, and Gabe felt a pang of sadness for the house as it slid into decrepitude.

The housekeeper, however, was already leading the way down a long passage to a set of double doors, and with a peremptory knock, she threw one door open and ushered them inside. Gabe blinked in the bright light, taking a moment to focus after the dark corridor. Four tall windows overlooked the Grand Canal, and for a moment Gabe drank in the view before he turned and took in the rest of the space. This room was also richly decorated, the walls a beautiful, soft rose pink. For a moment, Gabe thought it was empty, and then he saw an old man seated by a blazing fire, a rug draped over his knees.

"*Signor* Lamberti," the housekeeper announced, and literally pushed them to the chairs positioned next to him. "I will bring coffee."

Romola hurried over, heels clicking on the tiled floors before sinking into the plush carpet. She kissed him on either cheek. "*Signor* Lamberti. Such an honour to meet you. This is my esteemed colleague, Gabreel Malouf."

Gabe shook his hand, trying to hide his shock. Tomasso Lamberti was a sick man. He was thin, gaunt even, his skin clinging to his bones, his eyes large in such sunken features. Gabe could feel his fragile bones in his hands, and he immediately slackened his naturally strong grip. "An honour, sir."

Lamberti nodded and wheezed, gesticulating to the chairs opposite. "Take a seat. Aria will be back soon with coffee."

Romola took the lead as she sat elegantly. She wore a different suit this time; a skirt, jacket, and silk blouse, and her heeled ankle boots were of supple leather. She crossed her legs, but leaned forward attentively. "Thank you, *Signor*. I realise that this is an imposition to visit without an appointment. However, I was in Venice on business, and..."

He cut her off. "No doubt you are in Venice on business many times. If I remember The Orphic Guild correctly, you were always here, trading secrets and occult objects." He nodded to the bag at her feet. "You want to trade secrets now, I warrant."

Gabe couldn't help smiling. The old man may be sick, but he was fully in control of his faculties.

Romola also smiled, barely missing a beat. "You know the game well. I should have come to see you before. Obviously, our business lost touch with your family when your father died. My condolences."

He batted a hand as if brushing her words away. "That was years ago. His contact there came to see me months later. I sent him away. I had no use for your business then, and no need now."

"And yet you let us in," Romola pointed out.

He smiled, revealing yellow, uneven teeth. "I was curious as to what *gift* you had brought. Besides, Aria said you were beautiful. I have always appreciated that."

Before Romola could answer, Aria bustled in with a tray of coffee and placed it on the small table next to Lamberti. She poured their drinks, slowly and deliberately, and Romola reached into her bag for the delicate biscuits she had bought. One of her many gifts. "To go with coffee," she said, smiling.

Once Aria had gone, the pleasantries continued. Gabe was amused by it all, and he sat back, knowing the conversation would take its own course, and there was nothing he could do to rush it.

"I take it," Lamberti said, "that there are more than just biscuits in that bag."

"Of course, but let's not rush," Romola answered. "I must savour your delicious coffee first." She glanced around the room. "I reviewed your father's records. A few of the items we helped him find are in here. I saw some in the hall, too."

Lamberti's face twisted in displeasure. "Yes, he spent a lot of money on such things."

"You don't approve."

"I like beautiful things, as you can see, but his obsession with religious trifles was annoying."

Romola's face fell. "Ah. In that case, you may not want what I have brought you. Nevertheless, it is a gift."

"I shall hold my judgement until I see it. I have no objection to religion as such, we were brought up Catholic, but he was obsessed. It was unhealthy. When he died, I sought to distance myself from such things." His eyes clouded over, and Gabe paid closer attention. '*Unhealthy' was interesting. Was this about the ring?*

"But," Romola continued, looking puzzled, "you still have some religious iconography here. If you wish to sell it, I can help."

"Oh, I got rid of some. But tell me about The Guild. Are you still busy?"

For a while, Romola chatted easily about the market and the work they did. They talked of old names known to both of them, and Gabe realised that like in England, this world was tight knit, and old families all knew each other, despite Lamberti's protestations that he had left it behind. Gabe remained silent, focussing on feeling for any signs of Belial. The Fallen Angel, though, was stubbornly quiet.

With a shock, Gabe realised Lamberti was addressing him. "You don't look much like the office type."

He smiled. "I'm a field worker. I have a specific interest in Venice."

"Religious iconography, too?"

Gabe decided to cut to the chase. There had been a lot of endless chitchat. "Of a sort. Fallen Angels, actually."

Lamberti's hand shook violently and the small, delicate cup he was holding fell to the floor and rolled across the rug. Romola was also shocked, but she recovered quickly and instinctively lunged for it. Gabe's attention remained fixed on Lamberti's face.

Lamberti's voice was hoarse. "I knew you had come here for a reason. What do you want?"

"I heard rumours of a powerful and unusual ring that your family was supposed to possess. I would like to see it."

From the expression of dread on Lamberti's face, frozen in masklike horror, Gabe knew he didn't need to elaborate. However, he tried to lie. "I have no idea what you're talking about."

"Of course you do. I can smell your fear. I have no wish to drag up bad memories, or to cause you any harm. In fact, I will do you a favour and take the ring away. It has no place in civilised society."

A measure of calm returned to Lamberti's face, and he wiped his brow with a fine linen handkerchief. "What makes you think such a ring is here?"

"Aside from your panicked expression? Something recorded in a diary, years ago." Gabe gave him a brief explanation. "The entry was about your family. And then, of course, there's the ex-residence of your niece, now falling to ruin in Palazzuolo sul Senio. The temple in the grounds is of particular interest to me."

Lamberti started wheezing, gasping for breath, his wizened frame buckling over.

Romola glared at Gabe. "Are you trying to kill him? Grab some water." She pointed to the jug of water on another side table, and then scrambled to help Lamberti upright.

Gabe, feeling horribly guilty, but also vindicated in their investigations, poured a glass of water and helped the old man recover. "I'm sorry. Take a moment."

Lamberti glared at him, sharp black eyes boring into his. When he finally spoke, it was with a whisper. "How do you know about that damn temple?"

"Someone tried to kill me. I take it very personally. I decided to get to the root of it. Why don't you tell me what you know, and then I'll leave you in peace." He sat down again, knowing his bulk looming over the old man wasn't going to help him relax. "I have no issue with you. I just want the ring, and to find out why you seem to be linked to Belial."

"Not me!"

"Your family, then."

Romola was now looking at Gabe with tight-lipped annoyance. Not surprising, seeing as he hadn't mentioned anything about Fallen Angels earlier. He'd rather she didn't know now, but needs must. Plus, it was a good test as to what she knew. *Not much*, he'd say so far.

Tomasso's voice had become a dry rasp. "If I tell you, will you leave me in peace?"

"Of course. But I want the ring."

"It's gone!" he huffed, outraged. "I sold it after my father died."

Gabe leaned forward. "Who did you sell it to?"

"One of my father's contacts. One of the..." he faltered. "A business colleague."

"I think you were going to say The Brotherhood."

Lamberti blinked. "How do you know that name?"

"I do my homework. If you have heard of them, then you know what that ring is and why it's so dangerous. I bet you know a lot more, too. Where is it?"

"Somewhere you will never find it."

"You'll be surprised what I can find."

Sixteen

"This is unreal," Jackson said, blinking as he took in the entrance to the emerald cave in JD's marquee. "I think I'm hallucinating."

"In that case," Maggie declared, "we both are. What the actual fuck..."

"Anna," Jackson said, whirling around to look for JD's assistant who had walked over with them, "have you been inside?"

She puffed up. "No! I have nothing to do with JD's work. I just feed him and keep his house clean."

"But this is The Emerald Tablet! He's actually cracked it! I mean, you saw it, right? You know what he was doing."

"Of course I saw it. It was hard to miss. One of his more impressive results, I admit, but when you've known him as long as I have, it just becomes one of the many things he's achieved."

She really was an interesting woman. To live and work with a genius, and yet have nothing to do with his work. It was its own form of madness. And yet, maybe she was the sanest one of them all. *Best to keep out of JD's business.*

"I'll leave you to it," she said, backing away.

Then it struck him. "Holy shit! You're like him. Immortal." Anna smiled, confirming everything. "For how long?"

"Long enough." Her eyes sparkled with mischief, and suddenly Anna, the dour and disapproving woman, became far more interesting. *Another immortal...* JD must value her more than he had ever let on. Refusing to elaborate, she exited the tent, saying, "I'll see you later."

Jackson looked at Maggie. "Can you believe that?"

Her hands were on her hips, lips clenched tight, her eyes boring into his. "Fucking *immortal*? How many other fucking secrets are you keeping from me, Jackson?"

"Oh, shit!" *Why had he forgotten that Maggie didn't know about JD?* "Oh well, one less secret to keep."

Maggie didn't budge. "Anything else, before we step inside? And perhaps some details now might be nice!"

"Er, can this wait until we've seen JD? I promise to answer all your questions later." *Fuck.*

"No! How old are we talking?"

"JD is about five hundred years old. Give or take."

"Five hundred!" Maggie staggered backwards, hands gripping the back of a chair. "How?"

"He's an alchemist. I have no idea! But clearly, he values Anna. And no, I have no idea how old *she* is."

"How long have you known?"

"Years. A few of us in the PD know. Layla and Waylen. Russell never knew." *Thankfully. Although, would it have mattered? The Comte de St Germain knew anyway.* "Olivia, Harlan, and Gabe and his brothers know, too. It sort of came out during the jobs we did with him."

"You owe me!" Maggie prodded him in the chest, fury rising. "The last to know about that, too!"

"To be fair though, Mags, you don't know him or work with him. Your paths never cross. So, why would you know?"

She regarded him silently, obviously wrestling with her emotions. "I suppose that is true. I know him by reputation only as head of The Orphic Guild. Damn it, I'm still cross, though! Is he someone famous? I would like to know before I actually meet him."

"Well, yes actually, you might know his name. It depends how much of a history buff you are." Jackson knew most people would never have heard of him.

"Try me."

"He's John Dee. He was Queen Elizabeth's court magician."

"Queen Elizabeth the first?"

"Well, yes. It clearly wasn't the second, you tit!" He presumed shock was addling her brain.

Maggie took a moment to gather herself. "Well, obviously I have heard of her! But him, no. I have no idea who he is."

"Well, don't tell him that. In fact, just don't mention it at all." Jackson was sure she knew that the Count of St Germain was immortal because she'd helped his research. Consequently he'd assumed she knew about JD, too. His head hurt just thinking about it. "Can we go now? The big, green cave awaits."

"Just give me a moment!" She sat heavily on the chair, looking like a smaller version of the Maggie he knew. "You've had a long time to get used to this news. It's a shock to me. I know you've talked about him, and the advancements he's made with alchemical weapons, and that he's been tracking Black Cronos, but I didn't know he is immortal!"

Jackson rubbed his face and sat next to her, suddenly weary. "You know, I'd actually forgotten you didn't know, and to be honest, in the course of normal conversation, it doesn't come up. It's just JD doing his thing! I'm sorry."

"I'm in your pack! Your alpha—according to you. I feel an idiot."

"Maggie, you're not an idiot. I forgot. I bet Harlan and Olivia forgot, too. Well, maybe not Harlan. It's like he keeps lists of this shit. But you can't tell Stan or Irving."

"Of course not." *Blimey.* She was so shocked that she'd forgotten to swear. "So, his huge library and diaries, and all of that stuff you've talked about...did he acquire it over his lifetime?"

"Of course. He was there for a lot of it, or was passing through places and then heard news about various things. It's why he's so smart. He was already a genius in his lifetime. Now, with hundreds of years of study under his belt, well..."

"Wow." Maggie took a deep breath and exhaled slowly. "Okay, I'm fine. Let's walk into the Emerald Tablet, shall we?"

He grinned. "I bet you didn't think you'd be saying that when you woke up this morning."

"Oh, fuck off you smug bastard! Let's get in there."

She marched down the green passage, leaving Jackson running to catch up. He'd meant to savour this moment, and now he was rushing. *Bloody Maggie.* He slowed, letting her race off alone, and examined the walls and floor, trying to commit it all to memory. It was surreal. Like walking through a dream. It was an even weirder sensation when he actually reached the cave itself. The pillars towered around him, covered with endless lines of text. *Incredible.* It stretched in all directions. Harlan hadn't fully described the enormity of it. *But how could he?*

A bellow from somewhere ahead of him made him sprint, but it was Maggie's strident voice that set him in the right direction.

"Calm down! I'm not a stranger!" she yelled. "I'm Maggie Milne, DI with the Paranormal Policing Team. I'm here with Jackson Strange."

By the time he found her, Maggie had her hands up, backed against an emerald pillar, while JD pointed one of his weapons at her.

Jackson shouted, "JD! She's with me! It's okay."

"It's not bloody okay! I could have shot her. I thought she was an enemy agent!"

"From whom? Your house is wrapped up with state-of-the-art defence systems. It took me ages to get Anna to let me in the gate!"

JD scowled and lowered the weapon. "You can never be too sure! You're a detective?"

"Yes!" she said, still annoyed.

"You should have warned me, Jackson!"

"How? Anna left us here and there's no mobile phone coverage. Now, can we forget the mundane and talk about this!" Jackson stretched his arms wide and spun around, the height and breadth of the cave overwhelming. "This is insane! And you look terrible." He studied JD up close. The light made him look sickly. "Have you slept?"

"A couple of hours, perhaps. I'm trying to map this out before I do anything else. I understand hardly any of it, though. I'm waiting for the Nephilim."

"Nahum and Olivia will be here soon. Is there anything here that can help fight Belial and The Brotherhood?"

"I doubt it! You'll be better off looking in my library."

"That's what we were hoping to do, actually. You don't mind? We want the diary you showed Harlan."

"It's all on the table. I found a few other things for him about that alchemist. There might be more entries about Lamberti, too." He groaned, looking uncomfortable. "I slept badly. It's this place, I think. It manifests a weird energy."

Jackson had been so shocked by the enormous emerald cave with its towering pillars that he'd barely noticed the atmosphere, but now that JD had drawn his attention to it, he realised there was a strange hum that was almost imperceptible. "I feel it. Where does it come from?"

"I don't know. Magic, perhaps? I have found no obvious source of power. No sign of habitation, obviously."

"What about the fire?" Maggie pointed to a column of flame a short distance away. "And the lanterns? I presume you didn't light them."

"No. All already lit when I entered. It's as if Hermes walked out of here and just left it, and then shrank everything into the tablet. Brilliant."

"Or terrifying," Maggie said, looking darkly at Jackson. "What if there is a strange power here? It could blow up. Take half the county with it."

"There is no 'what if!'" Jackson pointed out.

"You sound as bad as Harlan," JD complained.

Maggie was right to be worried. The longer Jackson stood there, the more uncomfortable he became, and the more eager he was to leave. However, he had one more piece of news to share. "JD, I've accepted the offer to become Deputy Director of the PD. Russell's old job."

JD's eyes narrowed. "Have you now? Good. You'll do an excellent job. I told Waylen as much."

"You suggested me?"

"Why not? Your family has provided great service in the past. Your grandfather included. You deserve it."

"Thanks, JD! I didn't know."

"It was logical."

"So, has Waylen mentioned about the lab?"

"No, but I can guess what's coming. He's dropped some big hints."

Jackson laughed. It seemed Waylen had been having a few conversations lately. "Will you help, then? Oversee the lab? I can't."

JD's features softened. "I will. But they'll need to pull their socks up. That Lyn should work out, though. Diligent. Organised. I like her."

"Good. Thank you." Another weight lifted off Jackson's shoulders. *This might actually work out.* "Well, there's nothing we can do to help you here. We'll leave you to it, JD."

JD just nodded, already distracted, and Jackson and Maggie left him to his thoughts. By mutual agreement, neither said much, both absorbed by the enormity of what they'd seen. Jackson led the way to the library, feeling the residual effects of the cave slowly leave him. On arrival, he headed to the large table in the middle.

"You're as disturbed by that cave as I am, right?" Maggie asked, when the door was shut behind them and they were alone.

"Of course! It's unnatural, filled with all sorts of arcane knowledge. However, just because we don't understand it, doesn't mean we should be scared of it."

"Yeah, well, I'll reserve my judgement on that. And on him!"

"As unconventional as he is, I've learned to trust him. Over the years he has been an asset to our country, time and time again. He destroyed Black Cronos's stronghold. The Nephilim couldn't have done it without him. He founded MI6!"

Jackson had worked hard to put his kidnapping behind him. He was still left with a few nightmares. Occasionally, he woke up in a cold sweat. Over the past weeks he had dedicated time to tracking down any remaining Black Cronos bases, but it was hard. Belial was actually proving a welcome distraction—sort of. A large stack of books was on the corner of the table, and he reached for a sheet of paper perched on top of them with JD's familiar scrawl on it.

"Yep, that's the pile of new information he found for us."

"With lots of helpful little stickers," Maggie noted, thumbing the first book on the stack. "This will take hours."

Jackson nodded. "It will be worth it, though."

"Will it, if the information is years old?"

"This is no time to get picky." Jackson slipped his jacket off and reached for a thick, leather-bound volume. "Best get started. By the time Nahum gets here, we might have something useful to share."

Seventeen

Niel sheltered in a shadowed doorway, watching the main entrance of the Lamberti house. Gabe had entered a while ago, and the intersecting lanes had remained generally quiet, the foot traffic light.

He scanned the street, knowing that Ash was situated close to the front of the building, and Shadow had clambered up the walls to find shelter on a narrow balcony. She'd climbed like a monkey, frighteningly quick, reminding him of that fact she was a thief in the Otherworld, and to be honest, was here, too. He had lost sight of her, and presumed she had entered the *palazzo*.

He was uneasy about this situation, and wasn't sure what he thought of Romola. He wondered where she and Gabe were, and hoped that Gabe would learn something useful.

Movement down the narrow lane caught his attention. Six men were approaching, and they looked far from casual. They wore dark clothes, and their eyes darted everywhere. Niel drew back further into the deep doorway, glad that the lanes were so dark. They paused outside the main door and waited. In moments, the door opened, revealing a glimpse of the housekeeper, and the men slipped inside.

Herne's hairy bollocks. Something was wrong.

As a precaution they had packed their tiny earpieces that connected to their phones, and he quickly called Ash. His response was worrying. "Two men are here, too," he whispered. "They are blocking the escape route to the water."

"You watch them. I'm going in," Niel said. "I'll warn Shadow and Gabe."

After a clipped confirmation from her, and a quick text to Gabe that he hoped he'd see in time, Niel used the skeleton keys that they were all now familiar with, and entered the cool hallway. The six men and the housekeeper were nowhere in sight, but he could hear two voices from somewhere on the ground floor.

The stairs took up the bulk of the entrance hall, and he edged around them. The room to his right was empty, but ahead was another couple of doors. One door was shut, but the other was partially open, and the voices were beyond that. A rapid, almost whispered conversation was taking place in Italian—a man and a woman's voice. Glancing uncertainly up the stairs, Niel reassured himself that Shadow would be investigating, and he crept closer until he was right outside the door.

He caught flashes of the conversation. Whispers of a ring. Betrayal. Weakness. Stupidity. The woman was furious. "I should have poisoned him while I had the chance. Old, decrepit fool."

"We had our reasons for keeping him alive, but no matter. It will be done today. He will die with the others."

"But we need to know who they are, and how they know!" The woman insisted. "He is not alone!"

"Don't worry. We'll find out. Although, we already suspect. We have had trouble lately."

Niel gripped his knife, JD's weapon in his other pocket. Much to his annoyance, strolling the streets of Venice with his axe was not okay. With the rapid conversation still continuing, Niel pushed the door open, revealing a virtually empty room. A narrow window allowed for a view of the lane to the side of the building, and a sliver of the canal. The man's back was to him, but the woman was facing his direction. She glanced at the door and her eyes widened in shock. Niel threw his knife before she could speak. It plunged into her forehead, and she crumpled to the ground.

The man spun, a knife in his hand, too. He threw it with speed and accuracy, but Niel was already running to the side, and it hit the plaster behind him and embedded in the wall. Niel pulled it free. The man raced towards him, crunching into Niel, and they both hit the floor hard.

Niel, however, was bigger and stronger, and although his opponent was quick, he was no match for Niel's paranormal strength. He rolled, smashing the man's head down on the hard, tiled floor. He straddled him, pinning him into position, and covering his mouth with his hand so he couldn't speak.

The man bucked under him, trying to move, but Niel smacked his head down again, and he fell back, dazed. Niel listened for signs of movement, but the house was ominously quiet. He needed to get moving and see what was happening upstairs, but the man could have valuable information. Killing him was not an option. *Yet.*

Unless Shadow kept one alive. He almost laughed out loud at that idea.

Idiot.

"It's your lucky day, you shit-bag," he said to the man. He punched him, hard, knocking the man out cold. He retrieved both knives, locked the door, and headed upstairs.

The tall double doors that opened onto the narrow balcony did not fit securely, and Shadow had eased one open and edged inside as soon as she accessed the balcony on the second floor.

The bedroom beyond was filled with dark, heavy furniture, and looked unused. She crossed to the door and explored the upper floor, hearing faint voices from downstairs where Gabe was talking with Romola. She assumed this floor was hardly utilised. It was clean, but dust sheets covered most of the furniture. She hunkered down behind the wooden balustrade, safe in the knowledge that the dark landing and her own fey magic would hide her. The woman who had let Gabe in hovered on the hall below. She was listening to their conversation. When she disappeared into another room and made a hurried phone call, Shadow wasn't surprised when Niel texted ten minutes later. *Six men incoming. I'll tell Gabe.*

She heard the entrance door open below and the faint carry of voices. After a few minutes, five men ascended the stairs, and she readied her blades. *Who were they? What did they want? And why so many of them?* They clearly did not mean for anyone to escape.

Shadow calculated her chances. She could take out a couple quickly, but not without alerting the others. They were too close to each other. But did she care if she made a noise? *Yes.* She needed to allow Niel time to enter. The main entrance was out of sight from her position. With luck, he was already inside. Four of the men progressed down the hall, leaving one positioned at the top of the stairs.

Shadow jumped down, vaulting over the balcony and landing directly behind him, as stealthy as a cat. The man was short and stocky. "Is there a problem?" she asked, blades already in her hands, back to the wall so she could see the room at the far end where Gabe was, and where the four men had already entered. She should give them a chance to explain themselves. Who knew? It could be another business proposition.

The man whirled around to face her. "Who the hell are you?" he asked in broken English, a slim blade appearing in his hands.

"Your worst nightmare. And you?"

"You have no idea what you're dealing with."

"Then tell me."

"I'd rather kill you."

She smirked. "You can try." She released her fey glamour, her otherness flowing out of her as she spun her knives dexterously. He staggered back, eyes widening in shock, but he quickly recovered and lunged at her. He was far too slow. She cut his throat and he crashed to the floor, blood pooling around him.

Worrying what was happening with Gabe, she turned to run to the door, just as Niel rounded the turn in the stairs. "Gabe?" Niel asked, reaching her side.

"That way."

They turned and ran together.

Ash decided not to act against the two men who had arrived in a small motorboat, killing the engine and drifting to the wide porch that led into the Lamberti house. Fortunately, there were stacks of mooring equipment and old crates outside, all damp and rotten, and Ash sheltered behind them and huddled down to listen.

The men disembarked quietly, watching the river in case anyone else approached, but they didn't seem worried. They stood close, conversing quietly, and their conversation was revealing.

Ash and his brothers had thought there was only one family associated with Belial and The Brotherhood in Venice—the Lambertis. They were wrong. There were at least two other families involved, maybe more, and they were worried. The Nephilim and Shadow had created trouble, and the smooth running of their organisation was threatened.

Then Ash heard something else that made his blood run cold. There was a meeting that night on the neighbouring island of Murano to discuss *the Nephilim issue*. They were presuming one would be dead before the day was out. *Gabe.* Ash glanced up, trusting that Gabe could hold his own before the others arrived to help. In the meantime, Ash decided he would gather as many details as he could without being detected.

It seemed that Venice was a nest for The Brotherhood.

When Gabe read Niel's text, he realised there were two possibilities here.

Either Lamberti was stalling and had sent for backup via his house-keeper, or Lamberti had no idea that half a dozen men had just silently entered his house, betrayed by the woman who looked after him. Then he added a third option—Romola was in on it, too. Either way, Gabe needed to move quickly. He had mere minutes to act, and Lamberti had barely shared anything useful.

"On your feet, Lamberti." He grabbed the man's thin arm and pulled him up. He was astonishingly frail, and Gabe flinched when he realised how thin he was.

Lamberti cried out, sinking back into his chair. "Stop. What are you doing?"

"We have company. Is this your doing?"

"W-what?" He stuttered, outraged, looking from Romola to Gabe. "What is going on?"

There was genuine confusion and pain on his face, and suddenly Gabe felt like a monster. "You don't know."

Romola looked equally shocked. "Gabe! What are you talking about?"

"The door in the wall behind you. Where does it go?"

"It's my bedroom." Lamberti's face drained of what little colour he had. "They have come for me. This is *your* doing!"

"They have come for all of us!" Gabe didn't have time to argue. He weighed his options, and decided he had to protect Romola and

Lamberti. Once he had hidden them, he'd face the intruders alone. "Romola, get in that room and find a place to hide. *Signor* Lamberti, I'm going to carry you."

He scooped the man up like a child, aghast at how light he was, and ran into the bedroom, taking it in with one swift glance. Another door was on the other side of the room. Lamberti wheezed with pain.

"I'm sorry. Where does the other door go?"

"My bathroom. There's nowhere to hide in there. Or here! It's my bedroom!"

Romola had other ideas. "Gabe, the wardrobe. It's huge."

A monstrous, heavy wardrobe ran along one wall, deep enough to hide in. Romola had already pulled one of the doors open and started pushing clothes aside. Fearing the door to the other room would burst open in seconds, Gabe deposited Lamberti on the floor of the wardrobe. Romola clambered in next to him, pulling clothes over them, and Gabe shut the door, hoping he hadn't just locked Lamberti in with a killer. He then placed a heavy chair under the other exit, and ran back to the main room.

Gabe was just in time. He took his jacket off, prepared to unfold his wings if necessary, and unsheathed his short blades that were strapped to his forearms. He stood in front of the fireplace, facing the door. Four men entered, looking calm and composed, but their expression darkened as they saw Gabe waiting. All carried daggers.

The oldest man of the four, who had silvered hair at his temples but nevertheless looked fit and dangerous, paused just inside the doorway, and the others fanned out on either side.

"Can I help you?" Gabe asked. "I wasn't expecting anyone to join my meeting."

The man ignored his question, eyes darting around the room before settling on Gabe again. "Where is Mr Lamberti and the woman?"

"Busy. No introductions? Who are you?"

"Who we are is of no concern to you. You will be dead in a few minutes, as will the others. We *will* find them. I presume they are in the next room." He shrugged, his lips twisting into a grim smile. "It is just a matter of time." He stepped forward, the other men advancing with him, one heading towards the door to the bedroom.

"Not so fast." Gabe stepped across their path to block the door. "Ah, yes. Time. But *you* are running out of it, not me. I am on to you now. The Brotherhood. Or The Consortium, as you were once called. Your dirty little intrigues that are intent on spreading Belial's darkness. His tokens that you have sprinkled around. I will find them all."

If the man was surprised by Gabe's knowledge, he hid it well. "You pretend you act alone, but you don't. Is that how you knew that we were here? You have eyes on the building. No matter. We will find them, too."

Without another word he threw his blade with a deft flick of his wrist. His movement was so subtle, so smooth, that Gabe barely saw it, but he had faster reflexes than most. He dived to the floor, rolling behind the huge armchair that Lamberti had sat in. He threw one blade while in motion, aiming for the closest man. He struck him in the throat, and he crumpled to the floor, hands clutching at the hilt.

A flurry of knives followed, pinning Gabe in position. He picked up the chair, using it as a shield and a battering ram, and ran at the man who had been doing all the talking. Gabe crunched into him, knocking him to the floor.

Simultaneously, the door flew open and Niel and Shadow burst in. A short but furious fight followed. The men were agile and swift, but were ultimately no match for two Nephilim and a fey. Within moments, all lay dead.

"Fuck it," Gabe said, pulling his blades from the dead and wiping them on their clothes. "I had hoped to ask more questions. Where are the others?"

"I have one captive downstairs, Shadow killed another on the landing, but Ash is watching two more by the dock. The housekeeper is dead," Niel told him. "Where are Lamberti and Romola?"

"Safe, I hope. I'll check on them in a moment."

Shadow crossed to the window and looked at the Grand Canal below. "There's a boat down there. Must be owned by Ash's men."

"Go and check it out," Gabe instructed. "Be careful. Do not compromise Ash."

"You might need this," Niel said, throwing her the key. "I locked one room."

She nodded and vanished with her normal flash of fey glamour.

Gabe grimaced as he surveyed the dead. "I had hoped to avoid this. There must be others involved in Venice. Lamberti better start answering some questions."

Shadow avoided the locked room, and instead headed into the one next to it.

Its plaster work was crumbling, and the paint was faded, but one tall window looked out onto the small dock beyond. Two huge doors took up the rest of the space. It was a place to unload supplies. She crossed the floor silently and edged to the window.

Two men stood talking quietly as they overlooked the river. If she could open the doors, she could kill them easily, but the locks looked clunky and rusted, and no doubt that would make a noise. *Perhaps that wouldn't matter*, she reflected. *But where was Ash?*

Worried for his safety, she studied the shadows beyond the window. She doubted the men would have caught him off-guard, but where was he? The area was full of old crates, mouldering bits of rope, and other water-related paraphernalia. Fortunately, the men weren't looking in her direction at all. Plus, the windows were grimy, and the room was dark behind her. She pressed her face to the glass, peering to either side, and finally spotted a figure coiled in the corner.

Ash.

There was no way she could attract his attention. Any minute now, the men would be asking questions about what was going on upstairs. As she watched, one reached for his phone, and she heard the ringtone in the room next door. *Herne's hairy bollocks!* It belonged to the man Niel had knocked out. And it rang and rang and rang. The man turned, confused, and Shadow realised that he could hear it outside.

Not entirely sure what would happen, but fearing he might call for support, she acted quickly. She smashed the window with the butt of her dagger, and both men whirled around. She threw her knife at the man on the phone, and her blade plunged into his chest, killing him instantly. But before she could attack the second, Ash leapt from behind the crates and killed him after a very quick, muffled struggle.

Ash hauled the man behind the crates, and Shadow leapt through the broken window, helping him dispose of the other.

"I should have known it was you, Shadow. I was listening to them!"

"He could have been about to call for help!"

"You don't know that!"

"Oh, come on, the odds are strong. We've killed everyone except a captive. We do not want more turning up."

Ash paused, hands on hips as he surveyed the Grand Canal, but no one was paying any attention to their shadowed dock, deep under the overhang of the floor above. Shadow checked the dead man's phone, but it had stopped dialling, and she shoved it in her pocket.

"I guess not," Ash finally said. He lifted his chin, gesturing to the upper floors. "All dealt with?"

"Just the one next door that Niel punched unconscious. Want to help me take him upstairs? We have a lot of questions he could answer."

He nodded. "Oh, yes. I have lots of questions, too." And with that enigmatic response, he led the way back in through the broken window.

Eighteen

E stelle followed Barak, Nahum, Olivia, Lucien, and Harlan into Jenkins's office, somewhere in the labyrinthine passages of the British Museum.

He was a tall, rangy man who looked like he'd spent most of his life outdoors. He was, Estelle estimated, in his sixties, with tanned, weather-beaten skin and dark blue eyes surrounded by wrinkles. He had greeted all of them as if they were superstars, and they probably were to the museum community. Well, Harlan and Nahum perhaps, seeing as they had actually found the Templar treasure. Estelle was happy to soak it all up, amused by the excitement the find had provoked.

Before the appointment with Jenkins, they had all eaten a long, celebratory lunch, saying little about Belial, seeing as Theo was with them. However, once he had left them, Barak and Estelle had told them of their meeting, and the others had asked to join them. Fortunately, Jenkins seemed happy to entertain them all, dragging chairs from other offices to accommodate the group.

After some excited questions about the treasure, he said, "I understand, though, that you are interested in another type of treasure? Sumerian digs? Assyrian, perhaps?"

Barak took the lead. "I wouldn't know what age to categorise it, actually, but it is more Biblical in nature. It's regarding finds that have angelic symbols, or perhaps ancient jewellery—clasps, bracelets, rings of gold and silver, and other precious metals and gemstones. They would probably have been in a well-preserved state. Or maybe there was a horn? Something that you would use to call troops to battle. Potentially there would have been quite a hoard of jewellery, and it might have been found in the Middle East." He paused, glancing at Nahum, as if wondering how much to say. "Perhaps they would have had strange properties."

Nahum nodded. "Yes, as if they were cursed, like with Egyptian finds."

Jenkins leaned on the table, his hand stroking his chin as he considered their questions. "Well, as you know, Tutankhamun's tomb was considered cursed. I presume you refer to something like that?" They all nodded enthusiastically, but Jenkins frowned. "Are you on another treasure hunt?"

Barak smiled. "It's related to another case we're working. We're trying to find the source of a problem."

Jenkins cast Harlan a tight-lipped look. "Not planning on stealing antiquities, I hope? I know of The Orphic Guild's reputation."

Harlan sat back, affronted. "We delivered you Templar treasure! That's hardly justified."

"In *this* instance. I'm sure we both know there are others when you haven't been so forthcoming."

"That's unfair," Olivia said, glaring at Jenkins. "You have no idea what we do! Most things we find for clients are not significant enough for museums. And besides, you have so much stuff in your basement alone that will never be seen! Talk about hoarding treasure! Especially that which belongs to other countries."

Estelle winced. *Wading in on the Elgin Marbles debate was not the distraction they needed right now.*

Barak intervened, shooting Harlan and Olivia venomous looks. "We just want to know what has already been found, and what might be on display. You would know, I'm sure. A man of your vast knowledge and connections."

Jenkins rolled his eyes. "Flattery. You must be desperate." Estelle wondered if she needed to cast some glamour, something to oil his tongue, but Jenkins seemed to shrug off his issues with Harlan and Olivia, his interest piqued. He leaned forward. "There was a find many years ago that included just such treasures as you mention, and the dig was indeed believed to be cursed. It sends shivers through our community even now, over one hundred years later."

Estelle felt a stir of excitement, and leaned forward, too.

Jenkins continued. "The men on that dig ended up dead, all except for one, who disappeared."

Barak frowned. "They were murdered?"

"They went mad—or that was the theory, anyway, at the time. Some killed themselves, some killed each other. This find was in early 1800s. 1833, if I remember correctly. So, in the infancy of archaeology, when the profession was happy to trample over antiquities and raid other countries' culture." He shot Harlan and Olivia a narrowed glare as if daring them to contradict him. Fortunately, both remained mute. "It began when a rich Italian was touring the area and heard of an unusual cave that had intriguing markings on the walls. He hired a guide and went to visit it. Apparently, he was so excited by what he found that he harassed The Geographical Society, was given funding that he supplemented with his own money, and headed up there. He hired a group of men to dig. Not locals, you understand. They wouldn't touch it. A few reports were sent back, saying they had found a vast treasure of jewels. It mentioned a horn that was decorated with gold and silver leaf and had curious engravings on it. And then no one heard a thing. The Geographical Society contacted another group in the area—Turkey, actually—and they were sent to find them. It took weeks, of course, to get there. No planes and trains, like now."

"Where was the dig?" Nahum asked.

"Sorry! Didn't I say? The mountains of northern Iran. I can't remember exactly where. I could find out. Persia, of course, it was called back then. Anyway, when the expedition arrived and finally found the site, the team were all dead. The bodies picked at by vultures, and half rotted at that point. But it was obvious there had been a fight, and that some had killed themselves. One man appeared to have scratched his own eyes out. Evidence of the dig was still there—tools, implements, tents... And yes, there were indeed unusual markings on the walls of the cave. It went back quite a way. An ancient text no one could understand was inscribed on the walls. But there was no treasure, and the Italian man had vanished."

"How could they be sure?" Barak asked, exchanging a worried glance with Estelle. "Surely, decomposition would have confused things."

"Many of those there were Middle Eastern. It was obvious from their clothes. There were a couple of Europeans who had gone with the Italian man, but the Italian was older, and it was clear he was not amongst the dead. His body was never found."

Estelle's pulse pounded in her ears, and she was sure everyone had the same questions she did. "What was his name?"

"Beneventi. He never returned home, either. Well, at least no one admitted that he did." Jenkins threw his hands wide. "He had vanished. Poof!"

The group all looked at each other, their expressions saying everything. This had to be the source of Belial's jewels and his power. Beneventi must have opted to steal the treasure for himself, but the Italian name was unfamiliar.

"The horn had vanished too, I presume?" Barak asked.

"No, that was still there. Probably because of its size."

Harlan frowned. "How big was it?"

Jenkins held his hand apart. "A good two feet, and made of solid bone, mixed with ivory, pearl inlay, with gold and silver flourishes. It was filthy at the time! It had been covered by dirt for centuries. It took a lot of cleaning."

Estelle, aware her mouth was gaping open, quickly shut it. "It's on display somewhere?"

"Heavens no! It was taken to Turkey. That's where the team was heading back to. They already had an arrangement with a museum there. They hung around only to have the bodies moved, and then the locals sealed the cave."

It sounded exactly like the dig where the Igigi's underground home was discovered and the entrance was destroyed, but by the Igigi themselves to preserve their privacy. There, too, the locals had run in fear.

"Surely," Nahum asked, "The Geographical Society would have records?"

"I dare say they have, but with no one to report the actual events, I doubt that you would learn much," Jenkins qualified. "Anyway, the museum staff who cleaned the horn reported bad dreams. In the end, it was shoved in a box and packed away. No one wanted to touch it. Rumours were that it belonged to an angel." He forced himself to laugh. "A little far-fetched, of course."

The group was mute, fixed on Jenkins with rapt silence. *It had to be Belial's horn.* Estelle's mouth felt dry.

Nahum, however, was the quickest to gather himself. "Where is it now?"

"In the basement of The Oriental Museum in Istanbul. Or so I believe. No one mentions it anymore."

"So how do you know all this?" Harlan asked.

Jenkins gave a dry, almost embarrassed laugh. "Some digs develop an aura. A sort of myth. They capture your imagination, and the story becomes twisted. Your Templar treasure discovery will get a lot of interest, but when there's death and mystery, and talk of madness...well, that seals the deal. We curators gossip, you know." He smirked. "It's one of those things we whisper about over drinks. I got drunk one night with a Turkish curator who worked at The Oriental Museum. He told me about the rumours of strange whispers in their storage rooms, and how no one will touch the horn, even now. It even has an unofficial name. The Horn of Desolation. I have no idea if it's true, or whether he was just teasing me over drinks. I don't think he was, though." He laughed again, breaking the mood, and the spellbound listeners laughed with him.

Olivia scoffed to mask her probing for more information. "So, it's what? Just in a locked room where no one goes? Sounds highly implausible."

"Have you seen *our* basement? It's huge. I can assure you that it can happen. Half the time, museums even forget what they have. Or don't know. They obtain things in bulk, and no one ever goes through it for years! According to the curator, whose name I forget, it's on the lowest level and the furthest room. It's an old museum, set in an amazing building, so a warren of rooms in its basement is perfectly feasible."

Estelle's thoughts whirled, unsure of what to believe, but it was clear the story was beginning to fit together. *The question was, did they find the horn, or leave it safely buried in a museum?* One thing was sure. She didn't want Barak to have anything to do with it. She hated the effects that the jewellery had on him.

Jenkins addressed Barak. "Does that answer your question? No other discoveries quite like that one spring to mind."

Barak stood and reached over the desk to shake Jenkins's hand. "That does answer my question, thank you. It relates to another story we've been looking into. Unless anyone else has other questions, we'll leave you to it. I appreciate that you're very busy."

"It's been a pleasure." Jenkins smiled and walked to the door to see them out. "I felt left out of meeting all of you this morning, so it's great to have a private chat. I'll escort you to the lift."

After a few hurried thanks and reiterated goodbyes, they entered the lift alone. As soon as the doors shut, Barak heaved a long sigh. "So, who's going to steal the horn?"

Gabe pulled a chair close to Lamberti, glad the old man seemed to have composed himself after being shoved in a wardrobe, and then coming out of it to find dead bodies strewn around his house. He needed to resume their earlier conversation that had been interrupted.

Lamberti regarded Gabe with large, frightened eyes. His hands still trembled as he held a glass of deep red wine. "You have made enemies who won't rest until you are dead."

"That's okay. I aim to kill them first. But you need to get out of this house."

"No. This is my house, and I will die here. Either by their hands or God's. I will not be chased from my home. Those men," he nodded to the dead who had been dragged to the corner of the room, "come from big families. Powerful families. It is a miracle I am still alive after all these years."

Only Ash was still with Gabe. Niel and Shadow were watching for newcomers, either by water or land, and one of them was keeping an eye on Romola. Gabe wasn't planning on waiting around much longer. In fifteen minutes, they would be out of there. They had promised to dispose of the bodies first, as a courtesy.

Ash leaned forward, adjusting the rug over the old man's legs. "Did you know your housekeeper was working for them?"

"No, unfortunately. She was loyal at one point, I'm sure of it. But with our declining wealth and influence..." He shrugged. "Some people are easily swayed."

"Who are the other men?" Gabe asked. "I presume they were from the family you sold the ring to?"

"No, not these. Two families are represented here today. Arizzo and Carlucci. But there is a third. Marco Beneventi's family." He laughed dryly, and it set off a bout of coughing. "He leads all of it."

"Too big to dirty his hands with blood?" Ash asked.

Lamberti almost spat his wine out. "No. He has *plenty* of blood on his hands."

"I want details," Gabe said impatiently. "These dead men are in The Brotherhood?"

"Yes, along with the rest of their families, and Beneventi's, as I said. Four families set the whole thing up over one hundred and fifty years ago." He sighed. "My family was the fourth. They called themselves The Consortium then. I don't know why they changed the name. They exist to spread the word of Belial. The Angel of Death and Destruction. They are all consumed by him." Lamberti shrugged again. A pitiful gesture with his thin shoulders. "My father was obsessed with the whole thing. But me? I never saw the value of it all. I never touched the jewels, and I refused to be initiated. I distanced myself from it. My father was furious, but I didn't care. Beneventi has never had power over me. When my father died, I gave the jewel—the ring you asked about—to him. There was no sale. I wanted it gone from the house, and my obligation to The Brotherhood ended."

Gabe stopped him. "What kind of initiation was there?"

"You become eligible at the age of eighteen. There is a ceremony where you swear fealty, are draped in his jewels, and marked by him forever. It changes you. I see it in others. A sort of cunning behind the eyes."

"So they don't wear his jewels all the time?"

Lamberti shook his head vehemently. "No. It sends you mad. You touch them just once. That is enough. Only the truly devout wear them more often."

Ash exchanged a worried glance with Gabe. "How are you still alive?"

"I told Beneventi to kill me if he didn't like my ultimatum, but I warned him I had insurance. I said that if I died, information would get out about his deal with the devil." He smiled at Gabe's startled expression. "I know Belial is not the devil, but he's close enough. I also know he's behind the treasure that Beneventi's family and the others have spread across Europe over the last hundred years. I made it my business to know." He tapped his nose, a spark of malice in his eyes. "I have lists of where the jewels went, and where they could be now. I also have information on many of their dubious business dealings. That is what they are more worried about. I am the black sheep of the family, and glad to be."

"So Beneventi left you alone," Ash said, admiration in his eyes. "Well played."

"I was an idiot. It could have backfired at any moment. In the light of Aria's death and her betrayal of me, I suspect she has searched all over the house. I am not that much of an idiot, though. It isn't here."

"Hold on!" Gabe stopped him, needing to backtrack. "The ring that your family has owned for years is now with Beneventi?"

"Yes. It was a prized possession, one I'm sure he will have kept for himself. He's the descendant of the man who started it all. The man who found the jewels on a dig." Gabe exchanged a confused glance with Ash, but Lamberti hadn't finished. He took a breath and a sip of wine, and then related a fantastic story that left Gabe dumbstruck.

"Wait," Ash said, halting the old man. "They found everything in a cave?"

"High in the mountains of Persia. Everyone died, except for Beneventi's ancestor. He had a vision in which Belial told him to fake his own death and bring the jewels here. He was promised wealth. He formed The Consortium with three of his closest friends, and made a deal to spread the jewels far and wide. It became his personal mission for years. He spread the jewels around, planting them in religious objects. Icons. Places to infect those who already had religious faith, maybe even fervour."

At least now they knew who had planted the jewels in Olivia's relic, and no doubt many others. Gabe looked again at the once grand residence that now looked shabby. "By giving your ring away, you lost your wealth."

Lamberti nodded. "Yes. Our business declined. However, you need to know that there were many items of jewellery, many rings, bracelets, and other objects, but several were considered special. I don't know why. They all had influence. I could feel it. I refused to touch the ring we owned, though, as I said. I saw the effects it had. I told Beneventi to take it and he did. I presume it's in his house now."

"Here in Venice?"

"Murano, actually. It's more fortress than house."

"Murano?" Ash asked, excited. "I overheard a conversation downstairs. A meeting tonight on Murano. They have a problem," Ash's eyes slid to Gabe's before turning to Lamberti again, "that they need to solve."

"That will be Beneventi's home. You must have them worried."

Ash shrugged and said, "I'll tell you later, Gabe. How many people could be there tonight?"

"Perhaps twenty people, maybe less. The families are small now, but there are others involved. Acolytes, priests, and more. Not all local, of course. There are several spread across Europe."

"We'll deal with it," Gabe said. "Where is your *insurance*, as you called it?"

Lamberti sipped his wine again, and leaned forward, staring into Gabe's eyes. "If I tell you, what will you do with it?"

"I will hunt down every single object out there and hide them where no one will ever find them again. I promise."

"If you touch them, they will consume you."

"Not us. We are immune."

Lamberti studied him and then Ash. "I hope you're right. Okay. I trust you. You killed all these men, after all. My insurance is under the statue in the house my niece was forced to give to Amato. He is a dangerous and powerful priest."

"Not anymore," Gabe told him. He stared at him, looking for subterfuge. "Are you serious? Under the statue in the temple?"

"You've been there?" Lamberti's eyebrows rose in shock. "You have been busy. Yes. Under the plinth. It is the one thing they would never desecrate. I managed to hide it well, and I knew they didn't use the place anymore. They abandoned it years ago."

Shadow and Niel must have been so close when they destroyed the statue. Now they had to go back.

"But there's more," Lamberti warned them. "They raised more havoc. Beneventi, the original one who found the jewels, hired a conjuror to open a portal to the Underworld. He summoned a Nephilim. One of Belial's own. And he came." *Fuck*. "It meant that Beneventi wasn't in control anymore. He answers to Jiri. They all do. But Jiri lacks the one thing he really needs. Belial's horn. Beneventi found it on the dig all those years ago but when he went back for it, it had gone, and he had no idea where to. No one does. But when Jiri finds the horn that he has been searching for all these years, the *world* will answer to him."

Nineteen

N ahum took a long, deep drink of his pint of beer, and then leaned back in his seat, trying to absorb all the information that Jenkins had told them, and the news that Barak had relayed after a phone call with Gabe.

He, Olivia, Barak, Estelle, Lucien, and Harlan were now in a pub close to the museum where they had eaten lunch, and his companions looked as shocked as he was. Their mood was mixed with the excitement of discovering the root of where the Belial issues began, and the fact that they were now rich. The celebrations over their newfound wealth, however, would have to wait.

Barak looked thoughtfully at Nahum. "So, there's no doubt that the dig in Persia is responsible for the source of Belial's jewellery. The man who vanished matches the name that Gabe was given."

"I had my doubts earlier, but not anymore," Nahum agreed. "It all sounds right. It *feels* right!"

Lucien huffed and gesticulated in a way only the French could do. "Listen to you! Of course it is. They all went mad and killed each other or committed suicide. Plus, it cannot be a coincidence that there are Beneventis involved then and now."

Nahum laughed. "I'm actually relieved. We know the source of it! After what Gabe told you, Barak, we know that it's not some worldwide conspiracy. Just a few crazed families spreading havoc. It's still awful, obviously—people have died because of his influence—but we can manage it."

Harlan spluttered over his pint. "What about the damn Horn of Desolation that's locked in the basement of a museum? A horn that Jiri wants. If we know where it is, he might find out, too. And he's another Nephilim. Doesn't that bother you?"

"It worries me only because of Belial," Nahum said. "Nephilim are used to fighting each other."

"He could be juiced up on Belial's powerful jewels, like you were," Estelle pointed out. "That scares the shit out of me."

"And me," Olivia added.

"And me," Harlan and Lucien chorused.

"Okay!" Nahum huffed in annoyance. "I get it. Belial's jewellery has a weird effect on us, but we're still in control. If we have to use them to fight Jiri, then so be it. We'll even the playing field. I am sure that there will be more Nephilim, too. I can't believe only one is back. We just need to find their base."

"And unfortunately, I still have no idea where that could be," Barak said. Barak normally had a carefree attitude, and big laugh to match, but there was no evidence of that now. Nahum knew he was desperate to identify the city he had seen in the spell, but it was too hard without any landmarks or other clues. "We need to phone Jackson. With what Gabe has told us, maybe they should change their search in the references JD has found. We have other names to follow up. Maybe mention of Jiri and old cities."

Nahum nodded. "Good point. We should call them soon so they don't waste any more time on the Lambertis. Olivia and I will be driving there anyway, to look at the tablet. Or the cave? Whatever. We can catch up on their progress. What did Gabe say about the horn?"

Barak smirked. "He's calling Mouse. He wants a professional to steal the horn."

Estelle laughed. "Oh, Niel will love that."

"Yes, he will, because Gabe said he's going with her."

Nahum gaped. "To Turkey?"

"She can't get the horn on her own!"

"Why Niel?" Olivia asked, nudging Nahum. "I sense a story."

Nahum had forgotten she didn't know about Niel and Mouse. "He fancies her and she kind of almost betrayed him, but didn't really. This is Gabe's way of getting them together. I wish I could see his face when Gabe tells him." He laughed and winked at Barak. "We should put bets on it, like we did with Gabe and Shadow. And you and Estelle, too, actually," he added sheepishly. The brothers liked to place small wagers on each other's love lives. All in good spirits, of course.

"You *bet* on us?" Estelle's voice rose with indignation, and she drew herself upright.

Fearing she might cast a spell, he said, "Just for fun!"

Barak just laughed. "You might find that you're the subject of a little bet too, brother." He looked knowingly at Olivia.

"Well, you can bet," she shot back, "that I will do my utmost to confound all of you!" She looked triumphantly at Nahum. "We can all play that game."

Nahum felt another warm rush of affection and admiration for her—and maybe something else, too. To disguise his confusion, he just raised his glass to her. "Let's toast to getting them all to lose lots of money."

Harlan groaned, rolling his eyes at Lucien. "First, I want in on any bets. And second, just to get back on track, what can we do? Gabe and the others will be at Beneventi's place on Murano tonight. I feel like we should do something! The clock is ticking!"

"We need to find a way to neutralise Belial for good," Estelle said. "Even if you track all the jewels down and kill Jiri, the jewels still have power. How do we stop that?"

Olivia smiled. "The Emerald Tablet."

"What? We shrink it and wang it at his head?" Lucien asked sarcastically.

"No! It's a source of magic, right?" Olivia leaned forward, clearly excited, a flush on her cheeks. *She looks gorgeous*, Nahum admitted to himself. And he could see down her cleavage. He forced his eyes to her face. "Like Raziel's book, it lists the magic that underpins the world, right?"

"We think so," Harlan qualified. "That writing could also be an endless list of recipes."

Olivia poked her tongue out at him and continued. "Magic. Spells. As above, so below. Thoth was a God. There must be something in there about controlling angels. If the Igigi could do it, and Belial found a loophole, there will be a way to close that loophole in there. It's just a case of finding it."

"Holy shit!" Nahum said admiringly. "You're right!"

"No, no, no!" Harlan snorted. "You haven't seen that place. It's huge! Like half a dozen cathedrals, all mashed together. Thousands of pillars, with writing all over them. It's madness! It could take a lifetime to find the answer in there."

Barak shrugged. "We haven't got a lifetime. Like you said, we're on the clock. If Jiri's back is to the wall, he might well take matters into his own hands. I guess that answers what we can do. We are all going to JD's house to search the Emerald Tablet while we wait for further instructions from Gabe."

Niel's hand tightened around the handle of his axe. "You have got to be kidding me!"

"I'm not." Gabe folded his arms across his broad chest, not breaking eye contact with Niel. "I need you to meet Mouse in Turkey."

"*Anyone* could meet her. Ash could. You could. Or Shadow could. In fact, two thieves are better than one."

"No. I want you to go. The horn sounds heavy. Shadow and Mouse will struggle to lift it—and Mouse especially shouldn't touch it. You will not have such trouble."

"Neither would you or Ash."

"Ash is going to Amato's old place tonight to secure the paperwork that Lamberti hid there. Shadow and I will chase down Jiri—if we learn where he is after eavesdropping on that meeting tonight. He might even be there."

"There could be a lot of people there. We might make things a lot worse." Niel would have preferred Ash to be there too, but understood the need to secure the paperwork now that they knew where it was.

"Which is why we watch and listen," Gabe said. "You can leave first thing in the morning. I've already contacted Mouse. She's heading to Istanbul tomorrow. I'll let you know her arrival time when she tells me. Or, of course, she could tell you herself."

Niel put that suggestion aside for a moment. "You can't stay here, Gabe. They will hunt us down after today. No doubt Beneventi will have searched for the men he sent to Lamberti's place, and Lamberti could already be dead. He will have talked." Romola was safely out of Venice and heading to stay with friends in case anyone went looking for her. The old man, who Niel wasn't sure as to whether he was brave or stupid, had refused to budge.

"You don't know that."

"He's a weak, old man, and Beneventi will have tortured him."

"But he doesn't know where we're staying."

"It doesn't matter. It's a stupid risk to remain in Venice. You should have killed Lamberti. At least you would have made it swift and painless."

Gabe nodded. "I know, but I couldn't do it. He deserved to die on his terms, not mine. He knew what was likely to happen. As for leaving here, I haven't decided where we'll go yet. Maybe we'll leave Venice tonight, after we've been to Beneventi's house. We could book another villa and meet Ash somewhere. You, however, are getting on a plane tomorrow."

Gabe's dark eyes were almost unreadable. Except that Niel knew Gabe well, and understood just what he was thinking. He was fucking with him. "You are doing this deliberately. You know how I feel about Mouse."

"Yes, I do. That's exactly why I'm sending you. You like her. Your last meeting was just unfortunate."

"She electrocuted me!"

"To save your life." Gabe squared up to him, implacable. "I also know that you love to steal stuff."

"I love to fight more."

"And more than that, my friend, you love to *love*." Gabe's hard stare softened. "If you really hate the idea, then I'll send Ash, but I know that digging paperwork up is not your idea of fun, and that would mean you'd miss tonight's action *and* stealing from a museum. I also know that deep down, you want a chance to talk to her. Properly."

Bollocks. Gabe, infuriatingly, was right. He would love to see Mouse, both to gauge his own reaction to her, to see if he was mis-remembering how much he liked her, and also to see if Shadow was right. That Mouse did in fact like him. In this crazy, chaotic world of dubious morals they lived in, a little love would not go amiss. Besides, he would really like to get his hands on Belial's horn.

He sighed and walked to the balcony railing of their apartment to look over the Grand Canal. Darkness had fallen, and lights glimmered among the many houses, businesses, and boats. He and Gabe were the only ones outside. Ash was inside, preparing for the drive back to Palazzuolo sul Senio, and Shadow was checking their weapons.

Aware that Gabe had moved next to him, waiting for his response, Niel said, "Fine. I'll go. If we're successful—"

Gabe interrupted him. "You have to be."

"What if it's been moved to another location?"

"It won't. Not if it has a reputation. It will be there, and you will feel it."

"I guess that's true." *If the jewels gave off a wave of power and insidious whispers, what the hell would the horn do?* He shifted his position to look at Gabe, arm leaning on the railing. "What do I do with the horn? If it's that's big, I can hardly wrestle it on a plane."

"Can you destroy it?"

"With this?" He indicated the huge axe that hung at his belt. "I doubt it. This is not Mjolnir, Thor's hammer, and I am not a God. Except between the sheets." He winked at Gabe, his good humour returning.

"I am not even going to respond to that," Gabe said dryly. "Buy a big suitcase and put it on the plane."

Niel thought he was hearing things. "On a *plane*? Where its insidious whispers could cause the entire crew and passengers to have a melt down and we crash? I don't think so!"

"It might not have the same effect as the jewels."

"Barak told us they called it The Horn of Desolation. Does that sound harmless to you?"

Gabe clenched his jaw. "Now that we know where it is, we can't just leave it there."

"I know!"

Gabe turned away, also staring at the Grand Canal below them, as if seeking inspiration. Then he grinned at Niel. "Take a train across Europe. We're loaded. Maybe the Orient Express, or something else flashy. You could keep it in your cabin and bring it home. A train is better than a plane, right?" He put a search into his phone and started to scroll through the results. "Rough estimate, forty-eight hours of travel."

"Is that all?"

"Yep."

Niel felt the faint stirrings of possibility. *Maybe Mouse might want to travel by train, too.* "Okay. Something to consider. It will be even easier, though, if the others are successful in breaking Belial's power. Then the horn won't have any effect at all." Nahum's latest update had included an interesting idea. By now, all of their London team would be at JD's searching the fantastical emerald cave. "Or, we could ask Nahum to send the spelled box that he's not using anymore to Istanbul by special delivery. It could be delivered right to my hotel."

"Brilliant idea! Then, it goes in our bunker in the cellar."

"Are we really going to put a vault in?"

"Why not? Now that we're rich, are we going to stop treasure hunting?"

"I was thinking travel would broaden my horizons." Gabe just cocked an eyebrow, provoking a more truthful response. "Probably not."

"Then yes, we need a vault. Even if all of us end up splitting up and going our separate ways, it will always be our base." A maudlin mood seemed to have settled on Gabe.

"You think that's what will happen?"

"Of course it will. And it should. I mean, maybe not forever, but we're already drawing apart. Barak and Estelle spend lots of time in London—or in Cornwall, he'll be at her place. I'm pleased for him. Zee is already half moved out. Herne knows what will happen with Nahum and Olivia. I quite liked us all living together. It was chaotic, but fun."

"What about you and Shadow?"

"We like White Haven. We'll stay there, in and around trips and jobs, of course. I'm going to build, spruce up the outbuildings."

Niel smiled. "I like it there, too. I'll stay, around my own travel. It's home now. I don't think Ash is going anywhere yet, or Eli, with his bloody harem and his obligations to Ravens' Wood."

That seemed to cheer Gabe up. "I guess that's right."

"I like the witches, too. Plus, I want rooms in the barn."

"Done. You'll get to design them, too."

"Excellent. Besides, we still have a business. Shadow needs excitement, or she'll implode with boredom. So will I, for that matter. It doesn't stop us working together, even if we all start to do other things separately."

"True. But I guess we should focus on tonight. I meant it. We're *just* listening."

Niel felt the keen edge of his blade and sniggered. "Sure we are. And pigs are flying over Venice right now."

Twenty

Maggie snorted with derision, hands on hips. "Find a fucking spell to get rid of a Fallen Angel? You're all fucking mad!"

"Do you have to be so negative?" Harlan complained. "If the Igigi could do it, so can we!"

"The Igigi were half-Gods themselves, you oaf, you are not." She had only just found out about the Igigi, and she was pretty miffed it was the first she'd heard. *So many secrets.*

"But we have witches, and a bloody great emerald cave full of knowledge." Harlan swept his arms wide to encompass the cave they stood in. "And Nephilim, who can read any language in the world."

"I'm trying to be realistic."

"You're being a Debbie Downer. Or should I say a Moaning Maggie?"

"Actually," Jackson intervened, "in order to be grammatically congruent, it should probably be Maggie Moaner."

"Oh, shut the fuck up, both of you." Maggie glared at them, feeling overwhelmed and useless, which was partly the reason for her anger. She was also annoyed at having wasted hours looking for information on Lamberti, only to be told to search for Jiri and Beneventi references instead. Except, there were no mentions of Beneventi at all.

JD was making copious notes on an enormous roll of paper he'd spread across a long table in the centre of the cavern, close to the eternal flame, but he looked up then. "You have the mouth of a bawdy fish wife found in the back alleys of Spitalfields. It makes me quite homesick. If you threw in a few Elizabethan insults, it would be even better."

"Shut up, old man. You cock-wombling knave. Does that help?"

"Cock-wombling isn't quite Elizabethan, but I like it." JD wagged his finger at Harlan. "I like her. You can bring her back."

Harlan rolled his eyes. "Typical. I put up with months of crap from him, and you insult him and he likes it."

Maggie smirked. "I'm very charming, in my own way. So, you're serious? About the spell?"

"Yes." Harlan shrugged off his leather jacket and placed it over the back of a chair. "Jenkins gave us brilliant information. We know the source of the jewels now. It hasn't been an age-old conspiracy. Yes, there are a few families and their connections to track down, but now that Lamberti has told us where his list is, that makes things easier. Plus, we know where to find the horn, too."

"There's still a lot to do, though," Jackson said. He crossed to JD's side to look at the rough plan of the cave he'd started to make, and Maggie and Harlan followed him.

The London team, as Maggie called it, had arrived a couple of hours before, and searching and mapping the cave had begun in earnest. Jackson and Maggie had continued to read the selected books in JD's library, discovering all sorts of interesting snippets of information, but none particularly salient to their investigation. Reading JD's own notes from over a hundred years ago was weird. She'd also ended up searching for information on JD. He really had been the court magician to Queen Elizabeth I. Jackson wasn't lying. *Unbelievable.*

Their search had been fuelled by sandwiches and soup brought up by the immortal Anna. Maggie rolled the word around her mouth. *Immortal.* How weird would that be? *Lonely, perhaps. Or maybe exciting? So much time to explore and read and live expansively.* It seemed a very delicious thought. Maggie presumed that Anna must do more than cook and clean for JD, or she would have a very boring eternity. *The woman*, she decided, *had unknown depths.*

As had this place.

She'd been shocked earlier, and had barely taken the emerald cave in, but after hours spent buried in books, she and Jackson needed a break and had decided to see what was going on. Entering it again was actually intoxicating. She could lose hours here. Days, even. With no natural light, and with lamps burning constantly, and the smoky swirl of incense, she already felt disoriented. It was as if she had been transported back thousands of years. The rugs were of high quality, and she was sure the lamps suspended from the pillars and ceiling were of solid gold and silver. As for the flame in the centre, that was just weird. The place reeked of magic and knowledge.

"So," Maggie asked, inspecting the scrawl of JD's writing, "what have you found so far?"

"The cave is split into sections. Roughly. There are areas that pertain to countries, most of which have now vanished, or have changed their name, like Persia, for example. I guess Hermes would never have thought that Sumer or Assyria would vanish. There are areas that reference the elements, the base of everything and the root of all magic, and then there are histories. Endless histories." He sighed, his hands massaging his lower back as he straightened.

"Histories of who?" Harlan asked.

"Biblical figures. Adam, for instance."

Maggie was sure the room actually spun around her. "*The* Adam? As in Adam and Eve?"

"Yes. But, my dear, he was not the first man created from clay. Oh, no. Just a mortal who had evolved like all of us from the vast soup of the oceans. What the old God granted him was knowledge. And a not very compliant wife, eh?" He winked at Maggie.

"Women are not meant to be compliant. What would men have to complain about?" she shot back. "We're here to remind you not to be so fucking self-obsessed. That was a giant fail."

JD threw his head back, roaring with laughter. "Oh yes, you can definitely visit more often."

Harlan cleared his throat. "Anything about angels?"

JD pointed to his right. "Nahum and Barak are examining an area over there. There are lists and lists of angels. Fallen and otherwise."

Startled, Jackson asked, "Are there spells to control them, or lessen their influence?"

"Give us a chance! I am giving you broad brush strokes only."

"Are Estelle and Olivia with them?" Maggie asked.

"Yes, taking notes. Lucien, too, I believe." JD sighed, eyes narrowing as he stared at the flames in the centre. "But whether we find a solution for our most pressing issue? I don't know. We've barely mapped a fraction of it. With Nahum and Barak, however, we stand a chance. The rest will take me a lifetime." He smiled at them. "It's a good job that I have many of them. How did you fare with those notes I left you?"

Maggie scowled. "Badly. That first reference to the alchemist was interesting, but he didn't really give any details, did he? There was no mention of Beneventi or the other names, other than The Consortium. It was all very secret squirrel."

"We alchemists like our secrets, and clearly Lamberti did, too. What intrigued me," JD said, "was that the alchemist, Alfonso, said if the power could be tapped, it would be phenomenal, and may have several useful applications. He never said what they were."

"We noticed," Maggie said grimly. *More bloody secrets.*

Harlan had been studying the plan, but now he looked up. "Lamberti knew those jewels—specifically his ring—belonged to Belial. That's why Beneventi formed The Consortium, after all. Why even request the alchemist's help?"

"Maybe," Jackson mused, scratching his head and making an even bigger mess of his unruly hair, "some of them were having doubts and wanted to get rid of the power, but keep the jewels. Or maybe they wanted to use the power for themselves without Belial's influence. It could even be they just wanted to understand how it all worked. Unfortunately, nothing else we found could tell us. There were other hints about The Consortium, but it was frustratingly vague. There was no mention of Jiri."

Something had been tickling Maggie's brain for a couple of hours, and now it struck her. "What if the alchemist had been asked to help them use the jewels to find Jiri?"

All three men turned to her, eyes narrowed. Harlan said, "But he was an alchemist, not a witch or a magician, or whatever you want to call it."

Jackson nodded at JD. "Our friend here used scrying glasses and talked to angels. What if Alfonso did, too? Maybe he was adept at summoning circles? Like you say, JD, you guys have vast and varied interests."

"It's very possible." JD nodded, eyes distant as he considered the possibility. "He did have an interest in demons as I recall from his other manuscripts and treatises. Yes, that could well be the case. Perhaps he did summon Jiri. Maybe others. However, we'll never know for sure, unless someone talks." JD took a deep breath and straightened his shoulders. "There are things we cannot know, therefore we must focus on that which we can influence. A way to bind Belial for good."

"In that case," Maggie said, having had enough of chatting, "I'm going to find the others. If nothing else, I can take notes."

She set off between the towering pillars to find the Nephilim and the WAGs, as she now liked to call Estelle and Olivia. Not that she'd tell them that. *Yet.*

Ash pulled onto the side of the road that ran past Amato's country house, making sure it was far enough from the entrance not to rouse suspicion. The lane was deserted, and within moments, he shed his jacket and t-shirt, extended his wings, and rose majestically into the air.

It was a pleasure to be flying again. Venice was beautiful but cramped, and he'd missed the night breezes that ruffled his wings. He gave a wry smile as he studied them under starlight. He still wasn't used to the fact that his wings were now golden, courtesy of Belial. He had wondered if the colour would fade, but so far it hadn't. Fortunately, in darkness, there was little light to reflect, but by candle or firelight, they gleamed, much like his eyes.

Fortunately, there were no other repercussions from his use of Belial's token. No lingering after-effects or power, or whispers in his head. His wings, and particularly his injured shoulder, had healed well. The phrase, 'Broken Nephilim' still rankled, even though no one except Belial had whispered it. He cast his annoyance aside to focus on the present. He flew high, circling the grounds to make sure no other cars were there. The entire place still looked deserted and abandoned, and no lights glimmered in any windows. However, as he aimed towards the woods, he saw a flash of light close to where the temple was.

Bollocks.

He carried his sword, as always, glad that they could now transport their weapons in the plane's hold, and he withdrew it from the scabbard. He patted his pocket, checking that he still had JD's weapon, and felt its sleek outline. He also carried a backpack over his shoulder with a crowbar in it. He circled wide of the light, gliding silently over the thick canopy. From this distance the light had vanished, and he wondered if he'd imagined it, until it winked into view again.

But where could he set down? The canopy was thick, the temple overgrown. He had been aiming to walk along the forest path, but that seemed like a bad idea now. Taking another few moments to get his bearings, he flew lower and partially alighted on an uppermost branch, his wings supporting his weight. He waited, trying to see the temple he knew was somewhere close, but there was no other light or sound. Fearing a trap, he considered his options.

The deaths of the six men in Venice were already all over the news. They hadn't bothered to hide the bodies. Instead, they had piled them into the boat with a tarpaulin thrown over them, and pushed it out of Lamberti's dock and into the Grand Canal. Ash had volunteered to swim under water, and had tugged it out in the middle of the waterway before abandoning it and swimming back to shore. They had hoped there would be no repercussions for Lamberti, but that was stupid. Of course there would be. *But had Lamberti talked, if questioned? Was he already dead?*

Wary of making loud noises, Ash flew to the start of the path through the woods that led to the temple. On foot, he progressed slowly and softly, wings folded away, sword close to his side. The place seemed as deserted as when they had left it the other day. Huge chunks of Belial's statue lay on the ground, the paving cracked, and there, in the centre, was the plinth beneath which the paperwork should be.

Ash waited in the shadows, his eyes now fully adjusted to the darkness. The soaring columns could barely be distinguished from the trees, and there was no light or sound now, other than the nighttime chatter of animals and the sough of the wind through the branches. *How long should he wait? Or was he just being paranoid?* Checking that once again JD's weapon was in his pocket, he stepped from the deep shadows by the nearest pillar and onto the top step, the central, sunken area beneath him. Most of the fallen leaves had been pushed around the edge, thanks to Niel and Shadow, and the large central plinth was bigger than he remembered.

After casting one more searching glance around the edge, he progressed down the broad steps to the centre, wading through leaves and stepping over chunks of the statue. Up close, he could see a large crack ran down the centre of the plinth, and a seam had opened where the base met the paving. He squatted to see it better. It was wide enough to get his hand inside, and he reached in, hoping to feel a box or a package. Unfortunately, the space within was empty. Frustrated, he adjusted his position, wondering if the paperwork could be accessed from the crack in the plinth, or if someone had beaten him to it. The movement saved his life. An arrow suddenly whizzed overhead, striking the steps behind him and clattering to the ground.

Ash sheltered behind the high base, eyes darting everywhere. A bare whisper of noise to his right made him dive for cover again, and another arrow whizzed past him. He scuttled to the side, still unsure of how many men were out there.

He hadn't imagined it. Someone was here, waiting for him. Lamberti must be dead, and he must have talked before he died. That meant they might be waiting for Gabe and the others, too.

Gabe set Shadow down on the edge of Beneventi's grounds. *Lamberti had been right.* It was a large place, surrounded by high walls and thick shrubbery.

In fact, on first impressions, Gabe was sure that it had once been a religious building. A nunnery perhaps, or monastery. The main residence was built of old, thick stone, and cloisters stood to the side, a large statue of an angel with outstretched wings dominating the central space.

Murano was an island, one of several on the Venetian Lagoon, the second largest after Venice itself, situated very close to the city, and barely one and a half kilometres in size. It had approximately 7,000 inhabitants, and compared to Burano, it was nowhere near as pretty, but it was famous for manufacturing Murano glass. Not that Gabe would be buying any anytime soon. Beneventi's home was on the west side, bordering the lagoon. He wished he'd had more time to fly and explore. The lagoon was beautiful, serene, and he was able to take in the full scope of the area. It was also good to spend time with Shadow, alone, her curves pressed against him. He was determined that when this was all over, they would go away together, just the two of them.

Within moments, Niel landed next to them. "The roof is broad and shallow pitched. It will be a good place for one of us to hide."

Gabe studied the building. Several chimneys were on the roof, but one to the far end, closest to the cloisters, was the biggest. There was also a single storey building that edged the rear of the cloisters. *That could well be a good place to hide, too.* He nodded in agreement. "Looks good. That's presuming, of course, that they'll meet outside under that damn statue. If they do, I'd like one of us to get closer. On the ground, perhaps." He looked at Shadow, already almost invisible. "I couldn't get as close as you could get, though."

"But I won't understand a word they say, if they talk in Italian," she pointed out. "Let me enter the house, see if I can find the jewels in there. They will have stored them somewhere."

Niel shrugged. "Great idea. I'll circle overhead, and can drop down where I'm needed."

Gabe nodded. "Okay, but you must be careful if you find any jewels, Shadow."

"I'm not an idiot. Gabe, what exactly do we want to get out of this meeting?" Shadow asked him. "Names? Places?"

"I told you. I want to know where Jiri is, to get an idea of numbers involved, and to find their cache of jewels."

"But you don't want to kill them?"

"No."

"Despite knowing the danger they pose? The fact that they sent six men to kill *you*?" She cast Niel a long, sideways glance of disbelief. "Why not? This is the perfect time to strike." Shadow was beautiful and sexy, but she was also deadly. She had no compassion for those who had crossed her.

"They are enslaved by Belial. Not in their right mind. We might be able to save them."

"That's a big if, Gabe."

He bit back his annoyance, knowing Niel thought the same thing. They had argued about it earlier, and now it seemed they would argue again. "I don't care. If we're attacked, then go ahead, kill. But try to escape first. It may count in our favour later."

"And it may not. We should have killed Lamberti. He was weak and old, and whatever agreement he had with Beneventi before is gone now. They could torture him for information. They might know that we're coming here!"

Death did not sit so easily with Gabe as it once had. "He helped us, and that deserves our compassion."

"Beneventi will not agree. Six of his men are dead because of us."

The purr of boat engines out on the water interrupted their conversation. Like Venice, there were no cars on the island, and a series of pedestrian bridges connected the seven small islands that made up Murano. They had arrived as soon as it was dark enough, and Gabe expected they would have to wait for hours, but maybe not.

"Then we must be wary of subterfuge." Gabe nodded to the roof. "I'll find a spot to watch. Be careful, both of you."

With a single flap of his enormous wings, he soared high, watching a couple of boats pull up to the small dock. They had made it only just in time. Gabe wondered if this meeting might move indoors after the deaths earlier that afternoon, or even be cancelled, perhaps out of fear for their safety, but a couple of men were already in the cloisters, and a few lights illuminated the area.

Then, suddenly, lights were everywhere. In the garden, lighting up the house, and illuminating paths. He hoped Shadow had found a way into the house.

Twenty-One

E stelle placed her pen and notepad down and rolled her shoulders to ease the kink in her neck.

"I don't know about you, Olivia, but I feel useless."

"You shouldn't! At least you're a witch and have magic. I have nothing, except some expertise with hunting occult treasures. That's not exactly helping us now."

"Care to appraise this place?"

"You can't put a price on *this*!" Olivia brushed her long hair back from her face, her auburn highlights flaming as they caught the light from the many lanterns around them in the emerald cave. "I've given up trying."

They were both seated on large floor cushions atop a Persian rug that was spread in the centre of a group of huge, square pillars. It felt exotic, as if they were in some kind of Arabian tent, or palace. The light ignited the emerald columns, revealing flaws in the columns, and casting shadows on the archaic script. In the dancing flames, the elegant swirls of text shimmered as if they were alive. The whole place was intoxicating and mesmerising. She wished she had the Nephilim's skills with languages.

They were deep into the cave, the pillars running in all directions. Although Estelle couldn't understand the words, it was easy to see there was some kind of pattern to their placement. The pillars were grouped in shapes. Clusters of square columns, then plain round ones, fluted, spirals, thin, broad, gilded, unadorned... They all denoted segments of knowledge. The four of them had first spent time in an area that listed the thousands of angels, but then moved to another. This area talked about magic. Spells, to be exact.

Barak and Nahum were high above, inspecting the endless text that was written, well, everywhere. Both she and Olivia had started to make basic notes about the information on the pillars, but the sheer enormity of it was overwhelming. Eventually, Barak and Nahum had stopped shouting down information and had fallen silent too, except for short conversations between each other.

"Just think," Olivia continued, "what's written in here could rewrite history."

"And could destroy us all, too."

Olivia frowned as she sat cross-legged. "Do you think so?"

"People far cleverer than us could unlock the very material of our world. I'm not sure we should."

"Aren't physicists doing that right now?"

"You know what I mean. This is so much!"

"Someone could uncover the cure for cancer in here, or Alzheimer's, or all sorts of terrible diseases." Olivia's gaze drifted around the room. "It could change everything."

Estelle bit back her initial, scathing response. "You're so positive, Olivia. You see the good in things. I do not. Men would subvert this to their basest desires. Women, too. Wars, in fact, would be fought over this. We can never tell anyone."

Olivia looked as if she might argue, but then she just sighed. "I know. I can feel the tingle of it all on my skin, can you? It's like static electricity."

"That's the magic." Estelle stared around the vast cave again. "I can't decide where the source is. It feels everywhere. That seems impossible."

Olivia giggled. "We're in an emerald cave. That seemed impossible a couple of days ago. Men who didn't care for its secrets and knowledge would carve it up and sell it. We're in a billion-pound cave."

"I doubt it could be destroyed. I think the magic must protect it. Perhaps it would close itself up again and we'd be trapped inside."

"Would we know?" Olivia mused thoughtfully "Or would we be crushed to dust?"

"I guess if we weren't crushed, we would only know if we tried to leave to find food. We'd discover the entrance sealed, and we'd slowly die of starvation and thirst. Unless there's a kitchen here and an endless food supply we don't know about. Or if it granted us immortality and we'd never be hungry again." She laughed at her crazy suggestions. "I hope we don't have to find out."

"Well, I can absolutely say that hasn't happened yet." Olivia patted her stomach. "I'm hungry and thirsty. I might bring some food in for everyone. No one will leave here for hours. I don't even know what time it is."

They had realised some time ago that their phones and watches didn't work in there.

"Maybe we should check our messages, too," Estelle suggested. The cave suddenly felt oppressive, as if Estelle was in her tomb, and she wanted to leave, too. She looked up to see Barak soaring high above. "I'm surprised he hasn't complained about being hungry."

"He's obsessed now, like Nahum." Olivia hesitated, as if unsure of her next words, and then lowered her voice. "Is it really so bad when they use Belial's jewels?"

"Yes. I hate it." She saw Olivia flinch back in surprise and tried to temper her response. "They don't lose control completely, but it changes them. It gives them a hard edge. I see Barak's eyes change. He's not *my* Barak anymore. He's another man from another time. It's like I've lost him."

Estelle felt herself becoming tearful and tried to shake it off. She was never tearful, and she prided herself on it. But neither had she felt as comfortable talking to another woman before. She didn't get on with other women well, she knew that. The White Haven witches irritated her, and so did Shadow, although that was probably because they were horribly alike in many ways. Maggie was hilarious, and she respected her, but she wasn't sure they would ever be close friends. Olivia, though, was different, and she couldn't quite say why. Perhaps it was because they were of a similar age, and she felt no judgement from Olivia. Then again, Olivia had never seen Estelle at her spikiest.

"Sorry. I'm being stupid." Estelle looked up again at Barak, heart now thumping painfully in her chest. "I've never had anyone love me like he does. I don't think I could bear to lose it."

Olivia leaned forward and squeezed her hand, her warm tone reassuring. "You won't. They are...different, aren't they? They are like other men, and yet they're not. And I don't mean their wings and their strength that their half angel blood gives them. It's like this endless depth. I feel like I'm standing on a precipice, and if I fall in, I may never get out. I won't even want to get out."

She meant the precipice of love, of course. "It's worth it, Olivia. But yes. It's terrifying, too."

Olivia looked up at Nahum, and Estelle followed her gaze. He was hanging off another column, fingers gripped on some moulding, legs braced on the surface, his wings spread behind him, the lamplight burnishing his already olive skin as he studied a piece of text. His taut abs and muscled arms were more defined in the light. He was breathtaking. Not as breathtaking in her eyes as Barak, but these Nephilim were extraordinary.

She risked a question she wouldn't have dared ask earlier. "What will you do, Olivia?"

Her eyes never left him as she said, "I don't know."

Niel circled Beneventi's grounds, well above the reach of the garden lights.

They must suspect that he and the others would come here, or else having so many lights on was just a regular safety feature. It seemed excessive though, as did the number of guards. Men patrolled the dock, the area close to the gate, and the perimeter wall.

At least half a dozen boats were now at the dock, and people made their way to the house in small groups. Lights blazed at several windows, and there was a general air of hustle and bustle, and self-important posturing. Niel could also see more angel statues around the garden, but none so impressive as the one in the cloisters.

He wasn't sure whether the fact that the meeting was going ahead was a sign of utter naivety or sheer bullishness. Or a trap, of course. The cloisters, as they suspected, was their meeting place, and at least a dozen people were gathered there. He hoped Gabe could hear them from his position.

What Niel couldn't work out was why they weren't paying more attention to the sky. They must know that they were Nephilim. Belial would have told them. Or maybe their level of communication was far more basic. Perhaps The Brotherhood assumed that although he and his brothers had used Belial's jewels, that they also had a team of humans who they commanded, much like Jiri did them. Plus, according to Gabe, Lamberti had no idea that they were Nephilim.

Niel nodded to himself. *Yes, that sounded likely. Of course, only time would tell.*

Gabe lay flat on the roof of the single storey building that edged one side of the cloisters, watching the new arrivals.

The large, square space was edged with pillars that bordered a broad walkway, two sides of which were covered by a stone roof that backed up against the buildings behind it. The other sides were open to the gardens, partially shielded by trees and bushes. It would be a beautiful, restful place in the summer, with most of it in shade.

Half a dozen men and a couple of women were now in the cloisters. Belial's statue presided over them all, his wings spread wide, encompassing almost all of the enclosed space, but this time he didn't point anywhere. He carried a sword in one hand, and a huge horn in the other. *Interesting. Did this mark the last statue?*

A brazier blazed on the ground in front of it, and the group gathered in ones or twos as if they were waiting for someone else. Gabe wriggled forward so that he was close to the roof's edge, and voices drifted to him from the nearest pair. They were angry, speaking in Italian again.

A strident male voice that came from a portly, middle-aged man, said, "Amato's death has had catastrophic consequences! He must have left paperwork about, or else how could they have found Lamberti?"

"They are Nephilim," his companion, a tall, bearded man said, warming his hands by the fire. "Belial warned us that someone would know of the jewels' worth. They must have sent a team here."

"But *Nephilim*? How?"

"I presumed they were summoned here, just like Jiri was, but with no Fallen Angel to direct them, they are weak."

"They have smashed the statue in Palazzuolo! Stolen another ring! The temple beneath the church was destroyed! They are ruining everything!" Gabe's stomach turned. *So they knew about Palazzuolo already.*

"But they don't know all, my friend."

"They killed six men this afternoon, and pushed them into the canal on their own boat! You say they are no threat, but I do not believe it." His eyes darted about nervously. "They could even be here now."

"I doubt it, as Lamberti did not know of this meeting."

"But Lamberti knows about *us*! He could have told them everything."

The tall man leaned down, pressing his face close to the other man's. "Calm down. Armand does not like to see fear! It is why we meet tonight, despite their close proximity. At least old Lamberti is not a threat anymore. He is dead. Armand's nephew killed him. Not before he talked, though. We probably have his hidden paperwork already." The man scowled. "Armand should have killed him years ago."

"The risk was too great. The pact has served us well. We have thrived."

Gabe clenched his jaw, fearing Shadow and Niel were right. He should have killed Lamberti to protect themselves. He studied the people again, noting that although they wore jewellery, none seemed to be Belial's tokens. The men that afternoon hadn't wore them, either. *Interesting. It was just as Lamberti suggested.* He rolled onto his back, staring at the night sky as if he would see two glaring eyes watching him. He suddenly felt too vulnerable on the roof, and longed to crawl under cover. That was the thing with Fallen Angels. You were never sure how much they knew.

Then a door slammed below him, and a swell of voices carried to him. *Newcomers.*

A man spoke, his deep voice sounding older, mature. "Thank you for coming here on such short notice, especially after our losses tonight. Friends and family have died today. Aria must have been wrong. There must have been more than just one man and the woman there today."

"So, what are we doing about it, Armand?" a woman asked. "My son was one of those dead men."

"I know, and I'm sorry."

"Sorry doesn't help me! Belial is supposed to offer us protection! From *everything*. It's clearly a lie."

Even from the roof, Gabe could feel the tension. He adjusted his position, and caught a glimpse of the group. No one moved. It was a frozen tableau.

Armand, however, remained calm. "This is not time to lose faith, Emilia. The word has gone out. We are all on alert. Especially Jiri. Please remember that this is a relationship that has bound our families for years. We are rich and influential because of it. Of course there are risks, but..."

Emilia interrupted him. "Never risks like *this*! These men seem to have come from nowhere! They strike at the heart of us!"

"But they will not win. Georgio has the paperwork already, and they are waiting in Palazzuolo to kill whoever comes for it. We already are making headway on the others. They have friends and family, and they will die unless they leave us be. We have countermeasures. Whatever this is, it will be over soon."

Friends and family. His brothers, and maybe the witches in White Haven. Maybe even their London team.

Gabe's blood started to rage, the familiar, ancient bloodlust returning. He was insane for thinking that these people could be saved. They had all sworn allegiance to Belial, and no doubt had touched his jewels as some kind of initiation, just as Lamberti described. It was already too late to save them. They should just kill them all while they had the chance.

Belial was a cancer, and so were The Brotherhood. They had to cut them out, before they spread. *Change of plan*. As far as he was concerned, no one left here tonight. The house would become their tomb.

Ash edged around the side of the plinth, hoping he'd judged the direction correctly, and rolled onto his stomach.

He wriggled beneath the scant covering of leaves still left, now cursing the fact that Shadow and Niel had done such a good job of clearing the area. Abandoning the idea of using his sword, he pulled his alchemical weapon from his pocket.

Silence once again fell in the temple. He was a sitting duck, as the English so quaintly put it. Scarcely breathing, he focussed on the perimeter, and heard the crack of a branch. Another arrow landed within inches of him, embedded in the paving, but Ash had already spotted his attacker. He shot the branch above the dark figure and it crashed down, crushing him.

The flare of light from JD's weapon cast a harsh glow on the temple, partially blinding Ash. He used it to his advantage, trusting that everyone else out there would be similarly affected. He was on his feet in seconds, zigzagging across the ground to the edge. Arrows whizzed around him, all missing, and Ash ran up the steps and past the temple columns, then leapt over the fallen branches and the man beneath, using them as cover.

Keeping his body low, he reached between the branches, feeling for the man's pulse at his neck. He was sprawled awkwardly, but was still alive. Another arrow whizzed in his direction.

Ash shouted, "You risk killing your friend. He still lives."

There was no answer, only another arrow, this time very close. Ash cursed himself for speaking. *Idiot.*

He squashed himself to the ground, peering as best he could to try and see the second man, and hoping there weren't more. His assailant was either intent on killing him or was making his escape. If he had found the paperwork, he would have to follow him, but if he lifted his head to try to see him, he could die.

Another arrow flew above him, embedding in a tree.

Ash fired wildly, shooting haphazardly and not caring. He wanted to deter the assailant. Wound him, if possible. He had questions.

Then, in the flare of light, he saw why the other man was still attacking. There was an oiled package sticking out of the injured man's jacket, covered in leaf mould and dirt. *Lamberti's paperwork. It had to be.*

Ash gripped the fallen branch and reared up, using it both as a shield and weapon, just as a man came pounding out of the darkness. Ash ran towards him using the tangle of branches like a battering ram. He hit him with a huge crunch, and they both hit the ground hard. The man was still holding his crossbow, and the bolt flew past him, stinging as it cut his cheek. But that was the last thing the man did. He hit the ground awkwardly, his head striking the base of a pillar, and Ash knew he was dead, even before the blood pooled from his head wound.

Ash lay still, straddled across the dead man for a few moments longer, only standing when he was sure there were no others waiting. He strode back to the other man and retrieved the package. It was exactly what Lamberti had promised. A list of names, jewels, and where to find them, as well as business interests.

He crouched, moved the man's crossbow, and searched him for any tokens of jewellery, relieved to find there weren't any. The man groaned as he regained consciousness, and Ash put JD's weapon away and withdrew his sword. He placed it at his assailant's throat.

"Move slowly! I have questions for you."

The man took a moment to orientate himself, eyes on the sword. "I have nothing to say to you. You may as well kill me now."

He was young, maybe in his late twenties, and despite his bold words, he looked unsure of himself. Ash decided to try a different tactic. "You are a member of one of the three families who have vowed their lives to Belial, I presume?" His eyes flickered. "Or a friend, perhaps? An ardent convert? You have chosen badly. Belial is a harsh master, and he will kill you in the end, or send you mad."

"It's not like that," the man protested.

"Yes, it is. Were you promised wealth? A place of glory for spreading his madness?"

"He is one of the Fallen! To spread his power is for the good of mankind."

Ash sighed, withdrawing his blade by an inch. "I have seen the results of his power. People fight amongst themselves, or kill others, or are consumed by Belial himself. Have you touched his jewels?"

"Yes, months ago in a ritual when I was accepted into The Brotherhood, and I'm fine."

Then it was already too late. "Are you? Or did you see his eyes flash fire, and feel the beat of his wings, and hear the whisper of his voice? Can you feel him even now, as he sits deep within you? I think you can. He's whispering to you, isn't he? Urging you to act. Does he tell you who I am?"

The man's lips tightened as his gaze focussed inward. Then his eyes widened as he stared at Ash again. "You are Nephilim, like Jiri. Of the House of Raym."

A shiver ran across Ash's skin that had nothing to do with the cool night breeze. *So, Belial knew who he was.* "Yes, we fought against his House, and I know of Jiri." He spoke directly to Belial, knowing the sliver of his presence would register every word. "We will not rest until you are gone. You and Jiri, and however many other Nephilim are here."

The man writhed, eyes rolling back in his head, and suddenly his eyes flashed a pale, ice cold blue as he spoke in a voice that was not his own. A deep, commanding, and unearthly voice that spoke in the old tongue that Ash understood only too well. "*You will all fail. I will have dominion again.*"

Anger blazed in his eyes, but Belial had no power outside of the man's body, and no tokens to draw strength from. The man's skin became mottled, his breathing laboured as his body failed to cope with Belial's assault. Ash saved him from a painful death and cut his throat. Blood splashed into the cool, damp earth, and his head fell back as the light faded from his eyes.

Another death, among many. And there would be more.

Twenty-Two

S hadow crept through Armand Beneventi's house, finding little
to interest her.

He was rich, that was obvious; the furnishings were luxurious in a
tasteless, overstated way, and the whole place felt claustrophobic. That
was compounded by the men who guarded the exterior exits and patrolled the corridors, all armed with guns. She had successfully evaded
all of them, her fey glamour and stealth concealing her. Frustratingly,
she found nothing of use. No maps, no central area of command, only
endless angelic and religious iconography. Neither could she detect
any sign of power that would suggest there were more of Belial's jewels
nearby.

Eventually, she left the house through an open window on the first
floor, scaled a sturdy drainpipe, and made her way to the roof, where
she spotted Gabe on the level below, atop the roof of the single storey
building by the cloisters.

Keeping to the darkness, she dropped like a cat and edged towards
him, trying to catch his eye before he tried to kill her. When he did
see her, he edged back until both were at the rear of the building, well
away from the gathered group. Gabe looked angry, his eyes sharp flints
of obsidian.

"Something wrong?" she asked, her voice barely a whisper.

"Yes. We need to kill them all."

"So, I'm right?" She smirked. "Of course I am."

"Not the time, Shadow. They know who we are, who our friends are, and we need to kill them now while we have the chance. They have even set a trap for Ash, but I daren't warn him. Have you found anything?"

"Nothing of use. The jewels are either very well hidden, or elsewhere. But I agree with you. Let's tell Niel the new plan." Shadow looked overhead, hoping he was still up there. Her phone buzzed silently in her pocket, and she grinned when she saw his name. "Maybe he heard me."

"Spotted us, more likely."

He wanted an update, and she texted him Gabe's news succinctly, ending with, *We need to kill them.*

How many in the house? he asked.

Half a dozen. Maybe ten.

So, about thirty, maybe thirty-five in total. Nothing to worry about, then.

She rolled her eyes at Gabe. "He's cockier than I am."

"You're both too bloody cocky for your own good."

She texted Niel again. *Especially with JD's bombs.*

You've brought them?

Shadow sniggered, as Gabe looked over her shoulder at her message. *Of course! I'm not an idiot.*

I wish you'd have bloody given me some!

She turned to Gabe. "But that would deprive me of all the fun!"

"Tell him to wait until he sees us act, then he can, too. Where will he start?"

Niel's response to her typed question was swift. *At the dock, and then the gate. But there are many men on the perimeter, too.*

Gabe nodded. "We need to find where Jiri is first. Tell him I'll grab Armand out of the cloisters, and we can question him up there." He pointed upwards. "I reckon that will make him talk."

"Let's kill a few first, Gabe. He can see we mean business. Then you take him, and I'll clean up. Sound good?"

"Are you sure there's nothing in the house?"

"As much as I can be."

Gabe waited while she finished messaging Niel, eyes on the cloister again. Their angry voices carried to them.

Shadow pocketed her phone and checked her backpack. "I have ten bombs. Should be enough."

Gabe rolled his eyes. "You could take out half of Murano with that many. Let's not go mad, Shadow. A couple on the house, and maybe one in the grounds should do it."

"Fine. Spoilsport."

"All the more for later." He cracked his neck. "A few minutes just to listen to their discussion, and then we act. Ready?"

"Ready."

Niel watched Gabe and Shadow listen to the conversation in the cloisters for at least another ten minutes, and he hoped they had heard

useful information. Then Shadow dropped to the ground with her usual grace, and Gabe leapt down with outstretched wings.

Niel flew down over the dock, coming in low and fast, and struck quickly. The two men guarding the dock were dead within seconds, neither of them even able to fire their guns.

He then flew again, but not for long. A couple of men patrolled inside the grounds, just beyond the gated entrance. He killed one, but the second spotted him, and a spatter of bullets broke the night's silence, one catching his wing and splintering the tips of his primary feathers, but Niel covered the distance between them, killing him as swiftly as he'd killed the others.

He had hoped the sight of his wings would intimidate the men, but it didn't seem to. *Perhaps they were used to seeing Jiri, and maybe other Nephilim.* The gunfire set off a series of shouts across the grounds, and more men came running.

Damn it. Sheathing his sword, he pulled out his alchemical weapon. As he started firing, screams reached him from across the garden, and he hoped that Shadow and Gabe were okay. The distraction cost him. A bullet grazed his arm, searing his skin, and he dived out of the way, rolling behind some bushes before taking aim. The noise would carry across the island. If they didn't get this finished quickly, the police could turn up, or curious neighbours.

He focussed his mind. *Kill, survive, and get out of there.*

Gabe killed three men before they even realised that they were in danger. Shadow struck quickly, killing another three. Both used their swords, despite the risk of gunfire. Swords were quieter.

The screams were not.

Gabe grabbed Beneventi, arms wrapped around him, and holding him close to his chest, he soared upwards, leaving Shadow to kill the others. There was little resistance—at least from the group in the cloisters. Despite the fact that six men had already died that day, they clearly were arrogant enough to believe themselves safe. Gunfire, however, was ringing out across the grounds, and there was only a matter of time before they reached the cloisters.

Gabe kept well out of range and hovered above the lagoon.

Beneventi hadn't said a word after the initial yell of shock. Now he was as stiff as a board, and mute with terror. Gabe gripped him under the armpits like a toddler, and held him at arm's length. He looked into his eyes, seeing a spark of cunning in them as his terror subsided.

"So," Gabe said, "you are a descendant of the man who found Belial's jewels." He was older than Gabe had first thought. Late sixties, perhaps. Maybe older. But he was tanned and slim, with an air only the very wealthy could cultivate. *Arrogant prick*. He decided to goad him. "You look smaller than I expected. Insignificant. I can only presume your ancestor was more worthy."

"You know nothing about me or the power I wield."

"Not *your* power. Belial's. Without him, you would just be a mean little man who likes money. I knew Belial. I imagine he must despair of you. No wonder he brought Jiri in to manage you all."

"How dare you! We serve him and he pays us well! We do not need Jiri! Besides, Jiri arrived before my time."

"Yes, so I gather. Your other ancestors must have been weak and pathetic, too." Beneventi tried to kick Gabe, and swung his arms wildly, but his kicks were weak, and Gabe crushed his ribs even tighter. "Like I said. Weak."

"Even now my men are searching for your friends. You need to leave us alone, or they will die."

Gabe smiled. "I don't think you've done your homework, little man. My friends are Nephilim and witches. Powerful witches. Oh, and maybe an alchemist too, for good measure. You have no sway with me."

"Even if he sends Jiri after you?" Beneventi's eyes narrowed with cunning. "With Belial's jewels, he is unstoppable."

"You forget that I have his jewels, too. That's how Belial knows of us. It didn't save Amato, did it?"

"Amato was one of the most faithful. Belial is displeased."

"I couldn't give a shit. I hope he's fucking furious." Gabe adjusted his grip as if he might loosen Beneventi, and he gasped, clutching Gabe's arms.

"We can come to an agreement. We have money—a lot of money!"

"So do I. I don't need his money or influence. You see, many Nephilim, me and my brothers included, cast off the influence of our angel fathers millennia ago. I will not be yoked again. Now, where is Jiri?"

"You may as well kill me. I'll tell you nothing!"

"Oh, I'll kill you, there's no fear of that. The question is, will I kill you swiftly or slowly? It's your choice." Gabe had no intention of torturing him; it was abhorrent. Killing was brutal enough, but he didn't have to tell Beneventi that. Gabe squeezed the man's ribs even tighter, and discomfort flashed across his face.

He continued to plead, trying to catch his breath. "You don't understand, which surprises me. You are a Nephilim, with angel blood coursing through your veins. How can you settle for so little?"

"So little? You have no idea how I live. Instead, you listen to Belial's whispers. His jibes and taunts, and you think you know so much. But you are the one who knows so little."

"This world," Beneventi said, spitting saliva with frustration and pain, "is corrupt. We are cleansing it of the unbelievers."

"You are the corrupt one, you fool! Belial is the Angel of Death and Destruction. He didn't pick and choose his victims. He was indiscriminate, and so are you. You spread his jewels and his influence, causing arguments, violence, and confusion all around. But I care not to debate with a madman. Tell me where Jiri is."

"He has a stronghold that you will not penetrate."

"I've destroyed a Cathar castle. I can handle Jiri, and even his few supporters."

"I hardly call twenty of the House of Belial few. They are the equivalent of a hundred."

Twenty? So many? Or was he bluffing? Or even under-reporting? Twenty Nephilim could easily overpower his two brothers in Cornwall, and maybe even the witches in White Haven. And the Moonfell witches, too. His human friends would stand no chance.

"Where is he?"

"You will never find him. He will find *you* when you least expect it. When we have Belial's horn, then the world will quake."

"His horn?" Gabe feigned ignorance. "That is dust now. It will never be found. You're pinning your hopes on a dream."

"It's here. Belial knows it wasn't destroyed, and my ancestor had it for one moment before it was lost. It's just a matter of time before we possess it."

Beneventi's bluster and arrogance had returned. Gabe flipped him upside down, ignoring his screams, and took a moment to check his house. A sudden explosion ripped out half the building, and another blast destroyed the statue. Gabe winced. He had intended to read the plinth first. He hoped Shadow had thought to do so, too.

The bright plume of flames illuminated Gabe and Beneventi, and out of seemingly nowhere, a bolt from a crossbow whizzed past him. Gabe dived further over the lagoon, and Beneventi smacked into the water before he lifted him up again. Gabe scoured the sky, but there was no sign of a Nephilim. There must be a soldier on the ground that his team hadn't found yet. Already, he could see lights and sirens on the island from whatever small police force there was, and boats were mobilising in Venice. They had to leave.

Beneventi was screaming and flailing again. Gabe dipped lower, immersing him into the water for several long seconds. When he lifted the man clear again, he was spluttering and shivering. "Jiri?"

Beneventi gave Gabe a ragged grin, and open his clenched fist to reveal a ring. A bright light flashed out with a wave of Belial's power, almost blinding Gabe. He must have been waiting for when he was closer to the ground. Gabe dropped Beneventi in shock, and he plunged into the lagoon once more.

The man's eyes were glowing now, as Belial awoke within him. Gabe wrestled the alchemical weapon from his pocket and shot him, the weapon virtually eviscerating him. Then Gabe fled to find Shadow and Niel.

Shadow ran into Niel in the depths of the garden, both bloodied and bruised from their fights, and Niel's hand was pressed to his side, blood pouring from it.

"Niel! You've been shot?"

"A graze. I'll live."

"It looks worse than a graze."

"Sister," he said, glaring, "I'm *fine*. As long as my pretty face is still intact for seeing Mouse."

Another explosion by the gate rocked the grounds. "Perhaps we should discuss this later."

Niel frowned as he looked over his shoulder. "You've bombed the entrance?"

"Seemed logical. It's bought us more time." She glanced anxiously overhead. "Where is Gabe?"

But Niel didn't need to answer. A huge, winged shape came into view, wing tips gilded by blazing flames, and Shadow released a breath she didn't know she was holding. Gabe looked fine. Better than fine. His burnished muscles glowed in the light, and she wanted nothing more than to shower him with kisses and straddle him right there.

"Duck!" Gabe yelled. He fired over their heads to a man who had snuck up through the bushes. The man flew backwards, dead, propelled by the power of JD's weapon. Gabe brushed his hair back, smearing blood across his face. "Time to go."

"Wait!" Shadow turned away from them both. "I've found something."

Niel scanned their surroundings. "Can it wait? The police are virtually at the door."

"No, idiot. We're not coming back!" She ran, trusting the others would keep up, until she was standing in front of one of the other statues in the garden. Two men lay dead beneath it. "I thought that this was another statue of Belial, but I was wrong. Look at his face."

It was implacable, just like Belial's, but the face was broader, and his body was, too. His wings were outstretched, and he carried a sword in one hand, and a curved scimitar in the other.

"Herne's hair bollocks," Niel said, aghast. "It's Jiri. I'd forgotten he liked to use a scimitar."

Gabe agreed. "The face is his, too."

"Look at the plinth," Shadow urged them, scanning the grounds while they did so. She was pretty sure most people were dead here, but she didn't want to take any chances.

Gabe gasped. "Is that a city carved on the base? It's wreathed in clouds."

"It has a name under it, too," Niel noted, getting closer. "*Aethalia*. I've never heard of it."

"I think," Shadow said, "that it's where he is now. I've taken photos, and of the other sides. There's writing on it, but you can read that later. I nearly destroyed it, but I didn't."

Niel snorted with surprise. "Wow. Wonders will never cease."

Gabe, however, just smiled and opened his arms. "Now can we go?"

"With pleasure."

Twenty-Three

Olivia was halfway across the cavern, heading for the exit with Estelle, when Maggie joined them.

"Had enough?" Olivia asked her. She was pleased that Maggie had been brought up to speed on everything, especially now that they were a pack, as she, Maggie, Harlan, and Jackson called themselves after one drink too many one night. The thought made her smile. Maggie was being so supportive right now, she didn't know what she'd do without her.

"I was looking for you two, actually. I thought you were taking notes," Maggie said, as she fell into step next to them.

Estelle laughed. "We need food and drinks. The boys are totally absorbed in reading the pillars, and until they find something of use, it's a waste of our time. And besides," she glanced around as they neared the tunnel that exited the cavern, "this place gets claustrophobic after a while."

"I know that feeling," Maggie agreed. "I'll come and help you."

Olivia had her own reasons for leaving. She needed distance from Nahum. He was like a drug. The longer she spent with him, the more addicted she became. Her talk with Estelle had both reassured her and terrified her. She felt she was losing herself in Nahum, and that was ridiculous. Absolutely nothing had happened between them after that one, fateful night, and he had only been kind and solicitous since, and yet there was a growing connection between them that she couldn't ignore. Every time they touched, it was electric.

As they stepped out of the marquee and into the garden, she took a deep, cleansing breath, and stared at the spray of stars above her. *Calm down. Don't get ahead of yourself. It will all be okay.*

And then she blinked as something seemed to block out the stars.

Something about her posture must have alerted Estelle, who asked, "What's wrong?"

"I thought I saw something. Maybe it was an owl." By now all three women were staring up at the sky, and Olivia shivered, drawing her jacket around her. "Sorry. I'm just tired."

Estelle didn't move. "No, something is definitely above us. More than one, actually. I don't think those are birds blocking out the stars. They're Nephilim." Olivia's head whipped up again as Estelle said, "Look how high they seem, and yet the wingspan is too big. I can barely see them, though."

"I see them, too," Maggie said, voice grim. She grabbed Olivia's elbow and yanked her back into the marquee. "Get back here, Estelle. They're gathering, probably watching us as we watch them. With luck, they might not have seen us yet."

Olivia's mouth gaped open in shock as she peered up, head peeking out of the marquee. The figures overhead circled, getting bigger and bigger with every pass. "Holy shit. Could it be Zee or Eli?"

"No. They would have called, and there are more than two," Estelle said with certainty. "These are not our Nephilim. Olivia, go get the others. *Now!*"

"Let me," Maggie said, leaping into action. "You two watch them, but run for cover if they attack."

"Oh, they'll attack," Estelle said softly, still watching the sky as Maggie ran back inside. "They're observing, for now. Well spotted, Olivia." She dropped her gaze and ducked her head back inside. "You need to go inside, too. The cave, I mean. This could be a general attack, or they could have come for you specifically."

Olivia's blood turned to ice. "But what will you do?"

"Hold them off. I think JD has got some sort of defence system here. I hope it's activated." The witch flexed her fingers, and a pulse of power crackled along the tips before she balled fire in her hands. "Fire is my strongest element," she told Olivia, "but I have plenty of spells to use, too. It just depends on whether they wield Belial's power."

Suddenly, everything seemed very real and frightening. "They're Belial's Nephilim?"

"Do you know of any more?"

"Sorry! I'm normally cool-headed, but," her hand flew to her stomach subconsciously, "I have other worries now. I'm not leaving you alone, though. What can I do?"

"Arm yourself with one of JD's weapons." Estelle pointed at the tables that were still in the centre of the marquee. "I saw them earlier. Careful how you handle them! Unfortunately, mine's in my bag in the cave."

Olivia already knew about the weapons. Harlan and Nahum had told her all about them, and she had seen Nahum's. He had even shown her how to use it. "Not a problem," she called out as she raced to the tables.

A blast of fire ignited the dark behind her, and Olivia whirled around. Estelle was already hurling balls of flames skywards. Turning her attention to the tables again, Olivia spotted a series of the ovoid weapons, and picked up a copper one. It warmed in her hands, and she took a deep breath to stop shaking.

An enormous tearing sound erupted overhead, and she looked up in horror as a curved blade sliced through the marquee's roof. Without hesitation, Olivia fired, almost falling over in shock as a searing flash of red light sizzled through the marquee. A roar of anger followed.

But then more swords slashed through the tent's roof. Olivia fired as accurately as she could, running to the cave entrance. "Estelle! Get back here!" But Estelle wasn't even at the marquee's door anymore.

Olivia's voice was lost in the noise of sizzling magic, and despite her numerous shots, a Nephilim dropped through the roof and onto a tabletop. He was dark-haired, with eyes of flames, and his wings were pure white. He was clad in silver armour, and he carried two swords, almost as long as he was tall.

And then he saw her.

He grinned wolfishly, bounded off the table, and raced towards her.

Estelle ran onto the wide lawn that encompassed the marquee, and quickly cast a circle of protection around her.

At least half a dozen Nephilim were winging out of the sky, most aiming for the marquee, others for the house. Estelle knew she'd have the best chance of attacking out in the open. All the Nephilim were armed with either curved scimitars or broadswords. One dived down at her. She threw a cascade of fireballs at him, so many that he couldn't dodge them all. But he was shockingly quick.

He wheeled around and attacked again, while another Nephilim tried to distract her from a different direction. She attacked with a jet of wind. Caspian had taught her how to harness air more effectively, and she put it to good use now. Mixing fire and wind together, she sent a flaming tornado up and out, and the Nephilim scattered—but not for long.

Standing in the open was leaving her vulnerable to attack on all sides. She brought her hands together with a clap, amplifying it with magic. The sound thundered across the grounds as she cast the spell. The closest Nephilim's wings caught fire, and he screamed in agony.

However, she couldn't distract the Nephilim from the marquee, and more were dropping through the roof now. *Where were the others? Where was Anna?*

Lucien was wandering the cavern on his own, lost in his thoughts, and mesmerised by his surroundings.

He was beyond grateful that he had joined the others, fearing that he would be left behind in London. He still felt not quite part of the group, despite everyone's welcoming attitude, but Barak had just said, "You're coming too, right?"

So, here he was, a super-soldier who had no idea how to fight as well as the Nephilim, surrounded by ancient magic in a palace of wonders. There was no sign of the others now, however. He had left them behind, and he was now at the far end of the cave. At one point he thought it would go on forever. It was easy to get turned around and disoriented. However, the columns had ended, and a towering wall of sheer emerald stretched ahead of him, like a huge ice cliff in Antarctica. He walked along it, determined to map the perimeter. It was shadowy here, the lamplight barely penetrating. A fine powder was on the floor, like sand, and it crunched beneath his feet as he kept the wall to his left.

He crouched, filtering the powder though his fingers. *Emerald dust*, he was sure. It was fine, like the gems and metals that had been ground and added to ink to make his tattoos. His skin tingled, and with surprise he watched his skin change to copper—except, he hadn't willed it.

"No!" he shouted in surprise, trying to brush the powder away, fearing he was changing without control.

However, he didn't feel any different, and as he focussed, his heart rate settling, his skin changed back to normal again. *What the hell was happening?* His finger traced the fine design of the alchemical bracelet JD had made for him, and as the emerald dust rubbed into it, the metals glowed, too.

Suddenly curious, rather than scared, he rubbed the dust over his arms, and this time actively willed his skin to change. The alchemical reaction was like breathing to him now. He felt stronger, and his vision became more acute as he transformed. Where he'd rubbed the emerald dust, his skin and tattoos glowed with extra brightness and hardness. It had enhanced him even more. He peeled his t-shirt off, rubbing more of the emerald dust across his chest, and immediately saw the change there, too.

He straightened up, seeing the cave with new vision. The pillars had light within them, and the script etched on the surface glowed with an Otherworldly light. He was somehow attuned to the cave. He saw a broad archway a short distance ahead in the wall of the cave. It was twice his height, and the longer he stared, the more it seemed to solidify and yet shimmer all at the same time. And then he saw more of them. There were more rooms here, hidden within the walls themselves.

Unable to contain his curiosity, he stepped through an archway into a room beyond, and found a cache of weapons. Shields, swords, and daggers, all ornate, all ancient. He grabbed a shield, hefting it on his arm. It was lightweight and seemed to mould to his body. *More alchemical weirdness.*

He needed to tell the others. However, he had progressed only a short way across the cave when he heard Maggie's anguished shout, and he ran.

Nahum flew through the cave as soon as he heard Maggie's shout for help, Barak next to him. They left the others far behind.

As Nahum reached the end of the tunnel, he saw the dark-haired Nephilim advancing on Olivia. She fired JD's weapon at him as she retreated, upending chairs in his path, but he moved like the wind, his speed supernatural.

Fortunately, the intruder was so fixated on Olivia that he didn't see Nahum until the last moment. Nahum angled over her, slicing his sword at the Nephilim's head. With impossibly quick reflexes, his opponent's head whipped up, and he blocked him with one sword, while striking with another. Nahum wheeled around, using his wings as a weapon, dropped onto a table top, and pivoted on the balls of his feet. He launched at him again, keeping his attacker's focus away from Olivia. He glanced around, assessing the risks, and saw that Barak was tackling another Nephilim who had broken through the roof of the marquee. But more were arriving now, swords flashing as the marquee's roof was slashed to ribbons.

Nahum didn't know his opponent, but he recognised the insignia on his breastplate. *The House of Belial*. He didn't appear to be wearing any of Belial's tokens, though. But that was as much as he could take in. They met with a fierce clash of swords and grunting aggression. Fortunately, Nahum was used to fighting warriors after months of battling Black Cronos, and the Nephilim was distracted by Olivia, who was still firing at all the newcomers. Their armour was obviously enhanced, as they seemed impervious to JD's weapons.

"You will die here!" Nahum yelled. "Leave now while you have the chance."

"And leave your spawn behind in the human whore? I think not." His eyes sparked with malice as he slashed at Nahum.

Olivia shouted in outrage. "*Whore*? Who the fuck are you calling a whore? Get back, Nahum!"

The searing red light of the alchemical weapon sliced down the Nephilim's wing, leaving it shattered and broken. He roared in pain and shock. *Clearly, not everything was impervious.* Olivia struck again, hitting the other wing and making Nahum dive for cover behind a table. Her aim was scattered in her fury, but she had already caused enough damage. Nahum knew that the pain of severed wings would be immense. He leapt in and ended him, forcing his blade though his neck to behead him.

Then he swung around, ready to face another attacker.

Harlan sprinted towards the cave's entrance, flanked by Jackson, Maggie, and JD. The two Nephilim were already way ahead, and he had no idea where Lucien was.

"I have to get to my control tower," JD said, trotting to try and keep up with the others.

"Aren't your defences already on?" Harlan asked in horror as he contemplated the alternative.

"Only the ground ones! That will be of no use if Nephilim are attacking from the sky."

"Well, why the hell weren't they on already?" he asked, exasperated.

"Because of the birds, you bloody fool! They would be eviscerated!"

Chastised, Harlan fell silent, instead focussing on withdrawing his alchemical weapon, something he'd taken to carrying with him always now. *Thank the Gods he was paranoid.* "Maggie, you should stay in there!"

"Not a fucking chance!" She sprinted next to him, JD falling behind. "We need all the help we can get. I just need a weapon. We'll need to escort JD to wherever the fuck his control centre is."

"The roof." Harlan remembered the glass-walled control centre well. *The farthest damn point from here.* "Jackson, are you armed?"

Jackson nodded. "I have my handgun."

JD wheezed behind them. "I have some of mine on the tables out front."

Harlan slowed in disbelief and dread when they all reached the end of the cave's tunnel. Olivia was firing wildly, destroying tables and igniting the marquee, while Nahum and Barak battled with four Nephilim. Another was already dead on the floor, his wings shattered and smoking. Harlan wanted to shoot to try and help them, but all of the Nephilim were fighting so quickly they were a blur, and he feared he'd accidently hurt his friends.

"Olivia!" Harlan shouted. "You're a terrible shot! Stop!"

"Screw you, Harlan. I helped kill that one!"

"And you'll kill Barak or Nahum next, the way you're going. Come with me and JD. We're heading to the house."

"No! I'm staying with Nahum."

"No, you're not," Nahum yelled, grunting as he fought. "You go with them."

Jackson had already sprinted to the marquee's entrance, after weaving through the fighting men. "It's not looking any better out there. Estelle is fighting off more Nephilim. At least three."

"Help her!" Barak commanded. The big man was a blur of darkness, his huge wings sweeping tables and chairs out of the way as he fought. The marquee that had seemed huge before now felt far too small with the battling Nephilim in there.

"They must not get into the cave," JD said, wringing his hands. "They might destroy everything!"

"JD, we can't wait. We have to get to the tower, or we'll all be dead, and there'll be no one left who cares about the damn cave!"

And then Lucien suddenly appeared behind them all. "I will protect the cave. Go."

Harlan turned, and almost staggered back in surprise. Lucien was carrying an enormous shield, and he was a super-soldier once again, his skin glowing like burnished copper. But he looked different.

"Lucien? Where did you get the shield? What's going on?"

"I found something. Now go! I have this!"

Harlan nodded. "Thank you. Come on, Olivia."

"No!" She stuck her chin up, defiantly. "I'm staying!"

Harlan had known Olivia long enough to know when she wouldn't budge on something. "Fine! Lucien, you better protect Olivia, too!"

Harlan spotted alchemical weapons on the ground where they had fallen from an overturned table, and grabbing them, he handed them to JD and Maggie, saving one for Jackson. "Let's go. Maggie?"

Maggie cast an anguished glance at Olivia. "I'm not sure whether to go or not."

Olivia pushed her ungraciously towards Harlan. "Harlan is right. JD has to get to his tower. Go!"

"Be careful, Liv!"

Harlan led the way through the fighting Nephilim, and out onto the lawn.

Jackson didn't wait for the others. He sprinted across the lawn, firing his gun upwards as he ran. More and more Nephilim seemed to be arriving now, wheeling across the sky like huge bats.

Estelle was encased in a protective circle, three Nephilim trying to get close but failing as she attacked them relentlessly.

"Estelle. Get to the house! I'll cover you."

"But Barak is in there," she said, not stopping her attack.

"He's okay! Get moving." He fired at another Nephilim, and then rolled across the ground as one dived at him. They were too vulnerable out there. He looked behind him, relieved to see Harlan, JD, and Maggie closing the distance between them, firing wildly overhead.

Estelle didn't budge. "I'll wait until the others are close to the door."

As much as he admired Estelle's power and stubborn resilience, he knew she was wrong. "No, you'll end up stranded." He fired upwards again, most shots missing in his haste, and then glanced to the house to assess the distance. *Damn it.* A huge Nephilim had landed by the door, and was waiting for them. His outstretched wings blocked the door's entrance, and he twirled his swords as if taunting Jackson.

Harlan caught up and passed him an alchemical weapon. "Use this. Target their wings."

Jackson made a sudden decision as he blasted at the Nephilim on the door, combining his timing with the others. "You go. I can't leave Estelle. Run!"

It was growing increasingly dangerous on the lawn. All of them were firing at the Nephilim. A few were still flying, while others were advancing across the grounds. The alchemical weapons gave them a slim advantage, and were the only things keeping them alive. Jackson realised that staying out there was insane, but he couldn't leave Estelle alone.

Harlan knew it too, but he also knew they couldn't wait, and he ran, dragging Maggie and JD with him. "Stay safe, my friend."

Estelle yelled, "Get in here now, you bloody idiot!" He glanced over his shoulder, seeing Estelle slice open her protective circle with a cutting motion. "Now!"

He stumbled backwards, just about getting inside as a Nephilim took advantage of the lull in magic to attack. Estelle grabbed him by the collar and yanked him backwards, sealing the circle again with a word of command.

Instantly the noise muted, and her power crackled around them. *They were safe, but for how long*, he wondered as he studied the charging Nephilim.

Barak fought with increasing rage, aware that Estelle was outside fighting deadly Nephilim. He was not comforted by the fact that their friends were with her. They were all human and therefore vulnerable.

He needed to help her, but Nahum and Lucien were fighting another couple of Nephilim who had dropped through the roof. *Surely there couldn't be many more of them?* Four already lay dead on the floor, killed by a mixture of blades and alchemical weapons.

Barak caught sight of Olivia hanging back in the cave's entrance, desperate to fire JD's weapon. His anger at the assault fuelled his strength and increased his speed. These Nephilim, for all of their size, had clearly not fought like this in a long while, unlike he and his brothers, and they also had the advantage of JD's weapons that the Nephilim clearly weren't expecting. Barak had to thank JD later. They had definitely gifted them the advantage. And for some reason, their attackers did not carry Belial's tokens.

"Does he not trust you to wear his jewels?" Barak sneered as his sword sliced his opponent's arm before he danced out of the way.

"What we do," he replied, breathing heavily, "with his tokens is none of your business."

Barak smirked. "Perhaps you have run out because we have found them all."

The Nephilim lunged, and Barak stumbled back under his onslaught. He grabbed a table and used it like a shield. "You are a fool if you believe that, Barak of the House of Kathazel."

Barak was so shocked that he knew his name that he stumbled again, almost allowing his blade to reach him. "Have we met before?"

"No. Belial has his ways."

Barak was about to ask more questions when a sizzling, red beam of light struck the Nephilim in the neck, blowing a hole right through it. Barak followed up with a swing of his sword and beheaded him, even though he was already dead.

He looked around to see Lucien holding the gun, and Nahum breathing heavily as his opponent also lay dead at his feet. "Thanks, Lucien. I need to find Estelle. Can you stay here?"

"Of course. I have this. You too, Nahum. I will guard Olivia."

Nahum looked torn with indecision, but Barak checked the marquee one more time, and relieved that no one else was dropping though the roof, he nodded. "Thanks, Lucien. Get back down the tunnel. You'll defend the entrance easier than being here."

Lucien herded Olivia ahead of him. "Don't worry, I will."

Barak ran outside and immediately flew, taking in the scene, and Nahum joined him. He sought out Estelle, and found her in the middle of the lawn with Jackson, surrounded by a protection circle of shimmering, blue light. A few Nephilim were dead, while more still circled them. Others were trying to stop Harlan, JD, and Maggie who were almost at the door to the house, a dead Nephilim sprawled across the threshold, his body smoking from the many wounds that had been inflicted on him.

Without a word, they dived down to help.

Maggie sidestepped the Nephilim's body and threw open the back door of JD's house, her alchemical weapon raised.

A figure shouted, "Stop or I'll shoot!"

"For fuck's sake, Anna! It's me, Maggie. Are you okay?"

"Of course not!" Anna stepped into the light, looking terrified, her hands trembling as she held a shotgun.

"Get back. We're coming in." Maggie unceremoniously shoved JD inside. "Go. I'll follow." Harlan was still firing on the other Nephilim, and she was relieved to see Barak and Nahum fighting nearby. "Harlan, are you coming?"

"No." He glanced at her before firing on the diving Nephilim again. "You go, though, and make sure JD gets up there safely. And be quick! I suspect there will be more coming."

Maggie pounded down the hall, following JD who was barking orders at Anna as he ran for the stairs. "Head to the lab and grab the bombs. You know where they are."

"JD, you know I hate those weapons and your lab."

"I don't care! Get them, and take them to Harlan."

"I never signed up for this, JD!" Anna looked furious.

"Neither did any of us! Now do it. I have to activate the grid."

Maggie felt sorry for Anna, but JD was right. She had to pitch in and help. "Actually, Anna, bring me a couple of bombs, too."

Anna just huffed and headed down the stairs to the cellar lab.

Maggie shrugged it off as she followed JD, both wary, and with their weapons raised. Fortunately, it seemed there were no Nephilim in the house. On the first floor, JD went to flick the lights on, and Maggie stopped him.

"I wouldn't. It will alert them to where we are."

"They know we're in here."

"But not *where*, and," she added, catching a glimpse of the fighting through the hall windows, "I'd like to keep it that way."

In a few more minutes they arrived in the huge attic space. One wall was glass and opened onto a roof terrace. JD opened a door in the panelling and led them upstairs. *So, this was the control tower that Harlan was wittering about.* It was crazy. Like the controls of a spaceship—or so she imagined. It gave a perfect view of the grounds, and Maggie watched with increasing horror. Nahum was tumbling end over end, locked in a deadly embrace with a Nephilim. Three other Nephilim were still flying, frustrated at not being able to get close to Estelle and Jackson, but Estelle had gone very still, as if summoning her power for another assault. She couldn't see Harlan at all, and she realised he was still out of view, close to the house.

"Can I help, JD?"

He didn't answer, concentrating on flicking switches on his console. Lights flickered on the edge of the grounds.

"JD," she prompted, "did you say that you're activating a sort of dome?"

He kept working while he said, "Yes."

"How high will it be?" She kept an eye on the Nephilim flying outside the window, almost at their level.

"It will cover the whole house, obviously, another twenty metres above."

"So, Nahum and Barak have to keep below that?"

"Oh, yes. If not, they'll be caught in the beams and die."

"Do they know?"

"Well, they should," he answered grumpily.

"But they're fighting, which means they're distracted!"

"Well, you better tell them, then."

And that also meant any Nephilim still alive would be trapped inside with them. *Bollocking, fuckity fuck!*

The glass control tower was in darkness, but the flashing lights inside were drawing attention, and Maggie swore loudly. "For fuck's sake! I think they've seen us. Is there a window here?"

"Downstairs. You can get on to the roof through the sliding doors."

"Okay, I'm heading outside. How long will you be?"

"Two minutes at the most, just charging it all now."

Maggie raced back down the stairs, thudding into Anna at the base. Anna thrust what looked like an eggbox at her. "Here are your bombs."

"How do they work?"

"I don't know!" She was already bolting to the door.

"Anna, you're a bad liar. You must know!" Maggie wanted to slap her, immortal or not.

"You twist each half, in the centre." She mimed the action. "Ten seconds, and they blow."

"Thank you!" Maggie's voice dripped with sarcasm as she raced to the roof terrace. "Although, this is your home. Perhaps you should fucking help!"

The cold night air was bracing, and the battle cries were loud. Maggie fired at a Nephilim who flew at the tower, sending him wheeling. A bomb exploded below, and a Nephilim was thrown backwards. She fumbled for a bomb, too, planning to throw it at the Nephilim in the air.

However, in seconds, Anna was with her. She extended a hand, jaw tight, eyes full of fury. "Give me one."

Maggie smacked one into her palm, and with startling speed, Anna activated it and hurled it under the Nephilim that Maggie had fired at. It exploded below him, not quite underneath him, but close enough, and he shot skywards.

Impressed, Maggie passed her another. "Great shot!" Then she shouted to Nahum and Barak, gesturing with her hands, hoping they would understand her. "Nahum, Barak, keep low!"

What was taking JD so long?

Then Anna pointed upwards. "What's that?"

Two bright lights like shooting stars were hurtling towards the house from far above.

"Holy shit. They're Nephilim wielding Belial's tokens. They'll kill us all."

"Then we need to slow them down." Anna grabbed a catapult off the table on the terrace, twisted a bomb to activate it, and expertly fitted it into the catapult's pouch. In seconds, the bomb was hurtling upwards to meet the descending Nephilim. It exploded with shocking brilliance, the shockwave sending Nahum and Barak tumbling to the ground.

"Well, you're a dark horse," Maggie told her.

"Who do you think helps test these damn things?" She fired another with surprising accuracy, the shock of the explosion almost knocking Maggie off her feet. The flaming Nephilim slowed to divert around it. They were so close now that Maggie could see them in all their glory. Their outstretched wings were bathed in an almost incandescent white light. She could see the murderous intent in their eyes, and the flames dancing along their swords.

Another explosive kick of power rippled across the house and grounds, like a localised display of the Northern Lights. JD had activated his shield. Of the two Nephilim wielding Belial's power, one was caught in it, and he vanished, vapourised, the other was stuck on the outside.

For a brief moment, their eyes locked, and Maggie felt the full brunt of his anger. It was so palpable that she fell backwards into a chair, his eyes feeling like they had burned a hole in her head. He lifted his sword and pointed it at her, as if promising what was to come, and then he turned off whatever power he had used, his incandescent light diminishing, examined the view below, and in seconds, he flew away.

Estelle raced across the lawn to the last Nephilim she'd brought down. He lay on the ground, wings smouldering, his skin badly burned by the fire balls she had released.

Barak was also running over, his sword raised ready to dispense justice.

"No!" Estelle shouted. "Wait!"

Barak stood over the injured man. "Why?"

"Because we need him to tell us where the others are."

The Nephilim spat at her feet, barely hanging on to his consciousness he was so badly wounded. "I will tell you nothing!"

"Careful," Barak warned, sword at his neck, "or your death will be slow. Help us and I will show mercy."

The man laughed, blood staining his teeth. "I doubt that."

Jackson had followed her, and he asked, "How will you get him to talk?"

"Glamour. I need you all to hold him down—just in case." Although she doubted he'd mount much resistance.

By now Nahum and Harlan had arrived, and without argument, all four pinned the Nephilim down. Estelle crouched beside him, aware of the other dead bodies close by. She hated all this death and destruction. Excitement and treasure hunting was one thing, but this was something else. When this business was over with Belial, she wanted a new direction with Barak. She hoped he would want the same. This was not what her magic was for. For a long time she didn't know how she wanted to use it, she just knew she needed to use it to its full potential. But now... Well, this wasn't the way.

Pushing her objections to the back of her mind, she cupped the man's face in her hands and stared deep into his eyes. The pain he suffered was enormous. She had inflicted that. She took a deep breath and cast her glamour spell, feeling its power roll into the fallen man.

Nephilim were generally too strong to succumb, but this man was near death. Nevertheless, he tried to resist.

"Tell me where Jiri is."

He ground out words through clenched teeth. "Screw you."

Estelle decided to try another angle before she recast the glamour spell. "Belial's time is at an end, or should be, and you know it too. Is this really what you wanted when you came here? To be doing his bidding once again? Or did you want true freedom, like these Nephilim have?"

He gave a grim laugh, blood speckling his chin. "Belial does not offer freedom. Death is my only way out."

"It is now, for you, but not for the others. What if we could work together and defeat him? Would Jiri help?"

"Jiri would never help you."

"Would the other Nephilim help?"

"And betray our commander? Never."

Barak's deep voice rumbled a request. "Forget commanders. Forget rules! Make your own."

The Nephilim's eyes flickered with what looked like hope before it vanished again. "It's not possible."

"Yes it is, because we did it."

Nahum nodded, adding his own support. "Yes, we did. We have long lives, too long to live under the yoke of Belial."

Estelle turned the man's face so he was staring at her again. "Tell us where Jiri is, or who we can contact who will help us." She reinforced her glamour spell, and added one to dull his pain, but tried not to confuse him. Regret was the man's overriding emotion though, and she appealed to that. "Who would help us? I know someone will. I can see it in your eyes."

"Ozan. There will be a few others too." He gave the name up easily this time.

Estelle felt Barak flinch in surprise, but she didn't dare break eye contact with the injured Nephilim now. "Where are you based?"

"Cabo." His speech slurred as he slipped away, his eyes glazing.

"I need more details! Where is that?" Trying to keep him with her, Estelle asked, "What is your name?"

"Emre."

"Thank you, Emre. We need a number. A way to contact Ozan."

But Emre was already dead.

"No!" She groaned, head falling forward with disappointment. "Damn it!"

Harlan however was searching the man's pockets, and with a cry of triumph, he shouted, "Yes!"

He had found Emre's phone.

Twenty-Four

A sh opened the door of the rented villa for his brothers and
Shadow at two in the morning, taking in their dishevelled appearance, and cuts and bruises. They all stank of smoke.

"Good journey?" he asked, leading them to the small living room.

"Quiet. No one followed us." Gabe shrugged his jacket off and threw it on the sofa. "We took a circuitous route, just in case."

"Too bloody circuitous," Niel complained. He was streaked with sweat and ash. "We could have been here half an hour ago."

"Oh, stop whining," Shadow said, shutting the door behind her. "At least we're safe for a while."

"I take it," Ash asked, amused, "that you created a little bit of trouble?"

Gabe snorted. "We created havoc, although we made a clean getaway. At least, I think we did." Gabe pulled Ash into a hug. "I'm glad to see that you're okay after your own fight."

"It was touch and go for a while." Ash was bare chested, wearing only his jeans that he'd pulled on in a hurry, and the scratches on his arms and back were obvious, as was the graze along his ribs from the crossbolt.

As agreed late the previous afternoon, the group had decided that Ash needed a place to stay after his long drive to find Lamberti's paperwork, somewhere that Gabe and the others could get to easily if needed. It was obvious that staying in Venice for much longer was not an option. So, prior to leaving the Venetian apartment, Ash had made a short-term rental booking of a villa partway between Palazzuolo sul Senio and Venice, along with a second rental car for his own use. Fortunately, they had managed to secure a big enough place, deep within the countryside and far from neighbours. Not even Romola knew where they were now.

He rubbed the sleep from his eyes and brushed his hair back from his face as he headed to the kitchen. He had managed a couple of hours' sleep, far too tired to examine the paperwork he'd retrieved, and had placed it under his pillow.

"Coffee?" he asked.

"Very strong, please," Niel said, leaning his axe against the wall. Flecks of dark, dried blood still marked the blade. "I'll head to the shower first. I won't be long."

For the next few minutes, the group cleaned up and changed their clothes, and after making the coffee, Ash retrieved the paperwork from his room. He carefully opened the pages, relieved to see that the oilskin package had kept the information safe. He scanned the list of names, noting that Lamberti had even listed the type of jewel for each piece, whether it was a ring, torc, clasp, necklace, or even short, jewelled daggers.

Gabe took a seat in the armchair and poured himself a coffee from the pot on the table. He'd showered and was wearing clean clothes, although he needed a shave. Stubble lay thick on his cheeks, and his damp hair was unruly. More than anything, he looked tired, but he also looked hopeful as he saw the paperwork in Ash's hands. "Anything useful?"

"Plenty. Whether they're still where they are listed, though, is another matter. This is dated about five years ago. There are, I estimate, about thirty people that we'll need to track down. Have you found out anything?"

"Shadow did." Gabe looked up as Niel and Shadow entered the room, both wearing loose trousers and t-shirts after their showers. "We have a clue as to where Jiri is, but the name is unfamiliar to us. However, Estelle also managed to give us useful information. I take it you haven't heard from Barak or Nahum?"

Ash sat upright, alarmed. "No, why?"

"A dozen Nephilim attacked JD's place. It was touch and go for a while, but they're okay. Mostly. No serious injuries." Gabe outlined what had happened.

Ash felt terrible. His night had been nothing compared to everyone else's.

"I can't believe they attacked. Estelle did well to get Emre to talk." He could see the scene only too well. *The blood. The fear.*

"Very well," Gabe agreed. "If Emre is right, and some of them will help us, we can win this!"

"Have they called Ozan yet?"

"They're trying to decide on the right time." Gabe closed his eyes briefly. "Tomorrow morning, perhaps."

"If Ozan was a good friend to Emre, he won't take kindly to the call."

"He will if it gets him his freedom. But just in case, we need to find out where they are." He looked across to Shadow. "Show him the photos. If we can identify the island, maybe the place name that Estelle was given will make sense."

Shadow sat next to Ash on the sofa, and after accessing the images, she handed her phone over. Ash frowned. "Another statue?"

"There were several in the garden," she explained. "Most were of Belial, but this one was different. Gabe says it's Jiri. That's the base."

Ash enlarged the images. "If Jiri has his own statue, it must mean they consider him very important. Is that a cityscape?" The image showed the relief of a range of buildings, their silhouettes standing proud of the stonework.

"Looks like one, doesn't it? On the other side of the plinth is what looks like an island. Very stylized, with waves around it."

Ash kept scrolling, reading the words carved into the base. "It exalts Jiri as Belial's commander. It's a bit grandiose."

Niel grunted. "He was always a pompous ass."

"The text," Gabe says, "describes him as returning to the base of his power, where he will centre his command. A place called Aethalia. We don't know the name, so I've searched for it. It's the name of a few boats and tankers. That can't be right!"

"Aethalia." Ash frowned, knowing it sounded familiar. "It was the name of an island. It's Greek."

Niel had been slumped in the chair, but now he perked up. "A Greek island?"

"No, but it was in the Mediterranean, though." Ash was still tired, and his eyes felt dry. He needed more sleep. However, he handed

Shadow her phone and accessed his own, quickly pulling up a map of Europe. "It was in this area, I think."

"Could it be anything on that northeasterly line?" Shadow asked.

Ash glanced at her. "That's a great suggestion. It can't be further north from here, so we must have to go south. Just off the Italian coast is Sardinia, Corsica, and..." He frowned as he enlarged the image. "Elba."

Niel looked confused. "Elbow?"

"No! *Elba*. It's where Napoleon was exiled. That's it!" Ash felt more alert as excitement welled. "Look at the shape of it compared to what's on the base. It's the same."

Everyone crowded around as Ash showed them the image. Then he did another search of Elba and grinned. "I knew I recognised the name! It was called Aethalia by the Greeks. It was famous for its mines."

Gabe took the phone off him and scanned the details, while Ash looked at the photos of the statue's base again.

"So, we've found him?" Shadow asked, eyes sharp.

"Looks like it," Gabe answered, "if he hasn't moved. But why advertise where he lives on his statue?"

"It isn't so much where he lives, it's just about him! Of course," Ash said, as more memories returned, "I remember rumours that whispered while we had palaces, he had a bloody island. It was under his dominion for a while before the Flood. It all adds up."

"So, the statues pointing in one direction originate from Elba?" Shadow asked, confused. "Again, why?"

"Maybe they like games?"

"Maybe," Niel suggested, "they didn't think anyone would notice the statues aligned in one direction. I mean, they were supposed to be private. So, what now?"

"We have to go there," Gabe said. "If that's where he's based, we go to the source. The name that Emre gave Estelle was Cabo. Let's see... There's a place called Cavo! Could that be it?"

"Perhaps," Ash said. "You said he was dying. He could have mispronounced the place's name. Unless, of course, he was lying and just pretending to help. I'm certain of the island, though."

"Good. The rest," Gabe nodded at the paperwork that Ash had found, "can wait until afterwards."

Ash leaned back, hands behind his head, thinking through their options. "Did you kill all the humans tonight?"

"Most, I think," Gabe said. He looked uncomfortable. "I didn't want to, but they talked so remorselessly about their plans that I couldn't stand it. It was like a game to them, and Beneventi said their aim was to cleanse the Earth of unbelievers. He was deranged. There was no way to save them."

Shadow nodded in agreement. "If they had all been initiated as Lamberti suggested, they were already possessed by Belial's madness. It struck me that they were his eyes. He'll be weaker without them."

"Not weak enough." Niel poured himself more coffee. "He still has his Nephilim. Well, some of them. Even less, if Ozan will join us."

Ash hated putting his faith in others he didn't know, but if they had someone on the inside, it could change everything.

Gabe continued. "We stick with the plan. Tomorrow—or rather, later today—Niel, you meet Mouse in Istanbul, and we'll fly to Elba. Estelle, Barak, and Lucien will join us. Everyone else will remain at

JD's for protection, while Nahum will stay to help with the transla-
tions. Zee and Eli will remain in Cornwall. I don't want those jewels
to go missing. Then, if we can contact Ozan, well, we go from there."

"Which means," Niel said, darkly, "I can't join you in Elba, because
I have to get the horn back to Cornwall."

"Exactly. You cannot bring it to Elba."

"If I don't find it, though, I'm coming."

"Fair enough. And Ash, there's more news." Gabe looked at Ash
again, his expression unreadable. "They found something else in the
emerald cave. Something weird."

Olivia sipped overly sweet tea in the wreckage of the marquee, wishing
she could drink hard spirits like everyone else.

She wasn't sure why they were all in the marquee instead of JD's
house, but it seemed everyone wanted to be close to the emerald
cave and have a good view of the garden to ensure their attackers
wouldn't return. They had righted tables, swept broken glass aside,
and lit a multitude of lamps. The dead were on the lawn. Most of
their team were injured. She had cuts and bruises from where she had
rolled across the floor and dived under broken tables. Nahum and
Barak looked the worst. They were covered in cuts, grazes, and ugly
gashes. Nahum had an especially deep cut along his abdomen. It was
now bound and dressed, and Estelle had cast a little healing magic.
Fortunately, his own naturally accelerated healing was already having
an effect. Barak had glowed from within, his healing abilities different

to Nahum's, and it had healed an ugly cut across his forearm in no time.

Lucien had fared better. His weird, metallic skin rebuffed even the heaviest blows, and their Nephilim attackers had looked at him with ill-disguised unease. Estelle remained the least affected, but she was drained after using so much magic. Olivia also suspected that killing Nephilim had taken its toll. She looked defeated, despite their success. *At least they were safe.* The grounds hummed with power now that JD's weird dome had fully activated, and it was invisible, thank the Gods, after its initial pulse of green.

Nahum was sitting so close to Olivia that she could feel his heat, and her skin tingled as his arm brushed hers. He was solicitous, unconcerned about his own injuries. She felt loved. Seen. She liked it. But he didn't love her. He was just being Nahum, and that thought pained her more than anything.

Her thoughts were all over the place, but she focussed on the conversation as Jackson asked JD, "How long will the dome thing last?"

"As long as I want it to. It's a source of constant power. But, as I said, birds will die, and I don't like that."

"Better them than us," Harlan drawled sarcastically. He also looked rumpled and bruised after the battle on the lawn.

"They won't come back," Maggie said with certainty. "That remaining Nephilim, the one who was lit up like a bloody star, knew he couldn't cross your barrier. Unless they find a way, of course. Have you warned your brothers in Cornwall?"

Barak nodded. "The witches are confident that their protection spell will work. Plus, they might not have identified our home. With luck, this will be over in a couple of days if Ash is correct about where

Jiri's base is, and Emre wasn't lying. Let's hope we can contact Ozan tomorrow and make a deal." They had accessed Emre's phone using his fingerprint, and found the number of the Nephilim they hoped would help them. Barak stifled a yawn. "I need to go to bed and get some sleep if we're to be rested for our flight later today. JD, are you sure about having beds for all of us? You don't exactly own a hotel."

JD waved off his enquiry airily. "A couple of you might have to share, but it will all work out. Anna is organising it now."

"She is wasted as your housekeeper," Maggie said. "She's a mean shot with the catapult."

"Ah, yes." JD smirked. "She's helped me test things over the years, but she doesn't like violence."

"Well, she sure steps up when she needs to. With a little provocation," she added slyly. She cocked an eyebrow at Olivia, who laughed. There must have been a lot of swearing on Maggie's behalf.

Nahum spoke up. "Before we sleep, I really want to see what you've found." He directed this solely at Lucien. "Your shield was once a Nephilim's."

Lucien nodded. "I thought as much. Follow me."

They crossed the enormous cave and reached the back wall, where Lucien led them to a dark, shadowy area where the lamplight didn't reach. He pointed at the wall. "Can you see the archway leading to another room?"

"Archway?" Nahum asked, puzzled. "There's nothing there. Are you seeing things?"

Lucien just laughed. "Look at this." He bent down and gathered up a handful of emerald dust. "You've all said that I looked different. That my enhanced abilities looked, well, even more enhanced than normal.

Look at this." He rubbed the dust up his arms and onto his bare chest, and as he did so, his skin bloomed with a metallic hue. "I can't explain how, but it enhances me even more. It's like adding a double layer of metal skin."

"Herne's hairy bollocks," Harlan said, reaching forward. "Can I?"

"Sure. But it still feels like skin."

Harlan ran his fingers along Lucien's arms, pinching slightly. "It's so weird. But what has this to do with an archway?"

JD and Jackson were already tapping the wall.

"It's changed my sight," Lucien explained. "I seem to see with extra depth perception. The Nephilim we fought, even you two," he said to Nahum and Barak, "look odd. I can see your energy, the flow of angelic magic in you. As for this this cave? Well, everything is glowing. The pillars seem to have light inside them, and I can see that there are other rooms here." He laid his hand on the wall, and it shimmered and then vanished, leaving a doorway into a room beyond.

Rather than rush inside it, everyone hesitated at the threshold. Olivia shivered, suspicious that it would seal her inside somehow. It was twice as tall as she was, the archway oriental in design, the pillars that formed the frame, fluted and ornate.

"God's breath!" JD exclaimed, examining the entrance closely. "How did you open it?"

"I don't know, but the emerald dust makes all the difference."

JD stared at him, absently stroking his trimmed beard. "You must be attuned to this cave through your alchemical enhancements. This place is, after all, made through alchemical means, too. I was never able to completely determine exactly what gems were used to make your tattoos, but emerald must be one of them. It has interesting qualities."

"Such as what?" Olivia asked, intrigued.

"Well, it's always been popular in alchemy. We believe that it helps to manifest visions, and it also shields against conjurations and malevolent spirits. It provides inspiration and balance, enhances creative and mental abilities, and more importantly, increases psychic sensitivity and clairvoyance. What you are experiencing right now," JD said thoughtfully, eyes narrowed as he assessed Lucien, "is exactly that. You are seeing beyond the veil of normality."

"Will the effects last?" Nahum asked.

"Perhaps." JD shrugged. "Time will tell. I suspect, though, that once away from this place for a while, it will not. Unless you take the emerald dust with you." He patted Lucien on the shoulder. "Don't worry. None of it is bad. Now, let's see what's inside."

Harlan laid a hand on JD's arm, stopping him from crossing the threshold, his concerns echoing Olivia's own. "Is it safe? I don't want to get stuck in there."

"I'll come in with you," Lucien said, confidently, "just in case."

The room was circular, again carved from pure emerald, its surface polished to a glassy shine, and once again covered in lines of script. And there were heaps of weapons, much like in Raziel's Temple. They were piled on the floor and displayed on shelves carved into the walls. Everyone started to pick them up, examining the engravings and quality. They were in good condition, polished and untarnished, as if they had been stored there for hours rather than centuries.

"Herne's horns," Barak said, lifting one of the shields from a haphazard stack of them. "There are so many. I don't understand why they're here."

Nahum ignored the weapons and instead read the script. "Ancient Aramaic," he noted with a frown. "These are lists of Fallen Angel Houses and their Nephilim."

"All of them?" Jackson asked.

"Perhaps." Nahum scanned the walls. "There are hundreds, maybe thousands listed here. Unlikely that there are weapons for every House, though. There's nowhere near enough."

Barak nodded in agreement. "This is a sample. Why?"

"Thoth, or Hermes, or whatever the fuck you want to call him," Maggie said, "must have collected them. If there were as many of you as you say all those years ago, it would have been easy, right?"

Olivia nodded in agreement as she examined a richly engraved dagger with a polished horn handle. "This place isn't just a place of learning. It stores history, too." She glanced up, aware that the others were staring at her. "What? It makes sense. The lists of angels, the histories of Biblical figures, and probably those we've never heard of except in myth, and there's so much more here that we don't know about yet. It's like a museum!"

JD's mouth fell open in shock. "I hadn't thought of it like that, but yes, you're right!"

"Which means," she said, as she studied the hoard of weapons, "that these aren't here for any threatening reasons, they're here as a reminder of Nephilim might and power. That's all." She smiled at Nahum, noting his tension seeping from his shoulders. "You could use these, if you wanted. Maybe that's why they were in Raziel's cave, too. He must have known that it would take a Nephilim to enter. Perhaps they were a gift."

Jackson laughed. "I much prefer that theory." He nodded to the doorway, "It's still open. I suspect it will remain open, now that Lucien has activated it. We have earned the right to enter. I also suspect, JD, that you would have worked it out yourself, given time."

"Of course I would," JD declared imperiously, making Olivia suppress a smile. "Come, Lucien, let's open up the other rooms, too."

Twenty-Five

Niel landed in Istanbul at three in the afternoon. He'd showered off the stench of blood, alchemical weapons, smoke, and death, and was rested and wearing clean clothes, ready for adventure. For a moment he stood blinking in the sunshine, as the scents and sounds of Istanbul cast him back centuries.

No, he mentally urged himself, *do not get lost in memories*. This city did not exist in his time, but nevertheless, it triggered memories of other, similar places with equally evocative buildings and inhabitants. He hailed a taxi, and was soon threading through crowded streets that he longed to explore.

Unfortunately, time was short. Mouse had already been sent details of their plans, and he trusted she had researched the best means of entry. He adjusted his jacket again, and caught sight of his face in the rear view mirror. He looked fine. *Better than fine, actually*, he thought, grooming his beard.

Stop it. She nearly killed him. This is just a job, and then it's done. He wouldn't need to see her again.

He had texted Mouse a couple of times, deciding to organise his plans with her directly. He didn't need Gabe acting as a go-between. Besides, he knew his brothers and Shadow found it amusing. *Screw them.* He would rise above it. From Mouse's tone—if texts even had a tone—she was being just as professional.

He checked into his hotel, pleased that he'd organised it himself. It was a small, boutique place on a side road, and lowkey, just as he liked it. It was luxurious, though. He may as well enjoy their newfound wealth. According to the last message from Mouse, she was already there. Pausing only to unpack his scant belongings and observe the view from his window, he called her. Minutes later, he was heading up to the next floor, where her room was situated.

He knocked on her door, and then realised he'd never seen her face before, only her eyes. For some reason, this made him more anxious. He set his jaw, prepared for anything. Or so he thought.

The door swung wide open, and a startlingly pretty woman looked up at him. Her eyes were exactly as he'd remembered them. Almond shaped, dark pupils, teasing. But her lips were fuller than he'd imagined, her smile broader, her cheeks rounder. Her eyes darted to the hall. "Niel, you better come in."

"You arrived without any problems, then?" he asked, wondering why he was asking such a lame question. *Of course she fucking had.*

"Actually, I was a bit worried I might not get through passport control. I've had issues here in the past." She raised a groomed eyebrow, amused. "It seems my new passport is just fine."

"Great! On Europe's Most Wanted list?"

"Something like that." She walked to the coffee machine and kettle in the corner, and he took the opportunity to appreciate her figure. She was dressed in slim-fitting jeans and a fine knit jumper that hugged her petite, lithe figure. "Tea, coffee, or beer? My fridge is fully stocked."

"Beer, please." He studied her room. It was a mirror image of his own, and had a narrow balcony that looked over a side street. The furnishings were rich in colour, and he had another ache of homesickness before it vanished. Standing on the balcony, he said, "This is a little more sheltered than mine. If I have to fly, I can land here."

"Planning escape routes already?"

"I always like to be prepared."

She smirked as she handed him his beer and kept one for herself. "Aren't you the boy scout?"

It stung, for some reason. Like she was patronising him. It made him want to strike back. "Well, seeing as you electrocuted me last time, I always like to have options when working with you. I have a healthy sense of self-preservation. If it wasn't for Gabe, I wouldn't be here."

Her amusement vanished. "I told you, I did that to save your life."

He shrugged. "When you could have just included me in your plans."

"That was impossible! You are infuriating!"

"So are you. I'm still pissed off about it, so get used to it. I presume you have a way to get inside the museum?"

She glared at him for a moment longer as she swigged her beer. "Yes, actually. We're heading there very soon and strolling right through the front door."

"Why?"

"Because I have stolen from there before, many years ago. It was a nightmare. It has an excellent alarm system and a large number of guards. Our best bet is to walk in and hide until it's closed. Even then, we'll have to avoid the guards."

"Are you insane?"

"No. The museum closes at six, and I will get us into the staff areas. I know the place quite well, having spent hours in there just appreciating the displays."

"And the private areas?"

Mouse's arms were crossed, one hand gripping the beer bottle, a challenge in her eyes. "Less well, but I have a rough idea of the layout." Her fingernails were short and unvarnished, gracing slender fingers that were devoid of jewellery, and they tapped the bottle repeatedly. "Would you rather break in at night?"

He dipped his head in a sarcastic bow. "I will do whatever you advise, but if you set me up, I won't be half so accommodating with your health as I was before."

"I am not setting you up! We walk in there together, and we walk out of there together. You will need to take a backpack that's big enough to get the horn in. Maybe a change of t-shirt. They search bags on the way in, so no weapons."

Niel frowned. "Why a change of t-shirt?"

"Seeing as we're staying there overnight, I'd like to look different if we're spotted on camera. We'll emerge into the morning crowd and exit."

"Stay overnight? That's hours, which means ample opportunity for the guards to find us! Are there cameras?"

"Lots in the museum, but nowhere near as many in the staff areas. Especially in the old storage rooms." She seemed very confident.

"How many times have you been in the staff area? Really."

"Three—no, four times. The guards rarely open the locked rooms. We just need to get in one and hide. Then we explore later."

"And you stole an item every time?"

"Every time, undetected, from deep in the basements."

Niel drank his beer, watching her as he did so. It was a good suggestion, but being in the museum for so long, especially with The Horn of Desolation, didn't sound like a good idea.

Mouse picked up on his hesitancy. "If you have objections, say now, but this is the best option."

"Do you know what we're stealing?"

"No. Just something old and weird and bulky."

Niel kicked a chair out, putting aside his animosity, and sat at the small table. "Have a seat. This is no ordinary item. You've heard of Fallen Angels?"

"Of course. You're a Nephilim, and they fathered you." Her pretty eyes flitted over him, staring at his shoulders. "I haven't forgotten that, or your wings. It was a memorable night flight."

He wanted to add that he was always memorable, but decided against it. "Well, we are stealing a horn that belonged to one of the biggest and baddest. It's quite a story."

"Is it long? Because we have to go soon."

"I'll make it quick, but trust me, you'll want to hear this."

Nahum studied the script on the twisted stone columns, wishing Ash was here instead of him. These words were gibberish. He rubbed his eyes, blinked, and tried to focus. *Damn alchemists and their weird speech.*

"Are you okay?" Olivia asked, calling up to where he was studying, halfway up the column.

"Fine. I don't think this is what we need. I'll be down in a moment."

Olivia was another reason for his ill temper. She had shared a room with Maggie the previous night, and he hadn't had a chance to talk to her alone. He'd had some romantic notion that she might need his protection, and he could angle an excuse for sharing her room. Instead, he'd been relegated to a room down the hall. *At least he'd had a bed.* Lucien had slept on a sofa, admittedly a large one, while Harlan and Jackson had shared a room. Of course, Barak shared with Estelle, and both had already left for the airport with Lucien. He was worried about their safety and wished he could go, but someone had to stay and find a way to stop Belial for good.

When he finally flew down to the ground, Olivia looked pensive. "Nothing useful?"

"No. This is madness. Finding what we need could take years."

Olivia nodded absently as she took his news in. "Look, if we don't find a spell to negate Belial's power right now, it will be okay. The jewels have been around for years without causing outright destruction. We'll root them out."

"And my brothers? And Shadow and Estelle? If Jiri draws on Belial's power, it won't be a fight, it will be a slaughter."

"They have JD's weapons and bombs."

"It's still an unequal fight."

She swallowed, casting her gaze to the floor. "It's my fault. I wish I'd never have found those damn things."

He reached forward and lifted her chin so he could look her in the eyes. "It's not your fault. It's Belial's and the damn Brotherhood."

She nodded. "I know, but…"

"No buts. Where are Maggie and the others?"

"Maggie is dealing with the dead bodies. Her team is on the way, with Layla. Jackson is helping her. Harlan is with JD, working on other strategies."

He took advantage of their privacy, and stepped closer. "Are you okay after last night? I haven't really had a chance to ask."

"It was a bit of a shock to be attacked, but I'm fine. I need to improve my aim. It's shit."

He laughed. "Well, I didn't want to complain, but you almost killed me a couple of times."

"I had to try!" She scowled. "Harlan was extremely insulting. He almost wrestled the weapon off me!"

"Good. I owe him a drink. Probably several."

"You're both very cheeky. But how are *you*? You were fighting for your life." Her hand tentatively rested on his abdominal wound, and her touch was electric. A flare of desire raced through him, and he didn't dare touch her hand. *Or should he?* Her lips were parted as she stared up at him, a flush on her cheeks. *Fuck it.*

He took her hand in his left one and turned it over, the thumb of his right hand stroking her palm. Her breath caught in her throat, but she didn't pull away. Instead, she stepped closer as he said, "It's healing already. Don't worry about me. Look, Olivia, I don't know what the future holds, but I think..."

But before he could say anything else, JD yelled, "I've found something! Come and see!"

Nahum ignored him, his attention solely on Olivia, "I've been thinking about our living arrangements. I don't want to be away from you or our daughter at all. It feels wrong!"

"You want to move in? With me? All the time?"

"Is that so horrible? You're having my child. I'm excited and terrified all at the same time. And I think... I *know* that I'll miss you."

She smiled as she leaned into him. "You will?"

He lowered his head, desperate to kiss her, when JD shouted again. "Come on! It's important."

Nahum's jaw tightened. "I wish he'd shut up."

Olivia didn't speak. Instead, both hands reached around his head and pulled him towards her, kissing him with fierce intensity. His arm wrapped around her waist and pulled her closer, losing himself in the breathtaking kiss. He couldn't think straight. All he knew was that this felt right. When they broke away, he was breathless, his desire stoked, desperate to revel in her nakedness.

She spoke first. "Let's talk later?"

"Sounds good." He held her gaze for a few meaningful moments, hopeful of some kind of future together, and then after another annoyingly insistent shout from JD, led the way across the cave.

JD and Harlan were in one of the side rooms that Lucien had opened up before he left. He'd found another dozen that Nahum had barely glanced at, but it seemed JD had deemed them important enough to study further.

"Oh, good!! JD said eyeing them with annoyance as he turned to the doorway. "You took your time!"

Harlan snorted. "I think I know doing what, too." He motioned towards Nahum's lips. "You missed a smear of lipstick there, buddy."

Nahum grinned, refusing to be embarrassed as he rubbed his finger across his lips, and wanting to tease Harlan after putting up with weeks of his overprotective behaviour. "It was more fun than translating old text."

Harlan just rolled his eyes as Olivia poked her tongue out at him.

"Is anyone interested in this?" JD asked, hands on hips. "I might have found a way to stop Belial!"

Nahum focussed on the text inscribed on the walls of the cave. It was roughly the same sized space as the others, but this one was carved in the shape of a six-pointed star. "What a weird room. Aramaic script again."

"A language I understand reasonably well," JD said. He looked wild-eyed this morning, and Nahum realised he'd had little sleep. His hair was tangled and untidy, and his eyes looked red from too much reading. He scowled at Nahum and Olivia. "Does the shape of this room seem familiar?"

"It's the Star of David," Nahum said.

"And also," Olivia added, "it represents the alchemical sign meaning as above, so below."

"Exactly!" JD pointed to the main cave behind them. "There is one on the ground in the centre of the cave. This room is all about that sign!"

Harlan grinned at Olivia like a naughty schoolboy. "It's the key!"

Nahum frowned, confused. "To what?"

"The star on the floor, dummy!"

"And the wider cave," JD added, now bouncing on his toes with excitement. "It's the map room!"

Olivia traced a section of script with her fingers. "It's the map to the whole cave?"

JD pointed to the ground. "That is."

Nahum had been so focussed on the walls that he hadn't looked at the floor. He studied it now, JD and Harlan retreating to the walls to allow a better view. Patterns of dots in bronze were marked on the ground, and he realised they represented the columns. Seen from above, and at this scale, it was easy to see what they had missed in the larger cave. The columns were also arranged in the shape of a large six-pointed star, which explained why some areas of the walls did not have pillars close to them. In the centre was a smaller six-pointed star, representing the one in the cave that had the flame in the centre.

He shook his head. "I can't believe I didn't see the pattern!"

"It's too big to take in, even though you can fly," JD said, shrugging it off. "But now, it's obvious. The text on the walls maps out what is where. We were right with what we have found so far, and this gives us more details. There are sections on astronomy, geology, the Gods, Goddesses, the movement of planets, their correspondences, some in far more detail than even I have discovered. Some," he smiled smugly, "I already found out myself. And the mathematics here...breathtaking."

Clearly outraged, Olivia said, "So why hide it away? We could have made progress much quicker!"

"It's all about proving your worth. Knowledge is locked away behind layers of meaning. Lucien provided a shortcut, although I would have worked it out in time."

Nahum didn't doubt it. He scanned the text. "You said you have found out something to help us with Belial?"

He nodded, exchanging a nervous glance with Harlan. "I think so. The flame in the centre is the key. It seems that when used in the right way, it can undo great magic. Unravel it. But it might be dangerous."

"There's no *might* about it!" Harlan remonstrated. Unlike JD, Harlan looked refreshed and groomed, with no trace of stubble on his freshly shaved cheeks, but his eyes were shadowed with worry. "It essentially sounds like it breaks apart matter."

"As in 'unmakes' something?" Olivia asked, forehead creasing with worry. "Is that even possible?"

"No." JD jumped in quickly. "'Unmake' is the wrong word. Matter is matter. It can't go anywhere. But it can be rearranged."

Nahum's head was already hurting. "Like when you melt down metals to make something else?"

"No, that is still metal. Instead, you make something else entirely."

Nahum suggested something ridiculous. "Like cheese?"

"Yes, sort of. You change something fundamental. That's what one branch of alchemy is all about. Changing base metals into gold, amongst other things. It's what I did," JD added cautiously, "when I became immortal. I unlocked something at the cell source in my body. I gave it renewable energy. I switched aging off. I didn't turn myself into cheese or a chicken, but this formula here—" he tapped the wall, "suggests that is possible."

"Transmutation. Isn't that what some witches in fairy tales can do?" Harlan asked. "Become a frog or cat? Can any witches we know do that?"

"Not as far as I know," Olivia said, but she looked excited by the idea. "I'll ask Morgana!"

JD sighed. "I am, of course, explaining this at its most basic level, and clearly not very well."

"Because we're dumbasses," Harlan explained.

"Because it's complicated!"

"Hold on!" Nahum held his hand up. "Belial's jewels contain his power. How does that help us with them? Are you saying you have found a way to remove his power?"

"I think so. But I would need everything here to assess and try, because I need the eternal flame to do it. Even then, well, I'm not sure at this stage where his power goes..."

Nahum rubbed his forehead. "I think I'd rather leave it contained where it is until we know more. A bloody great cloud of Belial's power just wafting about sounds toxic. Like a cloud of nuclear waste."

"That is the issue," JD admitted. "We can melt down metals and destroy his jewels, but it's his power that creates them and holds them together." His eyes narrowed as his gaze sharpened, exacerbating his ferocious intellect. "Months ago, I talked to Gabe about the Igigi. He said that they used the Stone of Utu against the angelic horde, restricting their abilities. That precious stone contained the power of the sun, and unfortunately, I have no such thing, but we have an emerald cave..." He trailed off, thoughts clearly elsewhere.

Harlan regained his attention. "JD, you have harnessed the powers of gemstones in your weapons. Can you use gemstones in a similar way to make one that will destroy Belial's weapons, and diminish his power?"

"I've already considered such a thing, but the eternal flame could help. You know, what has just struck me is that this place is—as Olivia says—a repository of knowledge, but Hermes was an alchemist, too. If you're going to go to the trouble of making such a magnificent place, wouldn't you work in it? I wonder..." He paused, eyes vacant, and then spun on his heel and marched out of the cave.

Harlan rolled his eyes and then ran after him. "JD, I wish you'd finish your damn sentences!"

Olivia started to follow them, but Nahum grabbed her hand and pulled her back to him.

She looked confused. "Aren't we going, too?"

"In a minute," he said, pulling her close and wrapping his fingers in her hair at the nape of her neck. "I want another kiss first."

Twenty-Six

Gabe paced the terrace of their villa in La Calcinaia, a province of Elba where Cavo, the resort beach town, was situated.

Elba was a small island that was very popular with tourists, and Gabe was thankful that they were travelling in February, when tourism was low. Not only were there beautiful beaches and a pretty country-side, but there was also a huge amount of history and many ancient sites on the island, too. They had been able to pick up their accommodation through an online booking site at short notice, and the place was perfect for their needs. It sat on a hilltop with a huge swimming pool and a commanding view of the countryside and surrounding sea. Other villas and hotels were dotted about the hills, and Gabe wondered how close they could be to Jiri.

Darkness had already fallen, despite the fact that it was barely six in the evening, but the pool lights illuminated the paved area next to it. He was preparing to ring Ozan again, the third time he'd tried that day. He vowed this would be the last time. Either Ozan couldn't talk for some reason, or wouldn't because he didn't know Gabe's number. He didn't want to call on Emre's phone. It seemed cruel to offer Ozan hope that he was alive. Perhaps the deaths of the Nephilim who had attacked JD's house had caused major issues. Gabe knew the devastation it would have caused if his brothers had died, but perhaps Jiri's team was not like theirs.

Barak, Estelle, and Lucien had arrived only an hour after them, and all were inside, swapping stories with Ash and Shadow. As for Niel... Gabe checked his watch. He would be in the museum by now, and it would be closed. With luck, he would have hidden somewhere safe. It was pointless to worry about Niel; he could look after himself. Gabe had more pressing needs. Knowing he couldn't put it off any longer, he called Ozan again, running through his rehearsed conversation as he started to pace. Within only a few rings, a deep male voice answered in Italian, his tone short and clipped.

"Hello? Oz speaking."

Gabe was so shocked, he almost stumbled over his words. "Oz, my name is Gabreel, and I was given your number by Emre—don't hang up!"

"Emre? How do know him? Who are you?"

"I'm a Nephilim, like you, and I'm calling to make you an offer."

He didn't answer, and Gabe heard shouts and raised voices in the background.

"Oz! Please, hear me out."

"Wait!"

The background noise diminished, and Gabe imagined that perhaps Ozan was, like him, pacing a terrace on his own. He looked at the stars, paranoid that he might be ambushed, before shaking it off.

"I can talk now," Ozan said quietly, his tone dripping with menace. "I know who you are. You are in the group that is pursuing Belial. You are lucky not to be standing in front of me, or I would kill you for what you have done."

"I didn't kill Emre, if that's what you mean. I wasn't there."

"He is dead because of you."

"He attacked my friends, not the other way around. They defended themselves."

"If you hadn't started this stupid hunt, they would all be alive!"

"And hundreds or thousands of others would be killed by Belial's poison."

"Emre was my brother. You know the way of the Nephilim. Have you called to gloat?" His voice was hard, but Gabe detected a trace of tiredness. Of regret.

"No," Gabe said softly, "I have called to make an offer. He and all of the others are dead because of Belial and Jiri and their stupid need to destroy. You have been recruited to a cause that yokes you to them and stifles your independence. You know I'm right."

"I know that as a member of the House of Belial, that it is my duty."

"Is it? Or did that end with your death millennia ago?"

"Duty never ends."

"It ended for us when we decided to make our own rules. Many Nephilim did, but you know that."

"Belial is not your father."

"They all had their moments, mine included." Gabe heard the man's heavy breathing over the phone. His grief and anger. "Let us end this by stopping Belial's influence."

Ozan gave a dry laugh. "You speak madness."

"Do I? Or do I actually make sense? What do you and the others get out of this arrangement?"

"Life. Money. Power. The chance to live again. Like you."

"But are you free to do what you want?"

"Of course."

"So, you could leave right now and tell Jiri you want nothing to do with this?" Ozan didn't answer, and Gabe continued. "Or are you a soldier again, deployed to go wherever you're needed? I bet Emre didn't have a choice yesterday."

"We know the risks."

"You seriously see that there is a point to this? Does this make you happy, to know that you are spreading Belial's madness? That already happened once, a long time ago, but you do not have to play a part in it now. Especially seeing as his power is already diminished." Gabe had absently paced to a low wall while he talked, and he sat on it, overlooking the hills. The lights twinkled in the distance, and he could see boats out at sea; he suddenly felt very weary. "It's a waste of a life. It's wasting mine right now. I'd rather be doing a million other things than fighting you and trying to stop Belial. I think Emre gave us your number, because deep down he felt the same way, and knew you did, too. And others. Am I right?"

"It is not so simple."

"It can be, if we work together."

"Humour me, for a moment, Gabreel. How do you spend your life when you are not chasing us? Is it really a life of peace? You would be bored, I know it."

"I can't lie. We are violent men—it is our nature. There have been occasions when we have had to fight, but only to defend ourselves. We choose to spend our time hunting treasures and helping others, when we're not living in the countryside minding our own business. That's what I want to be doing right now."

"Then do it."

"I can't, not until this is done."

"And this is what you suggest I do? Hunt treasure?"

"You can breed pigs for all I care. It will be your life to do with as you choose. I can promise there is work for men like us. We have skills that not many have, and a paranormal community to welcome us."

"How many men have you?"

"How many have you?"

"So suspicious. All right, I'll start. Now, with so many dead, barely twenty. Jiri, his second-in-command, and the rest of us."

"There are five with me, others that I can call on if needed." Gabe didn't elaborate about witches and fey and enhanced super-soldiers. "How many of you would join us? If we work together, we could end this for good." Gabe hesitated to talk about Venice, but he sensed Ozan was interested in his proposal. "We have already killed many of The Brotherhood in Venice."

"We heard. It is fair to say that Jiri is displeased."

"Just displeased?"

"Fucking furious. He is raging right now with his innermost circle, deciding on what to do about you."

"Then there is no better time to strike."

"It is not that easy. It would take time for you to be here."

"It depends where you are. Are you saying," Gabe asked, feeling the tentative beginning of hope, "that you would help us end this?"

"I need to talk to the others who may want to join me. Maybe."

"So Emre was right. You do want out."

He didn't answer, instead saying, "I will call you back. One hour."

"Wait! I need to know where you are, just roughly?" Gabe wanted to finish this tonight. He was sick of it all, and he knew the time to strike was now. He could hear it in Ozan's voice, too.

Ozan was cautious. "I don't think so. Not yet."

"What if I guess?"

"By all means."

"You are on the island of Elba, off the Italian coast."

Ozan swore prolifically. "Emre talked."

"We picked some clues up, too. We're here already. If we attack tonight, while Jiri is angry and irrational, we can finish this quickly."

"Even though he has Belial's jewels? You know their power."

"We have options."

"Enough. I will call you." Ozan ended the call abruptly.

"So," Niel said to Mouse as he hunkered down in the back of a storeroom in almost complete darkness, "this is afterhours in a museum. Fun!"

"It's gets better, I guarantee."

"Good, because frankly, this is tedious."

Mouse smiled, amused. "Keep your voice down. The staff can hang around for hours."

"Even down here? In the bowels of the Earth?"

"Less so, fortunately." She paused, holding her hand up for silence. The light from a narrow window over the door illuminated her eyes, almost as if she had a mask across her face again. She was dressed all in black, as usual. "Guards."

There were two voices, conversational and relaxed as they rattled door handles and moved on.

Niel took comfort in the fact that so far, everything had gone smoothly. They had entered the museum an hour before closing time and wandered the halls and galleries, and occasionally Mouse held his hand, or looped her arm around his elbow. She had smiled playfully and said, "Let's pretend we're lovers."

His loins stirred again, even at the thought. His response had been harsh, though. "I'll pretend, but your nasty habit with a Taser has soured my ardour." A shutter had fallen across her eyes, and he kicked himself for his response. But she had been true to her word. She had accessed a staff door in a crowded corner of a large hall and snuck inside, pulling him along a short corridor and down a flight of steps until they were on the level they were hiding on now. They had passed no one, which seemed like a miracle. She obviously knew her way around well.

They waited until silence fell before Niel spoke again. "How much longer?"

"Another ten minutes. Normally, the guards settle into a routine. They'll come back this way, and then won't return for another hour or so."

Niel adjusted his position, stretching out his legs between tall stacks of shelving. A variety of boxes were stored on them, some were labelled, others were unmarked. "Do you know what's in this room?"

"Fragments of pottery, jars, vases, pots, some animal bones, sculptures, and figurines." She shrugged. "Most of it is uncatalogued, and nothing looks vaguely interesting to me. I picked this room to hide in because it's one of the biggest and the most unorganised. In fact, from what I can tell, most of the rooms on this floor are."

They were two levels below the ground floor. "All from archaeological digs, then?"

"I think so. The lowest level has the most interesting finds. The big ones." Her eyes gleamed.

"Like what?"

"Huge statues, massive stone blocks from digs, half destroyed pillars. Some were donated. I read the inventory when I can find it."

"You really are a little mouse, aren't you? Scurrying into dark corners. How did you get into this line of work?"

"Stealing, you mean?" Niel nodded. She intrigued him, even more so now that he was getting to know her better. "I had a poor childhood and was unattended for hours. It was a fun way to pass my time. And lucrative."

"How come you work for others?"

"Certain people always need a good thief, just like you do."

"But clearly you do get caught, which worries me, or else why do you need multiple passports?"

"It's an occupational hazard. Besides, I've never been truly caught. Just suspected. That's very different. Shush." She held her finger to her lips, and he heard the bang of a door from further down the corridor.

They both fell silent, and Niel used the time to try to feel for Belial's horn, but there weren't any tell-tale whispers or strange hums of power. After another few minutes, the guards returned, and eventually Mouse stood up. "Time to go."

She progressed stealthily to the door and peered into the corridor; satisfied, she stepped out and headed left. "The stairs to the lowest level are this way."

They passed several locked doors, finally reaching a lift with a staircase next to it. They ignored the lift and headed down the stairs. The lowest level was in darkness, and both accessed the torches on their phones.

"It's supposed to be in the end room," Niel said, wondering which end of the corridor that would be. Mouse had run through the layout earlier, but he was slightly disoriented now.

"There are two set of steps down here," Mouse told him. "One at the other end, close to the more populated areas of the museum, and this one. I suggest we try right, away from the steps. That way leads to the big service lift."

"Fine by me." He scanned every door they passed, noting that the place was a warren. Several smaller corridors led off the main one, and his spirits dropped. "This will take hours if the horn isn't where I expect it to be."

"We'll just be methodical," Mouse suggested. "Otherwise, we'll forget where we've covered."

They reached the huge doors of the service lift that opened onto a large, square area. "This is where the biggest pieces are stored," she said, gesturing to the rooms behind them. She accessed her skeleton keys and opened one. "Look."

The beam of the torch showed a large room filled with enormous stone sculptures, broken columns, and what looked to be the remnants of old temples.

"Holy shit," Niel said. "It looks like an ancient site."

"Probably several. Come on."

In a few minutes they reached the end room down a side corridor. There was nowhere to go from there. Mouse opened the door and Niel stepped inside, expecting to feel a blast of power, or something insidious, but still felt nothing.

"Bollocks." The room was a mass of boxes and shelving, and he progressed down them, looking into bigger boxes, and ignoring the rest. "It's not here. I'd feel it anyway, I'm sure."

"Okay," Mouse turned to the door. "I suggest we check every room in this corridor, and then head to the far end of this level. At least then you've checked the end rooms, as your source suggested. Then we work our way from there. We could split up, if you'd like?"

"No. I don't trust the horn, and if we're discovered somehow, it's best we're together."

It didn't take long for them to ascertain that the horn wasn't in their corridor, and with a weary sigh, Niel said, "The other end it is, then."

Twenty-Seven

arlan watched the last of the local police leave with Anna, feeling very relieved that Maggie was there to liaise with them.

He'd grown bored of watching JD investigate the central area of the cave, and desperate for fresh air had headed into the grounds for the latest news. There had, not surprisingly, been several reports of noise from the neighbouring houses, and a few reports of fireworks that would be the interpretation of the incandescent angels that attacked them.

"Is that it?" he asked her, as she turned back to him and Jackson.

"For now. They were a twitchy pain in the arse." She rolled her eyes as she pulled her jacket around her. It was another cold and misty day, and JD's grounds were barely visible. It was with the greatest difficulty that they had kept the police out of the marquee. Jackson was responsible for that. He'd flashed his government badge around, which had not impressed the local police at all.

"You two," Harlan said to them, as they headed back to the marquee, "make an impressive power couple."

Jackson exhaled, sounding resigned to the issue. "They didn't like being restricted, but Waylen pulled a lot of strings. It was still tricky, though."

"Fuck 'em," Maggie said with feeling. "No one sees that emerald cave except us. I don't care how much they complain."

"What did Layla say?" Harlan asked. She had arrived much earlier, when he'd been with JD.

"She'll do the autopsies on the Nephilim. She's quite pleased, actually, having obviously never done one on them before."

Jackson laughed. "It's a strange world we live in." Then his laugh was replaced by a frown as he looked beyond Harlan, pointing to the flower borders by the house. "Is there something in the grass over there?"

Harlan turned. "I can't see anything."

Jackson strode across the grass and other two followed, Maggie almost running to keep up with his long stride.

"There!" Jackson said, triumphantly. "That's a ring."

The ring was battered, its metal dull and the gemstone cracked, but it still exerted a trickle of power. Enough that Harlan could feel it, anyway. Jackson stepped towards it, but Harlan pulled him back. "Don't touch it! It must have fallen from the dead Nephilim."

Maggie's eyes widened with horror. "The one that died in JD's protective field? I thought it was destroyed!"

"If it was that easy," Jackson pointed out, "we'd be throwing them all at the shield. I need something to put it in. It could help JD."

Maggie pulled an evidence bag out of her pocket. "Use this."

"No." Harlan grabbed a stick from the shrubbery. "Use *this*. I wouldn't even touch it through plastic. Just poke it inside and hold only the bag. You two must be able to feel it, too. No whispers, though, which might mean it was affected by JD's alchemy last night."

Maggie nodded. "I feel uncomfortable. Like it's trying to draw my attention."

"It will be interesting to see what Nahum and Olivia think of it," Jackson said. With careful manoeuvring they swept the ring into the bag, and Jackson carried it gingerly in front of him, as if it might explode.

Their find subdued their mood, and when they entered the marquee, Maggie swore. "Herne's bloody horns! This place looks even worse than I remembered."

"JD lost a lot of equipment last night," Harlan observed. They had cleaned the place up, but many of JD's instruments and alembic jars were smashed. Fortunately, his alchemical wheel had survived, although it was covered in blood. "Not that he cares right now. He's too caught up in there, especially since he's discovered the map room."

Jackson cocked his head. "A map room? You didn't mention that."

"It's hardly a conversation to have with the police around. He thinks that there are instructions to find a hidden laboratory in there."

Maggie frowned as she led the way down the cave's long entrance passage. "What makes him think that?"

"The fact that so much information is in there, and that Hermes was an alchemist. I see his point. You'd want your lab close to all the knowledge. It's like being in the midst of a vast library or museum. He thinks the six-pointed star is the key."

Jackson stopped. "Can you feel something? Like a hum?"

"You can't feel a hum!" Harlan pointed out as he and Maggie stopped, too.

"You know what I mean. It's like the air is vibrating. Like there's a giant beehive somewhere."

"That's a really weird suggestion."

Maggie scowled. "If he's unleashed killer bees somehow, I'll never fucking forgive him. Fucking lunatic."

Harlan increased his pace, curious to see what the noise was about. "I applaud your imagination, guys, but surely not even JD is that nuts. And he's a genius, Maggie, not a lunatic."

Despite his reassurances to the others, Harlan couldn't help but feel trepidatious as they entered the cave. The humming sensation became more insistent, a dull throb, like a pulse. *Had JD released power, somehow?* Knowing that Nahum and Olivia were inside too, Harlan increased his speed, suddenly terrified at what he might find. However, when they reached the centre of the cave by the eternal flame, all three stopped dead in their tracks, eyes wide.

"What the hell has JD done now?" Jackson said, breathless from shock and the run.

The six-pointed star in the centre of the floor had risen out of the ground by about three metres on metal struts, leaving a gaping hole beneath it. Harlan stepped warily to the edge and saw stairs leading down to a large room, most of which he couldn't see, with more alchemical symbols inscribed in the floor, all arranged around the base of the flame. JD, Nahum, and Olivia were exploring the space.

"Herne's hairy balls, JD, you were right," Harlan said as he reached the bottom step. The chamber reached under the main floor by some distance, a dizzying number of symbols everywhere, and lots of tables filled with alchemical paraphernalia.

"Holy shit in a bucket." Maggie breathed out the words in a rush. "A lab?"

"Hermes's own, it seems," Olivia said, eyes sparkling. "I mean, find of the millennium, right?"

"I should think so," JD said as he handled some alembic jars. "There's still no sign of how the flame came to exist, though."

The flame's base was in the centre of the lower level, a round stone table encircling it, with a space for access. Close by was a three-legged stand holding a huge crucible. Harlan blinked as he tried to take it all in. It looked as if Hermes had just stepped outside, much as it appeared on the upper level, and Harlan couldn't help but wonder what other things the cave could be hiding. It was like a Russian doll. If anything, JD looked wilder than ever. His groomed beard and hair were dishevelled, and his flowing shirt was creased and stained with tea and ink.

"When I left you," Harlan said, studying the room in disbelief mixed with a degree of dread, "none of this had happened! How did you do it?"

"The map room, dear boy. It's the key to everything. After you all became bored and left me to it, I found the lock to opening this. The surrounding columns held the information, but I didn't fully understand it. Then something I read in the map room unlocked it all. There was a series of alchemical triggers I had to perform. Once I did that, this place revealed itself." He swept his arms wide, "It's the key to stopping Belial."

"How?"

"By removing his influence from his jewellery. Maybe all of it."

"Speaking of which," Jackson said, holding out the plastic bag, "look what I found in the garden."

JD's eyes lit up and he swooped on Jackson like a magpie on gold.

"Not so fast!" Nahum scooted in front of him, taking the bag from Jackson. "You didn't touch it, I hope?"

"Nope. I did not wish to end up possessed by Belial. Although, we suspect its power is muted."

JD bustled around Nahum. "Let me see!"

Nahum held it high out of reach. "No!"

His hands flew to his hips. "I just want to look."

"And that's all!" Nahum lowered it, and they all crowded around. "I think you might be right, Jackson. It does feel less powerful."

Harlan felt a little aggrieved. He had pointed all that out, not Jackson. "No whispers, right?" he added.

Olivia was behind Nahum, almost using him as a shield, but she nodded in agreement. "No whispers."

JD clenched his hands, a maniacal gleam in his eye again. "That means that I'm already on the right track. Good. I need to experiment—with your help, Nahum." He pointed to the floor that was inscribed with alchemical symbols. "Do you notice anything?"

Harlan frowned. "I see a lot of symbols."

JD tutted as everyone looked confused. "The patterns?"

"It looks," Jackson suggested, "geometrical."

"Just one design, or many?" He tapped his foot impatiently. "Use your eyes! God's pox, you all walk around with your eyes shut! The world works in harmony. There are patterns everywhere. One of the keys to life. Beneath our feet, many of these patterns, geometric nuggets of wisdom, are laid out and interlinked. It is a well of knowledge!"

"It is?" Harlan asked, his head already aching.

"Sort of like your wheel of correspondences?" Olivia asked.

"Far more complex. I have worked with geometric designs, obviously, but this is a work of brilliance. And have you noticed what the designs are made up with?"

"Looks like precious metals," Nahum said.

"And?" JD had become a mad professor. "Use your eyes!"

"Gemstones," Maggie said, frowning at the floor. "And some of them are pretty big."

"Exactly. We are standing on an infinite web of power that feeds *that*!" JD pointed to the eternal flame.

Harlan could see it now. If he squinted, it helped him see the interlinked circles and geometric shapes. He crouched down to examine the design in greater detail, and saw fine metal grooves. "JD, do these move?"

"What?" Jackson asked. "The floor?"

"Yes, I believe they do." JD started striding around the room again. "It's just a matter of finding the key."

"Another one?" Olivia asked, hands on hips as she watched JD. "This is insane! I don't understand how you can understand all of this already!"

"Harlan, tell her!" JD demanded, now completely sidetracked.

"Me?" Harlan wasn't sure whether to be flattered or annoyed. "Well, JD has been studying this for five centuries, Liv. He's a genius. Especially a mathematical genius. Geometry is math."

JD puffed up like a strutting pigeon. "Exactly. I am what used to be called a savant. Mathematics are easy to me. It's order and purity, and so much more. Like the elements, it's the root of all life."

"No wonder I fucking hate maths," Maggie complained. "What are you looking for? Can we help?"

JD didn't answer, instead focussing on the area around the eternal flame. After studying the ground for a few moments, he pressed his foot on a large, round gemstone, and a section of the floor started to move. Harlan leapt back, and Nahum pulled Olivia out of the way.

"Bloody hell," Jackson said crossly. "You should warn us."

JD was unperturbed. "I wasn't sure it would work. I'm wondering if there are walkways through all this." The section of floor continued to move, rearranging the circular table, and swinging the three-legged stand over the eternal flame, including the large crucible. "Ah, good. I was hoping that would happen. I suggest," he said, looking up at all of them, "that you leave me to it. I'll work it out better if I'm uninterrupted. You, Nahum, need to get your brothers to bring the jewels here. I think I know how to release them from Belial's grip. Or I will when I practise on *that* one."

"All of them?" Nahum had tipped the ring into his palm, but now he looked up, shocked.

"Why not?"

"I'm not sure I like that idea, JD. It's a long drive. If the other Nephilim come back..."

JD turned to him, lips pursed. "But it's all in a spelled box, right?"

"Yes, but—"

"Then it's fine."

"It really isn't. If Jiri and his bloody team are watching the house, they could pounce on them."

"I doubt it. They will have gone to lick their wounds. Besides, you said they didn't know where you live. "

"I don't think they do, but we didn't think they'd attack us here, either!"

"Do you want this to be over?"

"Yes, of course…"

"Then get them here. Now!"

"Are you saying you could do this tonight?"

"I thought you said the sooner the better? Aren't Gabe and your other brothers about to fight Jiri?" JD's foot was tapping the ground again, and Harlan wanted to throw something at him when he was in this mood.

Nahum remained calm. "Yes, they hope to."

"So, no time to waste!"

"But," Harlan interjected, "don't you need to experiment, or practise? Or just make sure you know what the hell you're doing?"

"Harlan, you blistering nincompoop, what have you just told Olivia? I have been studying alchemy my entire life. I am not coming at this blind! And this place offers me all the tools! I can do it. I know I can. Are you sissying out now?"

"Will there be consequences?" Harlan stepped closer, refusing to be intimidated by JD.

"To us, probably not. To Belial, yes. At least I bloody well hope so!" He looked at the group's uncertain expressions. "Well? Do you want to just sit around and twiddle your thumbs?"

"JD," Olivia said, laying her hand on his arm, "what you're proposing is big. We hoped that it would happen—we just didn't expect it so soon. All of this is incredible. I feel like I'm in a fairy story, or Aladdin's cave. It's the speed of everything that is so unnerving. You have to remember that we're not as brilliant as you."

JD liked Olivia far more than he did Harlan, and his expression softened. "Sorry. I know, but this is tremendously exciting. This is an alchemical playground for me, and it's exactly what we need. The important question that you must ask yourselves is whether you trust me, because there's no way that you will understand anything of what I will do." He stared at each one of them in turn. "I'm on your side, you know that. I helped you destroy the count. I will help you do this, too. And then," he grinned unexpectedly, "I wish to be left alone for months so that I can study this place properly, without interruption. Does that sound fair enough?"

"Well, I trust you," Jackson said, "and you're right, I have no idea what the hell any of this does. However, I'll help you in any way possible."

The rest of the group agreed with him, and Harlan smiled. "You're a mad old bastard, JD, but you're our mad bastard. I'm in."

"Wait!" Nahum demanded. "You can't handle the jewels. Belial will possess you. I won't allow it."

"Then you will have to help me. I have no intention of being possessed, thank you very much!"

All eyes swung to Nahum. He sighed, and then reached for his phone as he headed for the stairs. "I'll call them."

JD wafted his hands at them. "Shoo! Everyone else out, too. But be ready for my instructions!"

Harlan was the last one up the stairs, and he took a last look at JD exploring his new workshop. *What the hell were they getting themselves into?*

Shadow studied her brothers. She had rarely seen them so tense, but this wasn't any ordinary meeting they were waiting on. It was a meeting with Ozan. The Nephilim had phoned Gabe, and they had arranged to meet at a neutral location.

They were on the terrace, scanning the surrounding area, and checking their weapons. Shadow wished Niel was with them. She had absolute faith in everyone there, but Niel was a useful addition to the team.

"I suggest," Shadow said, "that only Gabe and I go. If it's a trap, then at least we won't be caught. Not that they'll catch me, of course. I am fey."

"Being fey," Estelle said with a bite to her voice, "will only get you so far."

"But I'm your secret weapon." She knew that statement would irritate Estelle, and although they had come to a truce, she couldn't resist teasing her. "Belial does not see me, and his tokens have no power over me." She tapped her long bow. "Plus, I have this. I can stay far enough away so that I am not seen, but still be close enough to be deadly if Gabe is compromised."

Barak shook his head. "I still think we should watch from above, but we'll keep our distance. I bet he'll have backup, too."

Gabe nodded. "Yes, he probably will. But just Barak. The rest of you stay here—including you, Ash."

"If you're not back within an hour, I'll come looking for you," Ash promised, "and I won't spare anyone if you're hurt."

"Where are you meeting?" Lucien asked.

"There's an old, ruined fortress on a hill, in the east," Gabe said, pointing across the dark landscape. "We meet there. You can't miss it, apparently, and I've looked it up on the map. We'll meet in front of it."

Estelle pointed at Shadow. "Where will you be?"

"Either on the roof, or in the trees. We'll assess it once we're there. Sound good, Gabe?" Shadow had no intention of giving Ozan any leeway, either. "If he steps a foot out of place, or you're surrounded, I'll take them all out."

"He won't. I could hear it in his voice. He wants an end to this, too. It sounds like others do too, but he didn't want to commit until he'd met me, which I understand. I want to meet him, too." Gabe rolled his shoulders, checked his weapons, and called Shadow over. "Let's do this."

In seconds, Shadow had wrapped herself around Gabe, legs around his waist, her sword in her scabbard, and her long bow slung across her back. He dived off the terrace, swooping down the hill before rising on a current of air. Barak followed them.

"You seem different, Gabe," she said, lips close to his ear. "Worried."

"I'm over all this, that's all. I want to spend time with you. Proper time, in which we're not killing people."

"Forever?" That sounded appalling.

He laughed. "Do you think just treasure hunting will fill your excitement void?"

"I suppose so. As long as you are with me, I can handle anything. I think it would probably be nice not to be fighting for a while."

"Good. There it is," he said, changing the subject abruptly.

She twisted in his grip and spotted the ruined building down below. A large courtyard was in front of it, partially surrounded by a stand of trees. "Put me down by the trees. I can shelter in the branches."

"Let me circle for a moment more."

Shadow spotted Barak hanging back, much higher than they were. In the opposite direction, she saw another winged figure. "I think I spot Ozan."

"Me, too."

Gabe angled around and down, the wind whistling through his wings, and he landed at the rear of the yard. Shadow nimbly unwrapped herself and kissed him quickly before heading into the trees. She took a moment to check her surroundings, back to a tree trunk, wary of anyone who might have had the same idea as them. Nothing moved, and she scrambled into the lowest branches, ensuring she had a good view of the front of the fortress, her bow loaded and ready.

Gabe stood in the centre of the courtyard, and within a few moments another Nephilim landed close by. In the far distance, a second Nephilim hovered on the air. Not Barak. Ozan, too, had brought back up.

Gabe focussed on Ozan. Like all Nephilim, he was tall and muscular, and he wore his dark hair long. It reached well past his shoulders, and he had braided part of it, so it was pulled back from his face. Like Gabe, he was Middle Eastern, and his wings were dark in this light. Gabe could not detect any sign of the power of Belial's jewels now. It was odd to be seeing another Nephilim besides his brothers. He hadn't thought it possible. Part of him was glad. There should be more of them. It was an abomination that so many of them had died.

Both kept a wary distance from each other, and Gabe called over to him, his voice loud in the still night air. "Ozan, I presume. I am Gabreel Malouf."

"Ozan Bakir." He glanced up above to the distant figure of Barak. "I see you brought another."

"As did you. I understand why. I hope you bring good news."

"You are committed to doing this, tonight?"

"I am committed to this any night. If you refuse to help, then we will be enemies, and I will find out your hideout one way or another. If I'm honest," Gabe said, stepping closer to Ozan, "I would rather not fight at all. It is as I said on the phone. I am tired of this, but equally I cannot let Belial continue to spread his madness."

"There are many in our House who will not know how to live without Jiri or Belial, and that is the simple truth of it."

"But there are others who feel the same way as you."

"Yes. There are six of us who want this to end. However, there are another dozen who do not." There was pain in Ozan's gaze, and now that they were closer, Gabe could see scars on his arms and chest. It was rare for Nephilim to scar. Those injuries must have been bad.

"Then the numbers are evenly matched."

"Jiri always wears Belial's ring, as does his own second-in-command, Pirro. They will use his power without hesitating. You know the consequences."

"Only too well." He wished he had some of the jewels with them, and cursed his weird moral decision not to carry them. Although, it was out of a sense of self-preservation, too. A need to hide from Belial. "Who were the Nephilim who wore his tokens yesterday?"

"Karim was one, Mikal another lieutenant. Mikal's death whilst wearing Belial's token was unexpected. It has caused much unrest. No one believed that it could happen. Or, in fact, that the team Jiri sent could die, The Brotherhood could be attacked so effectively, and the list of jewels discovered and stolen. Jiri has already instructed that all his jewels are to be moved again. You have caused havoc."

Gabe cursed under his breath. *Of course they were moving the jewels.* There would be no easy retrieval of all of them. He should have expected that. *Fool.*

Ozan stepped closer, examining Gabe as if he was hiding something. "I am as surprised as them. The Brotherhood has hid effectively for years, until you made it your business to find them. How did you destroy Mikal and my brothers? What weapons do you have?"

"I can't explain how Mikal was killed. The man we work with is a genius. As for the others, my brothers are hardened warriors. We have had many fights recently. It has honed our skills."

"While we have languished and fought only each other, not thinking that we would be fighting anyone as powerful as another Nephilim." *That explained a lot*, Gabe thought. It was what Nahum and Barak had suggested might be the cause. "But do you have more of that weapon? I ask," he explained as Gabe hesitated, "because it is that which swings us to help you. For the first time in a long time, we can see a way out of this. There is no way that we can walk away otherwise."

Ozan was a strong and powerful Nephilim, but there was no doubt that he was worried. Fearful, even. No wonder he wanted to meet

Gabe. If he didn't believe him, he would walk away. "Yes, we have smaller versions of these weapons. They are very powerful. I don't know if they could kill Jiri once he summons Belial's power, but it's possible. And there are other options." *Like bombs.*

Ozan took a sharp intake of breath. "Then it is true. This could work."

"I take it that you are not allowed to wear Belial's tokens?"

Ozan gave a dry, mirthless laugh. "No. Jiri rules by fear, like in the old days, and he is paranoid. He does not trust us, and with good reason. I would absolutely kill him. But I hide it well, as do the others. We bide our time, and that time is now."

Silence fell as Gabe contemplated his offer. The wood was quiet, and he trusted that Shadow watched them. Barak circled overhead, opposite to the other Nephilim, and it seemed as if the world hung on his decision. The ancient fortress that had no doubt witnessed many battles would now witness once more a pact between warring Houses. But Gabe trusted Ozan. He could see Ozan's need to rebel and find freedom, but he was just as worried at the prospect of betrayal. However, there would be no better time with Jiri angry and irrational, and weakened by the knowledge that he could actually be defeated.

"Agreed." Gabe stepped forward, hand outstretched. "Let us shake on this and plan our strategy."

"But there is one more thing you should know," Ozan said, gripping Gabe's hand between both of his own. "There are women at the villa. Human women. Playthings that he has...*acquired* in recent months, despite some of our protestations."

Gabe knew exactly what that meant, and his anger intensified. "Then I'll save them, too."

Twenty-Eight

As soon as Niel stepped into the dusty and neglected room at the end of the narrow corridor, he knew The Horn of Desolation was in there.

"Keep back," he warned Mouse. "It's here."

"Oh!" She followed him inside and shivered. "I feel it. It's like there's a presence here. A ghost."

"Ghosts are far preferable," he said, weaving through the crowded metal stacks full of boxes. It was clear no one had been in this room for a while. Dust lay across all the surfaces, eddies of it swirling around as he walked. He ignored it all, drawn to the horn like iron to a magnet. Despite his warning, Mouse kept following him. "I said to keep away."

"I can't. I have to leave here with you, and I need to know what we're dealing with." She looked up at him, a challenge in her eyes, a slight pout to her full and very kissable lips. "I'm not a wilting flower, Niel, despite my size."

"I'm well aware of that." He pushed his desires aside, annoyed that he still liked her despite the fact she had tasered him, and followed the trace of... *What?* It wasn't power, not like the hum the jewels gave off, or the insidious whispers. It was far subtler. An effect on his mood. It made him wary, suspicious, and paranoid.

A large box on a high, top shelf beckoned, and he clambered up the metal shelves, able to brace himself on the opposite shelving system, since the path between them was so narrow. He pulled the box towards him, noting it's weight. If the horn was as big as the box suggested, it would be too big to carry it out in his backpack.

"Pass it to me," Mouse instructed.

"It will squash you."

"Niel, it's a horn, not an anvil!"

"Be careful!" He handed it to her, still supporting much of the weight, but she helped enough to enable him to scramble down again. "Right, let's see what it looks like."

While Mouse held both of their phone torches, Niel used his blade to unseal the wrapping on the battered box. Inside was a nest of packing material, and he dug into it with his fingers, finally feeling the horn inside. It felt cold to the touch, almost like ice, and as he lifted it free, the precious metals that decorated it glittered in the light. The horn was, as he suspected from the size of the box, larger than he'd initially expected. It was about three feet in length, but the flared bell was narrower than described. It curved like a scimitar, and the entire length of it was decorated with precious metals in a curling design, inlaid with gemstones. The horn's material was thick, what little of the surface he could see, polished to a glossy finish. At least, most of it was. A section was still covered in a reddish dirt, and it seemed the museum had abandoned their attempt to clean it.

His feeling of unease intensified, and he looked over his shoulder, half thinking someone was watching him, even though he knew no one had followed them into the room.

"Ugh!" Mouse said, nose wrinkling in disgust. "It looks amazing, but it smells funky."

"Does it? I can't smell a thing." He lifted it to his nose, scenting at first only old bone and packing material. And then he detected a trace of musk in the binding of leather near the mouthpiece. Niel had a moment of complete dizziness, and he staggered back, assaulted by images of battle and bloodshed, and the keening war cry of Nephilim.

"Niel!" Mouse grabbed his arm, and her touch returned him to the present. Her pupils were large in the light, and she look scared. "What happened?"

"A flashback, that's all."

"It must have been intense."

Niel didn't answer; instead, he put the horn down and breathed deeply, trying to find fresh air, but only finding dust and mustiness. Finally, when he felt steadier, he asked, "You said it smelled funky. Like what?"

She gave a tentative sniff again. "Smells rotten. Like a rotting carcass, or...death, actually."

"Well, this horn has certainly been responsible for that. Do you feel odd?"

Mouse shrugged, looking around the room for a brief moment. "A little unsettled, as if we're being watched." She stretched her fingers towards the horn, but Niel grabbed her wrist.

"No! You can't touch it. I don't know what effect it will have." He pulled his backpack off his shoulder, but it was obvious that the horn was too big to fit in it. "Bollocks!"

"That is a rather large horn."

"Yeah, well, Belial always liked to boast. I can't exactly walk out the front door with it. Neither do I wish to sit in this room all night with it, either." His feeling of unease was growing, and he knew Mouse's was, too. She looked jumpy, and kept glancing over her shoulder. It wasn't just unease, either. He felt the creeping urge to be violent. To smash things, or people... He had to get out of this room. The confined atmosphere was making it worse. He had expected humans to be affected by it, but thought he would be okay. He shoved the horn back in the box and headed to the door.

"Where are we going?" Mouse asked, running after him in alarm.

"You are staying here, as planned, and leaving in the morning. I am finding another way out of here."

"No! I'm coming with you."

He quelled the urge to snap at her, internally cursing Belial. "It's dangerous. I can feel this damn horn's effects already, and it will intensify. You don't want to be around me then."

Mouse swallowed, and he knew how he must appear to her. He had a wild look in his eye already, he just knew it, and his jaw was clenched. Despite that, she said, "Actually, I think you need someone to keep you on an even keel. That's me."

"That's stupid. You're already twitchy, and you'll only get worse. The men who found this and the jewels killed each other, or themselves."

"But you are a Nephilim, and I trust you. I will remind you of that, and I'll keep you grounded, too. You can do the same for me." She stepped close, hands gripping his arms, eyes locked with his. "I can already see that you should not be alone with this thing."

"I can be a very dangerous man."

"I know, but you won't want to kill innocents. You need me. Besides, you hired me for the whole job. It's not over yet."

"I'm okay with that."

"I'm not."

Niel wanted to argue and shout, but knew she was right. He did need her around. He was reasonably sure he could control his violent urges, but with Mouse at his side, he'd try even harder.

He nodded. "All right. Any exit suggestions? I was thinking we should head up to the ground floor, and I'll just smash a door down and leg it."

"So sophisticated!"

"As long as we get out with this thing, I don't care!"

"I have a better idea that will be a lot stealthier. But it's also dark and damp." She pointed downwards. "There are extensive ancient water cisterns in Istanbul—huge, stone arched chambers and waterways. Most of them are abandoned now, but some are open to the public. This museum sits over one of them. I suggest we leave that way."

"Why the hell didn't we come in that way?"

"Because the entrance is impossible to get through from the other end. It's chained and padlocked on this side, and it's...tricky. I know because I checked once, years ago. You'll see."

"My way sounds easier."

"You're a smash and grab kind of guy, aren't you? No. You'd set alarms off, men will come after us, and it will create waves. We do this my way. That's why you hired me. And we have time. We found this pretty quickly, really."

He grudgingly had to admit she made a lot of sense. "Fine. Lead the way."

"The access is in the centre. I think I can remember which room." She pulled her mask over the lower half of her face again, eased the door open, and immediately frowned. "I hear something. Voices on the main corridor. I think the lights are on at the end, too."

She snuck out, padding silently up the narrow hallway, Niel right behind her. He felt like a giant in comparison. Carrying a backpack and a box wasn't helping.

"Well?" he whispered.

She turned to him with a look of resignation. "They're bringing in a delivery through the service lift."

"Now?"

"I told you, they work at night sometimes." She turned and glanced down the main corridor again. "Okay, only the area around the lift has lights on, and it's a good distance from here. We need to head about halfway down, and then duck into one of the side passages."

"One of them? You mean you don't know which?"

She glared at him. "I'll know it when I see it." She looked down the corridor again. "Okay, let's go now. They're out of sight."

He followed her as she sprinted down the corridor, quickly ducking into another passage just as a group of half a dozen men entered the big square area by the lift. Most boarded the lift, but one remained behind, returning to the room they had exited. Niel presumed it was the big one that Mouse had shown him earlier.

That meant only one thing. They were coming back.

Mouse didn't speak, she just continued, examining each corridor briefly before finally turning down one, just as the lift doors opened again. Niel saw the men wrestling a huge statue inside on a wheeled dolly before he followed her. He waited, wondering if he'd hear shouts or evidence of pursuit, his agitation and worry abnormally exaggerated because of the horn, but fortunately he hadn't been spotted, and he found Mouse entering another storeroom.

"This is the one, I'm sure."

He waited by the door while she searched the room. It was similar to the others they'd seen, containing big cabinets and long shelving. In here, though, there weren't any boxes. Instead, a range of textiles and paintings in frames were stacked haphazardly. *What a waste.* So much art going unseen. He should just smash it all. *That would teach them.*

Niel gasped in shock at his thoughts. *Damn Belial.* He was certain that being surrounded by old objects was intensifying his experience, but perhaps that was just stupidity. It really shouldn't make any difference at all.

"Niel! Over here!" Mouse summoned him with a raised whisper, and he hurried to her side.

A large, round metal cover was set into the floor, a padlock securing it in place. It was also partially covered by a long worktable. No wonder they couldn't have entered that way.

"I'll unlock the padlock," Mouse said, already on her hands and knees, lock picks in her hand, her face covering removed once more, "while you move the table."

Preparations complete, Niel lifted the heavy cover with a grunt of exertion, and edged it aside. Below was blackness, and the pungent scent of damp welled up to them. He flattened against the floor, gripped the edge, and peered inside, and as his eyes adjusted to the light, saw the reason why it was so hard to enter.

"For fuck's sake, Mouse," he hissed, "we're thirty feet off the ground!"

"I know." She crouched opposite him. "There used to be access, a ladder, I think; however, this cistern was dug very deep, and it's been built on over the centuries. Now there's just a big drop, but seeing as you can fly—"

"How do you know that there's a way out? It could be our tomb!"

"I found a way in through the other end. We're actually very close to one of the cisterns that's open to the public. We can exit to the street that way."

Niel didn't speak as he once again assessed the space. Below, he could discern the inky sheen of water, and enormous stone columns emerged from it to support a vaulted roof. There was plenty of space to fly, at least in the area he could see. The hatch he was looking through was set into the roof at the side of the room, and he could see evidence of where ladders had once been fixed to the wall.

He looked up at her, suddenly amused at the situation. "Are you sure you want to do this?"

"I want to get out without being chased or arrested. Yes!"

"You're plucky, I'll give you that. Potentially insane, but that works, too." And at least he'd have an excuse to hold her again. "Okay, I can't get in this hatch with my wings visible, which means I'm going to have to hang from the rim, then extend them. There is no way I can carry the box and you, so the horn will have to be wedged into my backpack. You will hand me the pack, then you have to clamber down and wrap yourself around me. You face me, and wrap your legs around my waist. Then you can make sure the backpack doesn't fall off."

"I have to hold the backpack and you?" She looked down at the drop and then at him again. "That's a big fall if lose my grip."

He smirked, feeling like he was getting his own back for the Taser incident. "Don't you trust me?"

"Yes, or I wouldn't have suggested it!"

"But the reality of it is becoming clear, right? Don't worry, I'll hold you. Whether I keep holding you when I think of what you did to me is another matter."

Her lips twisted with annoyance, and she jabbed him in the shoulder with her finger. "I told you, I did it to save you! When will you listen to me? I could wait here, let you exit in a blaze of fucking glory upstairs, and sneak out tomorrow, but no, I'm here, helping!"

That poke in the shoulder was enough to give him a thrill of desire again. *Oh yes, he liked Mouse a lot*. She was feisty, and the urge to kiss her was strong. Plus, she'd apologised plenty of times, so maybe it was time to move on. Time to flirt, instead. "You're just wanting to wrap yourself around my bare chest again. I get it. I look great naked."

A gleam of amusement flashed in her beautiful, almond eyes. "Perhaps we should talk about that another time."

"I like the sound of that." He leapt to his feet, stripped his jacket and t-shirt off, and then pulled the horn from the box again. Its touch slithered over his skin, but he ignored the sensation and quickly wrapped it in his clothes and stashed them in his backpack. He couldn't zip it closed completely, and the wrapped horn stuck out of the top, but it was reasonably secure. "Pass it to me when I'm ready."

He clambered into the open hatch, fingers gripping the rim, muscles straining as he hung from it. He unfurled his wings carefully, angling slightly backwards so he was almost horizontal as he looked up at Mouse's pensive face, because his wings extended above his head.

This was far trickier than he'd expected. He couldn't even use his wings to brace himself. The columns weren't close enough.

"You're going to have to wear the backpack," he told her.

She didn't question it, instead securing it tightly. "What now?"

"Lower yourself onto me, and grip very tightly."

"This is insane. You're taking up most of the space."

"Too late to change your mind now, so please, just get on with it! And just so you know, I'm going to drop pretty quickly."

Mouse rolled over the hatch, wrapped her arms around his neck while her legs braced on the rim, and said, "I can't get my legs in!"

By now, despite his considerable strength, the weird angle was proving too tricky to maintain. "Hold on tight, and when you can, wrap your legs around my waist."

Her face was inches from his, her eyes wide with genuine terror. He dropped, leaning backwards to allow her legs to slide through the gap, and they plummeted through blackness together. His arms wrapped around her body, clutching her to his chest as she screamed shrilly in his ear. With a flap of his huge wings, he suspended their fall, and she tucked her legs up like a gymnast, gripping his waist.

"Fucking fuckery!" she said, breath hot against his ear. "That was insane."

He adjusted his grip, so that his arms were wrapped around her and the backpack, the swell of her breasts tight against his chest. "It's okay. I've got you. Are you ready? It's going to get twisty."

Fortunately, the columns were set far apart, and he weaved through them, heading towards a tunnel that was lower than the vaulted roof. The columns seemed sturdy enough, but moss lay thick in places.

"How can you see where you're going?" she asked, her breath coming in quick, sharp bursts. "This is terrifying."

"I can see in the dark. Don't worry. I'm aiming for a tunnel lower down—is that the right direction?"

"Yes." She steadied as she talked. "I think you can fly through it. There is water on the ground, but it's shallow. It leads to another cistern, just like this, and then there's another tunnel that's gated at the far end. That connects with the next cistern that opens to the public."

"And you travelled through here on foot? On your own? I'm impressed."

"You don't know half of what I get up to."

"I'd like to," he said, lips brushing her ear.

She didn't answer, but she seemed to settle more closely to him, legs tightening around his waist. Then again, she was hardly likely to pull away.

He flew through the tunnel, which was just wide enough to accommodate his wings, eventually soaring into the next cistern. It was as stunning as the last one. It seemed incredible that humans had designed such beautiful places that were just meant to be filled with water. He wished he could linger, but focussed instead on getting them out of there. When they finally reached the gated entrance, he dropped to his feet, finding that the water came up to his knees.

"Let me open the lock again." Mouse slid down him, her breath catching. "Give me some light."

He took the pack from her, and in a few more moments they were through and Niel relaxed. He'd become used to the horn, and the effects seemed to diminish. Perhaps it was the circumstances, and he suspected it wouldn't last, but he'd enjoy it while it did. He took a moment to orientate himself, noting how this cistern had been cleaned, and walkways erected. Columns stretched ahead, and he couldn't see the way out.

"Where now?"

She pointed across the chamber using her torch. "That way. There are steps up to street level. We'll have to break out of the main entrance, but it opens on to the road, and then we can return to the hotel. But first, I want to show you something."

Rather than fly, they walked, using torches to highlight the details, and a peculiar feeling of peace descended over him. They were almost out. He'd secured the horn, avoided pursuit—for now—and he was with Mouse. And neither of them was unduly influenced by Belial yet.

The cistern was huge, and she chatted while they walked, talking about the cistern's history. When they reached the top of the steps, she flicked a bank of switches, and light bloomed through the chamber.

"Herne's horns!" Niel gasped as he took in the colourful, floodlit display. Shades of blue, green, red, and yellow illuminated the columns and the clear water at the bottom. The vaulted roof was also visible. It was breathtaking. "This is incredible."

"They spent years clearing this out. Amazing, isn't it?" Mouse's eyes shone in the light. "It's one of my favourite places in the world. Especially in private. Normally, it's full of people."

"Then I'm happy I get to see it like this, with you."

She smiled up at him. "You've forgiven me, then?"

"I guess I have. Shall we have one last flight while the lights are on?" He secured the pack over his shoulder and opened his arms wide.

"I sincerely hope it's not my last flight ever," she said, wrapping her arms around him again.

He lifted her up so she could slide her legs around his waist again, and he rested his hands on her slender hips, wishing he was cupping her pert bottom instead. He launched off the platform, hearing her breath catch again, and took a slow, circular route through the cavern, wishing he could spend hours with her instead of just minutes. When he finally landed again, his loins were aching with desire.

She didn't jump down straight away, instead extending her arms at full length so she could look at him, and circled back to his earlier question. "Do you really want to know what I get up to?"

"Yes. I want to see more of you—in all ways."

"You barely know me."

"I know. That's the point. I want to get to know you. You intrigue me."

Mouse leaned forward and kissed him, hands on the back of his neck and threading through his thick hair. He pulled her close, turning so that her back was to a stone column, and pinned her to him, kissing her like he hadn't kissed anyone in years, all thoughts of Belial's horn forced into submission. He wanted to drink her in. Actually, he wanted to take her right now on the floor of the chamber, in this place of light and water and stone. Instead, he eased back, both of them breathless.

"I think," she said, lips full, skin flushed, and her pupils wide with desire, "that we should continue this discussion back at the hotel. After one more kiss."

"Done."

Twenty-Nine

"I hope this isn't a set-up," Barak said to Estelle as they approached Jiri's sprawling villa.

It was several miles from their own place, but was high on a hill overlooking the sea. The coast spread below them, the lights of Cavo in the near distance. Ozan was meeting them all on the roof with another couple of Nephilim, and then they would split up to fight the others.

"Gabe is a good judge of character, and so are you. You felt you could trust him. Plus, he wouldn't have told him about the women."

"He would if he thought it would motivate him. It has certainly motivated me." Barak was as furious as Gabe at that news—all of them were, actually. Except perhaps Estelle, whose incandescent rage had settled into cold, determined intent to rescue them all and kill the Nephilim responsible. Barak had eventually been summoned to join the discussion at the ruined fortress, along with Ozan's friend, Nibal. Shadow had remained in hiding. "I believed him, but now I'm second-guessing myself. I know what Gabe saw though, because I saw it too, and we've both seen it too many times in the past. And experienced it, of course. Ozan and Nibal are trapped, and they hate it." He remembered the hollow sense of being unable to control their destiny, and how it ate away at him until he seethed with frustration and impotence. "I felt smothered."

"Much like I did with my father. We are doing them a service, as well as us."

Barak smiled at her words. Estelle was fierce with her enemies. She had a true warrior's soul. Her energy had been skewed in the past. Warped by frustration into taking out her pain on others who did not warrant it, but her balance was returning.

"Don't put yourself at risk, though," he warned. "I want a life with you after this."

"Same goes for me, Barak. Be careful."

He kissed her neck as he flew down to land on the roof of the small, round tower. "Always."

"Liar. If you see Belial's jewels, you ignore them, or I'll fry your balls. And you know I mean it."

They'd had a fierce argument after destroying the Cathar castle, and he wouldn't forget it easily. "Yes ma'am."

He spotted Ozan with Nibal and another two Nephilim, and checking his brothers were close by, they all landed together, Gabe with Shadow, and Ash with Lucien. There was a wary silence as they landed, the two Nephilim they hadn't met before hanging back with worried expressions. They all looked beaten into submission, eyes hard with suspicion, as if this was another trap. All had dark hair, and were very similar in appearance to Ozan.

Gabe stepped forward confidently, hand outstretched to Ozan, and Barak followed suit with Nibal. They needed to settle nerves and instil confidence—as well as assess the others. This was not the ideal time to put their faith in people they didn't know. Shadow hung back as was her way, sweeping the surroundings with her sharp eyes, and looking over the tower roof. It was a big building, all encompassed by a high wall, more fortress than villa. She finally joined them as they were introduced to each other.

"There are a few changes to our original plan," Ozan said cautiously. "Jiri is still with Karim, his lieutenant, in his War Room, as he calls it. A glorified study, really. But following Mikal's death, another Nephilim called Pirro now has Belial's ring."

"So, once more," Barak noted, "there are three Nephilim with tokens now?"

Ozan nodded, and Barak glanced at Gabe and Ash, noting they looked as disappointed as him. Despite the fact that they had lost a ring, Jiri had others, as they suspected. They had planned to approach all the other Nephilim and attempt to sway them to their cause. If that failed, they would have to fight. However, with another ring in the mix, that would be hard.

"Pirro," Ozan continued, "is in the main hall with the rest of our team, and my other two brothers who are with us are there, too. They are organising who to send to Venice. There are still some of The Brotherhood there, and they are deciding where to go from here, and how best to regroup with the survivors. They have every intention of continuing, and of course there are members spread further afield."

"Despite what happened in Venice?" Gabe asked, incredulous.

"Even more so, now," Nibal answered. "Belial, through Jiri, is determined he will not be thwarted. But," his eyes gleamed, "Belial frets and rages, and he takes it out on Jiri. That is why Jiri is so angry. Of course they discuss how to deal with you, but all we have achieved has to be restarted. Belial commands it. He is working on a bigger strategy right now."

"No," Gabe said abruptly. "This ends tonight."

"Jiri will do as Belial commands, and the others will follow."

Gabe squared his shoulders. "Take me to Jiri. I want to discuss it with him. I'm sick of sneaking around."

A ripple of unease ran through the other Nephilim, and Barak wasn't surprised. "Gabe! Are you insane?"

"No." Gabe turned to him. "Perhaps we can reason with him."

"You have clearly," Ozan said, amused, "never met Jiri. To parley signifies weakness, and to set foot inside his War Room will be suicide. You need to persuade him of your intent. Attacking him here, in what he considers his stronghold, will be another blow."

Shadow interrupted. "We need a way to draw them all out and cause maximum confusion. I suggest a bomb at the front door."

"Isn't that more likely," Ash said, "to get them to retreat behind closed doors?"

"No. That will definitely bring them out," Nibal said, "but our brothers must not be harmed."

"Why aren't they with us now?" Lucien asked.

"To listen, to watch. To ensure they all remain in one place. And to ensure the women stay together."

"Where are the women?" Estelle asked, her tone as hard as her eyes. "You need to take me to them."

Nibal studied her. "We didn't expect women would be part of the team. Neither of you are strong enough to fight."

Shadow didn't answer, only rolling her eyes, amused. Barak knew that Estelle did not want to reveal her power until she had to, and he respected that.

Estelle said, "Let me worry about that. Where are the women?"

Nibal glanced at Gabe, as if seeking approval. He said, "I suggest you answer her."

Nibal shrugged. "I will take you to them. They are safe, don't worry."

"Safe is a subjective word. Why isn't anyone keeping watch?" Estelle asked, as she observed their surroundings.

"Because they believe this place is still a secret." Nibal smirked. "Jiri is arrogant."

"Let's get on with this," Barak said, impatient to end it. "We do as we originally planned. Lead us to the room where all the Nephilim are gathered, and we will try to get the others to join us. If not, we fight. Pirro will die first. As for Jiri?" He cocked his head at Shadow, who was fully kitted out with sword, daggers, long bow, bombs, and JD's weapon. "Perhaps bomb his precious War Room."

"My pleasure." She pointed at a Nephilim called Dorian who hadn't spoken yet. "You can take me."

"Then I'm with you," Gabe said to her, clearly still determined to talk to Jiri. "Barak and Ash, you're in the hall with Lucien. Estelle, do you need assistance?"

She shook her head. "No. I just want to make sure they're safe, and then I'll join Barak."

Gabe nodded, then gripped Barak and Ash's arms, reinforcing his message. "Let's try and talk first, get them to come around. Help Ozan make them see sense. Especially if we negate Belial's power! They have nothing to fear, and everything to gain!"

Barak nodded, returning Gabe's strong grip with his own, and wishing he had half of his optimism. "We'll try our best."

Nahum met Eli and Zee at the entrance to the emerald cave. They carried the large, spelled box between them, and placed it down on one of the trestle tables to catch their breath. Anna left them to it with barely a backwards glance.

"An uneventful trip, I hope?" he asked his brothers in greeting.

"Unexpected, but yes, uneventful." Eli's lips were compressed into a thin line with resentment. "I had to dump my date."

"You're always dating, I'm sure she'll recover," Nahum said, smirking. "A new addition to your harem?"

"No. A regular."

"Lovely. I'm sure she's thrilled."

Eli gave him a slow, knowing grin. "Not all of us are a one-woman man. How's that going for you?"

"Just fine."

Eli leaned against a table, arms folded across his chest. "Just fine?

Nahum knew they were winding him up, especially as Zee had a goofy grin on his face, too. He arranged his features to an impassive stare, sure that guilty pleasure was radiating out of every pore. He'd eventually tell them that things had progressed, but not now. He wanted to luxuriate in their privacy for a while. *If Harlan kept his mouth shut.* "Yes. Fine. That's all I have to say on the matter."

"Oh, brother," Zee slapped him on the shoulder. "We'll just have to assess for ourselves. I take it," he cocked his head at the cave's entrance, "that used to be the Emerald Tablet?"

Nahum massaged the bridge of his nose, glad of the change of subject, but knowing it wouldn't last. "Yes. It still is! It's even crazier in there than when we first went in. JD has found the original lab, and it's nuts."

"The actual lab of Hermes Trismegistus?" Zee asked, almost scoffing in disbelief.

"Yes. And in the intervening hours since I called you, he has tested various alignments—I have no idea what to call it other than that—and has replicated the protective dome's effects and blasted Belial's ring again. He's weakened it further." He had already explained some of it over the phone hours earlier. "He's making a few minor adjustments, and then we'll try again."

Zee and Eli were both silent with shock, but Zee recovered first. "Are you saying he can negate Belial's power?"

"He has already weakened it. He's trying to eradicate it completely."

"So, we don't have to be dragons forever?"

"Hopefully not. Not to *his* treasure, at least."

"And what about the other tokens out there?" Eli asked.

"Herne's hairy bollocks! I don't know. Seems like a stretch, but ask JD."

They followed him into the cave, carrying the box between them, and after allowing them a few moments to gasp at their surroundings, he waited for more shock when they saw the lab.

"I must admit," Eli said, when he finally put the box down on the stone table in Hermes's lab, "I really have seen everything now."

Everyone was gathered down there after leaving JD alone for hours. Some had caught up on sleep, Olivia included, but Nahum had continued to explore the cave, trying to ignore the booms that emanated from the lab.

"Guys! Good to see you." Harlan marched over and shook their hands, and Nahum introduced his brothers to Maggie, JD, and Jackson.

"You've brought the box of tricks, then?" Harlan asked, eyeing the box as if it would bite.

"Everything we have," Zee confirmed.

Maggie, normally a stalwart in every situation, eyed up Zee and especially Eli. "Well, you two are a sight for sore eyes. Do you stir up as much shit as your brothers?"

"Sometimes," Eli confessed with a wink.

Nahum rolled his eyes as Eli exuded his normal charm. Fortunately, Olivia didn't seem the slightest bit interested. Instead, she watched Nahum out of the corner of her eye, and every now and again she gave him a teasing, shy smile that was for him alone.

"Whatever!" JD interrupted them. "Open the box. I need to see it all."

"In your dampening field first," Nahum reminded him. JD had set one of the geometric grids up with a protection field. "This packs a powerful punch."

"I really need to feel it first, if I'm to assess it properly." His stare was implacable.

Nahum relented, knowing it made sense, and addressed the humans. "Cover your ears. It will help a little."

Zee flipped the lid, and immediately Belial's power rolled out. Actually, *roll* was the wrong word. It reared up like a jack-in-the-box, and everyone except the Nephilim recoiled. Insidious whispers assaulted them like spears, and Zee quickly snapped the lid shut again.

"Enough?" Nahum asked JD, who looked pale with shock.

He swallowed. "They're more than I expected."

"I did warn you."

JD waved his concerns away. "I had to know." Wrinkling his nose with distaste, JD pointed to a hexagonal area to the right of the eternal flames. "Put it there for now. You all need to stand over there." He pointed to an area on the far side of the lab. "There's a line of pure obsidian. Stand behind it. I have one more test to make on the sample ring."

JD had made several alterations to the lab, and now had his mass of strange, gemstone-powered beams pointed at another octagonal shape laid out on the ground made only of precious metals. The ring they had found in the garden was at the centre, and JD had erected a forcefield around the whole area.

Everyone shuffled nervously back, and Nahum stood next to Olivia, ready to protect her.

"Er, JD," Harlan asked, "is it safe for us to stay?"

"Absolutely. But perhaps," he pointed to a box on the table close to where they stood, "wear those to shield your eyes."

The box contained dark-tinted goggles, and JD pulled a pair out of his pocket and set them over his eyes while the others followed suit. Immediately, the room was plunged into muted colours. Odd fields of energy were visible in different areas of the lab, and the obsidian line presented a dark shield in front of them. Nahum was well out of his depth. Nothing in this room made much sense, and only Jackson seemed to have some knowledge of what JD was talking about.

After a few moments of nervous anticipation, JD activated his beams that were directed at Belial's ring and a corona of light exploded around it, contained within the grid.

"What the actual fuck is that?" Maggie yelled, staggering backward into Jackson. "It's like a frigging bomb went off!"

No one answered, because no one knew, and JD was far too absorbed in his work.

The light swelled and receded, colours radiating with changing intensity as JD manipulated his instruments. For a brief moment, a writhing figure seemed caught in the glow, and then it blinked out as the light pulsed and then vanished completely.

JD whooped. "I did it!"

"Stay here," Nahum told Olivia, before racing after his brothers. He felt deflated, as if more should have happened. "Was that it? Belial is gone?"

JD had entered the grid, and he picked up the warped metal ring with tongs. The gemstone had utterly vanished, and the metal was cracked and charred. "What do you mean, was that it? Have you any idea of the power I used to do this? Yes! He's gone!"

Zee reached forward, plucking the ring from the tong. "Holy shit. He *has* gone. No Belial. JD, you're a bloody genius."

"I know."

Nahum couldn't quite believe it, and he took it from Zee. The ring was completely inert. "How?"

"The right combination of gemstones, set at the correct frequency, a combination of planetary energies, and the right conjunctions on the grid. A certain celestial combination. It's complicated."

Eli was flushed with excitement. "So, you can really do it? You can do the same to those?" He pointed at the box.

"I can indeed. But," JD wagged a finger, "this ring had already been weakened by the immensity of my field around the house. Those have not been. And there are a lot of them."

"So we do them one at a time," Zee suggested.

"Oh, no." JD shook his head, a spark of excitement kindling in his eyes. "We don't want a trickle effect. I thought you wanted to knock Belial off his perch?"

"Yes, especially seeing as Gabe and the others are attacking Jiri's stronghold tonight." Nahum checked his watch, fearful for their safety. "Right now, in fact."

JD rubbed his hands together. "Then let's tackle them all together."

"But will deactivating those affect all the others?"

"If we do it in one big strike, perhaps. Probably." JD nodded with conviction, eyes on the box.

Nahum felt renewed hope surge through him. *This could be the solution to everything...if they didn't bring Belial's fury down on all of them.*

His brothers, however, did not look reassured, and Zee asked JD, "Is it safe?"

"God's balls, no! I suggest we add a couple of extra protective fields, just in case."

Thirty

Gabe rested his hand on his sword hilt, eyeing the door at the end of the first-floor corridor.

"Describe the room's layout," he said to Dorian, who had escorted them.

"It's windowless. The desk is next to the wall on the left, and there's a seating area in the right corner, and a pool table on the right, too. It's a big room."

"A pool table? In his War Room?"

Dorian grimaced. He was leaner than Gabe, but still muscular, his dark hair tied back at the nape of his neck. "It's his private space for him and his lieutenants. He dangles it in front of us as some kind of private club. I want no part of it."

Gabe knew the type only too well. He loathed Jiri already. "And there's definitely only him and one other in there?"

"Yes. Karim, who was at your friend's place last night. He is also furious—and scared. It shook him up, although he hides it well."

"Perfect." Shadow readied her bow, a bomb in her palm. "Then let's rattle them some more with a bomb."

"No," Gabe stayed her arm. "I still want to talk to him."

"Gabe! You're insane. Let's really unnerve him."

"That bomb could kill him."

"I think Shadow is right," Dorian interjected. "Jiri won't negotiate. He's half-possessed by Belial after all these years."

Gabe felt sorry for Dorian, and that was hard to do with Nephilim. They had a presence, and were usually full of confidence. Dorian projected it, but it was a façade. He was over all of it and wanted his time with Jiri to be finished. *And he was scared*, Gabe suddenly realised with a shock. *Jiri ruled by fear*.

Gabe, however, was determined, and although worried about the use of Belial's tokens, he refused to be cowed by the possibility. "I don't care. I'm going in. Shadow, I'll open the door and head inside, but I'll keep out of the door's entrance and leave it wide open. If I come out running, send a bomb in. Dorian, you stay out of sight."

"My pleasure," Shadow said, adjusting her stance. She had become frighteningly efficient at loading her arrowheads with JD's bombs. She had spent weeks perfecting how they were carried.

Gabe marched down the corridor, took a deep breath, and threw the door open. Two big men, brutish in their size, were standing next to the pool table, hands resting on their pool cues, deep in conversation. They were halfway through a game, balls strewn across the table, and the room was low lit. It was obvious who Jiri was. There was a dominance to how he stood, hard eyed, staring at the man who was his lieutenant. *Karim*. Both were olive-skinned and dark-haired, and Jiri's hair was oiled into a long plait. His cleanshaven face was all sharp planes.

Gabe took it all in with one swift glance and stepped inside. "Jiri. It's time we talked."

Both men looked around in shock but recovered quickly, Jiri's face settling into a scowl. "How the hell did you get in?" He looked beyond Gabe's shoulder, but his angle was such that he couldn't see down the corridor, and he gripped his pool cue like a weapon. "No matter. I will find out and kill them—after I kill *you*."

"I want to talk," Gabe said, hand on his hilt, and stepped to the right of the doorway. "You need to walk away from Belial. I can help you do it."

Jiri walked slowly around the pool table, eyes not leaving Gabe's, his prowl like that of a lion stalking its prey. "Why would I want to do that?"

"Because this is another world, Jiri. Belial has no place in it, and you are free to build the life you choose." Gabe kept his eye on Karim, who circled the table in the other direction, watching Jiri as much as Gabe. Both wore gold rings, large emerald gemstones flashing in ornate settings. Gabe could feel their power from across the room.

"I wouldn't be here if it weren't for him. None of us would. I am loyal to my father."

"It's time to grow up and see him for what he is. A bully. You follow his orders like an automaton. Think for yourself for once!"

Jiri never stopped moving as his lips twisted into a smile and his eyes glittered viciously. He oozed danger. "I am thinking for myself, you fool. We have power here, spreading Belial's influence amongst the sheep in this society. I aim to continue our work of cleansing the weak for a long time." His eyes travelled up and down Gabe dismissively. "And you won't stop me."

"We stopped you last night." He switched his attention to Karim, and noted his fear that he tried to hide. "You saw it. Your brothers are dead. Even Mikhal, who drew on Belial's power. His time is over, and so is yours."

"It is not over," Jiri roared, "until I say so. And I say never!" He sprang towards Gabe, his pool cue raised, ready to swing, and Karim did the same. Gabe had expected as much. It was clear that Jiri was a power-crazed bully just like his father. He ran for the door and dived to the side.

An arrow whizzed above his head, and he scrambled to his feet to run up the corridor, looking back over his shoulder. He'd barely made a few paces when the bomb exploded behind him.

Ash entered the large, ground floor living area, one step behind Ozan, with Lucien, Barak, and Samir on either side. A dozen men were gathered in the room, either seated or standing. Some were at the window looking out into the villa grounds, and a couple sat at a large table. The atmosphere was tense.

At first, no one took notice of their entrance, and then a couple looked around and immediately rose to their feet. The movement drew everyone's attention.

Ozan spoke quickly, arms outstretched in a gesture of appeal. "Brothers. I am here to make a proposition. I suggest we leave Belial behind and forge a new life. This can be easy if we choose it to be, even for you, Pirro." He directed this at a Nephilim with high, sharp cheekbones and a clenched jaw.

"And who," Pirro asked, stepping forward with oily grace, "have you brought with you? Our enemy, I presume."

"They are Nephilim who want to live in peace, just as we should, without fearing Belial."

"Yet they are armed, and you have brought them into our home." Pirro's lips curled back. "You have betrayed us, you and Samir, and who else?" His eyes darted around the room. "Where are Nibal and Dorian?"

Ozan ignored his question. "We are on the wrong path, and have been for years. I am sick of it, and so are many of us. It's time to change direction, Pirro. That trinket on your finger is poison."

Ash watched the other Nephilim, spotting two who seemed to stand apart from the rest. He presumed they were Habib and Jabril, their co-conspirators. Ash leaned close to Samir, voice low as the other two talked, his eyes darting to them. "Those two are the ones on our side?"

Samir gave the briefest nod. Ash's hand was on one of the bombs in his pocket, ready to throw it to the far side of the room now that he knew who to avoid. Even though the Nephilim were in their own living room, all were still either armed or within easy reach of their weapons.

Pirro unsheathed his sword, pointing it at Ozan. "I have worked hard for this token, Ozan. Don't tempt me to use it. Stand down now, and you will survive. You too, Samir. Your friends won't, of course." His gaze swept over them all, and Ash knew, if given half a chance, Pirro would make them all suffer before death.

Ozan laughed mirthlessly. "If I stand down now, you will kill me. You have always been a liar, Pirro." Ozan withdrew his own sword, and the others did the same, all except for Ash, who cupped the bomb in his hand, judging when best to activate it. Ozan addressed the other

Nephilim. "Make a decision quickly. I know some of you are with me. This is no life anymore. It is a gilded prison, and we are chained to a cruel master."

Most Nephilim, however, fell in behind Pirro, armed with swords and daggers, and a couple of guns too, Ash noted.

"Have it your own way," Pirro said with a sneer. "I will kill you myself, but the others I want alive!"

A distant boom rang out across the house, just as Pirro charged. He halted for the briefest moment, confusion etched across his features, and Ash threw the bomb under the window. He'd timed it to perfection, and in seconds it detonated. The windows exploded and rubble flew everywhere, but Ash and his companions had crouched, braced for the explosion, and they regained their feet quickly.

Time to get to Pirro before he summoned Belial's power.

Estelle's rage increased as she observed the half a dozen women kept in a secure area of the villa. They were young, some barely out of their teens, and they all looked scared.

The series of small rooms were in the basement area, windowless and cramped, and the whole place stank of sweat and fear. A lounge area and TV comprised one room, and a bathroom was to the side. Through a partially open door, she saw that beds were lined up, dormitory style. A couple of other bedrooms with double beds were to the side. It wasn't hard to imagine what happened there, and rage welled up again.

She subdued it for now, far too worried about the women to be angry with Nibal at her side. "It's okay," she said, holding her hands up. "Do you speak English? I'm here to help."

The women had all jumped up and cowered back when they entered, but when they saw Nibal, they appeared to calm down. That reassured Estelle—slightly. One of them nodded at her. "Yes, I speak a little English."

"I am getting all of you out of here today, understand?"

The woman's eyes darted to Nibal and back again. "They're letting us go?"

"No. *I'm* letting you go." She glared at Nibal. "This is horrific! And you let it happen!"

"I was in no position to free them, but you can tell, they do not fear me."

She looked at the woman who had spoken. "Is that true?"

She nodded, eyes downcast. "Nibal is one of the kinder ones."

Fire flared along Estelle's palms as she said to Nibal, "But still a rapist?"

"No! Never. I feed them. I check their injuries. I try to keep them safe."

"He's right," another girl said. "He tries."

Estelle spelled Nibal back against the wall with a word of power. "It's not enough."

"I swear, I did what I could." Sweat beaded along his brow, pupils dilated with shock. "Are you a witch?"

"That's my business. When these girls are safe," Estelle said through gritted teeth, wishing she knew a spell to shrink testicles to dried walnuts, and penises to withered, flaccid skins, "I will burn everyone to ash."

"And I will help you, I swear." Nibal had flattened himself against the wall, hands raised. "They are all here. All safe, for now. We need to help my brothers."

An explosion rocked the building, and some of the girls screamed. Estelle was worried for Barak, but nowhere near as worried as she was for these abused women. She wanted to kill the men responsible, but it was clear it wasn't Nibal. She dropped her spell. "Tell me the best way to get them out, then you can help your brothers." She turned to the women. "Grab your belongings. It's time to go."

Nibal stepped onto the corridor and pointed up the stairs, back the way they had entered. "Turn left at the top instead of right, and you will find a series of short passageways and a few other storerooms. At the end is a door to the courtyard. It's locked on the inside." He thrust keys at her. "There's a way into the garage; there are cars there, and the gates out to the road." He flinched as another *boom* shook the building. "My brothers!"

"Fuck your brothers. Are there any traps on the way out?"

"No! Just locked doors. Lots of them."

She thrust the keys back at him. "I don't need these keys, only the car keys. And I want cash."

"The car keys are in the garage. Cash is all over the house."

"Down here somewhere?"

"The room above this one. There's a safe in the wall."

"You better not be lying, Nibal, or I swear I will kill you before all others, and it will not be swift."

"I'm not lying."

She nodded up the stairs. "Go. I will find you when everyone here is safe."

Nibal fled and she returned to the room. Most of the women were hastily grabbing clothes and toiletries, but two were just sitting rigid with shock. The other women were packing for them.

Estelle approached the woman she had first spoken to. She was young and pretty, but her eyes were shielded, and bruises marked her face and arms. "What's your name?"

"Chiara."

"Good." Estelle realised she was radiating power, and she took a deep breath and calmed down. *These women were scared enough.* "Can any of you drive, Chiara?"

"I can, and a few others."

"Are you all Italian?"

"No." She shook her head. "Some are Spanish, German, French... They took girls travelling alone, mostly." She clutched Estelle's hand. "We have nowhere to go, and no money, although," she glanced at her bag, "I still have my bank cards."

"I will find you money. Lots of it. You'll have to look after each other, but I swear that I will help. How long have you been here?"

"A few months, I think. I've lost track. Others have been here longer. They took our phones from us."

Estelle gave Chiara her own key and phone, after entering the directions to their rented villa. "Head here. It's about half an hour away. It's safe, and no one else is there. We will return there soon, and I promise to help you. Now, follow me."

In a few more minutes she had led them up the stairs as Nibal had directed, using magic to open locks, until finally they reached the garage. The half a dozen women squashed into one large four-wheel drive, the stronger women rallying the younger ones along. Estelle opened up the gate and leaned in through the window to Chaira again. "I'll be with you soon."

"Will you call the police? I don't think we can face that."

"We'll dispense our own justice, don't worry about that. Tell me, though...did these men hurt you?" She listed the names of Ozan and his friends.

Chiara shook her head. "It was mainly Jiri, Mikal, Karim, and Pirro. Nibal wasn't lying. He was kind. So was Ozan." Her eyes filled with tears. "No one crossed Jiri."

Estelle nodded, her resolve strengthening as she watched them leave, the car lights disappearing as they rounded a bend, and then turned back to the house. Now, she would unleash her vengeance.

Shadow rose from her crouched stance as the flying debris from the bomb settled, and cocked another arrow as a weird, hushed silence fell.

She spotted Gabe lying sprawled on the floor, half covered by the door that had been blown off its hinges. Another man had been blasted out of the room, too, and lay in a muddled heap. Dorian was at her side, still dazed, but she was clear-headed. She edged forward, seeing Gabe move beneath the rubble, and motioned to Dorian. "Move the door and help him up. Who's that behind him?"

"Karim." His voice was scarcely a whisper.

There was still no sign of Jiri, and keeping her bow aimed and steady, she kept moving forward. Karim groaned and sat up, his groan becoming a growl as he saw Shadow. She had a clear head shot, and she didn't hesitate. Her arrow pierced his forehead, killing him instantly, and he fell backwards.

Still no Jiri. She stepped around Gabe as Dorian dragged the rubble and door off him. The doorway was only feet away now, although less door and more hole. The room smouldered behind it and flames danced in patches, but where there had once been a wall was now a big, gaping hole to the outside, and Jiri was nowhere in sight.

Shadow ran to the gap in the masonry, scanning the area. A figure lay spawled on the ground, one arm at a strange angle. *Jiri.* But he was still alive, and he sat up, glaring at Shadow. She shot a volley of arrows, but it was already too late. Jiri was glowing with an incandescent white light, and his wings were unfurling behind him.

She couldn't stop him. He had already summoned Belial's power. She grabbed JD's weapon instead and fired.

Maggie had very little idea of what was going on, other than that things were about to get serious.

The level of worry and nervousness had escalated as the group in Hermes's lab watched and attempted to help JD's preparations. Now, it seemed, he was ready.

"Right," he declared, clapping his hands. "Time to play."

"I'd hardly call this *play*!" she remonstrated. "We might all die!"

"Hush woman, you nagging old rump-fed runion, it's all in hand. Back behind the obsidian line now. Well back."

It seemed JD had decided to use his choicest Elizabethan swear words on her. She found it quite endearing. "Screw you, you jumped up knave with a badger's arse."

"Nice retort, madam." He winked at her. "You may leave if you're worried, but I assure you that you will miss a treat."

"I'm not going anywhere!"

He flapped his arms at all of them. "Back!"

Harlan, Jackson, Zee, and Eli retreated with her to the back of the room. Nahum and Olivia had been banished to the garden, well away from the lab. Olivia had been worried about the effect on her baby, understandably, and so had Nahum. JD had fiddled with geometric grids, and adjusted his instruments that he hauled in from his old lab with their help, and now the place hummed with power, including that of Belial's jewels, of course.

They were heaped in the centre of the grid, and their strange energy had been temporarily dulled by a forcefield of JD's own design. Nevertheless, with hands clamped over their ears and the dark goggles on, they huddled at the back of the room. It was madness to stay, really, and they all knew it, but neither could any of them drag themselves away. Once her glasses were firmly in place, Maggie saw another three fields rippling between them and Belial's jewels. JD had retreated behind the second one.

His back was to them now as he held his controls, and he held one hand up, counting down from three with his fingers. With a terrifying display of light and noise, his alchemical weapons fired their beams at the jewels. The pressure built in the room, and Maggie's hair stood on end, even on her head. So did the others', their hair floating in a nimbus around them before settling again. The hum of power was still discernible despite the fact that they had their ears covered, and it wavered in volume, like musical pitches.

Then a boom rattled across the room.

They all staggered and jostled together, keeping each other upright. And then another boom resounded, and a rainbow wave of light flashed from the far end of the lab so brightly that Maggie closed her eyes and ducked her head. The pressure continued to build as her hair once again lifted off her skin. She felt breathless, terrified, and somehow exalted... As if in the presence of something great.

Exalted?

She lifted her head, blinking against the light, and saw an enormous figure almost as white as the light surrounding it, wrestling as if trying to break free. Wings caught in rainbow hues, and Maggie gripped Harlan's arm. He too lifted his head.

"Holy shit," she gasped out. "Is that a fucking angel?"

Eli was on her other side and leaned close, arms around her shoulder in a protective gesture. "Not just any angel." She glanced at him, but his eyes were fixed on Belial. "He doesn't want to let go."

"It's just like with Olivia," Maggie said, "although, that battle lasted for far less time."

JD fiddled with his controls as he staggered back. The play of light changed, and this time it was like the Northern Lights again, as a ripple of vivid green flashed across the room.

The writhing figure, wings outstretched, emitted a keening note of despair that Maggie knew she had felt more than heard, and then there was another enormous boom. The shockwave it released pulsed across the space, slamming through one protective wall after another, until with a dying ripple, it washed up against the obsidian shield and faded.

She closed her eyes tightly, and when she opened them again, Belial had vanished.

As the light dimmed, and the pressure decreased, Maggie tried to see JD. *Where was he? Was he dead? Unconscious? Pulverised into dust?*

She blinked with surprise as her focus returned. JD was none of those things. He was dancing a mad jig, kicking up his heels and crowing like a cockerel as he cavorted around.

"Well," Harlan drawled, "I guess it's a success."

But Maggie couldn't celebrate yet. "Has it worked on the other jewels, though?"

Lucien had turned into a super-soldier, confounding the fighting Nephilim, and that had worked to his advantage. With the addition of JD's weapons and the bomb blast, the fight quickly became uneven.

When the bomb exploded, Pirro had been thrown off his feet, and Barak had leapt on him. Lucien aimed at the men with guns. Both had been thrown across the room by the blast, but one still gripped his weapon. Lucien shot him before he could recover. The other man scrambled for it, but Jabril was already on him. Another Nephilim fought Habib, while Ash took on three of them all at once. Lucien ran to help him, shooting one with his alchemical weapon, battering the other with his Nephilim shield. Samir was also fighting his brothers, and it was ugly and brutal.

Lucien glanced over to Pirro, and with horror saw him stab Barak in the abdomen. He fell to the floor, hand pressed to his wound as blood poured from it. Pirro ignored him and started to glow with the incandescent light of angels that Lucien had been warned about. It summoned everyone's attention, and they all fell back.

Pirro roared with pleasure as his wings unfurled and his sword filled with light. "Now you will feel Belial's might!"

Ash grabbed Lucien, pulling him back as the two fighting teams disengaged. *This is it*, Lucien thought. *I am going to die at the hand of a Fallen Angel and his mad disciple.*

He didn't even think to use JD's weapon, watching instead with admiration and terror. His breath caught in his chest. Ash fortunately kept his head and shot at Pirro instead, but now that Pirro was drawing on Belial's power, the weapon had little effect.

And then something weird happened. The light faded, and Pirro's face turned from a mask of victory to one of confusion. "Belial!" he roared, face upturned to the sky. He looked down at Barak, incensed with rage, sword flashing as he slashed wildly at him. "This is your fault!"

"No!" Estelle cried out from the doorway. She hurled a barrage of fire balls at Pirro, and he burst into flames as his body was propelled across the room.

Estelle was consumed with fury, that spiteful expression that Lucien hadn't seen for so long etched onto her face. Magic radiated from her, and she turned her attention to the rest of the room. Noticing they had now split into two groups, she laid their enemies to waste with her power.

Gabe reached Shadow's side, pulling her back from the window as Jiri's glowing figure filled the view.

Jiri was airborne now, wings fully open, completely in possession of Belial's power. Gabe could see Belial in him, could feel him even, just as he had when Gabe had carried his token in the Cathar castle. Jiri's blades danced with angelic fire as he hung there, glaring viciously at Gabe.

"It's too late," Gabe said, drawing Shadow close. He had imagined a future for them, especially as she had returned from the Otherworld at Yule, choosing him over her other life. Now it all seemed futile.

Jiri would win.

"It's never too late, my love," Shadow said, breaking free of his grip. In a split second, her bow was armed with a bomb, and she fired directly at Jiri.

It hit his chest, and the explosion sent him cartwheeling over the grounds. He roared with fury, recovering quickly, and he flew with unbelievable speed towards them. Shadow fired again, and again, and again, driving Jiri back.

"It won't last," Gabe said. "It can't. He'll keep coming."

"Then at least I'll buy us time!"

Jiri was laughing manically through his fury, caught by some bombs, dodging others with lightning reflexes, until Gabe realised his glow was fading.

Jiri knew something was wrong, too. He twisted and turned, looking skyward as if for assistance, and then he stared at Gabe, arms outstretched as he held his two swords. "What have you done?"

Gabe felt the faint stirrings of hope as Belial's power faded. "We have friends. I think they've found success in your ultimate demise."

Jiri hung there, just a Nephilim, deciding whether to fight or flee, when Shadow made his decision for him. She released another arrow loaded with a bomb, too swiftly for Jiri to avoid. It hit him dead on, and Gabe averted his gaze as Jiri exploded. Shadow, however, didn't move. She watched, drenched in his blood and flesh.

Finally, she looked at Gabe. "It's done."

Thirty-One

"So," Niel said, rising up on his elbow to stare down at Mouse—a very naked Mouse, who was covered with the finest Egyptian linen bed sheet, "Belial is defeated, and I have a long train journey to look forward to. Would you like to come with me?"

"Well," she traced a finger down his bare chest, "you could catch a flight now. The horn has no influence."

Niel had texted his brothers to tell them of his success as soon as they arrived at the hotel room, and later had found out that they were fine. After that, he'd put all of them out of his head again. At some point in the night, and he couldn't honestly say when, Belial's power had vanished. By then, however, he was having far too much fun with Mouse to give it much thought. He had found out her real name was Anouk, and it suited her perfectly. It was Hebrew, and meant grace and favour.

"A train journey with you," he told her, "in a small room dominated by a bed, sounds much more fun. I have decided that I want to take my time returning home. I might even spend a few days in Istanbul first. It's unlikely they'll spot the theft for a while, or know we're associated with it."

"Those rooms are rarely used. They might not even notice the opening into the cistern for months."

"Good." He glanced across the room at the gilded horn. "When I get home, that's going on my wall."

"A trophy?"

"Yes. And a symbol of freedom."

Her fingers skimmed over his abdomen, stirring his desire again. "I admit, a train journey across Europe with you has its attractions. I'm not sure if I want to go to London, though."

"Where do you want to go?"

"I live in France. Provence, actually. I want to go home."

He caught her finger in his hand and pulled it to his lips to nibble it. "But you travel the world. Don't you fancy a trip?"

"You don't live in London. You live in Cornwall. You'll go home."

"Not forever. I like to travel, and we make a good team."

Her deliciously full lips curled into a smile. "We've crossed paths three times. I hardly think that's enough evidence."

"Yes, but this time surely proves it." He ran his finger down her breastbone to her navel and beyond, pleased to see a flush to her cheeks and hear her breath catch. "We work together very well."

"Are you suggesting some kind of partnership, beyond the physical?"

"Yes." His brothers had their own lives, and while he had no intention of leaving Cornwall for good yet, he needed to explore his options.

Anouk smiled again and pulled him close, and he rolled over her, pinning her beneath him, as she said, "I am open to negotiations. A train journey would be the perfect place."

"Excellent."

Barak prepared coffee in the rented villa on Elba, listening to the chatter of the women they had rescued in the other room. His wound ached, but was healing, thanks to his father's power. He had refused Estelle's help, wanting her to focus her time and skills on the women.

Estelle was still seething with anger, but her vengeance the previous night had assuaged much of it. However, once they were alone, in bed, after the women had been tended to, he held her as she cried. Huge, wracking sobs that encompassed her own experiences as well as the women's. He wished he could do more, but instead he just held her close. She had said only one thing before she slept, and that was, "*I want to do more for women like this. Will you help me?*"

He'd kissed her head. "*I will do anything you want me to.*"

She had cupped his face with fierce intensity. "*Thank you.*"

He shook the memory off, knowing they would discuss it further, and carried the tray containing the coffee and mugs out to the terrace and placed it on the table. Chiara and the others they rescued had already finished their breakfast and coffee. It was a cold but sunny morning, and the team were all keen for fresh air. The view across the hills was spectacular, especially with the sea sparkling in the distance. Spring was creeping closer. It was certainly warmer there than it would be in Cornwall; nevertheless, Barak was eager to be home. He needed time to decompress, to breathe again without fear of Black Cronos or Belial. He had no doubt that they would encounter other problems eventually, but for now, he would enjoy the peace.

Lucien, Ash, Estelle, Shadow, and Gabe were on the terrace too, debating their next course of action, especially how best to help the women, and Ozan had arrived to argue his point. He looked like a different man this morning. He stood taller, his expression hopeful, although right now, he was desperate to get Estelle's approval. It seemed Oz, as he liked to be called, and his companions wanted to help the kidnapped women, to atone for the others' treatment of them. Estelle was reluctant to let them near the women. Barak understood that. Their priority was to get the girls home. After that, they could go home, too.

"I see your point, Estelle, I really do," Oz said, leaning forward in his chair, "but we need to help them. We could do nothing at the time, and I hated it."

"You could have tried."

"It would have got us killed."

"Exactly. You favoured your own life over theirs."

Barak felt sorry for Oz, but equally he saw Estelle's point.

Oz wasn't done. "We took them extra food, and we gave them toiletries and medications."

"You mean to help with the wounds your brothers gave them."

"Do not call them my brothers. They were not."

"If I might intervene," Lucien ventured. "I experienced capture and degradation myself. I also want to help them, and Oz, I see that you want to help too, but it's not right. You have to walk away from this. We," he glanced at the others, "will do this. There are enough of us to make sure the girls get home or go wherever they want to."

Estelle smiled at him. "Thank you, Lucien."

Shadow reached for the coffee and poured herself a mug. "I agree with Estelle. We will deal with this. If you want to make amends, Oz, help us track down The Brotherhood."

He nodded, resigned, and accepted a mug of coffee that Barak offered him. "All right. We can do that. We know most of them, between us. Although, if the jewels no longer have power..."

Gabe glanced at Ash and Barak as he said, "We find them anyway, just in case. You know where they have been moved to?"

"Yes, mostly." A renewed determination settled over Oz as he said, "Yes, I like that idea. We will do that, and then chase up any remaining members of The Brotherhood in Venice."

Barak asked, "What about the dead Nephilim?"

"They are already in the sea. We carried them far out last night and dumped them. Nibal and the others are cleaning up the villa today. It's ours now, to do with as we please. Jiri bought it years ago, when he tired of living in Portoferraio." *The capital city of Elba – the city that Barak had seen in the images at Moonfell.* "It's a good place to rebuild."

Barak mulled over what he'd briefly discussed with the others the previous night. "Oz, it may be that we can put you in touch with someone who can offer you work, if you need it. It's not always honest," he said, laughing, "but I think you'll find it more honest than what you have been doing. We'll have to discuss it with our contact, but his organisation might want to use your skills."

Harlan might want to discuss it with Romola, too. They would see how they would fair with The Brotherhood first. See how trustworthy they could be. From his brief interaction with Oz, though, they all felt they could trust them. They had, after all, helped them defeat Belial.

Oz smiled, and it transformed him. "We would appreciate that. We have some money, but we'll give most of it to the women. Then, yes, we'll need work. Thank you. We are all curious to see this paranormal world you speak of."

Ash shook his head, perplexed. "You really haven't met many other paranormal creatures?"

"Very few. Jiri didn't want it. It's been an isolated existence, for the most part."

As the conversation changed direction to talk of the paranormal and the life they led, Barak realised they had been lucky with their new friends, and he wondered how his brothers were faring in London.

Zee pushed his empty breakfast plate away and reached for his coffee. The noise around the table was loud.

Everyone except JD and Anna was present in JD's dining room that overlooked the rear terrace and the battered marquee, and a range of conversations were taking place. Harlan, Jackson, and Maggie were debating how old Anna might be, whether the emerald cave would send JD mad eventually, and if he would ever actually leave it to help Jackson at The Retreat. Certainly, he had showed no sign of separating himself from it yet.

After their success at breaking Belial's control the previous night, they had helped JD put the slightly battered lab to rights before he shooed them out. He was a peculiar little man, no doubt, but Zee felt he owed him a debt that he could never repay. They couldn't have banished Belial alone. Now, Zee was eager to get home.

He and Eli would leave soon, needing to return to work in White Haven, but it seemed Nahum was staying in London for a while. He sat next to Olivia, and they leaned into each other; it was clear that they had come to some sort of accord. *The early beginnings of love, perhaps.*

Zee spoke to Eli, keeping his voice low. "Do you think Nahum will ever return to Cornwall? For good, I mean?"

Eli shrugged, smiling as he watched him. "Hard to say. Right now, I think not. Shame, really. I'll miss him, but change is good."

"But if the worst happens..." He didn't need to say what that would be. Eli knew. The death of their daughter was a distinct possibility. Sooner or later, it happened. It always did.

"Then we deal with it, but let's have a little hope, brother."

"I have a lot of hope, and so do they. That's what bothers me."

"They have Morgana and JD. Having met him, I now think he could do anything. But we have work to do when we get back, and I don't mean with the witches. The dryads need us. It's spring soon. Ostara. Nelaira has plans."

Zee nodded. Their promise of guardianship over Ravens' Wood was making demands again. They would honour it, of course. They had to. Eli also had his own reasons for helping Nelaira. An obsession that he kept under control, most of the time. More and more lately Zee suspected that Eli slept with other women to assuage his need for Nelaira, and he wasn't quite sure how that would play out.

"As long, brother, as it doesn't clash with a certain wedding." Reuben would be devastated if they weren't there, and so, in fact, would Zee. He was looking forward to it.

Eli laughed. "I'll make sure it doesn't."

Zee sipped his coffee as Maggie demanded Eli's attention. It would be almost a week before Niel returned home, and most likely Gabe, Barak, Ash, and Shadow, too. Nahum would return for the wedding. Zee decided to take advantage of the lull, and prepare to move into the apartment above The Wayward Son properly.

It was time to see to his own future, too.

It was a week after the fight on Elba and Jiri's defeat when Gabe finally walked into the farmhouse in Cornwall.

It was now March, and there were signs of spring everywhere. Early daffodils nodded at the base of hedgerows, and crocuses peaked from borders. Here, on the hills that surrounded White Haven, the fields and moors were fresh with green growth, and it soothed his soul. The courtyard was clean, and Eli—at least he presumed it was Eli—had been planting and tidying up the drive and courtyard. The house was clean and quiet, and it welcomed him. *And*, he thought, inhaling the scent of spiced meats, *Niel was home and in the kitchen.*

It hadn't been an easy week. Returning the captive women to their homes had been satisfying but traumatic. There were times when he felt ashamed to be a man, but it was done now. Oz, Nibal, Dorian, Samir, Habib, and Jibril, were fresh on their quest to end The Brotherhood for good. He had taken to calling them the House of Ozan. Oz was their undoubted leader, and they seemed to have forged a new strength together after the end of the House of Belial. They had all sustained injuries, some of them quite bad, but like all Nephilim, they healed quickly. Their mental injuries would no doubt take longer.

Ash nudged Gabe as he entered the hall behind him, carrying his bags. "Get on with it, Gabe."

"Sorry. Lost in my thoughts for a moment."

"Glad to be home?"

"Very."

Shadow followed Ash inside, silent as usual. She poked him. "I can't wait to tease Niel."

Gabe smiled. Shadow, as always, had rebounded from their situation with her usual ebullience. If it wasn't for her stubbornness, he might not be here. "After you, madam."

She kissed his cheek and wiggled her hips as she sashayed up the hall. She tossed her hair as she looked back over her shoulder at him and Ash. "I believe I won the bet, too! I haven't forgotten."

She meant the bet on Niel and Mouse. Gabe grinned as he and Ash followed her. "Some things never change."

Niel was surrounded by food when they entered the kitchen—bowls of salads, platters of breads, sweetmeats, and other delicacies. He looked up as they entered, a smile spreading across his face. "You're here already! I thought you'd be hours yet!"

"We caught an early flight," Ash explained. "Niel, you've outdone yourself."

"Well, it's going to be the first time we've all been together in months. It's a proper Middle Eastern celebration. And," he nodded to the fridge, "we've stocked up on champagne, too. I don't believe that we've all toasted to our newfound wealth yet."

"Or," Shadow said, "your successful liaison with Mouse."

He refused to be rattled by her double entendre. "Her name is Anouk. Mouse is her professional name."

"Oh. So nice you know details now."

He grinned. "Isn't it?"

"Hold on," Gabe said, confused. "What do you mean, we're all here?"

"Barak arrived last night, and Nahum this morning." He smiled at Gabe's confusion. "Barak came back from Estelle's place and Nahum has decided Olivia can cope alone in London—for a short while, at least. They're out there."

Gabe looked out of the window and gasped. "The loggia's been repaired."

"That's down to Eli and Zee. They're out there, too."

Gabe dumped his bag in the hall and headed out of the back door, Shadow already peppering Niel with questions about Anouk. His brothers were all seated around the table, and the barbeque was smoking. The scent of Arabic coffee came from the pot on the table.

Nahum stood and hugged him. "Good to see you, brother."

"You, too. Everything okay with Olivia?"

"More than okay."

Nahum was composed, always level-headed, but today he had an elevated level of calm and contentment that Gabe hadn't seen for a long time. "Good. You'll be going back, though?"

"Yes. I have to. I *want* to. But that's for another time. Today, I wanted to be here with everyone."

He and Ash greeted the others and Gabe settled at the table, looking forward to catching up with everyone's news, but a strange mix of sadness was tinged with it, too.

Change was coming for all of them. He may as well embrace it.

Thanks for reading *Brotherhood of the Fallen*. Please make an author happy and leave a review on a retailer of your choice, but I would especially appreciate one in my shop, Happenstance Books.

Newsletter

If you enjoyed this book and would like to read more of my stories, please subscribe to my newsletter at tjgreenauthor.com. You will get two free short stories, *Excalibur Rises* and *Jack's Encounter,* and will also receive free character sheets for all of the main White Haven witches.

By staying on my mailing list you'll receive free excerpts of my new books, as well as short stories, news of giveaways, and a chance to join my launch team. I'll also be sharing information about other books in this genre you might enjoy.

Ream

I have started my own subscription service called Happenstance Book Club. I know what you're thinking! What is Ream? It's a bit like Patreon, which you may be more familiar with, and it allows you to support me and read my books before anyone else.

There is a monthly fee for this, and a few different tiers, so you can choose what tier suits you. All tiers come with plenty of other bonuses, including merchandise, but the one thing common to all is that you can read my latest books while I'm writing them – so they're a rough draft. I will post a few chapters each week, and you can read them at your leisure, as well as comment in them. You can also choose to be a follower for free.

You can comment on my books, chat about spoilers, and be part of a community. I will also post polls, character art, share rituals and spells, share the background to the myths and legends in my books, and some of my earlier books are available to read for free.

Interested? Head to Happenstance Book Club.

https://reamstories.com/happenstancebookclub

Happenstance Book Shop

I also now have a fabulous online shop called Happenstance Books where you can buy eBooks, audiobooks, and paperbacks, many bundled up at great prices, as well as fabulous merchandise. I know that you'll love it! Check it out here: https://happenstancebookshop.com/

YouTube

If you love audiobooks, you can listen for free on YouTube, as I have uploaded all of my audiobooks there. Please subscribe if you do. Thank you. https://www.youtube.com/@tjgreenauthor

Read on for a list of my other books.

Author's Note

Thank you for reading *Brotherhood of the Fallen*, the seventh and final book in the White Haven Hunters series.

I wasn't sure how many books would be in this series, but it feels right to end it now. I love all of the characters, and although it's bittersweet, I believe that with so many of them pursuing their own lives, to try to wrestle them all into one book is madness. It won't be the end of the characters, though. They will continue to pop up in my other series, and some characters may well get their own short stories and novellas.

I have other books and series to write, and I'm looking forward to diving into them. I'm about to start writing the first full length Moonfell Witches book, and there will be more White Haven Witches and Storm Moon Shifters too.

If you'd like to read a bit more background on the stories, please head to my website, www.tjgreenauthor.com, where I blog about the books I've read and the research I've done for the series. In fact, there's lots of stuff on there about my other series, too. I have two websites, just in case you wondered! My other site is my shop, www.happenst ancebookshop.com.

Thanks again to Fiona Jayde Media who keeps producing such fabulous covers, and thanks to Kyla Stein at Missed Period Editing for sorting out my knotty sentences.

I must also thank my wonderful Happenstance Book Club members who read an unedited version of this book before anyone else. I loved hearing their feedback as I was writing it. Please join one of the tiers if you want to read early versions of my work, as well as receive other goodies!

Thanks also to my beta readers—Terri, and my mother. Their reassurance as they read each new book always soothes my nerves. Also, thank you to my launch team, who give valuable feedback on typos and are happy to review upon release. It's lovely to hear from them—you know who you are! I also love hearing from all of my readers, so I welcome you to get in touch.

I encourage you to follow my Facebook page, TJ Green. I post there reasonably frequently. In addition, I have a Facebook group called TJ's Inner Circle. It's a fab little group where I run giveaways and post teasers, so come and join us.

Finally, just a reminder to sign up to my newsletter, either through my shop, or at www.tjgreenauthor.com/landing.

About the Author

I am a writer, a pagan, and a witch. I was born in England, in the Black Country, but moved to New Zealand in 2006. I lived near Wellington with my partner, Jase, and my cats, Sacha and Leia. However, in April 2022 we moved again! Yes, I like making my life complicated... I'm now living in the Algarve in Portugal, and loving the fabulous weather and people. When I'm not busy writing I read lots, indulge in gardening and shopping, and I love yoga.

Confession time! I'm a Star Trek geek—old and new—and love urban fantasy and detective shows. Secret passion—Columbo! My favourite Star Trek film is the *Wrath of Khan*, the original! Other top films—*Predator*, the original, and *Aliens*.

In a previous life I was a singer in a band, and used to do some acting with a theatre company. For more on me, check out a couple of my blog posts. I'm an old grunge queen, so you can read about my love of that on my blog: https://tjgreenauthor.com/about-a-girl-and-what-chris-cornell-means-to-me/. For more random news, read: https://tjgreenauthor.com/read-self-published-blog-tour-things-you-probably-dont-know-about-me. To read about my journey as a witch, read: https://tjgreenauthor.com/leaning-into-my-witch/.

Why magic and mystery?

I've always loved the weird, the wonderful, and the inexplicable. Favourite stories are those of magic and mystery, set on the edges of the known, particularly tales of folklore, faerie, and legend—all the narratives that try to explain our reality.

The King Arthur stories are fascinating because they sit between reality and myth. They encompass real life concerns, but also cross boundaries with the world of faerie—or the Other, as I call it. There are green knights, witches, wizards, and dragons, and that's what I find particularly fascinating. They are stories that have intrigued people for generations, and like many others, I'm adding my own interpretation.

I love witches and magic, hence my second series set in beautiful Cornwall. There are witches, missing grimoires, supernatural threats, and ghosts, and as the series progresses, weirder stuff happens. The spinoff, White Haven Hunters, allows me to indulge my love of alchemy, as well as other myths and legends. Think Indiana Jones meets Supernatural!

Have a poke around in my blog posts and you'll find all sorts of posts about my series and my characters, and quite a few book reviews.

If you'd like to follow me on social media, you'll find me here:

f facebook.com/tjgreenauthor/

𝓟 pinterest.pt/tjgreenauthor/

♪ tiktok.com/@tjgreenauthor

▶ youtube.com/@tjgreenauthor

g goodreads.com/author/show/15099365.T_J_Green

○ instagram.com/tjgreenauthor/

BB bookbub.com/authors/tj-green

https://reamstories.com/happenstancebookclub

Other Books by T J Green

Rise of the King Series

A Young Adult series about a teen called Tom who is summoned to wake King Arthur. It's a fun adventure about King Arthur in the Otherworld!

Call of the King #1

The Silver Tower #2

The Cursed Sword #3

White Haven Witches

Witches, secrets, myth and folklore, set on the Cornish coast!

Buried Magic #1

Magic Unbound #2

Magic Unleashed #3

All Hallows' Magic #4

Undying Magic #5

Crossroads Magic #6

Crown of Magic #7

Vengeful Magic #8

Chaos Magic #9

Stormcrossed Magic #10

Wyrd Magic #11

Midwinter Magic #12

Sacred Magic #13

Storm Moon Shifters

This is an Urban Fantasy shifters spin-off in the White Haven World, and can be read as a standalone. There's a crossover of characters from my other series, and plenty of new ones. There is also a new group of witches who I love! It's set in London around Storm Moon, the club owned by Maverick Hale, alpha of the Storm Moon Pack.

Storm Moon Rising #1

Dark Heart #1

Moonfell Witches

This series features the mysterious and magical witches who live in Moonfell, the sprawling Gothic mansion in London. They first appeared in Storm Moon Rising, Storm Moon Shifters Book 1, and then in Immortal Dusk, White Haven Hunters Book 6, and features characters from both series. However, this series can be read as a standalone.

The First Yule - Novella
Triple Moon #1

Printed in Great Britain
by Amazon

43371358R00229